The GLORY of the EMPIRE

The GLORY *of the* EMPIRE

JEAN D'ORMESSON

A NOVEL · A HISTORY

Translated from the French by Barbara Bray

ALFRED·A·KNOPF · NEW YORK · 1974

THIS IS A BORZOI BOOK
PUBLISHED BY ALFRED A. KNOPF, INC.

English translation Copyright © 1974 by Alfred A. Knopf, Inc.
All rights reserved under International and
Pan-American Copyright Conventions. Published in the
United States by Alfred A. Knopf, Inc., New York,
and simultaneously in Canada by Random House of
Canada Limited, Toronto. Distributed by
Random House, Inc., New York.

Originally published in France as La Gloire de l'Empire
by Editions Gallimard, Paris.

Copyright © 1971 by Editions Gallimard

ISBN 0–394–48121–6   74–7756

Manufactured in the United States of America

First American Edition

To the great shade of Alexis

To his opponents as well as his supporters,
since that is how he would have wished it

To whom I love—and even to the others

History is a novel that happened; a novel is
history that might have happened.
E. AND J. DE GONCOURT

The future belongs to God, but the past belongs to
history. God can do no more with history, but man
can still write it and transfigure it.
JUSTUS DION

History, mother of truth—the idea is astonishing.
J. L. BORGES

Thus saith the Lord: . . .
Remember ye not the former things, neither consider
the things of old.
Behold, I will do a new thing.
ISAIAH 43:16–19

CONTENTS

I. THE PILLARS OF THE EMPIRE 3

II. THE EAGLE AND THE TIGER 11

III. ARSAPHES'S MERCENARIES 20

IV. AQUILEUS 32

V. THE BANQUET AT ONESSA 41

VI. THAUMAS AND INGEBURGH 56

VII. THE FOX OF AMPHIBOLUS 65

VIII. THE SIEGE OF BALKH 75

IX. THE WOLF HUNT 91

X. INITIATION 101

XI. FEASTING IN ALEXANDRIA 113

XII. THE YEARS IN THE WILDERNESS,
OR THE FOOL OF GOD 133

XIII. THE CALL, AND THE END OF EXILE 152

XIV. THE CONQUEST OF POWER 161

XV. THE KHA-KHAN OF THE OÏGHURS 186

XVI. THE DOUBLE DUEL 198

XVII. DIREITO POR LINHAS TORTAS,
OR THE NEW ALLIANCE 214

CONTENTS · X

XVIII.   SCIENCE, CULTURE, AND EVERYDAY LIFE
UNDER THE EMPIRE   236

XIX.   THE SPIRIT OF CONQUEST
AND THE MEANING OF DEATH   267

XX.   THE SACK OF ROME   283

XXI.   THE PEACE OF THE EMPIRE   307

XXII.   THE LEPER PRINCE   316

XXIII.   LOSER TAKE ALL, OR THE OTHER LIFE   338

XXIV.   THE POWER AND THE GLORY   354

NOTES   359

BIBLIOGRAPHY   371

INDEX   *follows page*   374

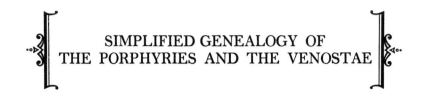

SIMPLIFIED GENEALOGY OF
THE PORPHYRIES AND THE VENOSTAE

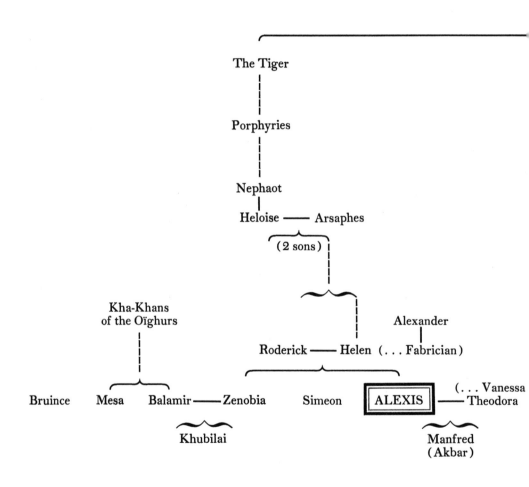

The Tiger

Porphyries

Nephaot

Heloise —— Arsaphes

(2 sons)

Kha-Khans
of the Oïghurs

Alexander

Roderick —— Helen (. . . Fabrician)

(. . . Vanessa

Bruince   Mesa   Balamir —— Zenobia   Simeon   ALEXIS —— Theodora

Khubilai

Manfred
(Akbar)

anabel
rotus?)

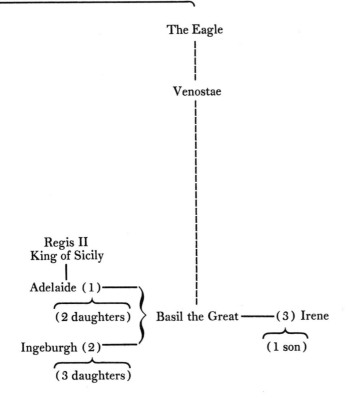

The Eagle

Venostae

Regis II
King of Sicily

Adelaide (1)

(2 daughters)

Basil the Great ——— (3) Irene

(1 son)

Ingeburgh (2)

(3 daughters)

The
GLORY
of the
EMPIRE

I

THE PILLARS OF THE EMPIRE

HE EMPIRE NEVER KNEW PEACE. FIRST IT HAD TO be built, then defended. From the depths of its history there arose the clang of axes, the hiss of javelins, the cries of the dying at evening after battle. Neither the forests to the north and east nor the high mountains in the south were proof against attack and invasion. In the great fertile plains at the foot of the volcanoes, massacre succeeded massacre. To the west, the sea too brought its share of dangers: suddenly threatening sails, pirates, surprise assaults at dawn. On the Empire's borders night never came without its escorts of dread and death. Even within, both in the country and in the towns, interest and passion raised up rival bands to fight for power with violence and arson. The Empire grew up on a foundation of flames and blood. From the time of Arsaphes to that of Basil the Great, a period of more than a century and a half, scarcely three or four years could be called free from war, foreign or civil. And peril came not only from men. Unbridled nature exacted a high price for an energy still youthful and powers as yet almost intact. Fire, packs of wolves, the eruptions of Mount Kora-Kora, hurricanes along the coast, earthquakes, and floods from the river Amphyses all left terror in the memories of one generation after another. It was said that on the snow-covered plateaus huge fighting eagles attacked women and carried off children, while in the sweltering southern plains beyond the mountains, warriors were devoured by tigers that appeared out of nowhere. Imagination hardly needed to improve on the horrors of the real. The violence of men, the seasons, and the earth took its place beside the dragons and monsters born of mirages, night terrors, and the tales of old men around the campfire. The second winter of Basil's reign was so severe that in the northwest the sea froze in the creeks and whole villages were buried under the snow. Cold, heat, flies, snakes, scorpions, plague, and epidemics killed off the least hardy. The strongest among the women often bore twelve or fifteen children, but it was rare for more than two or three of a family to survive. Most men died in war, most women in childbirth, most children never even had time to grow up. Just being alive was a triumph.

But under all these perils and threats the peoples of the Empire were cheerful. They were inhabited by a terrific will to live; they seemed to thirst to go on suffering. Nearly every ambassador's account speaks of the natives' gaiety, their love of pleasure, their bent for laughter and amusement. They forgot quickly—in that lay their strength. Every schoolboy knows Justus Dion's famous account of the death of Ingeburgh, wife of the Emperor Basil. Both he and his people venerated the empress. Her funeral was of a sinister grandeur. Twenty-four horses were slain, her two favorite maids threw themselves on the sacred pyre, women beat their breasts and tore out their hair. The emperor looked prostrate and old. In the phrase of the Pomposan ambassador, "age and sorrow had brought him close to dotage." But just at the end of the funeral celebrations the announcement of the great naval victory at Cape Pantama changed affliction to rejoicing in the twinkling of an eye. The emperor, suddenly rejuvenated, straightened up and even danced with the servingmaids around Ingeburgh's corpse. Three months later he married the prettiest of them—the madcap Empress Irene, as wild as Ingeburgh had been sedate.

This love of life, this gaiety in misfortune, this ability to find a stimulus even in obstacles and sorrows was profoundly characteristic of the peoples of the Empire. Games and feasting played a great part in their life. The whole Empire danced, the whole Empire watched horses race and bulls expire. Everyone seemed to want to savor the brevity of life to the utmost before quitting it himself. German historians in particular have pointed out how this love of feasting and games paralleled, rather than contradicted, the passion for war. War was a celebration and games were mortal. A thousand examples spring to mind of the cruelty of the public games, in which slow riders, clumsy handlers, and unsuccessful wrestlers were put to death by the crowd. The racing of bulls and horses, contests with wild beasts, ball games all produced favorites idolized by the public. But never was honor more dangerous or glory more deadly. At the least failure the heroes of the games were sacrificed in their turn. The greater their popularity, the more exaggerated the audience's demands of them and the greater the threat to their lives. In certain particularly febrile periods, fall followed apotheosis so fast that even the most ambitious or heedless were affected and sometimes faltered. But the peoples of the Empire prized fame so highly that the games never lacked victors or idols. Sometimes they would be executed the day after their fleeting triumph, but they died happy.

Conversely, war was a lighthearted butchery, full of color and movement. It was an honor, a competition, a game. It obeyed strict rules that, though largely arbitrary, were never broken. One stopped fighting when it snowed, when the moon was full, or if a fox crossed the battlefield. Basil the Great was suspected of taking cages of foxes with him on his expeditions to quell rebellion. He was even accused of having let one out to end the indecisive battle of Amphibolus. In any case, the fox of Amphibolus was one of the causes—at least one of the manifest causes—of the hostility between emperors and priests, which was later to have such serious consequences. The priests were involved in every aspect of the life of the Empire. If battles were games, like all games they had their rules, and these rules were closely connected with magic and ritual. As Professor Bjöersenson has put it, "The Empire rested on three pillars. It had three preoccupations and three laws that were really one: war, feasting, and religion."

Of the religion of the Empire we know little. The externals are evident, but the spirit escapes us. Texts and bas-reliefs show priests and their flocks in action, praying and dancing; we know their chants and rituals and instructions, but we do not understand them. Regarding their sense of holiness and the meaning of their rituals, there are diametrically opposed and irreconcilable opinions. Some, under the influence of Bayet or Guignebert or of Marxist thought, explain everything as sheer exploitation by greedy and fraudulent priests of a credulous and simple-minded people. Others, following the German Romantics, depict prophets and seers adept in secret rites and mystic revelation. The followers of Renan have seen the priestly caste as approaching a true mysticism which was yet very near collective hysteria and madness. We shall not try to resolve the question, but merely set before the reader what the records tell us of such great priestly figures as Thaumas, Isidore, and Bruince. In any event, they represent, beneath the splendor of wealth and the thirst for power, a sustained and sometimes successful attempt at a dream of order, and at the same time a suggestion of another world beyond order and even, sometimes, beyond the Empire. Order and another world: this dual aspiration not only ranged priests and seers sometimes for and sometimes against the emperor, but in the end destroyed itself.

War, feasting, religion. For a long time the history of the Empire was confined to anecdotes, genealogies of princes, roll calls of priests and victors at the games, and lists of battles and peace treaties. Bossuet reads in it the finger of God, Voltaire the struggle between man's folly and the slow rise of reason. Its welter of color and crime provided romanticism with a favorite occasion for the resurrection of the past. It was not until the arrival of the modern school that historians began to perceive, beneath the pomp and the blood and the hymns, both the everyday life of the common people and the often complicated system of rites and beliefs that governed it. Then the wave of interest in ordinary existence, in the preoccupations of classes so long ignored, in trade and crafts, in new techniques and group sensibility was replaced by a new phase of broad theoretical visions, comprehensive systems, total interpretations. One after the other, Marxism, psychoanalysis, and structuralism each inspired important works of sociology, cultural anthropology, comparative religion, linguistics, and semiotics, while at the same time researchers tirelessly sought for man and his workaday cares beneath the brilliant trappings of camp and court life. And so each day brought a further descent into the depths of concrete existence and a further ascent toward the heights of abstraction. A dual process of contrast and correlation at once brought man closer and set him at a greater distance. We shall make no attempt here to reproduce all the details of such excellent works as those of Bloch, Sommerfelt, Pierre Dupont, Weill-Pichon, and Rostopchin. But no one can now ignore the main results of their achievements.

The peoples of the Empire claimed to be autochthonous. According to legend they were born one spring morning between the warm plains and the great oak forests, when the demiurge, in the form of an eagle, let fall from its talons an acorn which was fertilized by a sunbeam. Hence the triple cult of the sun, the eagle, and the oak in the early religion of the Empire concentrated particularly on the heights of Aquileus, where priests and a shrine drew flocks of believers, invalids, and pilgrims. But modern science has not only thrown doubt on such heliocentric and arboreal theories of the origins of mankind, it has also demolished the national claim, of which the myth was merely a transposition, that the peoples of Europe sprang from local soil. It now seems certain that they came from Central Asia comparatively recently, that they wandered for a long time over the plateaus of Pamir and Altai, and came gradually to their ultimate habitat by a slow process of migration. Two points that still remain obscure are their links with the Ossetic people on the one hand and with the Etruscans on the other. But the airy ideas once entertained about kinship with the Basques and the Japanese can now be regarded as definitely ruled out.

Most of the languages in the Empire belong to the Indo-European group, with Semitic influences varying according to area. Recent works have pointed out a number of puzzling links with the pre-Columbian languages of Mexico and Peru, with Aymara and Quechua. This discovery has, of course, revived speculations about Atlantis, about the countries that emerged and the continent that disappeared between Brazil and Africa. It may be that research now in progress will teach us something more about the origins of the Empire and its linguistic structure. But for the moment it is best to abstain from farfetched hypotheses and stick to established facts—they provide so much material there is no need to let the imagination run riot or to resort to sensation mongering.

Many nations came together in the Empire, and about a dozen of them spoke quite separate languages, which, though coming from a common root, were often very unlike one another. Between them all, an official language served as a link. Greek was not only the language of the court and of lawyers, poets, and merchants, but also the *lingua franca* and medium of communication for a whole section of the known world. At their famous meeting in Cyprus, Basil the Great, the khan of the Oïghurs, and the king of Sicily all spoke practically pure Greek. Within the Empire, however, Greek did not reign alone. During the reigns of Basil and Alexis, a stroller through the metropolis would have heard a thousand different tongues. People from Brittany, Persia, Kuchan, Egypt, Syria, Bactria, and even from India, China, and Africa joined the vivid tones of the Mediterranean to the rasp of the steppes and the mountains in a great aural motley. In the provinces there were a variety of dialects, patois, and accents that foreigners, and even sometimes inhabitants of the Empire itself, found difficult to follow. The remotest areas presented a sort of patchwork of strange tongues, from Mongol to Aramaean, from the ancient sacred languages, mostly reserved for priests and liturgy, in which linguists detect old Sanskrit roots, to Phoenician and perhaps Etruscan, which, like Mayan, resists all the attempts of modern science to decipher it. Some people wrote from left to right, others from right to left, some from the top downward, others from the bottom up. Some still used ideograms or crude pictograms, or did not communicate in writing at all, or read alternately from left to right and from right to left, as in boustrophedon. It was at court, in the institutions of government, and in circles that prided themselves on refinement or efficiency that Greek had its revenge. Basil the Great did much to impose it as the common language of the Empire. It soon became essential to know Greek if one wanted an important post at court or in the army, or to represent the emperor abroad or in the provinces, or to aspire to fashion or notoriety. The measures to promote Greek were the making of great numbers of grammarians and masters of rhetoric—wealthy families and men of ambition paid the earth for their services. The peoples of the Empire acquired this taste for the spoken word, eloquence, and poetry at about the time of Basil's reign. Before, except in the capital, language and letters had been held in low esteem. Women talked and sang, men drank and fought. But the requirements of administration, the need to transmit orders and keep records, and the growing popularity of bards and minstrels who entertained the troops in the evening by chanting fabulous or heroic adventures, gave the written or recited word a new dignity, into which fashion and emulation also entered. We shall see later the extraordinary role that soon came to be played by a historian like Justus Dion, by the poet Valerius, and by Logophilus the grammarian. In less than a century language became a kind of craze. Basil the Great was not above singing before foreign ambassadors, Alexis's guests would include as many poets and historians as generals, and the sciences of language were soon as highly esteemed and as seriously studied as military science, medicine, and the interpretation of sacred signs and wonders.

The attitude of the soothsayers and the priests toward what, despite its humble origins, has justly been called "the rise of learning," was bound to be ambiguous. On the one hand, the rise of learning was also the rise of danger. It was a threat to customs and privileges that had only been established and preserved through secrecy, mystery, and exclusivity. On the other hand, the growing taste for words and writing lent enormous power to anyone who could make them his instrument. The priests were quick to see that here was something that had to be either annihilated or annexed. After a period in which they tried to fight against the grammarians and historians, they decided not only to make them their allies if possible, but also to become grammarians and historians themselves—and later, as we shall see, mathematicians and accountants too. They succeeded brilliantly. But throughout the history of the Empire, like a persistent thread, runs the equivocal interplay between priests and scholars, ranging from coalitions in which they were almost indistinguishable to more or less openly declared enmity. The most significant example of this ambiguity was to be provided by Greek philosophy, to which we shall return in due course. One influential sect of priests from Syria finally saw language not merely as the image, but as the very essence of the absolute. Their faith, a precursor of monotheism, conceived the Word as a special hypostasis of divinity. In contrast, in the wild regions of the north a schism raged for over thirty years, in which both books and anyone who could read them were burned, poets and singers were imprisoned, and axes destroyed any pictures or statues guilty of fostering man's taste for symbols and signs.

Through wars and feasting, under priests and generals, with poets and grammarians, with the occasional ruin or disaster, the two or three centuries spanning the reigns of Arsaphes and Basil thus witnessed the exaltation of the mind and the mind's possibilities—as also of its fertile contradictions. By the sort of felicity of which history affords other examples, everything seemed to be progressing in unison toward more knowledge, more wealth, more beauty. Violence and insecurity no longer damaged trade, but encouraged and, in a sense, created it. Priests sometimes burned poets, but they also made use of them and praised them. Emperors and seers did not always agree, but they knew they needed one another. And so slowly ripened that rare and precious miracle, a civilization. In it, emperors saw power, priests an order of things, scholars a culture, merchants prosperity. All were glad of it and moved in hidden concert, by different paths, toward one common goal. The struggles between them worked toward accord and resolved in harmony. Ships sailed in with saffron and pepper, gold and silk, amber and precious woods. They sailed out carrying ivory worked by craftsmen in the suburbs of the City, cloth of silver set with gems and mother-of-pearl, vases and goblets, weapons and statues. New metals, more ingenious and efficient tools slowly percolated to the countryside and into artisans' workshops. Smith and sailor, peasant and woodcutter, architect and musician, harvester and weaver all marveled at a world still full of secrets and wonders; they loved them to the point of fierceness, of the most extreme cruelty. For to survive meant choosing to suffer. In their shops, in their fields, in the forests, on the sea, they worked, and waited. Peace was not yet. Wars threatened and sometimes struck. But wars were often successful, and, most important, they did not leave behind them the poisons of fear and lethargy. The strength of the people was still new enough not to recoil before pain or death, but to rejoice in them as an honor and happiness. Life in the Empire was hard and gay. Death was common. Suffering and atrocities were accepted. War was a celebration. Rejoicing was cruel. Promise loomed larger than the past. The Empire was young and, even in its ignorance and suffering, dreamed already of the million golden eagles of its future strength.

II

THE EAGLE AND THE TIGER

 BOUT 350 MILES NORTH OF THE CITY AND THE mouth of the Amphyses, a modern traveler sailing past the shores of what was once the Empire suddenly sees a twisted promontory appear against a landscape of sun-scorched cliffs. If one manages, under the thin clouds that persist even in high summer, to reach this narrow headland, all one finds are heaps of rocks, scree, steep hillocks, and strange figures carved in the stone. The local shepherds are still ready to point out the Tortoise, the Throne, the imperial Eagle, and the recumbent Woman, all silhouetted against the sky. But the visitor, forewarned by culture-conscious guides, goes up and examines them more closely. And as well as these *paesine*, these stone landscapes in which fanciful nature imitates and invents harbors, houses, fleets in battle array, and Giotto-like visions, there suddenly appears, beneath the geological chaos, human hand and intention—the remains of a door, an arch, a fallen tower, a rampart: the ruins of Onessa. They tell the story of the struggle between the Porphyries and the Venostae, who for more than four centuries, by their mutual hatred and common violence, steeped in blood the land that was to emerge from their strife as the Empire.

The origins of the Empire, as related by Justus Dion or sung by Valerius, long remained buried in the legends and the fables which have proved so inexhaustible a source of inspiration for literature and art. Right down to our own day, men's hearts and imaginations have been fired by the story of the rival brothers, of which both source and illustration are to be found in the endless tales, tragedies, songs, poems, and accounts, epic or romantic, of their successes and reverses. When, at the beginning of the nineteenth century, rationalist criticism, and in particular the brothers Grimm, detected in this rivalry between symmetrically opposed champions one of the most classical elements in popular legend, this insight was enough to call in doubt the historical reality. But, as is well known, ever since the ruins of Onessa were discovered by Hiram Bingham and Schliemann, the latter a Mecklenburg pastor's son who had succeeded in business, modern scholarship has been unanimous in confirming the almost literal truth of the old tradition. All the hatred, fury, treachery, cruelty, daring, passion, and cunning was not invented by poets and dramatists, but inscribed in stone and time: it was humanity itself and its history. The birth of the Empire had not been just invented by literature and art. The crimes, achievements, follies, and legends involved were all lived before they were related.[1]

It is difficult to conjure up what the Empire was like before it became the Empire. The early poets, up to Valerius, speak of a mythical age when happiness reigned and work and war were unknown. The first historical accounts paint a less rosy picture. The country was ravaged by armed bands, descending on their victims at random. Insecurity was rife, a neighbor no less a threat than the enemy. Everyone's chief preoccupation was how to survive from one day to the next, and this precluded any larger enterprise, any exchanges, any thought for the future. The idea of happiness is not new—people used to be happy in the midst of want and danger. What is new is the idea of choice. The only choice open to a man in those days was between death or going on as he was. It was chiefly in this sense that he was unfree. Then, even more than now, everything was determined by chance and birth, situation and climate. The forests in the north and the east were impenetrable, the southern plains scorching, and the mountain ranges between impassable and terrifying. Everyone was governed by the earth and the sky and immemorial danger. It was naturally in the west, toward the sea, that trade, art, and working in wood and bronze were to develop. But even in the most favored areas some sort of order and security had to emerge before there could be any thought, any ambition, any appreciation of wealth and beauty. It is a terrible illusion to think that prosperity and culture can flourish except under the shelter of strength. In the Empire, whether by chance or necessity, power arrived in time.

The real name of the first prince of Onessa is unknown. Some call him Kanabel, some Protus, others Tarkinos or Hvotan.[2] In certain texts he even appears under the name of Kaisari, the anachronism of

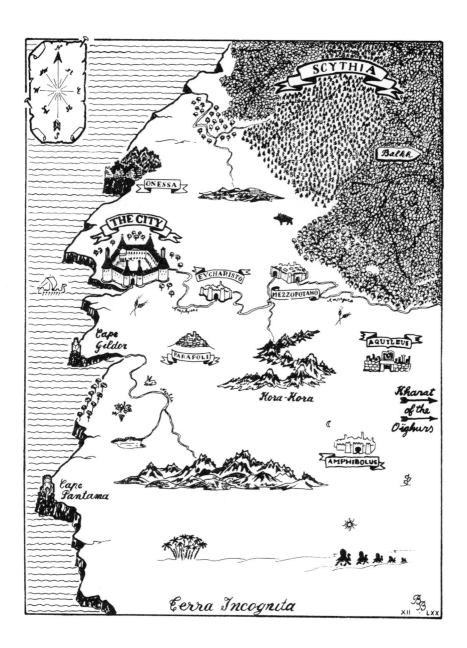

The Empire Under Arsaphes and Basil

which is glaringly obvious. What seems certain, at all events, is that all these different names apply to one war lord who brought under his command the whole northwest of what was to be the Empire. He chose as his residence the promontory of Onessa, and had it strongly fortified. It is the remains of this town which modern archeologists call Onessa III and IV (for two or three earlier settlements, of which almost nothing is known, had already succeeded one another on the same site). The whole cycle of Onessa legends, so extensively exploited, originates in the wars, splendors, and miseries of that era. Valerius's *Onessiad* will certainly remain its most outstanding memorial. It has been translated into French by the Abbé Delille, Burnouf, and Robert Brasillach; into English by T. S. Eliot; into Russian by Esenin and Mayakovsky; into German by Kleist and Rilke. These versions give us a glimpse of a daily life at once peaceful, ardent, and cruel, transfigured by a splendor of imagination and expression which translation still sometimes succeeds in transmitting through the ages.

With the two sons of the prince of Onessa, tradition emerges into a history still mythical but ever more thoroughly explored, and into family tragedy. Everyone in Onessa still knows the famous legend. The prince, on his deathbed, left his throne to whichever of his two sons most resembled, and could subdue, the tiger and the eagle. According to tradition, the elder, a gentle dreamer, was the first poet of the Empire. All the younger brother's thoughts were of war and of gaining power. A great clearing was made among the olive groves which can still be faintly traced to the northeast of Onessa. The two princes, unarmed, appeared simultaneously at opposite ends of the clearing, in the middle of which the priests loosed an eagle brought from the mountains and a tiger brought from the southern plains. The eagle flew up into the air, and after circling around three times came and perched on the shoulder of the younger brother. The tiger, after stretching itself, strolled to where the elder brother stood motionless, his sistrum or zither in his hand. Then the younger son, with the eagle still on his shoulder, came and strangled the tiger with his bare hands; and ever afterward the brothers were divided by a mortal hatred. The younger reigned at Onessa, which he had seized in the name of the eagle. The elder, taking the tiger as his emblem, went into exile, and for years, supported by just a faithful few, had to flee before the fury of his brother. He withdrew toward the south, and after a series of ambushes, battles, attempted betrayals, and narrowly escaped murders, he came and settled at last at the mouth of a great river. The river was the Amphyses, and the City was born.

That the Porphyries and Venostae are actually descendants of the two rival brothers is extremely doubtful. But what is certain is the persistence with which each party invoked one of the two princes and, in calling respectively upon the Eagle and the Tiger, fostered the enmity between the two factions. The Porphyries were masters of the City, while the Venostae ruled over Onessa and the surrounding region. As the years went by, the fratricidal struggle continued and developed. Each of the rival families had its lands, its fortresses, its troops and retainers; of each the only object seemed to be the annihilation of the other. There were traps and poisons, murders and reprisals. Every year at Onessa, on the first day of spring, a tiger and one hundred forty-four prisoners were tortured and put to death. The Porphyries were not so keen on killing. But the galleys of the City were full of oarsmen from Onessa.

The legendary and traditional motives for hatred eventually came to be only rhetorical. More real differences appeared and came into play. In a little more than two centuries the City, because of its climate and its position at the mouth of the Amphyses and as the outlet for the salt, spice, silk, and amber routes which wound north round the mountains and high plateaus, developed at a fantastic rate and soon began to enjoy an unparalleled prosperity. Onessa remained the war capital and unchallenged center of military power. But the City's trade and industry carried its fame far and wide. Another hundred and fifty or two hundred years, and its harbor gradually became one of the most important, then incontestably the most important, in the then known world. Pomposa alone could attempt to rival it. The ships of the City, their sails emblazoned with a tiger, scoured the sea to the northwest and pressed as far as Brittany, Barbary, and India. They came back laden with monkeys, parrots, ostriches, giraffes, breadfruit trees, coconuts, gold dust, ivory, wonderful tales, redheaded girls, and black slaves. The City was adorned with buildings each more huge and beautiful than the last; with temples, covered markets, circuses, hanging gardens. The philosophers and musicians came close on the heels of the merchants. Independently of the Arabs, Archimandrites discovered the theoretical rudiments of algebra and laid the foundations for calculating the probable losses of merchant ships; many centuries later, in Italy and

Spain and the distant Low Countries, this was to give rise to the insurance system. Almost simultaneously, Hermenides and Paraclitus founded their two rival schools of physics and metaphysics. The first maintained that the universe was immaterial like air and fire, that it was infinite, and that in it continuity reigned, there was room for freedom, and nothing ever repeated itself; the second declared that the world was like earth and water, that it was finite, composed of atoms, and ruled by necessity, and that history repeated itself cyclically.[3] Both schools were soon rent by schisms and heresies, and many apostates changed from one side to the other—atomists came to believe in freedom, while believers in continuity supported necessity.[4] The wild-beast shows, which throughout the history of the Empire drew huge crowds thirsty for color and blood, now no longer satisfied the more refined. Other kinds of entertainment grew up, to which merchants and their families went to give themselves a rest from trade risks and columns of figures. First came farces and panto-mimes, then satires and clowning. They were intended to evoke coarse laughter, but gradually became as cruel and harsh as the real world. Terror and tears gave even more pleasure than guffaws, and the adventures of the two princes of Onessa were revived in endless cycles where, intermingled with religious allusions, blood flowed in torrents and all was ruled by fate and the vengeance of the gods.[5] But beneath all the violence and roughness there were signs of the coming masterpieces of such dramatists as Menalchas and Polyphilus. After tragedy, comedy—nothing is subtler than a smile. Fun was poked at betrayed or beaten lovers, at misers and braggarts, above all at the audience itself. Sophistication was the order of the day: paradox, contradiction, and fine distinctions infiltrated everywhere. Moralists explained the whys and wherefores of events and feelings. Civilization was born.

Beneath the veneer of a skill and prosperity already widely famed, the City still lived under the constant threat of Onessa's enmity. It was a double danger, for as well as Onessa itself, other peoples were encouraged to take advantage of the rivalry between the Eagle and the Tiger. Every citizen tried to forget the fragility of fortune, and the tragedy of the City was that everyone succeeded. Yet the danger was always there, a faint background noise that all conspired to stifle. Pomposa never relented. Sicily, the islands in the northwest sea, the factories in Africa, and the sea routes to Syria and Scythia were all the subject of fierce, often violent, competition, and sometimes outright battles. Three times the fleets of Pomposa were victorious: off the Arginous Islands, at Maddalena Point, and in actual sight of the City harbor. In the east, the volcano district was uncertain, and the Aquilean Way was cut by roaming barbarians. In the north, the pressure from Onessa never relaxed. Prosperity and culture had come to the City too soon. After the first bright brief burst there came the resistance offered by men and things, adversity, the first setbacks, suffering, misfortune.

The history of the City and of Onessa now loses its early simplicity, only to recapture it again later at the same time as its grandeur. Meanwhile came dim ages of uncertain fortune, reversals, and confusion. The City was too weak to destroy Onessa. Onessa was not rich enough to master the City. Virtue reigned in Onessa, sharing the throne with cruelty and caprice. In the City, liberty and luxury verged on vice and weakness. While the first golden age of the City still showed legendary traces of its myths and origins, it also bore already the stigmata of decadence. Hardly was the City born, hardly had it begun to shine in the history of maritime powers and merchant republics, than it began to die. Historians later compared it to Tyre, Phoenicia, Venice, to England at the time of her triumphs. But now it was dying, dead. Confronted with the threat of the nomad barbarians, who had submerged Aquileus and were descending along the Amphyses to the sea, the City could only turn to one of its two enemies, Onessa or Pomposa. But the memory of the two rival brothers was still alive, maintained by literature and the arts, by the bitterness of old men and the raids that were a daily occurrence. Onessa was at once too near and too hated for its rigor, its obscure virtue, its austerity. So bitter was their hatred for the city of the Eagle that the rulers of the City threw themselves into the arms of the merchant warriors of Pomposa; with them, at least, drama and philosophy, easy living, and the trade in fine fabrics could go on as before. Capitulations were signed. The foreigners' ships appeared at the mouth of the Amphyses. A garrison disembarked. The harbor of the City became an annex of Pomposa. Though the appearance of well-being was preserved, the powers of trade and of the mind were sapped. By contrast with the roughness and pride of Onessa, the City showed the tinseled and torn façade of conquered splendor. The first act was over. The curtain fell on the City which had failed to create the Empire.

No one would dwell on this flash in the pan, these riches for a day, this weak showiness so soon swallowed up again in darkness, if the

Empire yet to come had not lent them significance. But every element in every story derives its meaning and importance from the ever-open future, which will give it its place, role, and rank. Nothing is ever complete at the time it happens. If the Empire had not come into being, if there had been no Arsaphes, no Basil, no Alexis, the City would have left behind only a minor trace. But the Empire did come into being, and Alexis did arise. And the first golden age of the City, instead of remaining in men's minds as a dead end and a failure, was transfigured into a sign and a promise.

In those far-off days, Onessa might have acted as an instrument of fate. The struggle between the Tiger and the Eagle was transformed into something resembling the dim beginnings of national sentiment. Onessa, still free while the City was under the Pomposan yoke, represented, as against the foreign invader, the spirit of the Empire that was to come. But Onessa had no navy. Pomposa could call on mercenaries from every quarter; the gold of the merchant warriors commanded power and interest, and was not without effect even on conscience. The attacks from the north continued almost without respite, but also without result. The paradox of the conflict lay in the position of the City, and in particular of the Porphyries. Every year, every month, the demands of Pomposa became more exacting, more unbearable. And the Onessan troops several times reached the walls of the City. Yet, caught as the Tiger was between two dangers, to give in and appeal to the Eagle was impossible. The past hung too heavy. Submission itself still had too many charms. In their palaces the Porphyries lolled inactive, in a sort of willful blindness, hovering between two dangers. As Weill-Pichon puts it, "The City, with a mixture of reserve and abandon, sampled the taste of slavery and collaboration." Pomposa presents a perfect example of colonialism before its time. Its shops and warehouses, its commercial and financial organizations, covered the country with a network of hangers-on. Wealth was skillfully exploited. Talent went into exile. The merchants and their High Council produced in the City a reign of mild and even smiling terror. Their barbarian mercenaries were the guarantee of an order that the Porphyries did not shake off because they could not, which they did not even decry because, in a sense, it suited them.

Everything is paradoxical and surprising about this first golden age of the City: that it came into being at all; that it lasted so short a time. Its good and bad fortune are equally improbable—as improbable as the ways of history, the ways of God and men. The City had thought that its fortune was made, but no—lack of courage had brought servitude instead. The City was to believe that all was lost, but no—everything would be saved. Saved? Yes. But by what deviousness, what tricks of history! There would have to be new tragedies and new actors. The curtain was already rising again; the theater was falling silent; the actors were taking their places. Each time the plot was a little thicker. History cannot advance without people, plenty of people. But beneath all the suffering and blood, beneath the luxury of palaces and the misery of slaves, beneath hatred, avarice, obscure religion, and the strangeness of men's minds, how simple things really are, how clear the designs of history, all ready to be inscribed in books and in human memory. The Eagle and the Tiger represent the rival brothers. Onessa, the City, Pomposa (or the Venostae, the Porphyries, and the merchant princes) represent a triangular and ambiguous combat. Then a fourth force comes upon the scene of the Empire—the barbarians.

III

ARSAPHES'S MERCENARIES

 HERE WAS NO GAYER OR LIVELIER SIGHT IMAGIN-able than the streets of the City, even at the time of its decadence. Every traveler's tale is full of surprise and wonder.[1] A unique prosperity and animation reigned there still, or already. According to the most conservative estimates, two or three hundred thousand people (some authorities say four hundred thousand) were engaged in trade, the arts, and entertainment, and they went about it with an energy, almost a frenzy, that was indifferent to servitude. From sunrise the harbor seethed with people, and long after night had fallen, mansions, palaces, and theaters rang with the echoes of banquets and revels which often went on until dawn. All night the watchmen would see people still on the streets—drunks, fops, wits, bores, people going home to bed late after a gay evening. The Pomposan merchants took good care not to interfere with this prosperity and these easygoing ways. They contented themselves with collecting profits and enormous taxes, and did their best to encourage pleasure and levity. True, there were two or three attempts at rebellion in the City, but they were crushed, and the roads leading into the town were lined with thousands of crucified rebels to serve as examples. The merchants did not soil their own hands with such unpleasant tasks. They left them to the barbarian mercenaries who occupied and controlled the country in the name of the High Council. Bearded, rough, often drunk, always cruel and brutal, they rode about on their little horses spreading terror. All the High Council had to do to intimidate everyone was bring in the mercenaries; all they had to do to reassure everyone was withdraw them. Everyday life and prosperity, the activities of docks and theaters, all presupposed the absence of the mercenaries. Any attempt at independence on the part of the

people, any thrust of ambition on the part of the Porphyries produced the mercenaries' presence and the threat of their violence. Once or twice a year the City was delivered over to them. Early in the morning, the sound of galloping horses would be heard on the outskirts. Panic would spread to the harbor, the City center, and the fashionable districts. The streets emptied. Every citizen peered out fearfully from behind barred doors at the wild hordes sweeping by.

The barbarians did not speak Greek. They came from Mongolia, Bactria, the Persian provinces, or Libya, and were grouped according to country and dialect. Their inability to communicate among themselves put them at the mercy of chiefs who spoke several languages and could thus command the movements of several divisions. Their chief general took orders from the High Council, who soon realized the power of the mercenaries. Army commissars saw to it that they were ruled with ruthless discipline. Several generals were summoned to Pomposa and tried and imprisoned. Some were executed, some were stricken with sudden mysterious illness—there was talk of poison. The object of the merchant warriors was to keep the mercenaries' power within the strictest limits so as to spread fear in the City and control the Porphyries without ever putting Pomposa's own supremacy in danger. The merchants were very good at such delicate juggling acts.

For several years the Bactrian troops were commanded by a young captain very popular with the women. His courage, intelligence, and good looks soon made him well known not only among the mercenaries but also in the City. Men of business and education began to invite him to banquets, to the circus, and even to the theater. The captain, whose name was Arsaphes, spoke several languages equally well: Persian, Libyan, Syrian, the far-off dialect of the Rhine, Latin, and Greek. He had distinguished himself on several occasions fighting against the Onessan army, he danced well, and combined the violence of the barbarians with the ease, charm, and breeding of the City and of Pomposa. On his return from an expedition against the armies of Venosta, he became the lover of one of the Porphyries' ladies in waiting. All the charms of garrison life then unfolded before the young captain. Feasting and pleasure were his for the taking.

After the violent incidents that accompany the beginning of any occupation, several barbarian officers had succumbed to the attractions of the City. Arsaphes differed from the others not only in his success but also in his steadfastness: he had become the most brilliant of the barbarians adopted by the fashionable world of the City, but he remained the most intransigent. After dancing with Aspasia in the Porphyries' palaces, he would go back to camp outside the City and sleep on a rough wooden cot.

The prince who then reigned, in name at least, over the City, was called Nephaot. He noticed Arsaphes, knew of his liaison with one of the ladies at court, and began to have hopes of an alliance between the Porphyries and the mercenaries against the domination of Pomposa and the High Council. By an already well-established custom, Nephaot's daughter, the princess Heloise, was being educated in Pomposa, as a sort of honored hostage. She was due to return to her father for her eighteenth birthday, and Nephaot planned, under cover of the celebrations and with the help of the mercenaries, to try to regain power. Aspasia, Arsaphes's mistress, was a key figure in the affair. She was admitted into the plot, and tried, by hints and allusions, to win over her lover. Arsaphes said neither yes or no. He was biding his time.

The arrival in harbor of the ship bringing back Princess Heloise was the occasion for one of those ceremonies that enchanted the crowd at the time, and later inspired the historical melodramas of Alexandre Dumas and Victorien Sardou, the once famous pictures of Paul Delaroche, Alphonse de Neuville, and Jean-Paul Laurens, and the Italian cinema between the two world wars. From early morning the port was full of people. It was spring, and the weather was already fine and warm after the rigors of winter. The sky had been clear for two or three days, and a mild breeze had coaxed open flowers and leaf buds. The crowd swarmed on the quays, children were perched on roofs and masts, and boats bursting with passengers set out to sea to meet the ship. The ocher cliffs to the south of the harbor, the white town on the hill, the high buildings along the shore, the colorful clothes of the spectators lent the scene the gaiety and liveliness so characteristic of the City. The women munched olives and dried fruit, the men drank the local rye brandy, so clear and pure it looked like water. As usual, a tent and a dais had been set up on the quay for the prince and the members of the High Council. As if display were inversely proportionate to real power, the prince was dressed in crimson, with high boots and a belt of gold. The merchant warriors wore their usual black, with white collars and strange round caps. The simplicity of their costume was enough in itself to set the people of the City murmuring with dread and respect mingled with an undercurrent of hostility.

When the princess's ship reached the entrance to the harbor a great shout arose from the boats, the quays, the houses, the hill, and the little boys perched in the trees. It took some time for the ship to berth, and the attendant dignitaries got through the deflating interval as best they could. At last a long gangplank was set up between the ship and the shore, and Princess Heloise, preceded by her nurse, her astrologer, and a Negro page, disembarked. With never a glance for the merchant warriors, she sank in so deep and graceful a curtsy before the prince that the crowd went wild. The prince raised her up and folded her in his arms.

The mercenaries, as always, had been kept well out of the way. Only their leaders accompanied the merchants on the dais. As Justus Dion describes it, with characteristic naïveté, "scarcely had Arsaphes laid eyes upon the princess than his heart was pierced with love—not merely the animal desire to embrace and possess her, but the fire that is at once grief and joy, the passion that defies death."[2] To judge by the coins and miniatures in which she is depicted, Princess Heloise was indeed a very beautiful girl. She was tall, very dark, with long hair down her back and a noble, not to say haughty, demeanor. Her striking carriage set off an exceptionally long neck, and her neck captivated Arsaphes, captain of the Bactrian mercenaries of the High Council of Pomposa. His reaction was to influence the fate of the City and of the Empire.

That evening in the palace of the Porphyries, Arsaphes had no eyes for anyone but the princess. Between dances, Aspasia sang her praises and tried to urge on him the exigencies of the plot. Arsaphes replied shortly that he had made his decision and was ready to serve the Porphyries. Aspasia lost no time in apprising Nephaot and Heloise of the success of her mission. A meeting was arranged at dusk the following day, attended by the prince and his daughter, Arsaphes, three or four nobles of the City, and two or three officers authorized by the High Council to discuss minor questions between the mercenaries and the palace. Arsaphes spoke with a lucidity and calm that impressed the prince. But the captain's only concern was with the princess. She had a passionate hatred of Pomposa and the merchant princes. She spoke fervently to the soldier, but seemed not to notice him as a man. The preliminaries went on for several days, and Arsaphes finally plucked up courage to face Heloise and assure her, with ardor, of his devotion to her. She replied loftily that devotion to the cause of the City and of the Porphyries was all that was required.

Arsaphes soon saw that although he was the linchpin of the whole military and political operation, he was destined to remain a mere instrument. But it was too late to draw back, and with despair in his heart he carried out his historic coup. Just before the critical moment, unable to keep silent any longer, perhaps fearing to die with his secret untold, probably thinking all he had suddenly come to care for was lost, he told Aspasia of his love for Heloise. The confession nearly wrecked the whole plot and cost Prince Nephaot his life. Aspasia had thought Arsaphes was doing everything for her sake, and his revelation of the truth drove her immediately into the other camp. Consumed with jealousy, she wanted only to destroy Arsaphes and his guilty passion, even if it meant bringing about the failure of the insurrection she had so much hoped for and in which she had played so great a part. The procurator of the High Council, secretly informed by Aspasia of what was in the wind, had the leader of the Porphyries accused of treason, arrested, and summarily put to death. Princess Heloise escaped only by a miracle. Arsaphes stabbed Aspasia to death.

Readers will already have recognized the main outlines of the tragedy of *Arsaphes and Heloise*, under which title Polyphilus, Garnier, the elder Corneille, and in our own time Anouilh all wrote plays. At the height of the imbroglio, when Nephaot had already been murdered by mercenaries loyal to the High Council, Arsaphes, still unsure of the issue, sent a messenger to the Princess Heloise to declare his love. The messenger's speech, as rendered by Garnier, Corneille, and Anouilh, has given rise to countless commentaries and comparisons. What is perhaps less familiar is the fact reported by Justus Dion that after the princess's indignant rejection—while the warehouses burned, the palace was occupied by rebel troops, and the members of the High Council were in permanent session in the camp of the Syrian mercenaries where they had taken refuge—Arsaphes, disappointed and temporarily discouraged, sent his aide to Heloise a second time. This time, as a token of his master's love, the messenger brought a handful of earth and a handful of salt, an ancient Bactrian custom that was observed persisting as late as the seventeenth century, according to the accounts of Tavernier and

Chardin.[3] But Arsaphes, driven by the obduracy of the princess and feeling victory within his grasp, added to the traditional offering two partridge eggs, one painted blue and the other red. The princess easily saw their significance, mysterious as it may seem to us. The colored eggs meant that though women may not look exactly alike, in the end they all taste alike.

Princess Heloise was worthy of the captain's admiration. She knew how to answer insolence. She sent back the lieutenant with two flasks which looked as though they contained water, but when Arsaphes tasted them, he found that while the first was indeed full of water, the second held the strongest and headiest rye brandy he had ever drunk. He then realized that while people may no doubt look alike, some are insipid and dull while others burn and intoxicate.

The battle for the City lasted five days and nights, and by dawn on the sixth day Arsaphes's mercenaries had gained the upper hand. It was a scene of utter desolation, of smoking ruins and ransacked houses. Fire and pillage had destroyed everything. Justus Dion says nearly a hundred thousand people—one out of every three inhabitants—died in the long struggle that had not really concerned them. When the survivors of the delegation of the High Council, who had taken refuge on a ship, sent to ask Arsaphes for peace terms and to spare the lives of prisoners, the City had ceased to exist. Its splendor, its prosperity in servitude, the monuments it was so proud of, the harbor buildings, the temples, the theaters, the palaces of the Porphyries —all were bespattered with blood, scorched, devastated, fallen. And so, in defeat, the merchant warriors of Pomposa found a bitter consolation.

It is not hard to see the reason for the violence of the fighting: it was not in anyone's interest to give quarter. For the merchant warriors it was a question of losing or keeping all; for the rebel mercenaries a question of losing or winning all. Neither side cared for buildings, works of art, ornaments, or ingenious devices which would never be of any use to them, and which, if they themselves were conquered and had their eyes put out, they would never even see. Their only interest in the City was either to get still more wealth out of it, or, having vanquished it, to exploit its riches. For both sides all these treasures were booty rather than heritage, and they preferred to destroy them rather than let them fall into the hands of the enemy.

As for the inhabitants of the City, their original attitude was one of indifference. For them it could only be a question of whether they kept their old masters or exchanged them for new. But it was difficult to remain neutral when battle was raging, arrows flying, and fire threatening at every moment. In taking sides, some were influenced by their hatred of the merchant warriors, others by fear of disorder. The City was the prize in a battle it only dimly understood, and it divided and destroyed itself in the service of interests that could never coincide with its own.

Perhaps the only person who saw in his victory a significance beyond pillage and loot was the victor himself, Arsaphes. For this attitude, which immediately gave him a distinctive place in the history of the City, there were several reasons. First, he was a man of vision, who saw further than the immediate satisfaction of minor desires. Second, he had come to appreciate the City, its civilization and culture, and even the love of pleasure that was also a love of beauty. The third reason was that he loved the Princess Heloise. History offers several examples of famous couples in which the woman is worthy of the man and vies with him in nobility: Ahasuerus and Esther, Alexis and Theodora, Hero and Leander, the other Heloise and Abelard, Justinian and the other Theodora. But none of their stories outdoes that of Arsaphes and Heloise.

Arsaphes put his life and career at stake out of sheer love for Princess Heloise. Naturally, some historians have denied the emotional and anecdotal aspect and advanced various other reasons connected with various philosophies of history. Some, like Robert Weill-Pichon, adduce religious motives, while Marxists see Arsaphes as the instrument of a popular revolt against the ruling caste of Pomposan merchants. But it now seems clear that the origin of what happened is to be found in Arsaphes's passion for Nephaot's daughter. Of course, it is also clear that the Porphyries made use of this passion to further their own ends. It is even fairly probable that Nephaot thought of getting rid of Arsaphes once he had served his purpose. But the rebel leader's momentary discouragement, his confession of love, and Aspasia's betrayal all paradoxically led to the murder of Nephaot and the victory of Arsaphes alone. And it was to love that the captain of the mercenaries owed his decision to act and, indirectly, his ability to use the advantages of victory for himself. The intermingling of politics, love, and victory made the story of Arsaphes and Heloise a matchless subject for the theater and romance. And for centuries, right down to our own day, historical sensibility and popular imagination were to be stirred by the famous triple interview after the battle, in the ruins of the Porphyries' palace.

Even with victory his, Arsaphes thought of nothing but his love. Justus Dion writes: "For the barbarian, the victory that gave him an empire was as nought. He had sought fame only to make himself loved." For another two days he hesitated. On the pretext of having to organize the situation and to negotiate with what remained of the High Council, he avoided the issue. Then on the third day, like a general naturally anxious about the fate of important citizens, he asked whether the Princess Heloise had escaped the fire and slaughter. No one could say. There was no news of her. Unable to restrain himself any longer, the captain commanded the princess to be brought to him at once, dead or alive. Let them send out patrols and search parties if necessary. Let horsemen scour the ruins of the City and the surrounding country. Rewards were offered. The person of the princess was declared sacrosanct under pain of indescribable tortures. Before night had fallen on the following day the princess was found in a house on the outskirts by the river. Arsaphes had her looked after with all possible attention and respect, and kept her waiting another three days. The delay was not so much designed to shake the courage of the prisoner as to strengthen that of the victor, suddenly terrified of the fruits of his victory. When the princess came to him at last, followed by her guards, the captain arose and went to meet her, bowed, and asked her to declare her wishes. Her answer was brief: she wanted either the throne or death.

The famous exchange between them, as reported by Justus Dion and endlessly reworked from Polyphilus down to Anouilh, tells us probably less about the mentality and manners of the City at the end of the Pomposan ascendancy than about the preoccupations of the dramatists and their audiences: in Polyphilus, the role of fate and the gods; in Corneille, the struggle between honor and passion; in Anouilh, the dignity of rejection. Somewhat paradoxically, Justus Dion's account suggests attitudes not so very far removed from the version we today might consider the most literary and artificial. The elder Corneille's *Arsaphes and Heloise* conveys much the same wild yet baroque grandeur as emanates from Justus Dion. We know that in its own day the play marked the final fall from favor of the aging poet. Madame de Sévigné and Saint-Simon, the one with emotion, the other with cold disdain, both refer to the play's hopeless failure. The marquise writes: "I am in despair and have been weeping like a fool since yesterday. What baseness! I could rail against God for having made our countrymen so feather-brained. . . . Indulgence toward friends is not, let me tell you, a weakness of which I am often accused. As Monsieur de Bouillon says, I have plenty of others. But I am enamoured of *Arsaphes and Heloise* and want everything to yield to the genius of Corneille." The duke says: "M. le Prince told Monseigneur, who again told Mme. de Saint-Simon, in the presence of a number of lawyers and authors, that most people, that is to say the fools, had condemned the play, judging it sometimes so unbridled as to be slightly mad, sometimes sickeningly sweet and insipid; and that poor Corneille, ill with shame and disappointment to see *Arsaphes and Heloise* plunged suddenly into the void after so brief a career, and himself used to praise and honor far beyond his rank and worth, declared that he knew the faults of the work but neither could nor would avoid them, carried away as he was by the grandeur and truth of his subject; and further, that his style had never more widely or deeply represented the human soul, the manners of the age, and the genius of monarchs." With Brasillach and Thierry Maulnier, posterity finally ranged itself against the cabal that opposed the poet and with the authors of the *Letters* and the *Memoirs*. And Corneille is saved not only by his style and imagery, but also, beneath the wigs and formality, by his historical accuracy. All doubt on the matter was removed when Professor Ritter, in 1953, discovered a fourteenth-century Arabic manuscript in the archives of the Sublime Porte. Justus Dion's account was discovered, almost simultaneously, by Robert Estienne and by Amyot in two monasteries in Flanders and Lower Saxony, in 1552 and 1557 respectively. So the Ritter manuscript represents a completely different tradition. And yet it has astounding parallels with Corneille.

Princess Heloise had lost everything, but she ruled the victor. All yielded to Arsaphes; Arsaphes thought only of Heloise. Nothing would have been easier than for the barbarian to seize his helpless prisoner by force; but the very love she inspired in him held him back. It was a marvelously simple situation that could easily be resolved by an agreement between the victorious mercenary and the fallen princess. But a moral obstacle prevented any simple solution of either the love story or the historical conflict. The princess was now powerless in the hands of the barbarian, and honor forbade her to give herself to him now she was brought low, after having scorned him at the height of her power. Could she who had scarcely glanced at him in her splendor contemplate changing in her distress? Or could she forget it was the rebel captain's confession of his insane passion that had been the indirect cause of Nephaot's death? Of course, her father had taken a risk in unleashing the revolt, but had it not been for Arsaphes's confession to Aspasia, Nephaot, instead of the barbarian, might have been the victor. Naturally, there was no lack of counselors to insinuate to the princess that Arsaphes's indiscretion was skillfully planned to rid himself of a master and a rival. Even if it was only through weakness, not guile, that he was responsible for her father's death, how could she now throw herself into his arms? The dilemma was all the more cruel in that—in Justus Dion, as in Corneille and in the Istanbul manuscript—through the surge of battle and the brilliance of victory, Heloise's heart gradually came to be touched. As danger mounted, so there was born and grew in her a love that she recognized at first with joy, then with horror. But when it had become so great she could no longer hide it from herself, it was too late. The trap had closed about her, victory was won, and the princess was no more than the prey of one whom rank, dignity, and honor all commanded her to refuse.

The story of Heloise and Arsaphes reaches its climax in the three interviews in which the princess struggles to get the better of her passion and the mercenary struggles to get the better of his victory. As we have seen, the first encounter—in which the princess claimed death or her throne—enabled her to keep her secret. She says she wishes to be spared seeing her conqueror again. But Arsaphes cannot bear not to hear the words that drive him to despair. Perhaps suffering only increases his love. Perhaps, too, he senses that beneath the cruel words the princess's will, struggling against itself, is weakening. The second meeting takes place the following day, and in it the feelings too long constrained by appearances burst forth at last. When the scene opens, both the barbarian and the princess still try to conceal their real sentiments. Arsaphes again assures Heloise of his desire to do all she wishes. Heloise answers with her usual haughtiness: if she cannot have either death or her rights, at least let her have less ceremony and fewer guards. Arsaphes, convinced that she hates and despises him, sees a victory that no longer holds any meaning for him snatched away. Unable to contain himself, he reveals his love and lays his newly won power at his prisoner's feet. She has only to speak and the City will be given back to her. She refuses all the more vehemently because she feels her resistance weakening. She will owe nothing to a conqueror she is forcing herself to hate. But when Arsaphes makes use of his last weapon and threatens to recall the merchant princes, surrender to them, and hand power back to the High Council of Pomposa, Heloise has no choice but to avow in her turn her ill-starred passion. Yes, she loves Arsaphes. He must rule the City, but she cannot give herself to him because he is the victor and she is alone and vanquished. But he must not recall the merchants of Pomposa; he must live, and go on fighting against them. He must make the City great. He must sire a new race and take the place of the Porphyries, whose day is over. But he must forget Heloise.

The barbarian captain is overwhelmed both by happiness and by a new despair. For a third and last time he meets the princess to try to win her over. But this time, as a sign of defeat and submission, it is he who goes to seek her out. Genius orders their exchange into a poetic yet real truth that echoes into eternity . . .[4]

These lines merit attention for several reasons. In the first place they, of course, illustrate the seventeenth-century antithesis, which found classical expression in Corneille, between love and honor, passion and duty. They also throw a new light on this opposition. But in addition, for anyone trying to understand the origins of the Empire, they show up clearly the historical position of Arsaphes, between the Porphyries' submission to Pomposa and the uncertain future he himself offered the City. The victory of the rebel mercenaries constitutes a decisive break. Not merely another family, but another people, another race, succeeds the Porphyries. But by a trick and paradox of history, the rupture, striking as it is, also illustrates a remarkable continuity in the development of the future Empire. The Porphyries had been subservient to Pomposa. No resurrection of what might later be called national feeling could be expected from them. We have already seen that Onessa and the Venostae might, and perhaps should, have filled that role. But they were not ready for so formidable a task. They had not the power; the City hated them too much—as much as, probably more than, the invading merchants. For the Empire to come into being there had to be some foreign element capable of driving out the merchant princes and the solidly entrenched High Council. This was the role played by Arsaphes, and Corneille shows it not only brilliantly but also with a political insight confirmed by the most modern research. We shall see later that Arsaphes's descendants were not always equal to their task, and justified the bitter doubts expressed by the founder of the new dynasty. But the step had to be taken. History still had more than one twist in reserve before bringing on Alexis, who never failed to claim kinship with the barbarian captain.

As we know, Heloise finally gave in to the combined pressure of Arsaphes's and her own love. There was no need for the semi-miraculous intervention of Corneille's high priest, reminiscent of that of the king in the epilogue of *Le Cid*. Justus Dion is more direct, and probably more accurate: "The princess resisted for three moons, and more. Then the desire she had for Arsaphes increased so irresistibly that one evening when he had come to see her quite unescorted, she threw herself weeping into his arms and became his wife."

The marriage of Arsaphes and Heloise took place in a ruined city, but amidst the enthusiasm of survivors who might at last hope for peace. Barbarian blood mingled with that of the last of the Porphyries and for a while gave the City back some of its old vigor. But the first golden age of art and culture was over. With Arsaphes, the City was to turn away from servitude, from overseas trade, from the theater, and from a life of ease. The mercenaries would begin to build the Empire that neither the Porphyries nor the Venostae had been able to create.

The idea of Empire, which was to have such a profound effect on political and social history, was first introduced into the world, though if not in its full and final form, by a jumble of Syrians, Persians, Scythians, Mongols, and Libyans under the leadership of a captain from Bactria. And as a further paradox, the love story of the barbarian who knew how to dance marked the entrance on the scene of a people who, in a new age of war and violence, aimed first at peace. As successor to the Porphyries, whose name, language, and religion he adopted, Arsaphes also inherited their traditional enemies. While the ravaged City still echoed with both the obsequies of the victims of war and the celebrations of the royal marriage, trouble was already brewing on three fronts. Pomposa, Onessa, and the barbarians were getting ready to combine their efforts against the City.

IV

AQUILEUS

 HERE IS A STRIKING CONTRAST BETWEEN THE CITY of the Porphyries and the Empire emerging under Arsaphes. Paradoxically, the mercenaries brought back liberty and independence. Servitude was over, with both its advantages and its disadvantages. At one blow the City lost the reputation for charm and easy living that had made it famous. For the one hundred fifty years between Arsaphes and Basil the Great, one can hardly name two or three philosophers, a single architect or painter, or more than three or four writers. The theater declined, night life faded. Before Arsaphes had been in power four years a kind of military and moral order reigned over the City. Justus Dion reports that prostitution, widespread in the Porphyrean golden age, though now not entirely abolished was very strictly controlled. The courtesans, whose houses by the harbor and in the fashionable districts used to be meeting places for elegant young men, important citizens, and officials (even the delegates of the High Council were occasionally seen there), now gathered together in special areas near the various army camps. The more fortunate among them took up residence near the temples, where the priests encouraged religious prostitution and regulated it for purposes of their own.[1] By another irony of history, this was one of the precedents—there were many more ancient ones—that made it possible for religious courtesans to play such an influential role, as we shall see later, in the Empire of Alexis.

The priests were building up their strength. The High Council had allowed them to celebrate their religion freely and to enjoy certain financial privileges and ostensible but empty honors. But it had taken great care not to let them acquire any influence over the masses. The merchant princes had regarded the soothsayers with the utmost suspicion, though they made no attempt to introduce into the City the gods of Pomposa, in whom they probably did not believe themselves. Two or three times in forty or fifty years the patriarch of Pomposa had been invited by the High Council to visit the City, but such visits were only the occasions for feasting and display. Trade was really Pomposa's religion. The High Council did not harass the priests; it simply ignored them. But it also kept a close watch on them; and when Pomposa's ascendancy ended, swarms of spies and informers in the pay of the High Council disappeared as if by magic. The priests at once seized the opportunity to establish their power on firmer foundations, and before another thirty years had passed they had become a formidable power in the State. Aquileus, their center, a town whose extraordinary fate we shall see later, grew ever greater in size and strength. Instead of the confusion that had reigned before, when there were many different religions and different gods, the priests combined to set up customs, rules, and hierarchies that were to last for many years. The role of priest came to be a coveted one, and young men of ambition saw it as either a career in itself or a springboard that could advance them toward secular power. Arsaphes, far from opposing this trend, encouraged and made use of it. Because he had to make war he needed soldiers, and if he needed soldiers he also needed those radiant yet undefined forces that make men want to live and enable them to die. He saw the priesthood, and an organized and obedient religion, as a very useful instrument of government. Of course, the danger was that a caste might grow up that would eventually threaten the central authority that had originally protected it. Historians and philosophers later criticized Arsaphes for giving the soothsayers so much power.[2] But it was difficult to see so far ahead. The main thing was to keep religion and the clergy under control, so as to maintain order and win wars. Arsaphes kept them under control.

Arsaphes himself changed greatly during the twenty-seven years of his reign. We met him as a young captain, fond of the rigors of camp life, yet dancing with his mistresses at the court of the Porphyries. But when the young captain became a prince he soon presented himself to his people as a symbol and example of austerity. Between the seventh and twelfth year of his reign he spent a total of only four months in the City. Always in the field, always fighting, he showed tireless energy and unflinching rigor. There are countless examples of his courage and endurance, of his violence too and the rigorous demands he made on others, as on himself. Once when his men seemed reluctant to set out on foot across a vast rock-strewn plain, treeless and waterless, he even stabbed his own favorite horse and led the way. It is hard to imagine how the same man who was so helpless before the princess Heloise, at the very moment when power was his for the taking, should suddenly have been transformed into this fabulous adventurer of the southern plain and the north and eastern forest. But he had never ceased to be an adventurer. It was just that passion struck and weakened him for a moment—the right moment for winning an empire. For Arsaphes, as later for Basil and Alexis, everything combined to go on adding to his power and strength. One seems to see a flaw, a mistake, a suggestion that his luck is turning, but it is always just one more step toward the realization of the Empire. For nearly fifteen years Princess Heloise was by his side, representing with unfailing dignity the survival of the previous dynasty. When she died of the plague, Arsaphes himself became the true heir of the Porphyries, and his and Heloise's two sons represented for everyone—except, perhaps, as we shall see, for themselves—the legitimacy of the princes of the City.

Even before the death of Arsaphes the Empire was beginning to take over from the City. The birth of the City had been linked with overseas trade. But Arsaphes looked chiefly to the east, to the land, to the deserts, and to the forests. Luxury was soon forgotten; pleasure was replaced by the disciplines of war. The harbor fell into disuse. Pomposa, unable now to profit from the City, was not content with ostentatiously staying away. By force or by persuasion exerted on allies, vassals, and rivals alike, she imposed a blockade that was sometimes very harsh. There were several clashes between the Pomposan forces and those of Arsaphes. At sea, Pomposa always won, so Arsaphes avoided maritime adventures and skillfully lured the merchants to attempt landings. Their third try was the biggest. One night at Cape Gildor, about 200 miles south of the City, the Pomposans landed five or six hundred troops which met with no resistance and seized several fishing villages along the coast without striking a blow. Strengthened by reinforcements, they thrust inland and after a few days had surrounded a camp of Syrian cavalry stationed there to defend the coast in depth. Arsaphes made no move. Several of his advisers begged him to attack as soon as possible and stop the merchants from setting up a dangerous new bridgehead so close to the City. Arsaphes paid no attention. On the contrary, he withdrew all reinforcements and fresh troops from the area. All he did was contain the landing by maintaining a firm hold on the coast north and south of Cape Gildor. The Pomposans fells into the trap. Reinforced by fresh landings at the same point, they skirted the Syrian camp, which was still holding out, and advanced farther inland. Arsaphes quietly watched the invaders pour into the pocket he had prepared for them. When he judged the prize big enough, and a fresh influx of the enemy began to look dangerous, he drew the net tight at Cape Gildor and sent in against the encircled foe the battalions of Parthian, Bactrian, and Numidian cavalry he had been holding secretly in reserve. Pomposa tried to land fresh reinforcements at the Cape, but the barrier of City troops now stretched across the neck of the headland prevented them from reaching the main battle area. There, the Syrians made a sortie that took the Pomposans in the rear and compelled them to surrender.

The defeat of Pomposa at Cape Gildor freed Arsaphes from any danger of attack from the sea. But it was not enough to enable him to compete with the Pomposan fleet. A tacit agreement was made: the sea belonged to the merchant princes, the land to the City and Arsaphes. In the course of years this *de facto* truce even became a show of alliance. Arsaphes had enough enemies already. He needed to be free to defend himself north, south, and east. The City ceased to be a port open to the west, and became a camp, a citadel, the base for long expeditions against the kingdoms of the barbarians.

It was as if, before it gave birth to the Empire, the City had to undergo two kinds of apprenticeships, one after the other: first trade then war; first sea then land; first art then asceticism. The strange thing is that in both phases the City came into immediate conflict with those who most resembled it. The Porphyries lived in luxury and a certain refinement, and they had a taste for maritime venture, intellectual activity, competition in trade; and they came up against the merchant princes. Arsaphes, a Bactrian mercenary, a soldier of fortune, a disciplined warrior although of rough origins, had to fight chiefly against the barbarians. The explanation is that it is rivals rather than enemies who hamper our beginnings, and it is against them we fight until the great conflicts arise which decide ways of life, modes of thought, and the meaning of history.

Under the Porphyries the City had many philosophers and architects. Arsaphes surrounded himself with soldiers. Hermenides and Paraclites were succeeded by Bogomil, Labianus, and Odier. They often came from the very places where they were to fight, and knew the climate, the roads, and the ways of the people. When victory was won it was not too difficult for them to establish friendly relations with the population. Barbarians in the service of the City, they came to act as representatives of the City among their own tribes or in the towns where they were born. At the death of Arsaphes the City had almost ceased to have any influence along the northwest coast. Its pottery and fabrics, the fame of its artists and writers were no longer carried far and wide. The foreigners who used to be attracted by the brilliance of the City and its reputation now came there only reluctantly, when business made it necessary. Barracks stood where once there had been temples and palaces. The gaiety, lightheartedness, and charm of the inhabitants had faded with the cessation of pleasure and the rigors of war. The harbor was dead. But to the north, east, and south, in the forests and the mountains, and beyond, in the desert, the armies of Arsaphes advanced. The whole Amphyses valley, and the Nephta valley too, now belonged to the City. The fertile plains at the foot of the volcanoes supplied the armies and their contractors with nearly all they needed of wheat and barley, rye and millet. In and around the City, in and around Aquileus, in Amphibolus, and in the camps around the temples, there was enough food for thousands of craftsmen to gather to make pikes, lances, bows, and javelins. Arsaphes personally supervised the workshops that supplied his weapons. Bogomil, who was responsible for equipping the army, became a veritable dictator in the matter of supplies. Barbarians skilled in the making of arms were grouped together at various distances from the City in what soon developed into new towns. This was how Amphibolus came into being, between the mountains and the forests and on the road to unknown deserts. Aquileus, originally a religious center, also soon developed into a garrison town and arms factory. The laborers and craftsmen who worked for the army enjoyed special status. In law, slavery did not and never would exist in the Empire. But, in fact, the position of many peasants, craftsmen, workers in quarries and silver mines and oarsmen in the galleys was very close to slavery. The makers of arms, in particular, were in a way serfs: they were forbidden to leave the towns they lived in, they could not change their occupation or have anything to do with foreigners. But their duties carried with them considerable privileges. The City provided them with food, pleasure, and entertainment. Some of them, inventors of devices or techniques useful to the army, became honored and important people. Thus, at Aquileus, chariots armed with javelins or joined together with chains trailing spiked globes made their appearance. The new way of living gave rise to new occupations. Bands of entertainers and tumblers roved from town to town to amuse the workers and soldiers. Peddlers brought clothes, furniture, pets, sweets, musical instruments. A kind of crude internal commerce replaced the great maritime trade which under the Porphyries had sent out, to the ends of the civilized world, so many masterpieces of art and so many marvels of taste.

To facilitate this traffic, and above all to facilitate the movement of troops and equipment so that they could swiftly be concentrated in any part of the country, Bogomil established a network of roads that was to be one of the most important legacies of Arsaphes's rule. From the City to Aquileus, then from the City to Cape Gildor, from the City to Amphibolus, and from Amphibolus to Aquileus, roads stretched out and multiplied, roads that were passable in winter as well as in summer, for chariots as well as for horses and foot travelers. They were several yards wide—sometimes 6, sometimes as much as 10— and they transformed both landscapes and living conditions. Chateaubriand, Lord Byron, and Théophile Gautier in the nineteenth century, and even Barrès at the beginning of the twentieth, took almost as long as Bogomil's soldiers to travel from Cape Gildor to Amphibolus and Aquileus. Sir Ronald Syme's excellent studies of roads in the Empire from Bogomil to Basil the Great[3] throw new light on the origins of the Empire; politics was so bound up with the means of communication that these essays constitute a genuine history of trade, manners, and administration in the Empire prior to the reign of Alexis.

There is also the question of water. Historians, especially in Germany, for a long time attributed the first great irrigation works outside the Amphyses and Nephta valleys to Basil the Great. But the work of the French *Annales* school has shown conclusively that it is necessary to go back far beyond the reign of Basil. Water was a primary necessity, in the first place for military reasons, but subsequently to support the colonies of veterans left behind to keep the peace and to make possible the agriculture and industry on which the craftsmen depended. Arsaphes surrounded himself with experts mainly from Egypt and the south of Spain, whose names have come down to us through various inscriptions, and as well as increasing the number of wells, springs, and fountains, began to sketch out the network of irrigation canals that Basil the Great later extended and was given the credit for. At the cost, no doubt, of countless victims, gigantic projects altered the courses of several tributaries of the Amphyses. Vineyards and cornfields multiplied tenfold the wealth and resources of a vast area between Aquileus, Evcharisto, and Parapoli.

What is striking about this phase of the City's history is its comparative simplicity. After the intrigues of the Porphyries and the merchant princes, after the subtle intellectualism of the City's first golden age, after opulence and luxury, after so much talent and imagination, it was as if the harshness of the early days had come back again, and with it not only hardship, but also unaffected and unostentatious pleasures. Genius now found its expression in military operations. The campaigns of Arsaphes against the Tartars and the Scythians, of Bogomil against the Oïghurs, of Labianus against the Hobbits, and of Odier against the Khazars and the Kaptchaks are still models of their kind. Like those of Napoleon later, they are all based on swift deployment of forces, massive attack on weak points, surprise. Everything contributed to make such military successes possible: rough conditions, the way society was organized, the progress made in the development of weapons, the network of highways, the irrigation system which brought bigger harvests and made it possible to build up the reserves needed by armies in the field. Hitherto the soldiers had been motley bands of mercenaries from the most diverse regions; now an iron discipline welded them into unity. At first Odier divided the army up according to language, as the Pomposans had done, but it was soon clear that this led to divided loyalties. So Bogomil and Labianus built up a system of groups, cohorts, and sections. Gradually a military aristocracy developed. Arsaphes encouraged it by giving its members official posts, strongholds to defend, provinces to administer. He appointed a committee of twelve, and a hundred and forty-four administrative officers; he set up a corps of special envoys plenipotentiary who represented him everywhere and took orders only from him. Into small towns and rural areas that had never had more than a vague, imaginary idea of what the City and Aquileus meant, these intermediaries introduced supreme power, with both its justice and its demands. The tribute of the conquered had to make up as best it could for the vanished profits of the maritime trade. Shopkeepers, big merchants, makers of luxury goods were ruined. The State was not rich, but it had enough to maintain a formidable army and an administration which, though rudimentary, was sufficient to dispense justice and collect taxes. The priests were powerful but obedient. And so the Empire was born.

The reorientation toward the east, the ruin of the City's harbor, Arsaphes's new preoccupations, and the influence of the priests all combined to bring about an important change: the court and the government moved to Aquileus. The declining City, while still influential, was valued mainly for its memories—it was the city of pomp and circumstance, but now overshadowed by Aquileus. The coexistence in the latter of the spiritual and temporal powers turned what was originally a religious citadel into the real center for military operations and administrative decisions. Aquileus, temple and fortress, dominated the whole of this age just as former ages had been delighted and fascinated by the City. Arsaphes's ambassadors, governors, generals, and envoys still spoke in the name of the City, whose Tiger still figured on official documents and flags. But the reality of power was in Aquileus. Until her death, Princess Heloise continued to live in her palace in the City, but afterward Arsaphes, who had always mistrusted the brilliance, levity, and insouciance of the inhabitants of the City, lived almost all the time in Aquileus. He only left his camp there in order to go on expeditions to the northeast or southeast, and he returned there with his booty and his prisoners, to recruit his strength and be able to push back still farther the frontiers of his power.

Clearly, the new dispositions and increased strength, the new way of life and military and territorial ambition, made new clashes with Onessa inevitable. The conflict soon came. The reason why it did not break out in the early years of Arsaphes's reign, despite constant brushes, was that the opposition between Onessa and the City did not preclude a deep hostility on both their parts toward Pomposa and the merchant princes. The break between Arsaphes and the High Council even seemed, at first, to foreshadow a rapprochement between the two towns: Arsaphes was not himself a Porphyry, and so the antagonism between the Eagle and the Tiger might die down. Arsaphes was abandoning the great maritime trade that had so annoyed Onessa; he was driving out the merchant princes; he was a protection against the common menace of the barbarians beyond the mountains, deserts, and forests. Perhaps some agreement was possible between those who alike turned their back on the seductions of trade, luxury, the refinements of culture, and foreign influences from across the northwest sea. Years went by in this mistaken hope. Matters were not helped by a rapprochement between Aquileus and Pomposa, slight though this was. But the truth became evident even before Arsaphes's death—there was no room for two powers, looking inward toward the land and both cultivating strict morals and military might. As Sir Allan Carter-Bennett put it, "After the City and its maritime dreams, Aquileus was merely another Onessa, still farther from the sea, more entrenched on the land, greedier for space and supremacy. The legacy of the rival brothers was the struggle for supremacy over the same continent." For centuries the Porphyries and the Venostae had fought because they represented the contesting powers of land and sea, austerity and luxury, boorishness and culture. Now Onessa and the City, in the guise of Aquileus, were to confront one another again because, at that time and in that part of the world, there could be a future for only one Empire.

V

THE BANQUET AT ONESSA

 RSAPHES LIVED LONG ENOUGH TO SEE THE DANGER grow and conflict break out. But it was not until after his death that the struggle began to rage in earnest between Onessa and the City—or rather, now, between Onessa and Aquileus. Arsaphes, having won a last victory over the Oïghurs on the edge of the Tartar desert, far to the south of Amphibolus, was just preparing in his usual way to switch to a completely different front, when he died suddenly on the way back to Aquileus. Once there he had intended to regroup his forces and strike northward against the Onessan army beyond the volcanoes and the Amphyses. Few deaths have given rise to so many legends and theories, both at the time and ever since. Whether caused by a rear-guard action, accident, poison, treachery, rebellion, or simple illness, it was a mysterious end, and we do not know what became of the Bactrian captain's remains. A black-and-white marble tomb had been erected for him in the great temple at Aquileus while he was still alive, but it was always to remain empty. The priests, true to the role he had allocated them, spread the legend that he had been caught up to heaven by a sacred eagle with outspread wings, which after seven times seventy-seven years would deposit the body in the tomb at Aquileus, where it would come to life again at moments of crisis. This was an example and a weapon that Arsaphes's successors, beginning with Alexis, were not to forget. At all events, it was clear that at a time when the heirs of the Tiger were about to take up the struggle once more against the city of the Eagle, it was good tactics to invoke the tutelary deity of the Eagle, at the same time patron of the priests of Aquileus. The question becomes somewhat more complicated if one allows, as some do, that the priests themselves might have had some share in the

Coin of the City bearing the likeness of Princess Heloise;
minted under Arsaphes.

Onessan coin representing an eagle.

death of a protector who had finally become an obstacle to their own soaring ambitions. It would take too long to discuss the point here.[1] And, of course, there is no inconsistency in supporting both the theory that Arsaphes was murdered by agents of the soothsayers, and the theory that his death, despite the ostensible affliction with which it was greeted in Aquileus, was exploited by the priests themselves for purposes of religious and political propaganda. In any case, for nearly fifty years, under Arsaphes's successors, it was in reality the priests who ruled Aquileus and, through Aquileus, the City and its possessions. The legitimacy of the power of Arsaphes's two sons, who succeeded one another with equal absence of genius, was not challenged, but it simply served to cover the real authority of the priests. During his own lifetime Arsaphes had been strong enough to keep their power within reasonable bounds. After his death, his memory was enough to maintain his sons on the throne, but not to curb the growing force that he had done more than anyone to foster. The priestly-*cum*-military government continued to follow Arsaphes's policy even though its author was no longer there. But instead of fighting in the east and southeast against the foreign barbarians, they turned, as Arsaphes himself had been about to do, against Odessa and its rulers. As Sir Allan Carter-Bennett says, in one sense the priests betrayed Arsaphes, and in another they continued his work. Or rather they tried to do so—success eluded them.

The phase of the Empire's prehistory that now began was one of the darkest and most cruel. For more than a hundred years there was nothing but fire and slaughter and armies sweeping back and forth, now victorious, now vanquished. Military anarchy was established everywhere as the principle of government. Year after year, from Onessa to the City and Aquileus, all along the banks of the Amphyses, farmers and craftsmen saw their crops destroyed, their tools confiscated, their houses burned down, and their wives and children carried off. Aquileus was taken three times—twice by the Onessan army and once by the barbarians—and three times recaptured by the armies of the priests. The City sank further and further into oblivion, almost into squalor. Only Onessa remained strong and intact. But the fate that seemed to dog Onessa made it yet again incapable of imposing its will on the territories formerly dominated by the City, Arsaphes, and the priests of Aquileus.

This century or century and a half of violence made the first splendor of the City seem like something belonging to the distant past. To minds dulled by privation it was like a mythical golden age. Philosophers, theaters, silks, statues of ivory, all the charms of culture and luxury—had they ever really existed? All that survived were the weapons and the feast days used by the priests for their own ends. The few texts we possess on the dark ages between Arsaphes and Basil constitute one long lament on the harshness of the present, one long yearning after the beauties of the past. Priests, writers, merchants, men of action and of thought all seem to have become suddenly incapable of hoping for or expecting anything from the future. They only dreamed of what was no more, what was being destroyed a little more each day by hordes of soldiers and incendiaries. Even memories scarcely survived the disaster. All through these endless years of extortion and murder, when rival bands of brigands carved out fleeting zones of influence in which all was subject to their greed and caprice, what is most striking is the absence of leaders. There was no one to command, to plan, to exact obedience to decisions which, rendered haphazard, tardy, and inconsistent by pressure of circumstance, usually remained dead letters. Naturally both Pomposa and the barbarians took advantage of this weakness and anarchy; and to internal strife were added raids and attacks from without, during which towns were captured and laid waste. It was a miracle that this disorder did not end in universal slavery. It was as if, from end to end of the lands that were soon to constitute the Empire, time had turned back to those first dreary ages later sung—and embellished in the singing—by Valerius. For more long years Onessa continued to be a bird of prey, capable of pillage and sudden boldness, but still unable to rise to real organization or peace. The City approached the end of its protracted agony. And under the long decrescendo of Arsaphes's descendants, struck suddenly with impotence, the priests of Aquileus began to indulge in sterile internecine struggles in the cause of theological influence or private interest. Not a single idea nor a single leader emerged—only, in the country, wolves, bands of deserters, famine and want; and, in the towns, insecurity, poverty, and fear. Then, at last, so many hundreds of years after its first prince, Onessa's hour struck.

Prince Basil was the direct heir of the Eagle and the Venostae. He was short, and, to judge by the likenesses on his coins and medals, rather ugly. Puny, with a red beard and a flat nose, he was sometimes sly and sometimes given to display, but always two-faced and cruel. He walked with a limp, and was to lose an eye at the battle of

Amphibolus. But that twisted body housed a will of iron, and by employing both battle-ax and murder he was to create the Empire. Historians have long differed over the nature of his ambitions and the role he played. According to some, including Sir Allan Carter-Bennett, Basil even as a boy already had a vague dream of unifying the Empire. But most French and German historians believe Basil was primarily a descendant of the Venostae, dreaming only of Onessa's greatness and the revenge of the Eagle over the Tiger. In any event, as soon as he appears on the scene of history a change is discernible in the formless chaos of intrigue and ambush. The fate of the people of the Empire found a center, their history found a pivot; in a very few years, everything would revolve around Basil.

Unlike Arsaphes, he was not an adventurer or a strategist. Nor like Alexis, later, was he a moralist and philosopher. He schemed, plotted, machinated, edged step by step toward his goal. Everything

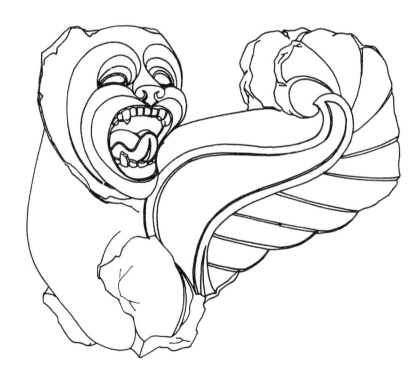

Broken capital with representation of a tiger.
Found in the ruins of the City.

served his turn. Not for nothing was he a descendant of the Venostae —he shrank as little from violence and cruelty as from guile and deceit. As soon as he came to the throne of the princes of Onessa, he calculated the risks to be run and those to be avoided, and drew up a list of objects to be attained. Amid the vast disorder in which all the peoples of the Empire had for years battled in vain, it was impossible to fight on all fronts at once. So at a single stroke Basil reversed the whole traditional policy of the princes of Onessa. He sought to come to terms with Pomposa; he sought to come to terms with the barbarians. Whether he dreamed of an Empire or confined his ambition to the fate of Onessa alone, his immediate object was to enable the Eagle to defeat the Tiger at last, and to rule over the City as it ruled over Onessa. Clearly such a plan entailed the humbling of Aquileus. To enable Onessa's supremacy to stretch from the Amphyses to the deserts, from the sea to the forests of the northwest, it was necessary to break the power of the priests. The fall of Aquileus would automatically bring about the fall of the City.

The simplicity of this plan was equaled only by the tortuousness of the means by which it was pursued. Ritter rightly compares Basil to Louis XI and Mazarin.[2] Sometimes he would appear to surrender everything in order to win more surely. Humility and lowliness were as much a part of his armory as pride and genuine grandeur. After the question of the scope of the young prince's ambitions, the next most interesting problem raised by Basil's devious policy is whether it constitutes a break with or a continuation of Onessa's previous history. The discontinuous aspect is clear: the alliance with Pomposa. But the continuous aspect is no less evident: in that this very deviation was made with the traditional object of ensuring Onessa's supremacy over the City. Basil's foremost gift was lucidity. Throughout his reign he never hesitated over what was essential and what might be sacrificed. To achieve his ends he hatched intrigues in which the chain of cause and effect was drawn so fine that only when it was too late did his terrified enemies discover the real meaning of stratagems, and even surrenders, that had seemed unimportant at the time. The most striking example of this long-range policy is the famous meeting with the king of Sicily and the Great Khan of the Oïghurs.

Sicily had long been under the domination of Pomposa and, in the heyday of the City's splendor and of the High Council, had maintained trade relations with the City and its port. But after the revolt of the mercenaries Pomposa took good care to interpose itself between

Sicily and the territories of the Empire. Then, under Arsaphes and his successors, the links grew weaker, and Sicily turned to the powers in the west and aimed at freeing itself from Pomposan influence. This policy was largely successful. Pomposan interests in Sicily were still extensive, but the old political and military domination were now only a matter of form, and the king of Sicily was almost free to rule over the destinies of his island. Regis II mounted the three thrones of Agrigentum, Palermo, and Syracuse almost at the very same moment as Basil came to power in Onessa.

While still only crown prince, Basil was betrothed to a Pannonian princess, a dazzling beauty as virtuous as she was fair. Her name was Ingeburgh, and Basil had never seen her. Ingeburgh herself was in love with a young Pomposan noble called Tybalt, a skilled harpist who had on three occasions accompanied trade and political missions sent by the merchant princes to Pannonia. The charming but poor Tybalt stood no chance against the dynastic necessities personified in the clubfoot of Onessa; and Ingeburgh, in despair, found herself promised to Basil, not knowing then that she would be immortalized as the Penelope of the sonnets Tybalt was to write under the name Mercutio of Verona. These sonnets have come down to us as one of the purest and most exquisite sources of our knowledge about the manners and feelings of that time. When, after a long voyage, Ingeburgh with her escort and attendants arrived at last at Onessa, Basil was already crowned and had begun to negotiate with Regis II. His minister, Gandolphus, sent as his envoy to Sicily, had just reported that King Regis had a beloved daughter, Adelaide, aged seventeen. At this point there occurs one of the most astounding episodes in the life of Basil, and one of the most striking examples of his decisiveness, lucidity, and lack of scruple.

Basil had welcomed Ingeburgh with all the honors due to her rank and the role for which she was destined. As soon as he saw her, he, like everyone else, was enchanted by her beauty and charm. We should try to imagine the feelings of a child of fifteen or sixteen, arriving almost alone in the Eagle's nest of Onessa. Princess Ingeburgh had never left her father and mother before, and the formidable appearance of both the place and its master was enough to make the stoutest heart quail. She doubtless thought of her handsome, mellifluous Tybalt as she gazed with horror on the deformed cripple now smiling on her. But despite his ugliness Basil was not lacking in charm. He spoke to her kindly, and Ingeburgh emerged from the first dreaded interview almost reassured. They had eight or nine such meetings in the course of three or four weeks. Meanwhile, through an intermediary, Basil continued his negotiations with Regis II. One evening he sent for Ingeburgh. The princess had almost begun to enjoy their conversations. She wondered innocently whether she might not be learning to love the terrible prince of Onessa. She smiled as she entered his presence, and dropped him the most graceful of curtsies.

"My child," said the prince, helping her to rise, "your beauty, nobility of character, and shining virtue have touched me deeply. I thought to make a marriage consonant with the dignity of our two houses and sure to add to their greatness. But the last few days, during which you have transformed Onessa with your gaiety and grace, have shown me that you would change what seemed a duty into an inexpressible pleasure. I have never before experienced the joy and richness of feeling that your presence bestows. I thank you for having revealed such sentiments to one who but for you would never have known them."

Princess Ingeburgh had almost ceased to think about Tybalt. She trembled with happiness at having touched the heart of the deformed prince of whom she had so long thought with horror. She vowed to herself that she would love him, and already felt with delight the first stirrings of her future affection.

"But princes are not born for happiness," Basil went on. "And it was with uneasiness and mistrust I felt it overwhelm me. For the great it can only be a sign of weakness, a harbinger of surrender. It makes them soft and distracts them from the great duties they have undertaken. I sent for you this evening," he suddenly concluded, "to tell you that we must both give up all thought of it."

Princess Ingeburgh could not have been more devastated if a thunderbolt had fallen at her feet. At the very moment when, after the sorrows of girlhood, her future seemed to be opening fair before her, the very man for whom in the last few days she had begun to feel the opposite of her former repugnance now stood before her as a tyrant who, after tearing her away from both her parents and her lover, rejected her. She had a sudden swift revelation of a future of humiliation and despair, and, bursting into tears, fell sobbing to the floor.

"My child," continued the prince in a voice that was almost gentle, "I don't mean to wound you or make you unhappy. Your sorrow delights me if it means I have been able to win your affection.

But I do not want the feelings that console me to make you suffer. You would have been the wife I dreamed of, and I could have been for you—or so your affliction now allows me to hope—something other than what you at first supposed. If I thus sever at a blow the relations that would probably have been dearer to me than to you, it is because the destiny of Onessa makes it my duty to do so, and because I would not, through cowardly shrinking from what has to be done, cause you perhaps to suffer even more in the future. Go, then, and remember that a prince who may become mighty has loved you as the humblest man may love the best and most beautiful woman he ever met."[3]

Four months later Basil married Adelaide. Ingeburgh had left Onessa, crushed and humiliated. But even the noblest women are fragile and she began to be consumed with passion and jealousy: she loved the ugly and cruel prince of Onessa.

Basil waited almost two years to meet his father-in-law, King Regis, and the khan of the Oïghurs. When he did decide on the encounter, he held all the trumps. Famagusta, in Cyprus, where the three met, never saw such splendors. The khan appeared, preceded by tigers and elephants; King Regis wore robes of gold and silk more sumptuous than any woven in the memory of man. Basil alone arrived on foot, limping slightly and stammering. The account of the interview, written in Greek by the anonymous clerk known as the Chronicler of Famagusta, gives a host of interesting and picturesque details on what the kings said to one another, and the dances, banquets, and other festivities that surrounded their meeting. Greek, of course, was the language used for the conference. But the only one of the three who could use it with both ease and elegance was King Regis. Not surprisingly, the Great Khan spoke Greek only with difficulty, but he made it a point of honor to use it, and the chronicler slyly reproduces the barbarisms and solecisms with which his flowery phrases were strewn. Basil spoke little. The more he wanted, the less he talked about it. When, after a week, the three princes quitted their golden tents, the rugs richly woven with hunting scenes and the combats of wild beasts, the dancers who had delighted and the tumblers who had amused them, and each king returned to his distant capital, Basil took away with him solid alliances on land and sea. He was protected both in the east and in the west. He had his hands free to move against Aquileus.

The agreement with the Oïghurs meant little to Pomposa. But the alliance with King Regis, reinforced by the marriage between Basil and Adelaide, constituted a direct threat to the naval supremacy and maritime trade of the merchant warriors. It is at this juncture that the depth and vigor of Basil's designs are strikingly demonstrated. Many of those about him, especially Gandolphus, urged him to take advantage at once of King Regis's friendly attitude and turn immediately against Pomposa. It was a good moment. Pomposa was then having to deal with the most violent mercenaries' revolt in the whole of its long history. The Illyrian crews of the Pomposan warships—the most skilled and highly trained of her sailors—had risen against the merchant princes, and a struggle of frightful cruelty was raging.

"My lord," Gandolphus would say, spreading out with his bony fingers a gold-illuminated map that King Regis had sent as a gift, "pray consider the relative positions of Onessa and the merchant princes at this moment. On the one hand, the barbarians are reduced to silence by your friendship with the king of the Oïghurs; Aquileus is divided by the rivalry between its prince and its priests, and the priesthood itself is rent by theological quarrels; and Sicily is not only your friend, but your ally. On the other hand, Pomposa is weakened by civil unrest and revolt within her forces—revolt in the most powerful of her forces, and, within that, in those Illyrian galleys which have inflicted defeat on the Phoenician, Carthaginian, and Irish fleets. Such a combination of favorable circumstances may not recur for a long time. Do not hesitate any longer, sire. Attack! And then, when you have rid yourself of Pomposa, who will dare to resist, let alone defy, you? Onessa will be mistress over both sea and land, and her prince the mightiest among the princes of the earth."[4]

But the wily Basil was not to be deflected from his original plan. He did precisely the opposite of what Gandolphus advised. And he sent Gandolphus himself, whom he trusted completely, on a mission of peace to Pomposa.

The merchant princes had argued like Gandolphus, and had been filled with apprehension. During a banquet given by the Council of Seven, Gandolphus and his opposite numbers spoke freely, amid libations and roars of mirth, of the preoccupations that had been preying on their minds. Pomposa, relieved of her deadly fears lest Basil should threaten her, was ready to agree out of hand to all Onessa's demands. So Basil had little difficulty in obtaining twenty galleys, twelve thousand men, and ample supplies of arms and provisions to help in the fight against Aquileus. The alliance with the merchant princes brought about a complete reversal of the situation.

Three events had sealed the fate of Aquileus: the marriage with Adelaide, and the meetings at Famagusta and Pomposa. Six months later, in the ancient tower of the castle of Sarmizegetusa, where she eagerly awaited messages from Pomposa or the City, Ingeburgh understood the deep designs of the lame prince of Onessa.

Arsaphes would have hurled himself on Aquileus. Basil went on maneuvering for several months, undermining the sacred town's resistance from within. Among the crowd of pilgrims who still flocked to Aquileus despite the danger and disturbances were numerous Onessan agents. Some were there to pick up and relay information, others to shake the morale of the army and the population. Even several of the priests themselves were in Basil's pay, and irritated or discouraged their fellow citizens by proposing measures either too drastic or not drastic enough. When Basil finally decided on action the battle was already won.

He entered Aquileus after a campaign lasting five weeks. The valleys of the Amphyses and the Nephta, the region of the volcanoes, and the plain up to beyond Amphibolus all now belonged to Onessa. Arsaphes's great-grandson, a dim young man who loved only horses, and perhaps their grooms, came with shaven head and white robes to offer his submission to Basil in the great temple in Aquileus. After all those centuries, the Eagle had conquered the Tiger. Basil had not hesitated to enter Aquileus, but the memories of the past glory of the City itself were still so much alive that he did not care to show himself there in person, and sent Gandolphus, together with some of his own priests, to take possession in his name.

But although all these regions had been conquered, they were not all ready to submit. Decadent though the City had become, it had still left an indelible mark on the vast territories once exposed to its trade and culture. Onessa, on the other hand, had never been anything but a strongly garrisoned fortress, and while Basil had turned that garrison into an army, it was still not big enough to occupy an Empire. From the beginning of Basil's rule, natural disasters rained down all over the country. The second winter of his reign was so severe that two or three centuries later it was still commemorated in the songs of the bards and in popular tradition. The sea froze for 30 or 40 miles along the coast between Onessa and the City. In the region of the volcanoes, some twenty villages and their inhabitants were buried under snow and ice. All that winter and the following spring, packs of wolves roved right up to the ramparts of Amphibolus, Aquileus, and Onessa.

Such extremities, together with a plague of locusts at the end of spring two or three years later, several bad harvests, and, at the end of Basil's reign, an unusually violent eruption of the volcano Kora-Kora, worsened the plight of the people, especially the peasants. There were several revolts. People murmured that nothing much had been gained by replacing the priests with Prince Basil, and that law and order were of no use if they did not prevent the poor from dying of hunger and cold. The ghost of Arsaphes began to haunt people's minds. Memories of happiness and ease in connection with the City were now too distant to exercise much power, but the legend of the captain of the mercenaries was still near enough to kindle, suddenly, the hopes of the hungry, the humiliated, and the wretched. Two or three years after Aquileus's surrender, rebellion threatened everywhere.

Once again Basil stood out against all the advice that was offered to him. Many wanted him to invade Aquileus, the obvious center of all intrigues and plots, and by noose and sword to drown in blood the calls to resistance and rebellion which, as yet, were still only being whispered.

"And then what, my good lords?" said the prince, his overlarge head drooping forward, and playing, as was his habit, with one of his rings. "And then what? No, it is wrong to devalue fear and repression by making unskillful use of them. What is the good of killing twenty priests if a hundred arise in their place, or of killing a hundred if they are replaced by a thousand? It is better to act coolly and have patience, to let things take their course. It is better to wait . . . and then we shall see." And those who knew the prince trembled at his good humor and his cruel smile.[5]

Basil, who no longer took any account of Arsaphes's successors and had decided once and for all to deal directly with the hierarchy, opened negotiations with the priests of Aquileus, who had been expecting to be crucified. He offered to set up a federation of all the territories over which they had ever wielded authority, and to link this federation somehow with Onessa, under his own authority. The federation would be autonomous, and all regional authority would be concentrated in the hands of the priests. Basil entrusted them with the task of bringing the population of town and country back to a peaceable frame of mind. The priests gathered in a shrine some 40 miles southeast of Aquileus to examine Basil's proposals. The oldest and the youngest among them were for mistrusting them and still preparing to fight. But the majority thought the proposals conceded all that any rebellion could reasonably be expected to achieve, and voted in favor of acceptance. Basil came to Aquileus in person to attend the first meeting of the new college of priests appointed to administer the federation. The more suspicious were alarmed by the size of the escort he brought with him. But cavalry and infantry alike did no worse than line the pockets of innkeepers and courtesans, and all went away again at the same time as the prince. Basil was cheered by an enthusiastic crowd of soldiers and priests. He had never been so popular in Aquileus.

After a year or two, civil peace was restored and a new stage began. Basil, alleging the external dangers that still threatened everywhere, the constant threat from the barbarians, and commercial competition from Pomposa, proposed a tighter link between the federation and Onessa. But he did not want, he said, to give with one hand and take back with the other. He was suggesting not only that Onessa be associated more closely with the affairs of the federation, but also that the federation be associated more closely with the affairs of Onessa. In short, he was asking the college of priests to participate in the government of Onessa just as he himself already participated in the government of the federation. Once more the college of priests wavered. Some wanted at all costs to keep Onessa and Aquileus quite separate. Others pointed out the inequality of their two forces and, since Onessa in any case already had power over Aquileus, were in favor of being able to exercise some inside influence over decisions made in Onessa. It was, of course, the latter opinion that carried the day, and by a large majority. Once more Basil and his troops were installed in force within the walls of Aquileus. And once again, to the surprise of the pessimists, everything went off perfectly smoothly. The priests of Aquileus and Basil's advisers spent nearly a week together, and the council of priests was invited, at the beginning of the following spring, to attend the solemn assembly that the Onessan leaders held every two years in the presence of the prince. To do away with all the suspicions Basil knew were aroused, he offered to hold the meeting in Onessa. The priests felt that they had got the better of their defeat.

On the appointed date, Onessa was *en fête* for the ceremonies. The usually sinister appearance of the Eagle's nest was brightened by sunshine and mild weather. Many priests came, attended on the journey by their chief captains and most skillful men-at-arms. On the evening of the second day a great banquet was held on the plain at the foot of the fortress, at which the guests were eight hundred priests and nobles from Aquileus, and an equal number of dignitaries and soldiers from Onessa. When the moon rose, young women from the mountains beyond the desert appeared in the vast circle formed by the guests, and began to dance to the sound of unseen music. Rye brandy had been flowing freely, and all these warriors and seers were seized with pleasant nostalgia. They all loved feasting, rich hangings, the music of their temples and camps, the bodies of women, and the comradeship of soldiers around the campfire. Every Onessan sat between two men from Aquileus; every Aquilean had an Onessan on either side. This symbolized the union between the two cities. Prince Basil, sitting between the eldest priest and the general of the Aquilean army, looked on in silence at the ebb and flow of the dance. In the pale light of the moon he could only just see the silhouettes of the dancers standing out briefly against the flames of the braziers before disappearing again into the darkness. A murmur arose from the circle of guests. One man from Onessa, one from Aquileus, one man from Onessa, one from Aquileus . . . The prince thought of the weight that rested on him, the weight of all those intermingled destinies out of which an empire had to be made. These destinies, these ambitions, these dreams, these apathies—all had to be welded together to form a single will. The women danced on. Among them the prince had noticed one, a child of about five or six. He had asked her name, and been told she was called Irene. Already she had great, sad gray eyes, though she laughed easily. She was beautiful. She came neither from the mountains nor from the deserts of the south, but from the sea, far north beyond Onessa, beyond the great forests where neither the City nor Onessa had ever reached. Forests . . . mountains . . . deserts . . . the little girl dancing. Suddenly, to the dreaming prince, the world seemed immense. Sometimes the prince did dream, and then all the serious, important things anyone said to him about his revenues or the discipline of his armies seemed to him futile and meaningless. He dreamed. The world was without limits; it offered no bounds to his formidable ambitions. It stretched out far, far, beyond seas and mountains, beyond deserts and forests. Already he had only to lift his hand and everything obeyed. The music had ceased. He lifted his hand and stood up. Every second man stood too. They all began to sing. Then Prince Basil, who had joined in the song, threw himself on the eldest priest, who was singing too, and thrust his dagger into his breast. And each man who stood and sang at the same moment stabbed the man who sat and sang on his right.

A fortnight later Basil had himself crowned emperor in the great temple at Aquileus.

VI

THAUMAS AND INGEBURGH

 HERE IS SOMETHING DISPIRITING ABOUT THE MARCH of history. That web which never alters despite an infinite range of motifs and variations: the same struggle for power under ever-different masks; the vain triumphs, the declines and falls; the ever-recurring myths; the straining toward a future that, though it always eludes the grasp, never ceases to exert its pressure and make its demands; the turning wheel which changes yet does not change; the hopes always disappointed, the victories foredoomed to failure—whether the picture they paint of man expresses his greatness or his weakness, we shall never know. Both, probably—and both at the same time. Nothing is more futile than history, and yet history is man himself. Nothing is more accidental, nothing more necessary. Everything could probably have been otherwise. But everything is as it is, and forever.

The emperor's first care was to undo all he had done and unmake all that had made him. He reconstructed the power of the priests, and he repudiated the empress. Immediately after his coronation, priests began to be hunted out and exterminated all over the Empire. The setting up of the federation and the emperor's apparent approval of it had encouraged all the supporters of the priests to declare their opinions freely, and this made them all the easier to track down and destroy. Justus Dion estimates there were nearly seventy thousand victims in about ten days. Although the actual figure has been questioned, it is certain there was terrible slaughter. In both country and town, blood flowed as freely as it had some two hundred years before, when Arsaphes captured the City. With the priests were slaughtered the women and children guilty of having lived with, protected, or served them. Many were crucified; others were impaled, had their eyes gouged out, were dismembered, or flayed alive. But almost as soon as the massacre had ended, Basil set about re-establishing the powers and dignities of the priestly order. In that time and place, the Empire could not exist without priests. Arsaphes had known, Basil knew, and Alexis would know this. The main thing was to have them on one's side or, better still, under one rather than against one. The emperor bent all his efforts to this end. And it is at this point that the great figure of Thaumas appears.

When Basil came to the throne of Onessa, Thaumas was only a young shepherd boy. Vivacious, quick, and of exceptional intelligence, he was one of those poor but gifted young men who saw the priesthood first as the goal and then as the instrument of their ambition. Unlike the great feudal families, jealous of their privileges and shut in on themselves, the priests welcomed new talents and strong wills. And for the poor, the herdsmen, and the shepherds, to be received into the priesthood was to emerge from their humble condition and to become someone who mattered. Thaumas, with his open countenance and his zeal in learning, had attracted the attention of an old priest whom his mother repaid with gifts of eggs and poultry, and at seventeen or eighteen, which was then quite late in life, he entered one of the most famous seminaries, where mathematics and philosophy were taught by scholars from Greece, Phoenicia, and Persia. In two or three years he learned to read and write and count. By the time he was twenty-five he could read the future in the stars and in the entrails of vultures. A little of the science and culture that had made the City famous lived on in him. Curious about everything, learned in a thousand secrets lost during the violence and disorder that had overwhelmed the peoples of the Empire, Thaumas found in the study of the City's past a learned serenity and peaceful richness that soon brought him reputation and honors. Besides quickness, talent, and charm, he possessed inflexibility of character and an unusually strong will. Ambition may have led him to the priesthood, but the priesthood, in its turn, gave him the strength of soul appropriate to his lofty conception of its functions.

At the time of the first struggles between Basil and the priests, Thaumas, steeped in the culture and glory of the City, was naturally conspicuous for his opposition to Onessa's designs. He was one of the leaders of the faction hostile to Basil, and when the prince conquered Aquileus for the first time, Thaumas resigned himself calmly to torture and death. But Basil included everyone in his clemency and forgiveness. Arsaphes's great-grandson, who still nominally ruled over Aquileus, then appointed Thaumas to welcome Gandolphus's army, come to take possession of the town for Basil. Not content with refusing this mission angrily, Thaumas took the lead in a new wave of resistance that was being organized around Aquileus against the power of Onessa. His reputation for wisdom and learning had led to his being included among the assembly of priests who governed Aquileus in reality; he was one of its most respected members, though the youngest. When Basil's proposals for federation came before this assembly, Thaumas fought fiercely in favor of refusal and war. But the majority decided otherwise. When Basil came to Aquileus again to attend the first meeting of the college charged with ruling the short-lived federation, everyone waited with curiosity not untinged with cruelty to see what would happen when Thaumas and the prince came face to face. The priest's friends feared the worst, and the prince's advisers urged him to a course that would have fulfilled those fears. The college of priests, riddled with Onessan agents, was so torn by fear and division that Thaumas's situation was well-nigh impossible, and he could expect no help in the present crisis from his own side. As soon as Basil entered the shrine near Aquileus where the priests were gathered, they all threw themselves at his feet in homage and submission, both those whom he had won over and those who had been most hostile to him. Only Thaumas still stood upright. Basil looked at him for a long while without speaking. Then he said:

"Thaumas, once before I might have punished you, and yet I spared you. You have always been among the most determined of my enemies. What should I do now—pardon you again or have you put to death?"

"Sire," answered Thaumas, "I was against you in battle. How could I be with you in defeat?"

Basil remained silent for several moments.

"If I pardon you again, will you still, will you always, be against me?"

"Sire," answered Thaumas, "if you put me to death, I hope others will remain faithful to my memory. If you spare me, I shall try to remain faithful to myself."

The prince was once more silent, then, turning to Thaumas, he offered him not his pardon, but his friendship and esteem.

"Sire," said Thaumas, "will you allow me in your presence to address my friends and brethren once more?"

The prince nodded. Then Thaumas cried out to all the priests still prostrate before Basil, and asked if any among them were still willing to follow him in resistance and in the struggle for Aquileus's freedom. There was a great silence. Then Thaumas turned to Basil and said:

"I will serve you as I should have liked to serve Aquileus, and I will be as faithful to your virtue as I have been to theirs."

When Basil returned to Aquileus for the third time to invite the priests to meet in Onessa, Thaumas came with him. He asked and obtained permission to speak freely once more to his old friends, and then delivered the most famous of all his speeches. After recalling his former devotion to Aquileus and solemnly declaring his loyalty to Basil, he warned the college of priests against accepting Basil's terms:

"One must know when the most honorable thing is to say no. . . . Cowardice never brings anything but tears and regrets. It is better to die free and conquered than to live enslaved and dishonored."

The prince heard him out in silence. When he had finished, Basil said so that no one else could hear:

"Then thrice, not twice, I shall have saved your life."

As we already know, the majority of the priests voted in favor of accepting Basil's plans and invitation. But Thaumas was not present at the banquet and the massacre at Onessa: he had gone on a two-year voyage to India and China.

On his return he was received by Basil, now emperor, with every sign of affection and reverence. The emperor spent three days with Thaumas, and on the evening of the third day, having summoned all the chief men and priests of Onessa together, he presented Thaumas to them as high priest of the Empire. It seems certain Thaumas had warned the emperor he intended to maintain his customary freedom of judgment and action. It may even have been his obstinate independence of mind that attracted, one might almost say fascinated, Basil.[1] As for the priests of Aquileus, they were so much under the emperor's thumb that they ratified unanimously and without a murmur of protest the decision on which they had not been consulted. They were only too pleased and surprised to see one of their own number, and the most independent of them, chosen for this high office. For twenty-seven years, Thaumas built up again and embodied in Aquileus the power of the priestly order. His reputation for wisdom and saintliness spread far beyond the borders of the Empire. Pilgrims came from Ireland, Ceylon, Ethiopia, and Scandinavia to touch his robe and kiss his feet. His miracles were too numerous to be counted, and his works, translated into every language, remain not only one of the main sources of our knowledge of the scientific and mystical thought of the period, but also masterpieces of writing still capable of moving us today.

Meanwhile Basil had put away Adelaide. He now felt strong enough to do without the Sicilian alliance if necessary. Adelaide had given him only two daughters, and the excuse for breaking with her was, of course, the need to provide a male heir. Gandolphus had no difficulty in getting the college of priests, meeting in special session, to declare the prince's marriage null and void. Adelaide went back to Sicily, where she arrived only a few days after the death of her father, King Regis. In spite of much opposition, Regis's nephew Tancred had just acceded to the throne of Palermo. He was already preparing to struggle against Pomposa for the settlements in Africa and the Levant, and had no desire to lose the alliance with Basil, who as emperor had now even more power and influence than before. Adelaide was a real threat to Tancred. As the only daughter of the dead king, she was the natural rallying point for all the new king's enemies and for all the inevitable malcontents, several of whom did not hesitate to refer to him almost openly as a usurper. So Tancred greeted his rejected cousin with great ceremony but little warmth, and lost no time in letting her understand that Sicily was not the best place of refuge for her. Adelaide was to end her days in Avignon, surrounded by a court devoted to music and the arts in which learned ladies and young nobles weary of war vied with each other in culture and fine sentiments. By one of those chances that history delights in, the most famous of the poets and composers who made Queen Adelaide's court at Avignon renowned in literature and art was a young man who came there from Pomposa, a young man of respectable family who during the few years he had spent at Verona had become one of the most celebrated men of his time. Accompanying himself on the harp, he sang sad and beautiful melodies that have survived into our own day. Between him and Queen Adelaide there was to spring up one of those equivocal loves whose mysteries are always being explored in histories of literature and the arts. For the young musician, later the more and more illustrious poet, and at last the old man laden with honors and crowned with laurels on the Capitol by an enthusiastic crowd, the man for whom the queen's passion never ceased to burn, the passion that generated so many gifts propitious to culture and the arts, remained faithful all his life to the radiant image that inspired him. And that image was not of the queen. He referred to it by the name of Penelope, and he himself, known north of the Alps as the Master of Avignon, was Mercutio of Verona, and none other than Princess Ingeburgh's Tybalt.

Throughout all these long years the castle of Sarmizegetusa, by the Danube, on its peak battered now by the sun and now by the snow, had remained closed in on itself and on the insult and humiliation inflicted by Prince Basil on Princess Ingeburgh and her noble family. The princess's father, a white-bearded old man called Liutpold, for a long while thought of mounting a punitive expedition against Onessa. But it soon became clear that the means at his disposal were ridiculously inadequate. A few quarrelsome barons, attracted as much by the thought of booty as by honor, would no doubt have been ready to follow their lord to the ends of the earth. But in all they never amounted to more than a few hundred, at the most a few thousand men—nothing that could begin to threaten a power such as Onessa. And with every year that passed Basil grew more formidable and the memory of the insult more faint. In the end, Ingeburgh's father came to live in a dream of revenge that his entourage respected as an honorable but harmless foible. Ingeburgh, as a matter of course, had thrown herself into a life of extreme piety and good works. She remained very beautiful, and it was not long before she acquired a reputation for great goodness, even saintliness.

One winter evening when it was snowing hard, a weary horseman knocked at the postern of the castle and asked for shelter. He was given a kind welcome. The grooms tended his horse, and the maids dried and cleaned his travel-stained clothes. He ate, then asked to see the owner of the castle. That evening a feast was being held at Sarmizegetusa, and Ingeburgh's father gave orders for the traveler to be brought to the great hall, where he took part in the rejoicings. The princess always attended with great grace and dignity on such occasions, but amid such rare pleasures and ceremonies she was like someone who was really elsewhere. At the end of the banquet, when the bear leaders and tumblers had made their last bow, the stranger asked to speak to the master of the castle. The princess's father had always been somewhat rough in manner, and his humiliation had made him even more unceremonious. He curtly asked his guest to explain himself. The traveler courteously replied that if such an honor might be accorded him, he would like to speak to the prince in private. He was then told he must say what he had to say at once, in public, and without further ado. The stranger then arose, walked amid a general silence to the middle of the room, and explained briefly that he had been sent by his master, the Emperor Basil, to take the Princess Ingeburgh back to Onessa.

A heavy silence fell. Everyone looked at Ingeburgh and her father. The princess, pale as death, had put her hand on the old man's arm. He had sprung to his feet and stood there still and silent, as if held upright only by the spell that had fallen on and petrified everyone in the room, the whole castle, and all the surrounding forest. The silence and petrifaction lasted a long time; then the mysterious thread that held them suspended suddenly snapped, and the room was filled with noise and movement. The prince cried out, but none heard him. The princess fainted. And in contempt of all the most sacred laws of hospitality, the knight from Onessa was attacked and slain among the remnants of the feast, and his bloodstained corpse was dragged past overturned tables, broken plates, and forgotten torches to the outer fortifications of the castle, where it was hurled down into the darkness.

During the days that followed no one dared speak of that strange evening or of Basil's messenger. It was as if no visitor had ever entered the great hall, as if nothing at all had happened during the forgotten feast. It was said that two tumblers who had been present at the scene had had their tongues and eyes torn out, and that two servants had been dispatched to murder a baron who had been foolish enough to spread the story of the knight from Onessa. But Sarmizegetusa secretly seethed with the subject. In the monotonous life of the castle, the story was a godsend to romantic young women and the knights who sought to please them.

Nearly two months went by. Sarmizegetusa had relapsed into dreary silence again. There was no more thought of feasting. Strangers, beggars, travelers, even pilgrims were kept far away from the castle, now sadder and lonelier than ever. Princess Ingeburgh spent all her time spinning; not a word ever crossed her lips. But her drawn face, her tear-reddened eyes, and her lassitude alarmed her father so much he had sent at great expense for one of the most famous doctors of Lombardy. The physician's arrival was awaited from day to day with growing impatience. One morning two breathless guards came to announce that a band of about ten people was riding toward the castle, through the snow that was still falling on the newly opened apricot and chestnut buds, and on the already flowering lilac. Everyone rushed to greet what they hoped was the arrival of the doctor. But the horsemen stopped at some distance from the castle, and sent one of their number with a message to be delivered into the prince's own hand. It was a letter from the emperor, offering pardon, friendship, alliance, a fortune, and titles, and asking Ingeburgh to ascend to the imperial throne at Basil's side. Ingeburgh's father summoned her and handed her Basil's message without a word. Ingeburgh read it, knelt at her father's feet, and said:

"Father, I have already unwittingly caused you so much trouble and sorrow that all I ask is as far as possible to repair the harm I have done you. Dispose, therefore, of my life, my feelings, and my future as best may serve your own reputation and interest."

She would not add another word, and, having curtsied to her father, returned with her ladies to the sad, dark room that for several years she had rarely left, and where her only pleasure was to look out on the forest she loved. The prince was a good and simple man. He knew his daughter's virtue and nobility and admired her greatly, and his only desire was for her happiness and the honor of the house of which he was head. He had often sought counsel of his daughter, who from an early age had given proof of wisdom and good judgment. Left alone now to deal with the problem that touched him most deeply, he was a prey to the most painful doubt and irresolution. It was at this point that the arrival of the famous Lombard doctor was announced.

The great man, whose name was Mirandola or Mirandolphus, had won a tremendous reputation in Padua and Bologna. He had traveled in England, Germany, Poland, and Persia, and had taught in Carthage and Damascus. At the age of fifty-seven he had behind him one of the most dazzling careers of the age. The prince welcomed him courteously and gratefully, and begged him to go at once and examine Ingeburgh, whose sorrows and character he described discreetly to the physician. Mirandola asked permission to be left alone with the princess. The prince hesitated. The doctor told him it would be quite useless for him to see the princess in the presence of others, adding that he himself was quite ready to leave at once for Andrianople, where important business and an urgent mission awaited him. The prince examined the famous physician narrowly. He looked old, weak, and ugly, and, though imposing enough, far from attractive. Permission was given for him to see Ingeburgh alone. He had no sooner crossed the threshold where she lay than Ingeburgh recognized Basil.

The emperor, of course, had had the messengers from Sarmize-getusa intercepted as they crossed the Alps, and he greatly enjoyed passing himself off as Mirandola. The epilogue of the story is well known, thanks to Augustin Thierry's account and the play in which Alfred de Musset represents Ingeburgh in the guise of Theodolinda, Florestan's daughter. Ingeburgh was to reign for twelve years on the throne of Onessa, during which time she was immensely popular throughout the Empire. She soon formed a close friendship with Thaumas,[2] and as long as the empress lived their combined influence on the emperor acted as a counterbalance to that of Gandolphus.

At Ingeburgh's death, which took place on the same day as the naval battle at Cape Pantama, the emperor married for the third time. This time his bride was the prettiest of the late empress's waiting women. Basil had known her for many years. It was he who had introduced her into Ingeburgh's service. She was none other than Irene from beyond the forests, whom we saw dancing before Basil at the banquet of Onessa. Of course, Irene could not replace Ingeburgh, or play the same pacific role as she had in the Empire. What is interesting about the reappearance of Irene is the light it sheds once more on the long meanderings of Basil's policies. These slow-maturing plans, in which each tiny, apparently insignificant event only takes on its true meaning in the context of later decisions, are absolutely typical of the emperor. In politics as in love, in war as in peace, nothing in Basil's life is ever wasted; all serves in the end to make his dreams come true and fulfill his design. Coming before the glory of Alexis, the reign of Basil the Great is nothing but a long patience. It is in this sense that people have rightly spoken of the genius of Basil preceding that of Alexis. Alexis was perhaps to be the negation of Basil. But he was also to be his heir.

VII

THE FOX OF AMPHIBOLUS

NGEBURGH, THOMAS, AND GANDOLPHUS EACH
played an important role in Basil's long reign—
Gandolphus primarily in the first part, Ingeburgh
and Thaumas in the second, up to the time of Gandolphus's final victory over Thaumas just before
his own death. The difference between the two parts
of the reign has given rise to endless discussion among historians.
Some—as, for example, Robert Weill-Pichon—see a clear break
round about the time of the emperor's marriage to Ingeburgh, and
attribute the new turn in imperial policy to the dual influence of the
empress and the high priest. Others recognize two different tendencies in Basil's governance of the Empire but refuse to admit this had
anything to do with Ingeburgh and Thaumas. Others again, following Sir Allan Carter-Bennett, categorically reject "the false distinctions introduced into the story of Basil by those who persist in dividing everything up into periods." Sir Allan Carter-Bennett's theory is
that Basil's whole reign consists of the harmonious and uninterrupted
execution of long-matured designs. Naturally, a time of war and violence is succeeded by a time of consolidation and peaceful administration. But they are not to be opposed to one another. Basil pursued a
single policy by differing means, but his objects remained unchanged,
and through altering facts and circumstances his direction is always
the same. At all events it is certain that Gandolphus, who had urged
Basil to attack Pomposa after the meeting at Famagusta, was always an advocate of violence and the harshest possible methods. It
is also beyond doubt that Ingeburgh and Thaumas encouraged Basil
to foster peace both inside and outside the Empire. The problem
resides in trying to make out the extent to which Basil was really
influenced by either party, or whether, as Sir Allan maintains, the

strength of his own purposes was enough in itself to determine all the developments as we know them. It must be remembered that even when making his harshest decisions, Basil never followed Gandolphus's advice blindly. We have previously referred to Gandolphus's efforts to make him go to war against Pomposa after the Famagusta meeting. There was a war, it is true, but only a few months later, and against Aquileus, and only after peace had been made with Pomposa. Thus even at the time of the early military campaigns, when Basil was accumulating territory and building up the Empire, Gandolphus can be more accurately described as in agreement with the main lines of Basil's policy—and with its main lines only—rather than as its real inspiration. In all, it is more a matter of occasional coincidence of views than of influence, and Basil spoke the truth in one of his favorite maxims: the emperor's horse carried his only counselor.

It is nevertheless true that up to the coming of Ingeburgh, which almost coincided with Thaumas's return from his eastern travels, Basil conducted a series of successful wars against Aquileus, against the barbarians, and against the cruel pirates who were just beginning their maraudings. These hostilities were interspersed, in accordance with Basil's natural genius, with often tortuous negotiations, lengthy preparations, violent intrigues, and underhanded subterranean dealings. Then, after he had married Ingeburgh and Thaumas was installed in highest office, Basil's first preoccupation became the organization of the Empire. The lame emperor now pursued for peaceful purposes the works Arsaphes had undertaken for military ends. Water, roads, the development of crafts and skills, provincial government, the organization of feasts and religious worship—nothing escaped his vigilance or his prodigious energy. Thaumas played the part, in fact, of his prime minister. It was impossible for Gandolphus not to take offense, and he often contrasted the length of his own fidelity and devotion, dating from the now distant time when the emperor was still only prince of Onessa, against the recent support, the fierce independence, and the violent and haughty character of the new high priest of the Empire. For by a strange paradox the belligerent Gandolphus was compliant and crafty in manner, while Thaumas, always bent on peace, was intransigent and abrupt, especially with Gandolphus. But to tell the truth, it is impossible to compare the two. From the very beginning Thaumas distinguished himself and rose to importance through the loftiness of his views and the nobility of his character, while Gandolphus was the bad angel, the doer of dirty work. As Justus Dion cruelly observed, "Nature for once showed herself equitable and straightforward, and set physical beauty and greatness of mind on one side, and on the other, a mean appearance and the heart of a flunky." We know little of what the high priest thought of Gandolphus. Thaumas's writings and official utterances are silent on the subject, except on the occasion of the battle of Amphibolus. On the other hand, we have plenty of proof of Gandolphus's hatred for the man who had supplanted him with the emperor. And when the day came that offered the possibility of revenge, he welcomed it with joy. The old counselor had been too long and too resentfully humiliated by the other's greatness not to seize the occasion with both hands.

The rivalry between Thaumas and Gandolphus is inseparable from the history of the Empire itself toward the end of Basil's reign. So long as Ingeburgh was there to keep the peace, the struggle only smoldered; but as soon as she was dead, open conflict broke out. Even before her death there were the first symptoms of an opposition between the two men that went further than mere antipathy or secret hostility. This was on the occasion of the last war against the pirates. A year or two before the empress's death, when the Empire had been enjoying a somewhat less precarious peace than before, there arose a danger not new in kind, but unprecedented in the scope it now assumed. The inhabitants of the coast had always been subject to raids imperilling their peace and prosperity. Once, it had been the fighting between Onessa and the City; then, the various invasions by the Pomposan army. Now they were continually harried by pirates who grew ever more bold, sometimes coming from far away to pillage ports and settlements. These pirates were what might be called marine nomads, with no fixed home, who might spend weeks and weeks at sea before putting in to land for a few months somewhere to repair their ships and replenish their stocks of food and wine. They came from Carthage, Syria, Ireland, the Gulf of Oman, and the Coromandel and Malabar coasts. Some historians maintain that they had crossed the Atlantic even, and that they originally came from the shores of the Caribbean or Greenland. They were fearless sailors and fighters, almost as formidable on land as at sea. Neither Pomposa nor Sicily had ever succeeded in subduing them, and the decline of the City and the Empire's turning inward on itself had left them masters of the seas and, to a certain extent, of the coasts as well.

Single attacks evolved into a kind of outright warfare with pitched battles that, just before Ingeburgh's death, reached the proportions of actual invasion. The whole southwest part of the Empire was vulnerable, and the inhabitants sent message after message imploring help from the City, Onessa, and Aquileus. Basil's first step was to prevent the pirates from penetrating to the interior; and in less than six months the scattered groups of pillagers, some of whom had gotten as far as the upper valley of the Nephta, were all exterminated. But the emperor soon realized that despite this success inland the pirates' pressure on the coast was as remorseless as ever, and that to rid himself of them he would have to strike them at the heart of their power—in other words, at sea. Thanks partly to the Pomposan and Sicilian alliances, he was able to build up a strong navy in less than two years. And it was on the very day of Ingeburgh's funeral that a breathless messenger brought the emperor the news of a decisive victory over the pirates' galleys off Cape Pantama.

As soon as the empress was dead the enmity between Thaumas and Gandolphus came out into the open. Thaumas urged Basil to offer the pirates peace and bring them virtually under the protection of the Empire. Gandolphus wanted them to be pursued and wiped out. For a few days the emperor hesitated, but in the end Thaumas carried the day. Gandolphus never forgave him. The matter was more important than may at first appear. In a sense it was a confrontation between two conceptions of the Empire. Gandolphus's would close the Empire, basing it on Onessa's domination of the territories conquered and grouped together after the victory over Aquileus. Thaumas's conception would open the Empire to all kinds of people and ways of life, in a kind of vast coexistence under the same laws and the same ruler. This is, in fact, the same problem and the same choice as had presented themselves to Basil at the beginning: was the Empire to be based on Onessa's supremacy over her crushed rivals or to be the birth of a new idea, a community of different races and nations? Despite his harshness and his bloodthirsty methods, the emperor had not yet really decided between the two alternatives, and the Empire might still have developed in either direction. So Thaumas's influence seems to have been crucial, and his example was to have incalculable consequences later for the Empire and for Alexis.

A similar situation was to arise again at the very end of Basil's reign, but this time on land, and with much more tragic results. All the time the pirates were attacking in the west, the barbarians continued to exercise pressure on the vague frontiers which ran through the deserts and forests in the east. As we have seen, as early as Arsaphes's reign there had been the beginnings of an interaction both subtle and violent between the barbarians within, who served the City and Aquileus, and the barbarians without, eager to share in the pleasures and powers belonging to what was to become the Empire. As the years went by, an ever-increasing number of barbarians infiltrated, and were finally absorbed into, the Empire. But there was always a new and more formidable wave ready to batter at the frontiers. To the invaders the frontiers seemed like some mirage of happiness and prosperity, where gold, wine, and girls were there for the taking. For years Thaumas and Gandolphus had been preparing for the crisis, Gandolphus by continually strengthening the army and its auxiliary services, Thaumas by using the power and prestige of the church and its ministers to weave a subtle but honorable web of expanding trade and religious and political relations with the barbarians. Between Aquileus and the barbarians there was a continual exchange of goods and persons, and, as in the time of Arsaphes, countless caravans began to cross mountains and deserts, following the routes of jade, amber, spices, and silk.

The situation in the area was suddenly transformed by far-off events whose repercussions finally spread to the borders of the Empire. These events were the thrusts made by the Ainus and the Khmers respectively toward China and India.[1] Few collective events have played a more important role in history. The terrified victims, fleeing before the invaders and rendered ruthless by necessity, soon became in their turn the scourge of their neighbors. A flood of migrations, in which the fear of one group was transformed relentlessly into the terror of another, began to break in wave after wave over vast areas. A large part of the world's population began to move across the steppes and the high plateaus, together with its sheep and cattle and horses, its carts and its tents of felt. In Justus Dion's image: "The weight of men fleeing made the earth tremble." Irresistible pressure was brought to bear on the portals of the Empire by the last to be stricken, endeavoring to be the first to be saved. For all the multitudes caught up in this military vortex, the Empire was at once forbidden territory and promised land, representing prosperity as well as safety and peace. But those who already enjoyed these treasures had no intention of sharing them with starving refugees, made dangerous by despair. Both those who came and those already there were afraid. All saw that the road to peace must lie through war.

Gandolphus prepared for war, and Thaumas, more farsighted, prepared for peace. It was as obvious to Thaumas as to everyone else that armed conflict was inevitable. But he believed that with such enormous forces involved—Justus Dion speaks, with apparent justification, of three or four million men—battles, even successful ones, could settle nothing. For Thaumas, as for Arsaphes before and Alexis after him, the only problem, the only solution, was the incorporation of the barbarians into the Empire—vanquished if possible, but in any case reconciled with the wealth, peace, and order their terrified millions sought to gain by disorder and violence. Gandolphus's one idea, on the other hand, was to fight and to exterminate the barbarians.

After more attacks, lulls, skirmishes, and intermittent parleys than can be gone into in detail, one of the bloodiest battles in history took place in the late autumn on the plain south of Amphibolus. Thaumas had never given up negotiating with the barbarian leaders, and Gandolphus had never given up representing this to Basil as treason in the height of battle. At first the imperial army withstood the barbarians' onslaught; then they drove them off in disorder and passed to the attack. Basil's forces were far superior to the enemy's in discipline and equipment, and by midday it seemed as if the battle was over. It was at this point that Basil's troops, established on a hilltop, saw a sea of barbarian reinforcements sweeping toward them over the plain. In a second the news spread through the ranks that five, seven, eight hundred thousand, perhaps a million men of the most savage appearance, yelling war cries already faintly audible in the distance, were about to hurl themselves into the fray. There was a moment's confusion, and this was the moment Thaumas chose to suggest that Basil should meet the barbarian leaders, who were ready to negotiate.

This was just what Gandolphus had been dreading. He was a clever and cunning strategist, and had soon realized that the tide of battle was turning. This meant it was necessary to regroup and rally the men, prepare new moves and attacks, anything rather than negotiate. The army had to take a breather, not lay down its arms. It was then that Gandolphus had an idea which was to have sweeping consequences for the history of the Empire.

For a long while the relations between the barbarians within and those without, and more generally between the Empire itself and its nearest neighbors, had exposed the religious unity that revealed itself ever more clearly as characteristic of the period. No one either in the Empire or outside it contested the religious pre-eminence of Aquileus. Even when pressure by the barbarians was at its height, thousands of pilgrims and sick people still flocked to the shrines at Amphibolus, Parapoli, Mezzopotamo, and above all Aquileus. By his policy of rapprochement with the barbarians Thaumas intended not only to serve the Empire but also to fulfill his role as spiritual leader of both sides. Even those fighting against him recognized his authority, and revered him as the guardian of myths in which all alike believed. This is a difficult concept for the modern mind to grasp, conditioned as it is by national and economic conflicts in which clearly distinguished interests are ranged one against another. We must cultivate a kind of intellectual empathy in order to understand those equivocal conflicts in which the adversaries, though aiming at mutual destruction perhaps even more determinedly than enemies do today, both wished to share a supreme good whose value neither side denied.

Religion was mixed up, in a way incomprehensible to us, in certain rituals that, no matter what sphere of life they belonged to, literally could not be disobeyed. It was unthinkable not to observe them, whether in sport, marriage, or trade, or in any aspect of economic, social, cultural, or everyday life. In a no longer exclusively religious context we probably still obey similar imperatives today, though they are so taken for granted we are not even conscious of them. And so it was with the Empire and with the barbarians who wished to become part of it. Religion was so closely bound up with life and custom it was indistinguishable from them.

Feasting and war were the two spheres most deeply impregnated by religion: feasting, war, and worship were but three different aspects of a single reality. All were, therefore, dominated by a number of sacred rituals also observed by the barbarians—or at least by those in direct contact with the peoples of the Empire. Things were to be very different with the other barbarians who emerged later from the depths of Asia. All hostilities, for example, came to a halt if snow began to fall on the battlefield, or if three eagles in succession flew over the opposing armies. And if a fox happened to pass between the two camps, the sun must rise twice before fighting could begin again. On this occasion the wily Gandolphus, who stuck at nothing and whose only rule was to succeed, had, as usual, brought along a heavily guarded chariot that was kept well out of sight. It held half a dozen foxes in cages. At the very moment when discouragement had seized the imperial army and Thaumas was trying to arrange for Basil to meet the barbarian leaders, Gandolphus had the foxes secretly released by his trusty henchmen. No sooner did the emperor and the enemy generals catch sight of the foxes streaking between the two armies than they gave orders for all activity to be brought to a standstill. Thaumas, informed by his spies, soon saw through the trick. The suspension of the fighting did not really mean there was to be negotiation and peace; it was only to provide a lull before fresh attacks. Thaumas hastened to Basil, told him of Gandolphus's deceit, and begged him to make use of the coming hours to restore peace while there was yet time. But Gandolphus was there before him, reporting on the fresh reserves he had called up from all the camps and fortresses between Amphibolus and Aquileus; within twenty-four hours nearly one hundred and fifty thousand reinforcements would arrive ready to go into action, and the imperial army's inferior numbers would be amply compensated for by its tactical superiority. A violent dispute broke out between Thaumas and Gandolphus. Basil took Gandolphus's side, and gave orders halting both the fighting and the preparations for a meeting with the enemy. Gandolphus had at last won the revenge he had been waiting for ever since the affair of the pirates. The reinforcements arrived as planned by the following sunset. By dawn on the third day the emperor had been hit by an arrow and lost an eye, but the barbarians had been cut to pieces.

Such was the origin of the phrase now found in almost every language, "to let loose the fox of Amphibolus," which has come to mean merely to slide out of something, or, more precisely, to use underhanded means to escape from a difficult situation, and, by extension, to betray or desert a cause, to leave the weak and innocent to their fate. Time and circumstance have gradually turned the fox of Amphibolus into a symbol of cowardice and indifference. Such are the paradoxes of living language that the phrase has come to refer not to the power of guile but to that of baseness or even impotence. Napoleon still used the expression in its proper sense when he suggested it to Las Cases for his *St. Helena Memoirs:* "The armory of the Prince of Beneventum must have included the fox of Amphibolus." But it was unfortunately both a misapplication of the term and a vain hope when, after Munich, on a front page still usually devoted to personal advertisements, the *Times* printed an eight-column headline that read, "The Fox of Amphibolus Again."

The irony of history and linguistics had transformed what was originally a military ruse, disgraceful but successful, into a symbol of desertion. But Basil's and Gandolphus's contemporaries, including the barbarians and the priests, understood clearly enough: it was the shame of victory, not defeat, that they blamed Basil and Gandolphus for. Only much later did the fox of Amphibolus completely change its meaning. One can easily understand how and why, and at least history and language preserved the element of shame and dishonor in the trick that marked Gandolphus's triumph and Thaumas's defeat and decline.

But the future soon brought the very results Thaumas had predicted for the battle and for the fox of Amphibolus: the vanquished barbarians returned in even greater numbers than before and ceaselessly harried the borders of the Empire. Gandolphus's victory was not only a trick, it was also no more than a respite before the onset of new ordeals, the magnitude of which we shall see in due course. But it did Thaumas little good to be in the right. The rise of truth and justice in the world is slow, and when they do prevail it is often too late. Thaumas, pursued by Gandolphus's hatred, rejected by Basil, who did not care for being told that his victory was precarious and won only through deceit and contempt for religion, was forced to quit the service of the emperor and take refuge in Aquileus. The clerics there were torn between the fear that Basil still inspired and the enormous prestige of the priest, now fallen from favor. They took Thaumas in, but in fear and trembling.

Thaumas's dismissal brought a tremor in the structure of the Empire. The edifice was still sound enough, and for some time withstood all doubts, fissures, and divisions—but only with difficulty. As barbarian pressure on the frontiers increased, discontent grew within the Empire. The memory of the great days of Aquileus and Arsaphes, even the memory of the City, was not quite dead. Gradually, within the very borders established by Arsaphes and Basil, the barbarian mercenaries, moved by a secret solidarity with their brethren still outside the Empire and exposed to every kind of danger, began to resent army discipline and to claim a bigger say in the decisions of the imperial government. After years of acquiescence, the priests began to allude to the emperor's atrocities. As Justus Dion says, "The fox of

Amphibolus suddenly woke the guests of Onessa from their drunken stupor." And all along the frontiers there was nothing but insecurity, raids, wars, and rumors of wars. The end of Basil's reign is full of ghosts: the specters of barbarian horsemen ever rising to life again out of steppes already drenched in their blood; the specters of barbarians within the Empire who had no rights but who yearned for the possibility of wealth and prosperity as well as military glory; the shameful specter of the fox of Amphibolus; the gory specters of the banquet at Onessa. Ingeburgh was no longer there to advise the emperor. One winter's night three messengers from Gandolphus arrived just as everyone in Aquileus was about to go to bed. After a few hours' sleep and a meal of mutton, dates, and rye brandy, they mingled with the pilgrims come to take part in certain ceremonies that Thaumas was due to conduct. When Thaumas appeared the three men hurled themselves upon him and slew him. According to the legend the dying Thaumas, his hands still resting on the altar at which he was officiating, turned first to the priests and then to his murderers and cried out before he collapsed: "Weakness, where is thy victory? Victory, where is thine honor?" So ended the struggle between Gandolphus and Thaumas. Less than three months later, Gandolphus, in his turn, was assassinated by a barbarian chieftain in the pay of the Empire. And a fortnight after that, Basil died of the plague. And with Ingeburgh, Thaumas, Gandolphus, and Basil all gone from the scene, the Empire was once again exposed to the grave dangers of earlier days. The pirates reappeared. The barbarian troops mutinied. The priests plotted. Between Onessa and Aquileus the old hatred revived. Agitators went about the City uttering fiery prophecies and speaking again of enmity between the Tiger and the Eagle. Everywhere, unity was dissolving. As always, history seemed to be hesitating at the crossroads. It was as if the Empire would have to be built all over again.

VIII

THE SIEGE OF BALKH

 N THE NORTHEAST, THE EMPIRE WAS BORDERED BY great forests, bounded on the south by plains of wheat, with Aquileus in the center. Watered by streams that were mostly tributaries of the Amphyses or the Nephta, the plains stretched as far as the eye could see toward the deserts of the Kirghiz and the Tartars. But in the north the forest had no bounds. Neither ancient tradition nor travelers' tales ventured to assign its limits, or to describe anything but its outskirts and the few winding paths that soon lost themselves in its depths. Few men dared enter far enough to tell what it was like. All anyone knew was that deer and wolves, boars and bears were more plentiful there than sheep upon the hills. The armies of Onessa and Aquileus had made only rare thrusts in that direction, and but faint echoes had been heard there of the great battles of the Empire.

A few hundred kilometers from the most northerly reach of the Amphyses the forest was still penetrable, consisting chiefly of great oaks in their prime mixed with fir and beech and an occasional ash or birch. It was a wild region, very cold in winter and hot in summer. The small but belligerent population lived scattered about in shacks, from which they would descend at regular intervals to ravage the fertile plains in the south. Once they had carried out their raid and gathered up their booty the warriors from the north soon left the burned-out villages and withdrew to their forest fastness. Little is known of the language they spoke, and they left no written records. They had neither king nor assembly, but were divided into tribes each with its own absolute ruler. Under Basil, the most important of these tribal chiefs was a leader whose power and reputation were already spreading far. He was a tall, strong fellow, selfish and cruel, and his men feared rather than loved him. His wealth and the promise of power had enabled him to marry one of Arsaphes's great-grand-daughters, the sister of one of those insipid princelings who dragged out showy but poor and useless existences in Aquileus, openly scorned and sometimes even referred to as mere puppets, under the thumb first of the priests and then of the emperor. It was not long before Princess Helen was as much beloved by her subjects as her husband Roderick was hated. Almost as tall as he, very fair, and at once vital and gentle, Princess Helen was a direct descendant of the Porphyries of the City. The men of her race seemed to have handed over all its virtue to the women, and Helen was its most dazzling incarnation. Her great beauty, her courage, and the simplicity of her demeanor, whether in adversity or success, lent her husband a prestige and authority he would never have won for himself but of which he made skillful use. Despite the mistrust of the emperor, who naturally feared a revival of the power of the Porphyries, Roderick was able to add to his lands and resources through successful campaigns and well-planned alliances. Basil's triumph had compelled Roderick, like many others, to recognize Onessa's supremacy and pay tribute to the emperor; but up there, in the distant forests of the northeast, no one could yet challenge the lord of Balkh's unashamed exploitation of his rights and privileges. Always engaged in some battle, or some raid against a poorly defended township, Roderick was really no more than a kind of brigand chief. One of his favorite exploits was to descend on the markets and fairs held where plain and forest met. He would suddenly appear at the head of his band of horsemen, seize all the merchandise, bales of cloth, and weapons, kill anyone who resisted, and vanish again into the depths of his forest as swiftly as he had come. Whenever he took a few days' rest from plundering the rich merchants or the flocks and herds of the plain, his chief amusement was the chase. He was a hunter of prodigious skill and strength, and dozens of tales were told of boars he had strangled barehanded and bears and wolves he had slain with cold steel. While her husband and his men were away on distant expeditions, Princess Helen looked after everything. She dispensed justice, tended the children, visited women in childbed, and could keep order over a territory that was by now extensive. But in the evening, after a tiring day spent with stewards, captains left behind, physicians, and shamans, what she really liked was to sit before a fire of blazing oak logs and talk with priests and scholars of travels in far-off lands and of what became of the soul after death. From her childhood in Aquileus she retained a respect for the priesthood and a taste for theological discussion. Twice for certain, perhaps three times, Thaumas came and spent several days in Balkh. And for years Helen and the high priest kept up a regular correspondence, which unfortunately has not survived.[1]

It is very likely, though not sure, that Helen consulted Thaumas over the problem of her son's education. Young Simeon was very like his father. Dark-complexioned and very strong, at the age of seven he had had a servant whipped to death for failing to comply quickly enough with his already crazy whims. At the age of eleven or twelve he was said to have raped a shepherd's daughter who was his play-fellow. He showed promise of being a splendid archer, he had the gift of command, and even as a child was an indefatigable horseman. But he was false and cruel, and his mother could hardly believe he was her son. She tried to surround him with good influences, and trusted much to that of two or three lads of Simeon's own age with whom he had made friends. One in particular became almost another son to her. This was Nandor, the son of one of Roderick's lieutenants, a bold, lively boy a little older than Simeon, who had lost both mother and father. Then an incident occurred that seemed slight enough at the time but was to leave its mark. Roderick had a dagger that he greatly prized. It was inlaid with ivory and precious stones and had been given to him by a prince of Bukhara. One day he noticed it had disappeared. Under torture, two or three servants on whom suspicion first fell revealed evidence pointing to the group of lads surrounding Simeon. Roderick questioned his son at length, no doubt with his usual harshness, but Simeon knew nothing. Roderick was wild with rage. He had brought before him one by one all who could possibly have had anything to do with the affair. He received them whip in hand, and did not always refrain from using it. But when Nandor's turn came the boy did not remain passive. As soon as the thong touched him he seized it with all a boy's courage and strength, and tore it out of Roderick's hand. Roderick, furious, tried to wrest it back again, but Nandor snapped it over his knee and threw the pieces away.

"You would not have dared to touch me if my father were still alive," he panted. "But because he's dead you think you can do anything." And without another word he turned and walked out.

Roderick was still stunned by the lad's resistance, and a touch of admiration was beginning to mingle with his anger, when his son asked to speak with him. Simeon confessed he had told Nandor where the dagger was kept in Roderick's absence, and said Nandor had taken it one night after they had both drunk the leavings in some glasses of rye brandy they had found lying about. A confrontation between the two boys in Roderick's presence produced little result. Nandor only shrugged his shoulders and gave Simeon a look of the utmost scorn. Helen tried talking to the two separately—she loved them almost equally. But they would only stick obstinately to their contradictory stories. Then the men Roderick had ordered to find the stolen dagger at all costs discovered it hidden under Nandor's bed. And despite Helen's entreaties the boy, who was only twelve years old, was executed before Simeon's eyes. The executioner cut off his hand and tore out his tongue before decapitating him.

A few months later, one of Helen's old servants fell dangerously ill. Helen was very fond of him, and was sitting by his sickbed when he indicated that he wished to speak to her. She bent over him and listened with horror as he told, in a voice broken with fever, how Simeon had forced him, by the direst threats, to hide the dagger under Nandor's bed. Helen seized the dying man's hands and begged him to tell whether it was Simeon alone who had stolen the dagger in the first place. Summoning his remaining strength, the old servant said it was so. One night he had heard a suspicious rustling and, creeping toward it, had seen, by the light of a dying fire, that Simeon was searching the chest where Roderick kept the dagger. He had gone up and tried to reason with him, but Simeon had only insulted him, threatened to accuse him of the theft, and forced him to swear secrecy. A few days later, seeing his father's wrath, Simeon had sought out the old man and made him plant the evidence that led to Nandor's death. With his last breath the old servant begged Helen to forgive him the sorrow he was causing, but he could no longer hold back the truth. He asked Helen to forgive Simeon, too, for a sin he put down to youth and a temporary aberration. Then the old man fell back dead.

Helen never dared tell her husband what she had just learned. But she sent for her son and spoke to him sternly. He denied everything. His pretense of innocence was sufficiently unconvincing to make his mother certain of his guilt, but at the same time skillful enough to horrify her at such duplicity in one so young. That day saw the end of any bond between them. Dozens of times Helen felt an impulse to tell Roderick everything, but she always drew back because of the pitiless punishment she knew would follow. As a result, Roderick came to reproach her for her strange harshness toward their son. And Simeon played off against his mother the indulgence of a father from whom, but for her, he would have had so much to fear, but whose cruelty and violence he now exploited for his own ends. It was at this point, perhaps on Thaumas's advice, that young Fabrician arrived in Balkh.

Fabrician was the great-grandnephew of one of Arsaphes's generals who was killed near Aquileus in a battle against the Oïghurs. Alexander, the young man's father, had been a friend of Thaumas's, and Thaumas had always helped him, even during the darkest days in Aquileus. Alexander's death left Fabrician very poor. He was thin, tall, full of fire and ambition. He looked like a skinned rabbit, but had lively green eyes that attracted women and impressed men. Thaumas took him under his wing and sent him first to the priests' seminary, then on various missions to Mursa, Ctesiphon, and Caesarea. After that he gave him administrative posts in the City that involved a great deal of responsibility for one of his age. Fabrician had fought against the pirates and been taken prisoner, then exchanged and repatriated after the battle of Cape Pantama. Then Basil, on Thaumas's advice, had summoned him to Onessa, and it was from there he set out for Balkh. Fabrician revered Thaumas, but had mixed feelings about the emperor, and hated Gandolphus. Some say it was Gandolphus who sent him to Roderick, in order to get rid of him. History is full of such ironies.

Simeon did not react too badly to his new tutor. Roderick, perhaps warned against the newcomer by Gandolphus, who might have commended Fabrician for his learning while alerting Roderick to the ambition and independence of mind that could prove dangerous, received the young priest with a mixture of roughness and contempt. But he was gradually won over by the young man's courage and keenness. For Fabrician, who was rather delicate, threw himself ardently into the hunting parties and military expeditions in which Roderick had included him in the hope of putting him to shame. He ended up by acquiring great skill in riding and throwing the javelin, and by becoming Roderick and Simeon's boldest and most dashing companion-in-arms and in roistering. Only Helen was not won over by the newcomer. She found him insolent, frivolous, and self-satisfied, and his cool gaiety frightened her. Justus Dion tells how one evening when she was complaining of him an old servingwoman told her, "But you will come to like him, madam. He is like Thaumas."

THE GLORY OF THE EMPIRE · 80

And in a way it was true. Beneath a brilliant and sometimes sarcastic exterior, he had the same strength of character, the same sense of destiny, the same ability to forget himself in a greater cause. But he hated any affectation of virtue, and preferred to hide his own under a mask of cynicism and pleasure-seeking. Danger and adversity, however, were soon to show his true worth.

Less than a year after Fabrician's arrival, Roderick set off once more on a long expedition against the bands of Ossetes and Alans who, for some time past, had been harrying his domains. Most of his soldiers went with him, leaving Helen to take charge of Balkh with the help of a handful of veterans and young men. All went well for a few weeks, and then one spring morning Fabrician was told that two horsemen were asking to see him. He had them brought in, and immediately recognized one of them as Gandolphus's agent. The two envoys began by showering Fabrician with compliments and precious gifts, and then came out bluntly with the proposition that he should hand Balkh and its possessions over to the emperor. In return, they promised in Gandolphus's name that Fabrician should be made ruler over Balkh and given half its revenues. The young man had a swift vision of power and fame, but then he recalled the trust reposed in him, and remembered Thaumas and all he had learned from him. He was astonished that Thaumas should countenance such dealings. But as the conversation proceeded he realized it was a personal maneuver on the part of Gandolphus and not an official move on the part of the Empire. Basil might be shutting his eyes to it; Thaumas, at any rate, could have no part in what was probably just one more episode in the hidden struggle between him and Gandolphus, in which the latter never let slip an opportunity to try to better his position. Seeing all this, Fabrician soon made up his mind.

"I have been entrusted with the task of educating Simeon and preparing him for life," he said. "What future should I be giving him if I deprived him of all his possessions? As for myself, if I betrayed my present masters, how could the emperor or Gandolphus ever trust or respect me again? It is more reasonable to value servants for their loyalty than for their treachery. If I were Gandolphus's man I would serve him against Roderick, but since I am Roderick's I shall defend him against Gandolphus."[2]

Then he summoned Helen, and, saying nothing of what had passed, they offered the imperial envoys a banquet and beds for the night before they continued on their way. As soon as they vanished among the trees, Fabrician told Helen that the emperor's, or rather Gandolphus's, troops, were probably about to attack. Two or three weeks later the lookouts on the edge of the forest galloped up to report that detachments of armed men were moving in the direction of Balkh.

Balkh owed its strength to its position at a point beyond which the forest became impenetrable. The site was of almost unbroken flatness, with just a few shallow depressions whose streams emptied into ponds or lakes. But the trees were already so thick that it was difficult for troops to move. Fabrician organized the defense of the city around the resources supplied by the forest. He had moats dug and lined with pikes and wolf traps, then covered with leaves and branches. Huge nets were spread among the trees in such a way that one man, releasing a spring, could enmesh a whole detachment. Oak trees were chopped so that they were only just left standing and the slightest touch would bring them crashing down. Ravening bears and wolves were shut in an enclosure ready to be loosed on the attackers. Palisades of the stoutest wood were put up all round the outskirts of Balkh to stave off the assault until reinforcements arrived. While taking all these precautions, Fabrician had also sent off a messenger with orders to find Roderick at all costs, as soon as the difficulties of the journey permitted, and to tell him of the dangers threatening Balkh, Helen, and Simeon.

Gandolphus's army was large and well equipped, but through Fabrician's snares they lost at least a hundred men in a few days. Fabrician, surrounded by a handful of old men and youths, had brought Simeon with him almost into contact with the enemy. Simeon loved trickery and violence and had a passion for weapons, but Fabrician found him less apt and inclined for war—this war at any rate—than for pleasure and distraction. But, in fact, there was no major confrontation. The enemy's superiority was so crushing that Fabrician did all he could to avoid a pitched battle. The ground kept giving way beneath the assailant, and the forest echoed with oaks crashing down on terrified groups of enemy soldiers. A week or so after the first skirmishes, scouts from Balkh were still finding parties of Gandolphus's men half buried in the ground and hidden by the branches. Their companions had deserted them, and they lay there with broken limbs, covered in blood, and gnawed at by wild animals or ants. When the enemy finally reached the fortifications improvised around Balkh itself, where Helen and Fabrician had spared no effort to organize resistance and keep up the morale of the defenders, the attacking force had already lost a good deal of its strength and spirit. But for the besieged few the danger was still great, and there seemed to be little hope.

Balkh resisted the invader for twenty-seven days and twenty-eight nights. The moon, which had been new at the beginning of the siege, shone brighter and brighter over nights filled with alarms and fighting, and then began to wane. It was fine May weather. The nights were still cool, but in the daytime the new buds basked in the sun. The whole forest was gay with rebirth; but lances and javelins flashed among the branches and the singing of the birds. Helen and Fabrician were everywhere at once, tending the wounded, encouraging the youngest and oldest, promising the imminent return of Roderick and his men. Though neither spoke of it, both were afraid lest the messenger had been killed or lost his way, or for some other reason had not been able to reach Roderick, who might, all unaware of the mounting danger at home, be pressing on deeper and deeper into the vast steppes of the Ossets and the Alans.

The end of the day was not the end of anxiety. Every night Helen and Fabrician listened through the darkness for sounds threatening attack. After distributing supplies and inspecting the defenses, they would settle down again to wait. The enemy knew, too, that time was against it, and that it had to reduce the town before Roderick's return. Each side could well imagine the hopes and plans of the other. What the besieged did not know was when the attack would begin, whether at dawn or dusk, by day or night. During the whole twenty-seven days of the siege Helen and Fabrician never slept. They waited.

Trouble and adversity, which men fear and try to escape, unite them much more strongly than all the charms of indolence and ease. During those days and nights when they were alone, dependent just on their own resources and their own courage, a feeling of mutual trust and respect grew up between Helen and Fabrician. Fabrician, like everyone else, had always greatly admired Helen, but her unvarying nobility and simplicity now turned his admiration into a kind of devotion, so that even the thought of dying for her was not unattractive. This feeling, still hidden under a mask of detachment, eventually overcame Helen's original dislike or even hostility toward the young priest. His constant cheerfulness, resolution, and loyalty first impressed and then moved her, and she began to fear for the life of one who took war so lightheartedly. Danger brought them together. Both, in their different ways, had always led a rigorous and often austere life, and the great peril they had faced together was for both a source of exaltation. One day Fabrician told Helen he enjoyed taking any kind of risk so long as it was for her. It was sweet to laugh at death, or to fear it only for the other. It was intoxicating to be in action. Tomorrow they would be either dead, enslaved, or victorious—there was no other alternative. The life being reborn all around them in the forest affected them too, filling them with a kind of joy in the midst of misfortune and transforming the siege into a test that had to be gone through, whether the issue were triumph or disaster. They vied with each other, and all the defenders of Balkh tried to show themselves worthy of their example. "It was an epidemic of courage," wrote Justus Dion. "Valor and the will to resist spread like a beneficent plague sent by the gods."

Only Simeon stood aside. Some authors say, without very much proof, that he was on the side of Gandolphus and the attackers, who had gone to him after Fabrician rejected their proposals. Others see his attitude as a desire to avenge himself on both his father and his mother. Others again see him first and foremost as a victim. What is certain is that after a few incidents inside the besieged town—Simeon got into a fight with two soldiers, and, on another occasion, against the express orders of Helen and Fabrician, organized a sortie that was bound to fail—Simeon disappeared, and turned up again in the enemy camp. Here, again, there are various different interpretations. Some people say he was kidnapped, some that he voluntarily went over to the enemy. Legend relates that a messenger was sent to the princess saying the boy would be put to death if Balkh did not surrender. Helen's reply is said to have been: "What does it matter? I am still young enough to have others." This answer on the part of the mother may throw some light on the attitude of the son, in whom ingratitude and thirst for affection may have been interdependent.

The whole incident is obscure. Later, Roderick, of course, tried to account for it in terms of deception and violence, but the theory of deliberate treachery on the part of Simeon has retained many supporters. It is perhaps not impossible that, jealous of both Helen and Fabrician, Simeon aimed at bringing together Roderick and Gandolphus against the defenders of Balkh. Simeon's hypothetical plans and vague projects were long treated as adolescent dreams or the whims of a mischievous child, but recently they have given rise to a substantial body of serious work.[3] We must not omit to mention the explanations derived from psychoanalysis and depth psychology, which depict a child terrified of his father, separated by a lie from his mother, and among clever enemies who dangled before his eyes a picture of himself as a hero destined to save the family heritage for the general good, despite and in opposition to his parents.

All the historians more or less favorable to Simeon and anxious to excuse him have insisted on what lay behind the horrors of war and the glory of the resistance in Balkh. If the siege went on, life went on also. What triumphed in the doomed city, exalted by its own valor and by the imminence of death, were not merely noble sentiments of mutual trust, but, rather, normal human nature and passion. It took a long time and much violence for anyone to admit the truth, especially Helen and Fabrician. Perhaps it was Simeon who first saw or guessed the powerful new bond between them that made them scorn danger and rise to such heights—perhaps he saw it even before they did so themselves. But what was the use of going on trying to deceive themselves or others? Full of joy and terror, Helen and Fabrician discovered they were in love. The war and the siege were now only an excuse for them not to part, and to enjoy at last, alone, away from everyone and everything, the glimpse of happiness paradoxically made possible for them by the encircling armies. Could that have been the secret reason that made Simeon go over to Gandolphus's camp? Though one or two authors, like Prosper de Barante and J.-J. Ampère, continue to resist the evidence, the great majority of historians nowadays agree that Helen was passionately in love with the young priest. Their love, as often happens, was hidden at first under detachment and irony, then under mutual admiration and unspoken understanding; then danger and the nearness of death made it burst out into the light of day. He was about five or six years younger than she, but everything combined to make them feel they were made for each other. Neither had ever known much happiness. There is ample evidence of the affection and esteem they came to feel for each other. Their life was to end there, deep in the forests in which they were both foreigners. It was spring, and between them and death there still remained a few nights of courage and happiness. Before dying together they wished to live together. Danger, youth, even fear and anxiety gave them the right, and helped to throw them together.

The encircled city presents a strange image of man's dreams and man's limitations, his greatness and his illusions. The title of Apollinaire's short play, *Balkh, or A Brief Happiness*, summarizes the theme of a whole line of plays about the siege and the lovers of Balkh, from Lope de Vega to Hugo, and from Shakespeare to Maurice Barrès and André Suarès. For Dante and Montaigne, Helen and Fabrician were symbols of human dignity and weakness. At the beginning of the nineteenth century they became archetypes of the romantic hero. Chateaubriand drags them into his *Genius of Christianity*, with which, as Maurice Levaillant and André Maurois have wittily demonstrated, they have little to do. Byron eulogizes them; Stendhal obviously uses them as the basis of one of his most successful *Italian Chronicles*, in which Balkh is weirdly transmogrified into a Tuscan princedom; Lautréamont himself evokes them magnificently in the famous imaginary conversation between the forest lovers surrounded by wolves and bears. True, a few pages further on, thirsting as always after life's contradictions, he praises in the same breath "viper-faced Simeon" and "his infernal need for cruelty and the infinite." But fame, even posthumous fame, is always dearly bought. It was not long before reaction set in. In about 1918 or 1919, in Switzerland, anonymous and undated, there appeared one of the masterpieces of erotic literature. This little, oblong yellow book, recently reprinted,[4] definitely not for the general reader, is a skillful broadside against conformism in love and war. It has the charming title of *Go F——Yourselves, Helician and Fabrine*, and in it the exploits of the lovers of Balkh outrage respectability in a style altogether dazzling.[5] Such are the splendors of literature and history.

But let us set aside these cumbersome chroniclers, and imagine, behind the inventions of legend and print, the spring nights around the besieged city. Nothing stirred in the forest. All seemed to sleep under the ancient oaks, changeless through seasons and through centuries, under the impassive moon. Nothing moved, but all trembled: the trees, the wind, the buds, the leaves, anxious wide-eyed does, birds on the branches, Gandolphus's warriors tossing impatiently in their felt mantles as they lay at the mossy foot of oak or birch. They came from Onessa and Aquileus, from plain and desert. They knew nothing of either Helen or Fabrician. They were paid to kill, and that was what they would try to do. A bit of human history was being enacted in an almost virgin setting. The weather was fine. Roderick was galloping on the margin of steppe and forest. A young man rode after him to try to bring him back in time. Simeon had vague dreams, in one of Gandolphus's tents, between two of Gandolphus's men. Was he a prisoner? Guest of honor? Ally? He loved neither father nor mother, and would take his revenge on them by saving, for himself and despite them, all that they would have lost. Mysterious threads led far from the forest itself to Gandolphus and Thaumas, and to Basil, pondering in his habitual pose, chin in hand, on the destiny of the Empire. All were dreaming. Of their lives, their loves, what they would do with their money, their land, their future, or the world. Some did not dream—the dead, or the dying. A wolf had leapt at their throat and they had failed to fight him off with their javelins. Or traps had opened under them and their blood had slowly ebbed away. Or they were still imprisoned by a net or an oak tree that they did not see falling until it was too late—they were in a leafy cage which kept out the light of sun or moon. They had broken legs and hips. They did not even cry out. They shut their eyes and uttered the low groans that make it a little easier to die. Such is war. Such is life. As Simeon put it at the sight of three corpses mangled by traps and wolves, "Ah, well, to live is to die."

And in the besieged city itself? Inside Balkh, too, nothing moved. Nothing moved, but all was alert. Children of eight or nine stared into the night to see if it really slept. Old women who could not sleep crawled secretly up to the ramparts to take a drop of goat's milk to their grandsons. Two soldiers who were homosexuals made love under the boughs. Two soldiers who were gamesters threw knuckle-bones into the air. Two soldiers who were tired slept for a while before dying. It was fine. Roderick galloped on the margin of steppe and forest. If only the messenger might find him and bring him back! If only the messenger might never find him and never bring him back! Helen and Fabrician thought only of loving and dying. By now they were defending Balkh only because they wanted to go on loving. They would have liked to live together, but would rather die than be separated by victory. They had defended Balkh for Roderick. They had defended Balkh for Simeon. They had defended Balkh for its own sake. And now they were defending it for themselves and their own happiness, against Simeon and probably against Roderick too. All they asked of life now, and they asked it passionately, was a little time in which to love. If only Roderick would suddenly appear in the midst of the forest! But their lips and hands, their bodies and souls had already answered—if only Roderick would go farther and farther away, into the steppe, far from the forest! And if only we might die! They listened for the sound of a familiar horn, desperately longed for and now, suddenly, desperately dreaded. But there was nothing.

Nothing but silence in the forest, and men-at-arms asleep. Then, solaced by this silent proclamation of disaster, the raised heads were lowered again to the outstretched lips, to the soft thigh, to the already bared shoulder, and the anxious bodies yielded to, harmonized with, one another. Once more, perhaps for the last time, the kiss, the slow caresses, the still and sudden flame.

The messenger had overtaken Roderick, who was already hastening back. He had left the steppes, and was deep once more in the gloomy forest where he felt at home. But the forest was vast, and it took a long time to ride as far as Balkh. It had taken sixteen days for the messenger to catch up with Roderick. To save time, Roderick and his men returned by shorter but more difficult ways. More than one exhausted steed died under them, but in eleven days they reached their point of departure. The outward journey across the steppe and the forest—interrupted, it is true, by fighting and various successful excursions—had taken over three months. Now it was no longer possible to ride. The trees and undergrowth were too dense. So the men had to dismount and lead their horses in single file through the luxuriant wastes. But what was impenetrable they crossed, from what was inextricable they emerged. Twenty-five days after the messenger's departure the army suddenly found itself in familiar surroundings—it was approaching Balkh. Another two days' riding and they would be in the city.

On the twenty-third day of the siege Gandolphus's men lost patience and went over to the attack. It began with a hail of arrows loosed on the fortifications and their defenders. Fabrician recognized the tactics of the Scythian archers Gandolphus liked to use. As the enemy drew closer, arrows were followed by javelins. Twenty men were laid low behind the ramparts. But the most pressing danger came from the flaming torches fixed to the enemy's spears and arrows. Balkh was built entirely of wood. The same readily available material had been used not only for the cottages of the soldiers and their families, but also for the dwellings of people like Roderick and Helen, for Fabrician's house, and for the buildings where religious ceremonies were performed and ambassadors received. Stone was scarce around Balkh and oak cost nothing. Everything came from the woods and the forest—chariots, weapons, cisterns, even shoes. Only the chief warriors used swords or lances made entirely of bronze or sometimes iron. Ordinary soldiers used mostly wooden weapons, the most common types being clubs and cudgels. The wood-handled pike or ax was comparatively rare. Only princes and chieftains were allowed to use ivory. But in the hands of the warriors of Balkh and the surrounding forest, all weapons were formidable and wrought havoc.

One can imagine the destruction caused in a few hours in that city of wood by the brands of Gandolphus's men. From the age of eight or nine, the boys fought in the front line of the city's defenders. The younger ones, and the girls, were the firefighters. Little girls of six or seven, helped by broken old men who could scarcely stand, might be seen dragging buckets of water that they could hardly lift to throw on the flames. By the evening of the first day of the assault, half of Balkh was already burning.

The attack went on during the whole first part of the night. The sky, which had been clear for week after week, grew gradually overcast, and javelins and arrows traced fiery trajectories against blackest darkness. The children had been quick to grasp what they had to do. They watched out for the brand's trail, calculated by instinct where it would fall, sheltered themselves behind a tree or a wooden shield, and pounced on the torch as soon as it touched the ground. Thus half or three-quarters of the firebrands were quenched before they could spread their dancing destruction. But the rest, those that the children and old men could not extinguish in time, were enough to turn Balkh into a furnace.

On the twenty-fourth day the fortunes of battle changed. Some twenty of the attackers managed to get through a breach in the fortifications and reach the outlying cottages of the city. But they were wiped out by Fabrician and his men. The evening was quieter. Both sides were getting their breath back. The next night was favorable to the besieged. Ever more threatening clouds had been massing in the sky, and soon after midnight the rain began to fall and quench the fires that had not yet been put out. Hope revived in the hearts of the forest warriors. Perhaps every hour that passed brought Roderick and his army nearer. All resolved to hold out to the limit of their strength. And the twenty-fifth day did not go too badly. At sunset, taking advantage of a lull both in the weather and in the fighting, the defenders gathered in the public square surrounded by wooden huts and, standing in front of the big mansion with double staircase and oak balcony that Justus Dion calls the palace, they cheered Helen and Fabrician loud and long. The princess and the priest heard the shouts of those who were about to die, and who included them both in the same devotion. It was the culmination of their strange, brief encounter, which in any case was already over. Those who acclaimed them knew nothing of any hidden love. They knew their own true life had only just begun, in tribulation and courage, and that it was drawing to its close.

At nightfall, when the rain had begun again, Fabrician sent a boy of eleven or twelve through the enemy lines to meet Roderick. It was impossible to remain in doubt any longer; they had to know if he was coming. But unknown to Fabrician, the child was killed a couple of hundred yards outside the *enceinte*. Roderick was now only twenty hours' ride away by paths he knew by heart. He had slept for three or four hours among his men, sheltering as best he could from the rain that was still falling. The sun was shining when he awoke and sprang into the saddle. He would be in Balkh by next day.

It was the twenty-sixth day of the siege. The weather was fine. Pressure on the city became more and more severe. The defenders had now lost more than two hundred men, women, and children, killed or seriously wounded. The wooden dwellings and the towers on the ramparts were afire again. At two or three points at least the defense was weakening. Toward noon Fabrician attempted a sortie on the side of the town backed by the forest at its densest. The object of the operation was a kind of outflanking movement that would take the main body of the enemy from behind and make them think Roderick had come. The diversion was a partial success. It sowed panic in the enemy ranks and killed many of their men. The vise was loosened for three or four hours. But before dark, the assault began again.

It was the nightmare everyone had already glimpsed in their worst dreams. Balkh burned more fiercely than ever. There was fighting in the moats, on the ramparts, on the palisades, on the barriers improvised from the ruins of burned-out houses. Fabrician joined two horses together with a rope to which were tied clubs and big pieces of wood. Then he loosed them into a gap a hundred yards wide that had been reduced to ashes by fire and through which the enemy was pouring. In a few minutes the horses were laid low, but not before, maddened by the whip, the din, and the flames, they had knocked down and trampled on whole rows of enemy soldiers. The battle went on all night. The defenders fell back step by step, hiding in holes and attacking from the rear the assailants who had already passed by. People were fighting now with lances, clubs, axes, and bare hands. Women threw live embers and firebrands into the enemies' faces.

Children fought with slings, wooden swords they had plunged into the flames, any toy that came to hand. But the odds were too unequal —the defenders were outnumbered. Huge Syrian and Scythian archers swung children round in the air and hurled them as missiles. It is said one little girl of five or six was saved by her grandfather, who caught her in his arms. When dawn broke, the fortifications hastily erected by Fabrician were breached on almost all sides. Gandolphus's troops had entered the city and were converging on the center and the palace, where a few fanatics, led by Fabrician and Helen, still fought on. Helen sent to ask for a truce in which to gather in the dead and tend the wounded. But the enemy refused, anxious lest the main body of Balkh's army return, and eager to end the siege and either raze the city to the ground or fortify it for their own fight against Roderick. Fierce fighting broke out again. By noon only the palace was resisting still, together with a few strong points nearby. Helen and Fabrician had already bidden one another farewell, in haste, with the noise of battle at the very doors of the palace. Feelings find swift expression in the face of danger. They exchanged a last kiss.[6]

"I die happy," said Fabrician, "because I have known you. Do not die. Remember."

"I shall not die," answered Helen. "I shall live on, to remember you, and that you may not quite die."

Helen kept her word and did not die. Fabrician was killed by a spear thrust, defending the palace, at the very moment when the distant sound of Roderick's horn announced his entry into the ruins of the city. Some say the priest deliberately sought death. Gandolphus's men were taken in the rear and slain—every one. Roderick found Helen in the palace, with Fabrician's corpse in her lap. She was motionless, calm, unweeping. But the ordeal of the siege and the fighting had left her as if unconscious. The young priest was buried at night by torchlight in the midst of the ruins, with a hero's honors. Three years later Roderick was murdered by one of Nandor's brothers. He had made peace with the Empire and died rich and powerful, but he had never been able to rebuild Balkh, which had suffered such destruction and lost so many of its women and children. A son had been born to him during the winter following the siege. Helen had named him Alexis.

IX

THE WOLF HUNT

 EACE AND SILENCE HAD RETURNED TO THE GREAT forest. The oaks were recovering slowly from their wounds and the tempest. The memory of massacre had gradually faded, and the cries of the dying had been swallowed up into the past. Those who still heard them during sleepless nights found a kind of pleasure in recalling the siege and its sufferings. Even cruelty and horror come to inspire in the human heart something of the affectionate melancholy that belongs to things past. Time and life had done their work. Balkh, destroyed by the flames, was abandoned—for the young it was no more than a far-off and even somewhat tedious myth. History, though it consists of memory, has a poor memory. Death and disaster come fast, and so do forgetfulness and the wish to survive. Roderick and Helen had taken up residence 100 miles to the northeast of Balkh, in a great house flanked by wooden towers and surrounded by moats, where life must have been very grim. But those who were loyal were there, and so were the trees and the forest.

We know little of the relations between Roderick and Helen after the siege and destruction of Balkh. The evidence that survives speaks only of the renewal, less than two years after the conflict, of the alliance between Basil and Roderick. Roderick recognized the supremacy of the emperor and agreed to pay him tribute, but the Empire granted him various new rights and the enjoyment of extensive territories and their resources. Politics and history offer almost as many examples as love does of reversals that would have appeared incredible a few months or days or hours before. Men's hearts and men's interests seem to vie with each other in inconsequence and to share the same liking for the unforeseen and unforeseeable. Imagination exhausts itself trying to guess the course people and things will take. Logic and reason seize on them only afterward to give an appearance of order and necessity to the seething abundance of life. We meet Roderick again in Onessa, where several accounts bear witness to his presence and where he very probably met both Thaumas and Gandolphus. But we know practically nothing about the end of his life, apart from the fact, already mentioned, that Nandor's own brother stabbed him to death with a dagger. A romantic reader who saw this as a passionate act of revenge would be jumping to conclusions. It seems the deed arose rather out of a conflict of interests, probably aggravated by overindulgence in rye brandy.

Meanwhile Alexis was growing up in the forest with his mother. Many years later, when he had reached the heights, he was to speak of his obscure childhood as the happiest time of his life. There is nothing very unusual about that. Childhood escapes history; it belongs to the magic world of poetry and, even in lives most brightly lit by fame, retains an aura of happiness that neither power nor glory can destroy or tarnish. Alexis's childhood was bound up with the forest. How he loved it! Whether in Tartar or Kirghiz desert, amid the splendor of the cities of the East or on the shores of the Mediterranean, Alexis would always miss his birches and oaks. Right up to the end of his life he would talk of the sights of the forest: the hunt after roebuck and young boars, the sky seen through the leaves, the sweet melancholy of evening, the snow on the bare branches, the brilliance of light and the sun as the sap returned with the spring. The forest mingled with his games, his walks, and later with his rides and earliest adventures—it was first and foremost his youth. When, many centuries later, in the spring of 1847, Turgenev followed Alexis's footsteps through the forest, he experienced, or thought he experienced, some of the feelings the son of Helen must have known. But he attributes inclinations to the future emperor that belong rather to himself, as when he describes to Pauline Viardot-Garcia, pupil of Liszt and sister of La Malibran, the beauty of the birches and oaks, and Alexis's horror of aspens. Right up to the end of the last century the vast forest between Balkh and Tsarkozy-Wilozlaw remained almost unchanged.[1] In 1869, Alexandre Dumas conjured up forest life during the time of Alexis in a witty, lively, and imaginative letter to George Sand in which the past of the world came to be identified with his own.

According to the evidence available, Alexis, at the time of the death of Roderick or a little later, was a shy, dreamy child, subject to

*Persian miniature inspired by illustrations from the Ritter Manuscript.
Note variations of detail; e.g., Alexis, lower left,
with falcon but on foot (Louvre).*

sudden fits of terrible anger. He seems to have had fair or chestnut hair and to have been rather small for his age, with deep green eyes and an insatiable curiosity about horses, arms, and travelers' tales. The mutual affection between him and his mother never faltered for a day, until, toward the end of Helen's life, circumstances and life's cruelty finally separated them. The child's passionate attachment to his mother was one of the essential traits in his character, and Freud, in a little-known essay written near the beginning of his career,[2] saw it as one among many clues to the life of the future emperor.

At the end of his *Histories* and the beginning of his *Chronicles*, Justus Dion recounts a whole series of anecdotes about Alexis's youth that many historians have called into question because they are so typically traditional. The lovesick nursemaid who lost the child in the forest; Helen's distraction; the finding of the child on a bed of leaves, cared for by a she-wolf who kept him warm with her breath; Alexis's first attempt at archery, when his arrow split an acorn in two at a distance of a hundred paces—these and other stories are too familiar in popular legend everywhere and in every age to be taken very seriously. The only surviving feature that deserves real attention is the revelation to the child that he was a bastard. Of this there are two fairly late, but important, accounts that give versions slightly varying in detail but basically in agreement. One is a mystery play called *The True Mystery of the Destruction of Balkh*, of which a study was made in 1949 by Prof. E. T. Jones of the Institute for Advanced Studies, Princeton University. The other is the fourteenth-century Arabic manuscript mentioned earlier in connection with Arsaphes and Heloise, and discovered in 1953 by Professor Ritter in the archives of the Sublime Porte.

Simeon had returned to his parents, in somewhat mysterious circumstances of which we know little. The most popular theory is that his return was negotiated by Basil and Gandolphus at the time of the rapprochement between Roderick and the Empire, when Simeon was of no use to the emperor or his minister either as a hostage or as an ally. It is likely the negotiations were so protracted that Simeon reached home only a short while before Roderick's death. The question of whether Roderick ever had any suspicions about Alexis's birth gave rise to countless contradictory theories, all more or less inconclusive until quite recently, when the problem seems finally to have been settled. The theory encountered most frequently in the chronicles and courtly songs of the early Middle Ages is that Alexis was sired by a god or born by spontaneous generation. Some later historians, including Voltaire himself, even maintain that toward the end of his reign Roderick deliberately fostered the rumor that Helen had been miraculously united with the Eagle of the Empire, which had come to the aid of the unjustly attacked city of Balkh. The legend did him more good than harm and added to the prestige of his family name. At the beginning of the nineteenth century the brothers Grimm related the imperial Eagle of the legend to the fact that Fabrician was a priest from Aquileus or the surrounding region, and, like all priests, dedicated to the Eagle. What is certain, at all events, is that despite his treachery and the proofs he frequently gave of instability and weakness of character, Simeon always remained his father's favorite. Roderick never liked Alexis. But this may simply have been because he never had time to watch him grow up, since he spent most of the last part of his life hunting and drinking with the elder son now restored to favor. It is also certain that during his last years Roderick neglected Helen for numerous courtesans and several favorites whose names are known to us and of whom one, perhaps even two, seem to have been elevated to the rank of wife in a period of less than three years. Even before Roderick's death, Helen, for her part, made no attempt to conceal her preference for Alexis. Her highly developed sense of duty and justice prevented her from favoring the younger son at the elder's expense, but she had been disappointed so often by Simeon's brutality and falseness that her trust and hope and affection had long been concentrated on Alexis.

One autumn morning Simeon, with a large escort, set out early to hunt wolves, a sport he loved as much as his father had. Alexis, then eleven or twelve, or perhaps a little older, went with his brother at his own request. A miniature in the Ritter manuscript shows him dressed in green and blue, with a strange turbanlike headdress, and a falcon on his wrist, riding some way behind Simeon among the huntsmen and men-at-arms. The elder brother is alone at the head of the procession, squat, black-bearded, fierce. But though swallowed up among the soldiers and grooms, Alexis is naïvely depicted as slightly larger than the rest, including Simeon. All around them beasts disport themselves; they can just be made out as boars and wolves. In one corner there is even an elephant together with a leopard or tiger—creatures quite foreign to the northern forests of the Empire, but no doubt included by vague association with the legend of the Porphyries. The sky is full of warblers, tits, and partridges, some of them

pursued by falcons. The whole has a pleasing freshness oddly evoca-
tive both of the miniatures of Samarkand and Bukhara, and of the
Emperor Frederick II's treatise on the art of falconry.

When the little troop had advanced some way through rides and
glades into the forest, there was an incident.[3] Alexis was carrying on
his wrist Simeon's gyrfalcon in its leather hood. As was the custom,
the elder brother owned this highest-flying of birds and allowed no one
else to use it. But just as they were crossing a meadow, the hunters
suddenly flushed a covey of partridges, and in the excitement of the
moment Alexis loosed the gyrfalcon without waiting for his brother to
give the order. The falcon flapped its wings two or three times, rose
into the air, then swooped down on the partridges, which were as if
paralyzed by the falcon's swiftness. Simeon, turned in his saddle,
looked back on the scene with displeasure, and sent for Alexis.

"Do you not know, brother," he said, "that the gyrfalcon is mine
and I alone have the right to say when he should be unleashed?"

"I ask pardon," said the still breathless Alexis. "I was carried
away by youth and excitement."

"If you really wish to pass for the son of my father," answered
Simeon roughly, "you had better learn what you ought to have known
already."

The insult and the threat were still disguised. The likeness between Simeon and Roderick was plain; that between Helen and Alexis
struck even those who knew nothing about them. Justus Dion tells
how a Greek traveler who was a friend of Helen's recognized Alexis
from among a score of playfellows of the same age. It was as if an
image of Helen as a child had risen before him. But Simeon's phrase
could also be taken as a reminder of Roderick's marked preference for
his elder son, who took every opportunity of boasting of it. Whether
through affectation or indifference, the escort showed no sign of
noticing anything. Alexis bowed his head and without replying rode
back to his place in the midst of the troop.

Since childhood Alexis had often pondered on his own lack of skill
for activities at which Simeon excelled. Lack of skill is hardly correct,
for Alexis's dexterity and even strength were themselves remarkable.
But to hunting, roistering, and the other rudenesses of the age, he did
not bring the same single-minded enthusiasm as his companions.
Already as a boy he was interested in ways of life very different from
the customs of the forest. He inherited from his mother an insatiable

curiosity about distant lands, for what happened elsewhere, for travelers' tales and chronicles of times past. When still young he loved, like Helen, to talk with pilgrims and scholars about nature and about the inventions of man. Amidst uncouth warriors thinking only of the present, he nursed dreams that often wafted him far away in space and time. Sometimes he would find himself wondering about his own life and destiny; and he would feel vaguely uneasy. He would suddenly find himself less comfortable, less at home in the forest than the others. He loved it passionately but it did not wholly contain the world he longed to find. One day the old Greek of whom Justus Dion speaks jestingly asked some of the forest children which words they liked best. Some said *oak* or *clearing* or *roebuck*, others *war* or *javelin*. But Alexis answered *sun* and *far away*. Life did not seem long enough to get to know the great universe of marvels eager to be seen that lay beyond the forest, beyond the mountains and the seas. In everything he felt a yearning to go further. And to this was joined a reflectiveness, a meditativeness even, which led sometimes to sudden moods of excitement. The forest, the sun, the thought of the sea would inspire him with enthusiasms that made his mother tremble. Already, within him, he could feel dawning those dreams of knowledge, contemplation, and sympathy with the universe which drew him both toward the fascination of adventure and toward the peace of the priests and monasteries of Aquileus.

So Simeon's rebuke had shaken him. Not because he saw in it an allusion to his birth that he could not understand, but because it seemed to widen the chasm, of which he was already only too aware, between the tasks fate held in store for him and his own unworthiness to fulfill them. Everyone about him was satisfied with familiar horizons, and wished for no others. They were sure of themselves and of the world they lived in. He alone suffered because of something he did not understand. And Simeon's anger was a sharp reminder of his clumsiness, of his occasional sense of strangeness in the midst of an order whose laws and meaning he did not always comprehend. The boy Alexis was full of a vast eagerness—but he did not know for what. The world was a summons to an unknown future, full of questions, difficulties, trial and error, but also full of delights. Alexis, despite his uneasiness, was brimming with gaiety. The others were gloomy in a world without problems that suited them exactly; he, never quite at home in life, was always experiencing the joys of wonder. Existence troubled him, but he laughed at it. And now his brother's roughness taught him once again that both his questioning and his cheerfulness were wrong, and that the thing to do was to submit silently to the exigencies of the world in which he felt at once so strange and so happy.

It was noon, toward the end of autumn. There had already been some snow, but the sun had come out again in a pale, cloud-driven sky. On and on they rode. One of the men sent in advance announced that there was a pack of wolves not far off to the east, near the gullies by the marshes. Simeon quickly consulted with the most experienced hunters, then ordered the company to divide into two. The first went off to the left. Simeon himself led the second toward the marshes. The first group, mostly on horseback, were to cut off the wolves' retreat and drive them toward the gully where Simeon awaited them. The two brothers soon heard the distant sound of horns coming half muffled through the trees, on which the leaves were still thick and only just turning color. A few more moments went by. Then the wolves suddenly burst into a clearing only a few paces from the ravines. There were three big wolves, with thick coats and bright eyes. Simeon seized his pike and ax and spurred his horse toward them. The rest of the party rushed after, Alexis among them. It all happened very quickly. The wolves fell back and began to flee under the trees, by the ravines, hotly pursued by the horsemen. But the pursuit did not last long. The wolves soon came up against the line formed by the first group of hunters, deployed in a semicircle to bar their way. The three wolves hesitated, halted, then, with their backs to the ravine, stood at bay. Simeon selected the finest beast, and while five or six of his companions rushed on the other two to separate and strike them down, he lunged at it with his pike. As soon as the blow went home, he sprang from the saddle with a lightness astounding in a man of his weight, and attacked the wolf with his dagger. Man and wolf rolled over and over on the ground. A brief struggle, and Simeon stood up. He was covered in the blood that was spurting from the wolf's throat.

The hounds, still in full cry, hurled themselves on the wolves and tore them to pieces with howls of joy and fury. They were mastiffs, just as savage as the wolves themselves, and rent their prey so furiously that the huntsmen had to shout and haul at them to control them. Simeon tossed his reeking dagger to the groom who had charge of his weapons, and went a little way off to enjoy a spectacle "rendered most noble and pleasant," says the Ritter manuscript, "by the dusk and the blood." Simeon adored the end of the chase, the phase that came after the effort and the struggle. He leaned against a tree, tired and happy, and looked on. Men and wolves had fought honorably, he thought, and the forest was beautiful. It was true—the forest was beautiful. Night began to fall. The trees made a dark background for the maddened hounds, the carcasses of the wolves, the outlines of the hunters gradually disappearing in the gathering dusk. A groom lit a torch. Then another. An improvised pyre began to burn. All that could be heard were the dogs and the crackling of the flames rising up into the night. Alexis felt mounting up in him a kind of tenderness toward the brother who did not love him. They were both standing a little way off from the pyre and the dogs, and the sound of the hounds at their quarry reached them but faintly.

At that moment Alexis saw two eyes gleaming in the now almost total darkness. It was a wolf, a monster—the three others seemed puny and weak beside it. It stood motionless, still half hidden by the thicket from which it had emerged. Simeon could not see it. Alexis stifled a cry, and grabbed his brother's arm. Too late: the wolf had already sprung on Simeon, who had neither pike, ax, nor knife to defend himself. The animal knocked him sprawling, and he struggled under its claws and fangs, protecting his face with his arm and trying vainly to get at the wolf's eyes or ears or throat. Alexis, speechless with terror, had jumped back under the trees. Thirty or forty years later he used to say that that backward spring was the greatest acrobatic feat of his life. Then, in a flash, he leaped on the beast. Simeon had by now swooned, and Alexis, imitating his brother's and his brother's huntsmen's familiar gesture, plunged into the wolf's throat the hunting knife Helen had given him for his tenth birthday. When the huntsmen and grooms came up, drawn by the muffled sound of the struggle, their torches lit up the senseless form of their master lying beneath the corpse of a gigantic wolf, and beside them, petrified, his knife in his hand, Alexis, scarcely trembling. He said he had been very frightened.

Simeon never forgave Alexis for having saved his life. His first words, when he regained consciousness, near a spring in the forest, were insults and abuse. It was then, in his wrath and humiliation, that he uttered in public, in his brother's very presence, the word *bastard*.

For Alexis, it was a thunderbolt. The day after the hunt, he asked his mother for permission to leave the forest. Helen thought about it for three days, and on the evening of the third day she sent for him. They had a conversation which went on into the night and of which we know nothing. Alexis left at dawn.

X

INITIATION

 HILOCRATES WAS A GREEK. HE WAS BORN IN MURSA, between Pergamum and Ephesus,[1] and he was ugly. His mother was a fishwife, and for thirty years she had cried her wares on the quays of the port—the catch of one or two dozen boats which set sail before sunrise to spend half a day, a week, even one or two months along the coast or out at sea. Some never came back. A few returned with miraculous hauls that made fortunes. But none of this ever did Alfrania any good—she was to remain poor the whole of her life. She did not even own the wooden stall from which she sold her fish, nor was it on her own account that she stood there in the wind and rain and scorching sun behind her reeking wares. The stall, the bench, the fish, she herself—all belonged to two or three wily merchants whom she had never seen and who doled out each month, from their carefully guarded profits, enough to keep body and soul together and go on. She had known little happiness, but she rarely complained. She was very pious and resigned to the will of the gods, and whenever there was a new moon, or at the beginning of every season, or after a storm, she would always go and burn rare herbs or sticks of incense outside the temples. Twice in her life, with terror and wonder, she had witnessed eclipses of the sun and moon and, when the planet of day or night made its blessed return, had gone with the rest of the faithful to give thanks to the gods who allowed the world to continue. She used to listen to the sailors talking of monsters and splendors, and would dream a little and sigh. And every day her customers would find her there selling her fish to the motley crowd, whose cheerful, noisy animation gave Mursa the reputation for energy and gaiety that drew travelers and merchants thither.

One evening when a storm was raging on the coast, a fishing boat from Delos came and took shelter in Mursa harbor, where for several days it waited for the weather to improve. The crew took advantage of their enforced leisure to caulk and repair their ship, which had been very much knocked about; they also spent their money gaming and drinking. They came from Syria, Phoenicia, and Crete, and had been to Cyprus and Rhodes. Some had gone as far as Malta and Carthage, or even Sardinia and the Balearics. One, even rougher and gloomier than the others, was from Delphi. He was the son of a prophetess-*cum*-courtesan who had fallen on evil days. He had gone to sea at the age of nine, and for fifteen years now had been going about from one port and ocean to another. He believed in nothing and did not hope for much. He spoke little and seemed to be dreaming of distant seas and unknown shores. The mixture of rapture and bitterness that emanated from him dazzled Alfrania. She gave herself to him by the harbor because he was poor and lonely like herself. And she learned what passion was. They made love five or six times on the deck of the ship or in the country, behind the temples. And then the sun returned, the sea grew calm, and the man sailed away with his companions to new harbors and new tempests. Alfrania did not complain. He had made no promises, and she had known their happiness would be only a brief interval in their wretched lives. She went back to selling her fish; but now she had memories and vague and sunny dreams. She looked out to sea with patient resignation; she was scarcely sad; sometimes she was almost happy. One morning she felt faint and lost consciousness for a moment. A few months later she gave birth to a son.

From earliest infancy Philocrates was ugly and a dreamer. He was clumsy, his sight was not very good, and he did not worry about the future. Winning, being first, was a matter of indifference to him. He couldn't swim or run as fast as the others; he wasn't ashamed of being frightened; and even as a child he despised money and honors. A few priests who had a regard for his mother found him odd jobs around the temples that enabled him to earn his living. When he was six or seven, he tidied up after the faithful and lit the torches on evenings of special ceremony. He would sit for hours on the steps of the temples, motionless and staring into space. If a worshiper or passer-by asked what he was thinking about, he only smiled. Many supposed him backward or deficient, and it was easy to see why. His greatest pleasure was listening to the priests. Instead of going and playing with the other children, who were somewhat suspicious of him despite his gentleness, he would settle down in one of the holy places and listen, without moving or speaking, to endless discussions on the origin of the gods and the order governing the universe. By the age of eight he could already silently make distinctions between things and between men. He scorned many, but when he admired he did so with a fervor and constancy unusual for his age.

At that time Mursa, like many eastern and Mediterranean cities, was divided by a famous quarrel that went back to the days, distant even then, of Hermenides and Paraclitus. The reader will perhaps recall the part played by these two philosophers in the first golden age of the City. The schools they founded had gone through many vicissitudes and different incarnations and still survived; they had even developed and spread. Countless sects and schisms had complicated the relations between the various thinkers and systems involved, and their quarrels, their points of agreement and disagreement, and their doctrines on the history of the world and the relations between gods and men had given rise to a considerable body of literature. With the help of some of the priests, Philocrates had learned to read the texts that set out, with many and often contradictory arguments, the nature of things and the destiny of the soul. The ideas of free will, salvation, identity and otherness, the one and the many, the mixed, mediation, dialectic, and universal harmony were as familiar to him as knucklebones and mora were to the other boys. One summer morning when preparations were under way for some solemn ceremony, Philocrates, then aged twelve, managed to slip into a corner in the great hall where priests from all over the country were meeting in private before appearing to the people. He listened with passionate interest to one young priest sent by the Emperor Basil, who spoke of the destiny and dignity of man. The child's face showed such attention, such intentness, that the priest was struck by it even as he spoke. As soon as he had finished he sent for the boy to question him. An aged priest from Mursa brought Philocrates to him, whispering that the boy was a kind of idiot whom they allowed into the temples out of pity. The young priest gave a gesture of impatience and asked that they be left alone.

"My child," he said kindly, "you were listening to me, and I was looking at you. And I think your face said more than my speech."

"My lord," stammered the child, "I love words above all else, and yours were like music to me, like honey. You spoke, and I understood."

"And what was it you understood?" asked the priest, smiling and stroking the lad's hair.

"It seemed to me," said the child, "that the skies opened and the order of things which is written there was unfolded before me, like stars around the sun. You spoke of beauty and the honor of men, and I wanted to weep."

"How old are you?" said the priest.

"Twelve, my lord."

"And what do you want to do when you grow up?"

"I want to learn, like you, and know, like you."

"I know nothing," said the priest. He was no longer smiling.

"I should like to learn," said the child.

"Do you want to learn words, and how to hide that you know nothing? Do you want to be able to argue and convince and get the better of others? If you do, I will teach you."

"Oh, no, my lord!" said the boy quickly, "I don't want to convince or get the better of others. I just want to know how far it is possible to know."

The priest looked at the boy and took his hands in his own.

"That is really what you want?" he said quietly.

"Just that," answered the boy.

"It means suffering, too," said the priest.

"Suffering?" said the boy. "Not knowing is suffering, too. And I would rather know and suffer than not know and not suffer."

"You will know only one thing—that you know nothing."

"That in itself is knowledge," said the boy.

The priest was silent a moment.

"If I had a son," he said, "I'd wish him to be like you."

The boy looked at the priest. Both remained motionless, then the child threw himself into the priest's arms and began to weep. The priest clasped to him the little body shaken with sobs, and stroked the dark, tousled head lifted toward him. From outside came the chanting of the faithful, making the rounds of the temples. The priest set the child on his feet and kissed his brow.

"Come," he said.

And they went out together.

The crowd made way for them to pass, and when, hand in hand, they reached the front row of priests, they, too, made room for them both.

"I have a disciple," laughed the young priest.

Philocrates felt joy explode within him. He held the priest's hand tight, and looked up at the sun to stop himself from crying.

The procession continued, led by the chanting priests, whose song was echoed in chorus by their flock. They came to the altar, where a sacrifice to the gods celebrated both the solstice and a recent victory over a rebel city. A dazzling sun shone in an almost cloudless sky. The priests mounted a few steps. At the foot of the altar were a white heifer, a he-goat, and six prisoners in chains. Two of these were handsome, with a proud, bold bearing. The rest seemed overwhelmed by hardship and privation and cast terrified looks about them. The sacrificers arose, each robed half in white and half in red and with a knife in his hand. Beasts and men were slain together, and their blood mingled to run down the garments of executioners and priests. Philocrates was covered with it. He averted his head, and seized the hand of the young priest beside him. The crowd began to chant again.

"The blood . . . ," gasped the child.

"Courage . . . ," murmured the priest. And he clasped more tightly the little hand that trembled in his.

Eight priests, their faces hidden by masks and carrying knives hollowed out like spoons, had approached the corpses. As one, they tore out the eight hearts and threw them to the crowd, who began to clap their hands and shout with joy.

"Why?" said the child, looking up at the priest. "Why?"

"That is the secret of history," said the priest, bending close to him. "Religion is the secret of history. The future will explain the present. But it will no longer understand it. Perhaps you will change all that. But later on others will come who will explain you in your turn. But they will no longer understand you either."

Gradually the shouting and excitement died down. The eight hearts were passed from hand to hand, and traces of blood could be seen on breasts and brows.

Two old men came and bowed before the young priest sent by the emperor. He returned their greeting and stepped forward on the platform in response to the acclaim of the crowd, which was redoubled when he stood alone before the altar. He was the bearer of a message from Thaumas, whose reputation was as great in Mursa as in Ctesiphon or Alexandria, in Caesarea or Babylon. Men, women, and children all applauded, crying out "Thaumas . . . Thaumas . . ." Another name was intermingled with this—the name of the young priest. Philocrates, who had not quite been able to make it out, strained his ears to hear and to remember. It was thus he learned, from the countless throats of the faithful, intoxicated by sun and blood, the name of his new friend and protector. The crowd was calling: "Thaumas . . . Thaumas . . ." and "Fabrician . . . Fabrician . . ."

Fabrician took Philocrates back to Onessa with him, and two or three years later sent him to Aquileus. Philocrates astounded the priests by his zeal. He rose with the sun, and went on studying late into the night by torchlight. Soon he knew as much as the most learned among them. Before he was seventeen they offered to have him initiated into the mysteries—a very rare thing for a foreigner as young as that.[2] But he declined. He had made friends in Aquileus with a young man of about his own age called Isidore, who was preparing for the priesthood, and to him he wrote a famous letter explaining his decision:

"Do not suppose I scorn or disdain religion and those who serve it. I owe them too much not to love them; I respect and revere them. I believe with all my heart they approach as near the truth as man is permitted to approach the light. I think power without fear of the gods is a great evil, and that if priests themselves cannot rule, at least kings and princes should possess the piety and justice taught us by the gods. And so you will ask me, why do I refuse to serve these gods and to bend to their laws? The reason is that the truth of the gods can only ever be, for us, the truth of the men who translate and interpret it. No man will ever become a god. The gods will never descend to man. I believe only in that unknown inner god who manifests himself dimly in the reason and the heart ($\chi\alpha\tau\grave{\alpha}$ $\phi\rho\epsilon\nu\grave{\alpha}$ $\chi\alpha\grave{\iota}$ $\chi\alpha\tau\grave{\alpha}$ $\theta\upsilon\mu\acute{o}\nu$). He has no need of mysteries or initiation; he needs only tears and hope, affliction and lucidity. And even if this god himself were, in his mercy, to offer to reveal himself to me in all his splendor, I verily believe, Isidore, I should still refuse the gift of his goodness. For man is made to seek, not to know; knowledge is only knowing how far it is possible to know."[3]

Pascal and Renan both admired this letter, which echoes the conversation between Fabrician and the young Philocrates in the temple at Mursa. It has given rise to the most diverse interpretations. Marxist historians, including Engels, have detected traces of atheism in it; the Jesuits have given it a Christian twist; Protestants have seen it as one of the origins of the spirit of the Reformation; rationalists and believers have all laid claim to its author in endless treatises and exegeses. At all events, Philocrates did not give way—he never became a priest. But his decision to remain a philosopher made his position in Aquileus difficult, and when Fabrician suggested he should go with him to Balkh, he eagerly accepted. He joined Fabrician between Onessa and Balkh, and they entered the great forest together.

In Balkh, Philocrates was very close to Fabrician. He rarely saw Roderick or Helen or even Simeon. Because of his youth, he was one of those who remained behind instead of accompanying Roderick into the steppes, and he was in Balkh throughout the battle against Gandolphus's men, the siege and fall of the city, and the passion of the two lovers. During the siege he did all he could to protect Fabrician and Helen, and he was probably the only one to whom Fabrician confided his secret before he died. Fabrician had told Helen the story of the meeting in the temple at Mursa, and praised Philocrates' learning and wit. After Fabrician's death, Philocrates went with Helen as a matter of course when Roderick abandoned the city of Balkh. And when, many years after the feast of the summer solstice in the temple at Mursa, and many years after Fabrician's death even, Alexis, following the wolf hunt with his brother Simeon, decided to leave the forest, Helen was happy to keep faith with Fabrician by entrusting his son to Philocrates.

The young Greek and the boy traveled together. For Alexis they were long years of apprenticeship. The two companions crossed oceans and visited cities. They were seen in Vienna, Adrianople, Como, Avenches, Autun, Cologne, Trier, Carthage, Dura-Europos, Samarkand, and Bukhara. They thirsted in the desert, and were often so weary they threw themselves down fully dressed in miserable inns, barns, wayside ditches. They mixed with pilgrims, armies on the march, artists, and vagabonds. They worked in circuses, with jugglers and ropewalkers. They hired themselves out to farmers, rich herdsmen, woodcutters, and owners of boats. They were attacked by brigands, and killed some of them. They went to war in order to eat, and to survive they sacrificed to unknown, savage gods. They went through the world, and wondered at it. They saw strange animals, signs in the heavens, all the miracles of nature. Men seemed to them varying yet alike, always different yet everywhere the same. Their houses, clothes, speech, and beliefs altered from town to town, valley to valley, from one bank of a river to the other. In one place the women slew their children, in another the men burned their wealth to dazzle their rivals. But the women still loved the children they offered up to their gods, and the men still prized power and glory and supremacy. Poverty, laziness, or humiliation explained the vagueness or extravagance of the meanings they attributed to their lives. The travelers saw something of everything in this world they went through, and often one day's revelation was the opposite of what they had seen the day before. But these differences, paradoxes, contradictions, marvels were everywhere similar, and Philocrates explained to Alexis that the world was the dream of a god, and its diversities the image and reflection of an unknown unity of which all men formed part. Absurdity, the ridiculous, cruelty, ugliness, pain, and death all had a hidden meaning. We could not know what that meaning was. But there still remained the world where the sun shone for all and only died to be reborn.

One evening, after years of weary wandering, the master and the disciple came to a big city full of stir and activity. The relevant texts do not allow us to identify it for certain: some historians think it was Alexandria, others Emesa or Edessa, others again Antioch or Tarsus. It was a place where there were soldiers and merchants, slaves and judges. There were also many priests, some of whom ministered to the worship of the sun. Though not the most powerful or influential, these had a great reputation for wisdom and learning. Philocrates had long been in communication with some of them, and they now welcomed him as one of themselves and opened their schools and temples to Alexis.

Alexis had always been attracted by sun worship. In his native forest he used to bask in the sun with an abandon at once wild and voluptuous. He may once or twice have yielded to a sort of ecstasy, an illumination which later took on the sense of a mystic communion with the sun. In all events, he saw in the sun the principle of unity toward which a nature like his, solicited on all sides by passionate curiosity, eagerly aspired.[4] The triple cult of the sun, the eagle, and the oak practiced in Balkh as in the rest of the Empire may have directed him when still young toward a kind of religious experience in which solar myths played a part. But despite appearances the religion of the Empire, which did not concern itself with any ideas of order or unity in the universe, accorded only a very minor place to the veneration of the sun. Not only had the oak and the eagle ultimately eclipsed the sun in the pantheon of the Empire, but the dissipation of godhead among a multitude of different divinities had deprived the sun of that primary function as source and rallying point which for real sun worshippers was its essential. But in the temples of Emesa, Alexandria, or Antioch, Alexis found the sun exercising undivided rule over the world and its inhabitants. Philocrates, too, inclined toward a solar-type monotheism for which he had been prepared by a whole group of thinkers no longer satisfied with the old religious traditions of the Empire or the controversies between the supporters of Hermenides and those of Paraclitus. Still faithful to the views he had expressed several years earlier in the letter to Isidore, he refused to be initiated into the mysteries of sun worship as he had refused to be initiated into those of the priests of Aquileus. But faithful also to an almost relativist conception of the relationship between nature and truth, he thought the problem was not the same for Alexis as for himself, and that the path of the disciple was not strewn with the same obstacles as his own. Philosophers, moralists, and historians of religion have all expressed surprise at Philocrates' dual attitude, and many have found it incomprehensible and disappointing that he should have encouraged Alexis to accept an initiation that he refused himself. But this indignation takes too little account not only of what would now be called Philocrates' liberalism, but also of his explicit doctrine on the diversity of approaches to the divine. He played the same role toward Alexis as Fabrician had played toward him. Thus the disciple of the father was the master of the son, and thus was begun the long and lovely concatenation of culture and tradition, which required, in the name of Philocrates' open skepticism and relativism, that Alexis's longing for unity and peace should be assuaged by initiation.

Alexis was initiated into the cult of the sun at noon on the day of the summer solstice, twenty-five or twenty-six years to the day after the bloody ceremony in the temple at Mursa.[5] He was eighteen years old. A maiden led him blindfolded and walking backward to the mouth of a cave in which incense was burning. He wore a white robe and a thin white fillet around his brow; his head and feet were bare. He went alone into the cave, whence he had to crawl along a path, or rather an underground tunnel, to a large, dark, silent chamber full of rough pillars painted red and black. The walls were covered with representations of sphinxes and griffins, horrible grimacing heads, masks, and bones. Bats fluttered about unseen. Slowly burning herbs made him cough at first, then brought about a state of intoxication or unconsciousness full of flames and torrents from which he was aroused, he never knew whether it was hours or minutes later, by a voice calling his name from on high.

"Alexis!"

The young man raised his hands palms upward in a gesture of prayer. The voice pronounced his name three times and began to question him.

"What are you doing? What do you want? What are you waiting for?"

"I seek," answered Alexis. "I hope. I believe."

"Where do you come from?"

"From darkness and the depths of night."

"Where are you going?"

"Toward the light that calls me."

"May it be yours if you obey."

"I shall obey."

"May it be yours if you command."

"I shall command."

"Whence come the oak and the acorn?"

"From the sun which feeds them."

"Whither fly the eagle and the eaglet?"

"Toward the sun which draws them."

This catechism went on for some time. Then two priests brought the young man some ears of corn, a handful of earth, a pinch of salt, a vessel of wine, and a shell full of seawater, and led him to a fire giving off sweet odors, in a smaller room with stone columns carved in the shape of lotuses and palm trees. They left the young man praying before the dying fire, which slowly went out, plunging the whole cave once more into utter darkness. Then Alexis fell asleep.

He had a dream. A dazzling light spread through the cave and drew him toward itself, so that he seemed to be rising into the air and merging with it. The universe and all the ages unfolded before his eyes; all the secrets of the world were revealed to him. He floated. At his feet, everything was reduced to the smallest dimensions, and yet each detail was minutely visible. All was limpid and clear, and the marvelous multiplicity of beings and things reduced itself into beauty, light, and order. He could see roads where travelers hastened toward their inns; kings on their thrones; girls waiting for their sweethearts. Money flowed everywhere, like rivers; many suffered and wept; others sang, to the gods or to their lovers. Battles, births, children playing, sailors at sea, villages scorching and still in the midday sun. Snow on the mountaintops, valleys of violets, great cities with prisons, cunning, chance. Everything constantly moved and changed, but in an immutable harmony. At each moment the world was born and vanished in order to be born again. Slaves became rich, the powerful became slaves. Plowmen, fishermen, craftsmen in their workshops, merchants in their countinghouses, hope and movement, and sorrow and death. Philosophers thinking, and the ambitious, and the lovers, and the madmen, and those who built bridges, houses, aqueducts, and temples. In his dream he saw other dreams, and pangs, terrors, lies. He saw the fish of the sea, and the carp and pike and eels and toads. He could even see the trees, the flowers, the pebbles, the coral in the lagoons, the grains of sand on the shore, the drops of water in the ocean. He saw his own life, stretching out vast from his birth in the forest to glory and death, just like one of those grains of sand or drops of water. He saw his place in history and the echoes of his life across the years and the centuries. He saw all those, in the ages of ages, who would write his name and invoke his memory; all those who would read the books he would appear in; perhaps he saw you, at this very moment, thinking of him. Justus Dion tells us Alexis had, in a flash, a complete prophetic vision of all that would be contained in all the volumes future historians would write about his adventures. Measureless space, limitless time were to him transparent. He called to himself—"Alexis!"—and his name rebounded to the ends of the universe. All trembled at his voice and at his look; the world was his voice and his look also. Then he knew that both men and things were his.

Six white-robed maidens came to him in the cave, and he made love to each of them in a different position.[6] Then a seventh appeared at the entrance to the cave, in a blaze of light. She was more beautiful than all the others, with fair hair falling about her shoulders, her green eyes, and a noble and winning mien. He would have liked to rush and take her in his arms, but he knew he was forbidden to possess her. She was the symbol of those distant limits where power, will, and life all are halted. He asked her name. She answered that he would know soon enough, and took him by the hand. She led him into another room, so small it was scarcely more than a widening in the tunnel and he could hardly stand, and there she left him.

As soon as she had gone, two wooden grates came down over the two exits. With one outstretched arm the voluntary prisoner could now touch all four of the narrow walls enclosing him. A dull noise came from overhead, like stamping interspersed with raucous breathing. Alexis looked around and then above. The ceiling of the room consisted of a sort of open grid. As he looked up at the gleams of light filtering through, something heavy fell from above and made all dark again. At the same moment Alexis felt some warm, sticky liquid running over his brow and cheeks and chest—first a few drops, then a thin trickle, then a stream. In a few moments the neophyte was drenched from head to foot, and when he tried the liquid with his tongue it was thick, strong, sweetish. It was blood.

He fell to his knees beneath the bloody baptism. His eyes gradually got used again to the dark, and he thought he could make out, above him, the inert form of a white sacrificial bull. When its sacred blood stopped flowing, he seemed to fall asleep again. He awoke in broad daylight, lying laved and perfumed on a flat stone, wearing a blue-and-red tunic and a crown of laurel and flowers. Sweet music sounded in his ears, and he felt pure and strong. Beside him he recognized a man still young but very ugly whose familiar face smiled at him kindly and with a shade of irony—it was Philocrates. There were two others standing beside him: a man with long hair and a white beard, and a radiantly lovely young woman. The first was the chief priest of the temple of the sun, and the girl was the seventh maiden, she whom Alexis was forbidden to love by all the laws of heaven and of earth. The look she bent on him was gentle yet lofty, and there, under the sun at its zenith, washed clean of the blood of the bull, and still intoxicated with having soared above space and time, he thought how beautiful she was, and how beautiful the world, with its mysteries and miracles.[7]

XI

FEASTING IN ALEXANDRIA

 HIS WORLD LIT UP BY BEAUTY AND WONDER SOON offered Helen's son attractions other than holiness. It seems that Philocrates, once having urged Alexis to be initiated, set about weaning him away from religious mysteries and reintroducing him to the charms, and perhaps the follies, of everyday life. The four or five years following Alexis's experience in the temple of the sun appear to have been devoted to every kind of pleasure. We possess two or three letters from Helen to Philocrates in which she actually reproaches him with abandoning Alexis to temptation and loose living. Philocrates' reply to Helen is as famous as his letter to Isidore:

"The gods have granted each of us but a few years upon earth, and what awaits us after death is revealed to none. But what we have always known is that life is short. You know it, madam, and I know it too, and not a day passes but I say to myself: My soul, instead of harking after eternal life, exhaust the sphere of the possible. Though we know nothing of the gods and the mysteries in the beyond, they are present here below in their reflections, mysteriously lighting up our path across the earth. That is why I did not feel it my duty to deny Alexis what I have always denied myself, and he dedicated himself to the gods and their service. For a life without the gods is an impoverished one, and to be really a man one must look toward them. But to serve them also means, in a way, to turn aside from men. I did not help Alexis to approach the gods in order to drive him away from men, but in order to bring him nearer men, too. If he plunged into pleasure as if death and heaven were only tales for children, I would put him to shame for his folly. But if he devoted himself to the gods and to uncertain hopes as if life and the earth were mere mirages, I would remind him that he is a man, and that laughter and women and wine and horses were created by the gods for men to enjoy. Alexis already venerates and serves the gods. So now let him live, and let his life serve him."[1]

This and other letters, and certain occasions on which Philocrates seems deliberately to have urged Alexis on to pleasure and perhaps to a certain form of vice, have been used by several historians as evidence that Philocrates was Basil's or even Gandolphus's agent, whose object was to divert Alexis from nobler ambitions.[2] But this theory does not seem to bear examination. All those who put it forward see Alexis's youth in the light of his future glory. But at the time, when Alexis was unrestrainedly indulging in all the pleasures proper to his age, how could Basil and Gandolphus have seen him as a possible threat to their own supremacy? The emperor, Thaumas, and Gandolphus were all aware of the existence of Helen's son. They had had dealings with Roderick, Simeon, Fabrician, and Helen herself, and the slightest evidence of ambition on the part of a descendant of the Porphyries would have aroused mistrust and even hatred—perhaps not in Thaumas, who would have been more likely to favor him, but certainly in Basil and Gandolphus. But up till now had the young man manifested the least desire to assert any rights at all? Had he given the emperor and Gandolphus the least occasion for displeasure? A document by Thaumas, which Renan uses in support of his theory, does show a certain reserve toward Philocrates, while at the same time valuing him as Fabrician's disciple. But Thaumas certainly does not accuse him of alienating the young man from affairs of state and political ambition—the idea of such a plan apparently does not even enter his head. He merely wonders whether the Greek philosopher does not lay too much stress on nature rather than the gods in the instruction he offers his pupil. It is perfectly natural that the great priest should be preoccupied about the feelings and actions of a young man who was dear to him. Nor is there anything to suggest some mysterious ambitions which might be causing concern to the young Greek tutor. At the time of the initiation, such ambitions were still nonexistent and imaginary.

Sir Allan Carter-Bennett gives a diametrically opposed and much more convincing explanation. He, like Robert Weill-Pichon, believes that if anyone was able to divine Alexis's future destiny even while he was still a boy, it was not Gandolphus but Philocrates himself, who knew him best and was closest to him. And far from distracting him, he prepared and armed him for the struggles to come. Seen in this light, what happened takes on a coherent meaning. If Philocrates encouraged Alexis to undergo an initiation he himself avoided, it was because the role of a prince and leader is different from that of a scholar. The philosopher prefers problems to solutions, whereas the man of action must settle questions and make definitive choices. In action the essential thing is to keep going always in the same direction and never hesitate. For a thinker the important thing is always to leave every issue open, to call everything into question, and to admit no impossibilities for the mind. Mind seeks, action decides. For himself, Philocrates had every right to adopt a task that was infinite, a quest to which he set no bounds. But Alexis had to be led away from endless speculation and offered at once the comforts of religion and all the help that spiritual certainty can give to action. And religion and the gods gave Alexis not only a way out of the metaphysical torments that so preoccupy youth, but also the backing of a strong organization, a hierarchy, a system of values and authorities. If, immediately afterward, Philocrates encouraged Alexis to return to the world and its pleasures, it was because there is temptation in certainty no less than in seeking. When once you have found the answer, why bother any more about all life's vanities? One can lose one's way in solutions as well as in problems. If Philocrates had wished to spare the young man the anguish of chaos, it was not in order to let him be swamped in the contemplation of certainty. So the philosopher set before his pupil all the marvels of nature and men as seen in the order of the world established by the gods.[3]

It is not certain the initiation into the cult of the sun took place in Alexandria, but we do come upon Philocrates and his pupil there eventually, plunged in the welter of pleasure that made the great city the scandal and wonder of the world. At this period Alexandria presented a dubious yet fascinating spectacle. It embodied what Athens represented at the time of its splendor, or Rome at the time of its decline, Florence under the Medicis, Venice in the eighteenth century, or Paris under the Second Empire or after the First World War. But Alexandria had sunk lower into abjectness and self-contempt, and offered the world a rarely paralleled example of excess, in which debauchery and lust held undivided sway. "It was," says Renan, "an incredible collection of mountebanks, quacks, mimes, magicians, healers, sorcerers, and false priests. A city of racing, gaming, dancing, processions, feasts, and bacchanals; of unbridled luxury, all the follies of the East, the most morbid superstitions and fanatical orgies. The Alexandrians, sometimes servile and cowardly, sometimes ungrateful and insolent, were the very model of a mob without country, without nationality, without family honor, without a name to preserve. The great *corso* that ran through the town was like a theater traversed all day long by wave after wave of people, frivolous, fickle, unstable, riotous, and sometimes witty, entirely taken up with songs, parodies, jest, and impertinence." On anyone attractive or amusing were lavished the loveliest women, the most sumptuous ceremonies, all the delights of food and flesh, refinement combined with luxuriance, the extremes of excitement and novelty. Alexis was very attractive and amusing. And he had scarcely emerged from the revelations of divinity before he plunged into the vortex of pleasure with all the ardor of his twenty years.

Among the pleasure seekers and debauchees money flowed like water, and Alexis did not lack for it. Helen regularly sent Philocrates large sums, which he could put to all the better use now because he had scarcely touched them during the long hard years of wandering apprenticeship. He had gone to usurers and pawnbrokers not, like most young men, to borrow money, but to offer to lend it at reasonable interest. The interest had been accumulating, and now Philocrates began to enjoy the profits of those comfortless years of travel and living in the open. His reputation also was beginning to spread in the same way as that of Thaumas in the previous generation. And instead of using it in the service of political ambition, he offered people his services as a teacher of rhetoric or literature, and asked for very high fees. To do him justice, the veritable fortune he amassed from the sale of his learning was exclusively devoted to paying for Alexis's pleasures. Words of wisdom were converted into extravagances, and Alexis's chariots, clothes, jewels, servants, and horses were soon the admiration of the city. It was all processions, races in the arena, boating parties at night, fireworks, masquerades, and feasts. In the midst of this pomp and luxury, Philocrates never lost his head. He gave Alexis enough to dazzle Alexandria, but he kept enough to plow back into speculations that he managed so skillfully they always provided what was required.

During the years of apprenticeship the Greek had mixed with men of every trade, and learned which were the most profitable. The ones he had chosen were sea-borne commerce and marine investment. While Alexis amused himself, Philocrates acquired two or three ships which he sent out to Pomposa, Sicily, and the City laden with rare woods and rich vases. The fortune they earned him he divided into two, the smaller going to swell Alexis's supplies, the larger going toward the purchase of a veritable fleet of ships which, in two or three years, grew to be one of the largest in Alexandria. Hard times were over. Thanks to Philocrates and his talents, Helen's son reigned over the gilded youth of Lower Egypt.

In his celebrated study *Masters and Disciples*, Paul Bourget examines one after the other the relationships between Mentor and Telemachus, Aristotle and Alexander, Saint Augustine and Adeodatus, Heloise and Abelard, Descartes and Princess Elizabeth, the Abbé Vautrin and Rubempré, M. Hinstin and Isidore Ducasse. He gives a good deal of space, with reason, to the influence of Philocrates on Alexis. The philosopher kept in the background, but he was always there. Two or three times, even before the final disaster, Alexis went too far and was involved in shady or improper affairs that might have caused a scandal. Each time Philocrates intervened and got him out of it. He advised him, schemed for him, acted as intermediary in such murky plots that he might have been thought to be helping him to his ruin. But in fact he was guiding him and saving him.

A moving piece of evidence has come down to us from these years in Alexandria. This is the famous cameo from the Dresden Museum that shows Alexis standing in his chariot, probably after some procession or a race in which he had been the winner. He is handsome. His long fair hair streams in the wind. His young face wears an expression of gaiety and pride. He was not very tall, but he was supple and beautifully proportioned, and attractive to both men and women. Though thin and slight when very young, he had been hardened by experience and practice until his exploits rivaled, often to their fury, those of the most famous athletes. But most of his strength went toward assuaging a thirst for pleasure and sensuality that often reached terrifying proportions.

He who had been, and was to be again, so sober and even austere, was seized with a sort of frenzy of luxury and lust. He moved house several times in Alexandria. His last residence there was a palace of unsurpassable richness. His bed was covered with cloth of gold, and all his dishes and plates, some of which depicted scenes of great license, were also either of gold or solid silver. He gave banquets the splendor and daring of which have come down in history. One of the most famous, echoed right down to the epics of the later Middle Ages, had as guests all his mistresses, their husbands and lovers, the wives and other mistresses of these husbands and lovers, the husbands and other lovers of these wives and mistresses, and so on. In this way Alexis gathered round him a vast crowd of guests many of whom did not know each other despite the intimate links between them. He called these gatherings, to use the neologism invented by Amyot to render the Greek expression (an invention much admired by Malherbe and Vaugelas), his "connubial banquets." The menu of the most successful of these feasts has luckily survived. The drinks were extremely select: resinated wines, wines made of pennyroyal, roses, and crushed pine cones. These accompanied sausage made of oysters, conches, crayfish, and squill; dromedaries' heels; the combs of living cocks; nightingales' and peacocks' tongues, offered as a preventive against the plague; mules' innards; sows' dugs and vulvas with lentils and rice; ostriches' and phenicopters' brains; partridges' eggs; parrots', pheasants', and peacocks' heads; and, instead of cress and fenugreek, mules' membranes—"quite astonishing," as one of the chroniclers comments.[4]

Alexis, like Alcibiades and Brummell, saw surprise and boldness as the key of his entertainments. What he liked to do was astonish people. Barbey d'Aurevilly[5] very subtly perceives in this a secret desire for power. Alexis loathed habit and routine. He threw himself into pleasure as if it were a substitute for fame. And in sensuality at least he needed no teacher.

He carried eccentricity to the point of never making use more than once of the same clothes, the same shoes, the same jewel, or the same woman. It was said he excreted into goblets of gold or silver, and urinated into vessels of jade and onyx inlaid with precious stones. He was passionately fond of dressing up, and would disguise himself as a pastry cook, perfumer, innkeeper, or pimp, and was so punctilious in debauchery as to enter into the activities belonging to the disguise he wore. After nights of infamy, when he did not shrink from wallowing in filth at his companions' feet, he would be overcome next morning by storms of weeping and despair at his own degradation. But the next day he would start all over again. And despite the fact that he humiliated others and himself, Alexandria and all Mediterranean Egypt were full of friends and admirers whose only wish, usually vain, was to imitate or rival him. This was because his generosity was as boundless as his self-abasement. After terrifying his guests by loosing leopards or snakes into the banqueting chamber, he would

make it up to them with little presents of eunuchs, mules, rare ornaments, or chariots. True, some of his gifts were tacit insults, as on the
night when, having gotten them drunk, he shut up some of his friends
with a group of lewd black prostitutes, aged and repulsively ugly,
who had been instructed to carry out certain farfetched practices no
matter what the resistance. From time to time he would organize
lotteries that gave free scope at once to his imagination, generosity,
and scorn: one contestant would win twenty pieces of gold, another a
hen's egg, a third a wolf, and a fourth three strokes from a cudgel.
The first prize on one of the most famous evenings hatched by
Alexis's imagination, after a good deal of drinking, was the virginity
of a girl of twelve or thirteen whom her mother had sold to a young
rake for a few pieces of silver.[6] One of these lotteries led to a scandal
that was to have an important effect on Alexis's career. We shall
revert to it in due course.

Alexis's real passion was women. He loved them to distraction,
and they loved him madly in return. Alexandria then shared with
Antioch and Pomposa the reputation of being one of the most depraved cities in the world. It is not difficult to imagine how every vice
proliferated in such a setting. Homosexuality was held in honor, and
very probably Alexis, like the rest, joined in worshipping the beauty of
boys. But it was toward women that he was drawn both by temperament and taste, and into the love of women he put a kind of fury that
inspired his contemporaries with amazement and even terror.

Though Don Juan is probably a modern invention, André
Maurois is right when he says that the young Alexis shows more than
one trait characteristic of Don Juan or Byron. He loved to please,
conquer, and dominate, and, unlike Philocrates, he liked to get the
better of other people. An acute observer might have seen his follies
and excesses as signs of his future greatness. Vice, debauchery, the
most impure love can also be a kind of glory in reverse, and an avidity
for every sort of love may be closer than we think to a fascination with
death and a longing for power. Alexis was not yet thinking of power,
but under his passion for women there was certainly an ardor for
living and a thirst for the world that might well have made the
Venostae uneasy, and that would later, under the influence of mysterious demiurges, change their motives and objects and be directed
toward very different conquests. In the forests of his infancy, Alexis
had appeared a dreamy child unattracted to violence or the chase.
And now, in his youth, love appeared to him as a kind of chase, but

one that was a matter of persuasion rather than constraint. In the depraved Alexandria described by Renan, kidnapping and rape were not exceptional, but there is not one example of Alexis ever taking part in the nocturnal expeditions in which wild young men struck terror into the hearts of mothers and breathless duennas. Like all great seducers, Alexis never used force or threats. In fact, he did not even need to seduce at all, but simply agreed to let himself be seduced. He used to say, "No one has been so ravished as I since the Trojan War." In order to make these ravishments possible, he was almost forced to apply the rule already mentioned, never to make love more than once to the same woman or girl. This peculiarity soon became known. The news spread first through the city itself, and finally became a subject for jest and more or less horrified admiration throughout the eastern Mediterranean, from Alexandria to Tyre, Antioch, Chalcis, and Tarsus.

Man thinks it is he who leads his life, but his life also leads him. A few months, a few years of a regime by which Alexis is supposed to have entertained brief relations with one hundred forty-four young women (or, according to other traditions, three hundred sixty-five, or even one thousand and one)—we may notice in passing the mythical significance of the numbers—and change itself had become routine. Thus, in spite of all, everything is transmuted into order, even disorder itself. By a strange and probably revealing paradox, it came about that Alexis, who had more women at his feet than he desired, could only endure the company of courtesans and prostitutes. There was no lack of them in Alexandria, and Alexis was their master, their hero, their god. The future emperor's first taste of celebrity came to him from brothels and houses of ill-fame.

To carry paradox to its furthest extreme, the young man forbade himself to touch prostitutes whose services he had bought at an exorbitant price. He would just load them with presents and send them away. To anyone who expressed astonishment at this he would say: "Must one sleep with all the women who are one's friends?" One of the most famous courtesans of Alexandria, who has left a name behind in the history of manners, was called Imperia. The lovely Imperia was born in Genoa, where, when still very young, she had been the mistress of a nobleman called Philippe Mala or de Mala. The hazards of war brought Philippe de Mala to Africa, where he met his death outside the walls of Pelusium. Imperia, whom he had brought with him, settled in Alexandria, where her charm and beauty soon made her the first among the city's daughters of pleasure. Alexis sent her the rarest perfumes, precious stones, a pair of murrhine vases, and a crocodile, which much to the horror of visitors she installed in her swimming pool. Imperia was seized with a violent passion for Alexis, who was a good fifteen years younger than she. But he never touched her who had received into her bed every man of any note in Alexandria; he respected her as if she were a virgin. This strange form of homage nearly drove Imperia mad. He would accept only one favor from her, and that she granted with pleasure: one evening on which there was a masquerade, he had her harnessed, bare-breasted and together with three common prostitutes, to a chariot decked with flowers and silks. He took his place quite coolly in this conveyance, and drove in it through the streets of the city.

When, as usual, he was indulging in drinking and debauchery, and had begun with his own hand and his own razor to shave the crotches of half a dozen prostitutes, explaining that a bastard could not aspire to the noble profession of barber for men, he suddenly took a fancy to visit a banquet, to which he had been invited, in one of the most respectable houses in the city. He had stayed away in order to get drunk in bad company, and now he proposed to go to sup with the severe and highly esteemed judge who had invited him, accompanied by the half-naked courtesans who were with him. Two or three soberer friends tried to dissuade him, but in vain—it was very difficult to make Alexis change his mind once it was made up. His only concession was to cover more or less decently the prostitutes he had been amusing himself with; and then the whole party set out—it was already after dark—for the gardens near the gates of the city where the banquet was being held.

By a miracle, their arrival first in the garden, then in the hall, caused no particular stir. Even in the best society in Alexandria, manners were very free, and the judge's guests, too, had already partaken not wisely but too well of the wines and fermented liquors poured without stint by enormous Negroes from the Sudan, clad in short jackets and red trousers. Alexis started to drink again and to divert himself by introducing the courtesans under assumed names to all the tipsy Alexandrian dignitaries, pretending they were foreign ladies visiting the city. The local worthies took great pleasure in discussing the weightiest subjects with such charming creatures; some of them even remarked on the visitors' elegance and distinction.

The night was drawing to a close, and the young Alexis felt

himself beginning to be overwhelmed by the familiar depression and lassitude. He went out alone into the garden. It was a spring night. He lifted his head and inhaled the scents of jasmine and honeysuckle that floated everywhere. The stars were still shining. He tried to recognize those he used to see in his childhood above the oaks and birches. He often used to think of the forest, of his mother, and of the dark shapes of the wolves gliding over the snow. What a strange world it was that contained wolves and honeysuckle, death and priests, pleasure and the sea and prostitutes! He felt rising in him once more that strong and mysterious sense at once of the diversity of the world and of its unity. In that feeling were intermingled anguish and happiness together with a kind of insatiable thirst for all that was to be done in space and time—a space to be abolished, a time so brief before death. He suddenly felt as if he were simultaneously in the gardens in Alexandria, in the forest of his childhood, in the fields and cities through which he had traveled with Philocrates, in storms at sea, in deserts and harbors. What was suddenly missing, as if the ground had disappeared from under his feet, was the time to grasp everything, do everything, know everything. Twenty, he was twenty, and then he would be twenty-one or twenty-two—and he was shaving the bushes of Alexandrian harlots dressed up as Athenian ladies at a gathering of magistrates in a suburb in Lower Egypt. Why? Why? And all these men and women everywhere. And this need for happiness, money, love, and glory. And history marching on, with its victories and its ruins. The sun came into view over the orchard wall, and Alexis had to lean for support against some statue or tree. He passed a hand over his brow, overcome with the vertigo of the world. It was then he saw a white shape moving at the bottom of the garden. It was the seventh maiden of the night of his initiation, she whom he was forbidden to love.

He loved her. All his life Alexis was to drag behind him a weight of darkness and secrecy: the dual scandal of the nights of debauchery in Alexandria and the forbidden love. Not least among the paradoxes of abasement and crime is that they bring into great lives a trace of the human mystery that seems more akin to weakness and sin than to power and glory. Vanessa was the great-niece of the high priest of the sun who had presided over Alexis's initiation. She belonged to the caste, still shrouded in mystery even today, of the "guardians of the flame," whose links with parallel institutions in India or Rome have been the subject of many studies. Savage, and what seem to us now obscure, rules forbade the guardians of the flame, on pain of death, to have sexual or emotional relations with men, especially the neophytes with whose initiation they were entrusted. According to certain scholars they had to remain virgin until their thirty-seventh year; according to others they were deflowered by the high priest in person on the day of their own initiation, usually their fifteenth birthday. At all events, they were dedicated to the sun, and all defilement was forbidden them between the ages of sixteen and thirty-six. They washed in rain water only, ate nothing but food prepared according to the strictest rules, wove their own garments, and were not allowed to touch pigs or oxen or reptiles or amber or corpses or unweaned infants. In exchange for having to observe these restrictions, they were surrounded by universal consideration and respect, and upon retiring, often to marry, when their period of service ended, they were given enough in presents and gold to live thereafter in comfort and almost wealth.

Vanessa was eighteen. She was beautiful, and famed especially for her green eyes, long fair hair, and an incomparably noble mien. Alexis's reputation had naturally both horrified and attracted her. As for him, the idea that a woman, one woman, was forbidden to him was enough to make him decide secretly to abandon everything for her and for what was an impossible dream. But he made it possible. As may be imagined, we know very little of the story of this love, at least from direct sources. But legend took up the tale with delight. The poem *Alexis and Vanessa*, by an unknown author who mysteriously signs himself Turolde and ends his work with the famous and mysterious line, "Ci falt la geste que Turoldus declinet"; the well-known romance by Demetrios de Jamblée; the discreet and respectful allusions made by Valerius in several of his works, in particular *The Birth of the Empire*—all these have made the love of Alexis and Vanessa one of the most familiar examples of the "romance" common to almost all the world's cultures. One finds traces of it in many Indian and Arabic texts, and one of the most frequently performed Nō plays today is a Japanese version of the story dating from the beginning of the fifteenth century. Mystery, secrecy, prohibition, the frenzy of the lovers, the revelation of passion to one who knows nothing of love and to the other who knows too much, the story's tragic end—all called forth many interpreters as well as many readers and spectators. The story has been set to music more than a score of times, by artists from Lorenzo de' Medici (whose version was performed in Florence in 1492 before a dazzling audience that included Pope Alexander Borgia, his son Cesare, his daughter Lucrezia, Marsilio Ficino, Politian, and Cardinal della Rovere, later Julius II) down to Erik Satie and Georges Auric.

The counting rhyme

> One and two and three
> Alexander and Venishee
> And out goes she,

which has presented linguistics experts and sociologists, misled by the modification of the names, with so many problems, obviously derives from the source we are discussing. Like the loves of Arsaphes and Heloise, Basil and Ingeburgh, Fabrician and Helen, the passion of Alexis for Vanessa is linked to the history of the Empire, and so to the whole aggregate of masterpieces, anecdotes, and traditions that makes up a culture and belongs not merely to an individual civilization but to the common memory of mankind.

Let us try to imagine the meetings between Alexis and Vanessa in that wild city of Alexandria. Into the midst of tolerated debauchery and established disorder, crime and sin brought a little silence and beauty. It all happened very quickly, that night at the banquet when he saw her again, that night to the bitter, dazzling memory of which he was so often to refer, obliquely, all his life. He was drunk, filthy, haggard. He saw her, and from then on he loved her. Perhaps he had loved her ever since his ordeal in the cave. Probably there was the sound of music in the distance, and the coolness of the fountains soothed senses irritated by the crowd, the wine, the noise, the glare of the torches, the violence of the perfumes. Under the fading moon and stars, the rising sun spread a single scent of jasmine and honeysuckle mingled. It was the hour when despair and self-contempt always seized Alexis. He would feel weak and wretched, and suffer intensely from the three diseases that rarely relent, and accompany man to his grave: dissatisfaction with himself, a sense of the passing of time, and a vague lack of which he knows neither the meaning nor the name. For a moment he thought he saw his mother's shadow passing far off through the garden. He ran toward it, but the shadow had already disappeared. He stood there motionless, arms dangling, hesitant, as if something was missing from his life. He could not bring himself to leave the garden. The sun was rising and it was almost light. Day shed on Alexandria, on Egypt, and on the world a pale and silent menace. It was at this moment that the shadow reappeared in the garden. The sun and the light brought out its youth, its beauty, its calm and noble mien. Alexis realized that, through the illusion that it was his mother, he had already recognized her before in the darkness now fading. It was Vanessa, and he loved her.

Not all the resources of science and history, nor all the treasure of folklore and popular tales will ever tell us why Vanessa came back into the garden to meet passion, endless anguish, and death. Some will say chance, others fate, others that she was already a prey to the most ordinary and violent of passions and had returned to the garden to see if the debauchee she had heard so much about was still wandering there in the dawn. Yes, he was there. He went toward her and greeted her in a voice that was indistinct, even thick, but burning with anticipation and anxiety. Words launch men on terrible paths where they sometimes meet their end. They send them to death, madness, glory, despair. Alexis and Vanessa did not say especially fine things to each other. They had very little time. They only exchanged the simple words that make possible exquisitely organized catastrophes. He asked if he could see her again. She said yes. When? Tomorrow. Where? Behind the temple at the city gate, on the road to Saïs, just to the right of the copse, at sunset. Everything was already in place for a most cruel end.

They met, and met again. Of course, she thought at first that her only object was to help him escape, in secret, from the depraved world that so shocked her innocence. He was attracted by her—but it was something more. He told himself he was attracted by her, but he had only to hear her name or think of her for his heart to be shaken by a strange tempest that astonished even himself. He went through all the anguish and exasperation of waiting. He would watch the sun go down, and count the moments that still separated him from that fair hair, that clear soft skin, that form only guessed at through the long robe that fell to her feet. It was no longer even desire, but almost painful impatience, apprehension. At last he would see her, she was there, and calm, a deep delight, peace, would take the place of torment. She was there, he would speak to her, their hands would meet and touch and remain clasped one within the other. And it was as if each recognized at last in the other that other half of their self for which they had been searching.

She knew already what was at the end of this love. Perhaps he knew, too. They struggled, but reluctantly and feebly, against themselves. He had taken her, and she had given herself to him, as a sacrifice to a forbidden god, adored no matter what the cost. He would say to her:

"We'll go away. To Carthage, Syracuse, Onessa, the City, or to the forest of my mother."

And she would answer gently:

"I shall stay here, with my temple and my gods."

Then he would take her by the wrists, angrily, and all the lovers in the world would speak their eternal chorus through his lips. He would say she did not love him, that he needed her, that she was playing with him and did not understand him . . . She would look at him and listen without speaking. He would fall down and embrace her knees, and lie there motionless, his head buried in her, breathing in the scent that obsessed him all day and intoxicated him all night. She would slowly stroke his hair, looking far away and sad. She would bend over him and brush his brow with her lips.

"I do love you," she would say. "But I shall stay."

They loved each other in the city, the night after the feast. In the fields; by the temples; in the forest; on the moss; on the sand; by the sea. In spring; in the heat of summer; in the cool evenings of autumn. Wealth, birth, their position in society were all at once a hindrance and a help. A help because they had spare time, servants, the means of buying silence and assistance. A hindrance, because they were spied on by the whole city and were so well known they were recognized everywhere. Through pleasure and danger, the nights, the months, the seasons, the years flowed by, given over to delights and to that elevation of the soul which despite sin or even crime belongs to passion.

To avoid causing suspicion, Alexis did not entirely stop seeing his old friends. He still went to feasts, banquets, orgies, but taking with him only the shadow of his former frenzy. He would absentmindedly stroke someone's hair or wrist, or drink priceless wines from golden goblets, and all the while be thinking of Vanessa waiting for him on the beach or among the trees at the gates of the city. Several people noticed his weariness and apathy, interrupted by flashes of joy and transports of happiness he could not always hide. They put his oddity down to dissolute living, exhaustion, or perhaps some secret malady. He, tired of these vanities and follies and the play-acting involved, would sometimes indulge in acts of cruelty or brutality which his friends and guests had never seen in him before. He would break valuable objects, beat prostitutes till he drew blood (though, as a matter of fact, they asked nothing better), or, among his familiars, lose the sang-froid that should be preserved even in the deepest abysses of pleasure and debauchery. The smallest events of his secret life with Vanessa were translated, magnified, in his public life: when she had been tender, he became almost cheerful again; but if he had found her elusive and preoccupied, he would fall back into the depression that spread questions and idle speculation all over the city.

Things remained like this for some time. Secret meetings in the forest or behind the temples alternated with suppers and masquerades. From time to time the two lovers would both be present at official ceremonies. They would go with mixed feelings, in which the happiness of seeing one another was inextricably entangled with the almost unbearable irksomeness of social and religious duty. They felt the madness of their love all the more keenly when they saw one another decked in ceremonial robes, surrounded by a respectful crowd, encased in ritual and tradition, and playing their assumed parts. How joyfully they would meet again on the morrow of feasts and sacrifices, alone, naked, far away from everything and everybody, drunk with freedom, drunk with love and pleasure, forgetful of the city and the gods, each present only to the other, body, lips, and hands, and to the low murmur in which a whole world vanished! Remorse, quarrels, the uncertainty of hour and place, were only a spur inciting them to love one another more and more so as to escape from the world and other people with their rules and their laws, and to put off the mysterious reckoning they dimly feared.

At last, one morning beside a brook in a little wood near the sea, Alexis was told by his mistress, at the end of her tether, that the high priest suspected something and was having her watched. She could not endure all these dangers and lies any longer, and in a broken, almost inaudible voice, interrupting herself with kisses and tears, she asked Alexis if they should not end their relationship. It was like the blow of a whip to Alexis, like a red-hot iron on his heart. He leaped to his feet, staggered for a moment as if he could not breathe, came back, stood there pale as death before his mistress, and began to revile her. She didn't love him any more. Why didn't she say so instead of looking for pretexts to get out of an affair that was beginning to bore her? Let her speak out and dismiss him. He would go back to his low life and his masquerades. Perhaps he would kill himself. He loved her and would never forget her. He would think of her in his promiscuity as he had thought of her in his passion. She wept without a word. Tears ran down her cheeks and wetted her white robe. She stood there without stirring. He seized her, twisted her arms, all but struck her. Speak! Say something! She stood there silent, weeping. A fine time to weep! What was she crying for? Herself? Their love that she was condemning to death? The end of their happiness? But she could hardly be crying for him, since it was she who was rejecting him. No doubt she didn't love him any more and could do without him. Let her forget him then and be happy.

"Forget you!"

That was all she said through her tears.

"Forget you!"

He looked at her. She wept. She raised her eyes and looked at him, still weeping. Then he fell at her feet, brought her down into his arms, and asked her forgiveness. In tears both lay on the ground.

"I shall die," she said. "I shall die. But I shall die happy."

He put his hand over her mouth, already soothed by his victory. She took his hand and kissed it, and he watched her. They smiled. Above her, beyond the body of the lover lying gently over her, she saw the sky. He blocked out her view of the sky, but she could still glimpse it, all blue, there on the right, there on the left. And the sun, already high in the heavens. She clasped him in her arms, she could scarcely breathe, she uttered a cry. What does the price of happiness matter when one can taste it on one's lips!

The love of Alexis and Vanessa had all the bitter strength of passion in jeopardy. Vanessa could feel the suspicion of the high priest lurking around her. Alexis had conceived a hatred for the old man who opposed their happiness and hopes. He had gradually taken again to drinking, to occupy the endless waiting, to forget the obstacles bristling in their path. On the pretext of misleading the high priest's spies he started to frequent bacchanals and orgies again, and if necessary to sponsor them. It was during a night of unbridled drinking that the disaster happened.

Alexis's friends and admirers, clients and parasites, were wearying him with their questions and sympathizing. Did he not feel well? Had he reason to complain of his fortune or his fate? Was he worried about something? He looked tired, not well. Why did he not give more of those feasts at which he used to be so brilliant? To cut short gossip and cross-questioning, to mislead people, to distract himself, perhaps also, deep down, to avenge himself for the tears of Vanessa and the harshness of fate, Alexis decided one day to give a banquet in his old style. It was a big party and a great success. The women were pretty. Everyone drank a good deal. The high priest was there, and so was his great-niece Vanessa. Alexis and Vanessa did not exchange one look. It was torture. Vanessa bore it in silence, speaking just a word to this person or that, standing motionless most of the time beside the high priest. But Alexis fought against pain with drink and excitement. He seemed to suffer less when he saw Vanessa suffer. So he went on drinking, and caressing young women, and roaring with laughter at the coarse pleasantries of his reeling hangers-on. In the middle of the night there was a general cry for a lottery like the ones that had caused such scandal before. Alexis resisted at first, then began to yield. In his drunkenness and exasperation a terrible idea had come to him. He suddenly made up his mind, called for scribes and slaves, and issued whispered orders. From the guests who had already understood, there were cries of joy and frenzied activity, and the servants set about organizing the lottery, preparing the prizes and the bits of parchment or hide that were to serve as chances.

The lottery began amidst drunken laughter. Alexis looked on, somewhat distant. In growing chaos the minor prizes began to be distributed—parrots, cameos, stone scarabs, forfeits that carried derisory consequences, like pieces of cloth or fines. The roistering grew louder, but Alexis remained strangely calm. The tumultuous night seemed about to peter out in weariness and depression when the high priest and his great-niece came to take leave of their host. Alexis got up to accompany them to the door, but after a few steps he turned, as if surprised, to the old man.

"But you are not going to leave empty-handed?" he said. "Without a prize or a jewel or anything? Didn't you take part in the lottery I organized for my friends?"

"Thank you," said the high priest. "I'm too old for that kind of amusement."

"I want you to join in," said Alexis. "I insist." And he clapped his hands.

A huge Sudanese emerged from the shadows, followed by a young girl, almost naked but for her golden necklaces, and carrying a basket. There were two bits of folded parchment left in it. Alexis leaned toward the high priest, seized him by the wrist, and cried with blazing eyes:

"Choose! Choose!"

In the light of the dying torches, Alexis's face was swept with waves of excitement and madness. The old man fell back, hesitated, then, with his eyes fixed on Alexis, stretched out his trembling, wrinkled hand toward the girl, who, smiling, tendered the woven basket lined with gold-threaded scarlet silk. He drew out one of the two parchments. Alexis snatched it from him and read it aloud. It didn't take long. All that was written there was "Death."

"You are fortunate, old man!" cried Alexis in an unnaturally shrill voice and turning his back on him. "You have drawn a lot which is only that of all men. God knows what is on the other parchment! I wish you a peaceful death when your hour comes."

The priest did not answer—he suddenly seemed very old. Vanessa had turned pale. She was obviously ill and looked as if she were about to swoon. There was something sinister in the way the feast was breaking up, amid mockery, exhaustion, and the kind of trembling insanity generated by alcohol just before daybreak. The old man and his great-niece went out together into the darkness, deathly tired, confused by the noise and commotion, appalled by Alexis's behavior—like ghosts of suffering and death who had somehow strayed among pleasures.

A few moments later, on his way home, the high priest was set upon in the street and beaten by four or five unidentified men. Vanessa, terrified but unhurt, managed to get the old man to his house, covered in blood. He died that day. The young priestess could not be present because she was forbidden to look on a dead body. Rumors about the banquet and the lottery had already spread from house to house, and the affair caused an enormous scandal. Though Alexis had long been a topic for talk in Alexandria, he seemed to have grown quieter the last year or so. But his past had been so lurid that now, though the city was used to every kind of excess, an outcry arose that was all the louder because it had been held in check so long by friendship or astonishment. Philocrates suddenly reappeared, now that his pupil was in danger, and spared no efforts on his behalf. He besieged the priests, the judges, the city authorities: there was nothing to prove that the young man was guilty, no evidence of any connection between the lottery and the attack on the high priest. Of course Alexis's behavior had been disgraceful. But the Alexandrian nights were so full of such insults and indignities that people had ceased to take any notice. The murder of the high priest was altogether more serious than any childish prank, in however bad taste. Although many tried, no one succeeded in implicating Alexis directly in the old man's death. The affair was a nine days' wonder, and then would probably have faded out and been forgotten if it had not been revived in an unexpected fashion. The high priest had left behind a secret will which he entrusted to a young pupil and confidant of his who was both violent and ambitious. This will accused Vanessa outright of treachery and murder. The young man handed the document over to the college of priests, and in less than five days Vanessa was arrested, imprisoned, tried by a tribunal of priests, and sentenced to death.

The punishment for guardians of the flame convicted of serious dereliction of duty was prescribed down to the last detail. It consisted of a dreadful kind of death of which vestiges are found in various civilizations, including that of Japan a few centuries ago. The victim was both stoned and buried alive. A hole was dug in the ground and filled with clay and rubble, and in this she was buried up to the hips or shoulders. Then, on the trunk and arms and face still left exposed, the assembled crowd threw stones, branches, and missiles of all descriptions until the victim died of injuries or asphyxiation. Sometimes she would be wounded in the head and die quickly, but in other cases she would suffer an awful, long-drawn-out suffocation as she was gradually submerged beneath an incongruous mass of old rags, mud, wood, broken toys, bricks, refuse, and rubbish.

Alexis could not have been ignorant of the fate in store for Vanessa. If we know next to nothing about his horror at the end he had brought upon his mistress, who did nothing to resist it, we may suppose it is because any documents or other evidence were sought out and destroyed later by envoys of the Emperor. We shall come back to this point. In any case, we can easily imagine how for Alexis it must have been like awakening out of a drunken dream. There is an indication of this in a letter written by Isidore, who, probably kept informed by Philocrates, is found a few months after the tragedy still expressing the gravest anxiety for the young man's health and even life. How could one doubt that Alexis wanted to save Vanessa or to die with her? And how can one doubt, either, that Philocrates, caring only for his pupil's best interests, used all his wisdom and firmness to dissuade him from desperate acts that could not have saved the priestess from torture and death, and might have involved Alexis in the same fate? A persistent tradition, in which it is difficult to distinguish legend from fact, has it that on the night before the execution Vanessa was kidnapped from the prison by means of a mysterious plot, and her place taken by a young hysteric, a girl insensible with drugs and wine, who was killed in her stead, wearing the ritual veils that hid the victim even from her executioners. It is of course impossible, so many years later, to hope that the truth will ever be known about this historical enigma, which has given and continues to give rise to so many theories and to so much passion. What is certain is that an execution did take place. As dawn was breaking, a long procession went from the prison to the lonely place still known as "Qabr al-fatat" or "Torbat el-bint," both phrases meaning "the girl's tomb."[6] A white shape, half fainting, was buried in the earth freshly dug in accordance with the law, and the execution began. Apparently a fatal blow was struck quite soon, and the stones and branches only fell on a corpse. The body was left buried under the heap of missiles for three days and nights, and on the fourth day it was burned by the priests. Some maintain that Philocrates and his pupil secretly attended the execution, and that the fatal, liberating stone was cast by Alexis.

XII

THE YEARS IN THE WILDERNESS,
OR THE FOOL OF GOD

 REAT DESTINIES AND PROMISED LANDS ALWAYS LIE on the other side of a desert. For seven years according to some, twelve years according to others, Alexis vanished from the scene of history. It is as if he were taken from the land of the living by a premature death.[1] We are sadly lacking in details of time and place for this mysterious phase in the life of the future emperor. Until 1952, all attempts at historical reconstruction of the missing pieces in the puzzle were merely shadowy conjectures. The most one could legitimately do was question, for chronological and internal reasons, the theory that twelve years was the length of time Alexis spent unheard of in unknown countries. According to Justus Dion, Isidore, and Philocrates, Alexis was eleven or twelve when he left his mother and Simeon. Then came the years of apprenticeship and wandering through Europe and the Near East with Philocrates, and when he was initiated into the cult of the sun he was eighteen. The Alexandrian period lasted between three and five years: one or two years of dissolute living and roistering, two or three years of passion for Vanessa. At the time of the execution of the guardian of the flame, or perhaps of the unknown substitute, Alexis must have been about twenty-two or twenty-three. Twelve years of exile in Asia would bring him up to thirty-four or thirty-five. For reasons too lengthy to go into, it is very unlikely that Alexis could have been as old as thirty-five when he emerged into the daylight of history again. It is much more likely that he was about twenty-nine, or thirty at the most. That brings us back to the theory that it was seven years that he spent in secret. It is not impossible that the length of this period

was exaggerated by successive historians and mythologists in order to create a parallel between Alexis and Christ. For many years nothing is known of Jesus and the secret life he lived between boyhood and the period of his death. Those who wrote about Alexis may have been trying to allege a symmetry. Of course, both seven and twelve are figures with a symbolic connotation. In any event, in the case of Alexis seven seems nearer to the truth.

After time—space. Where did Alexis take refuge during his voluntary exile? Here, again, the most arbitrary hypotheses have long been advanced. Some claim Alexis can be traced in the Maghreb, Sudan, Yemen, the Arabian deserts, or on the shores of the Persian Gulf or the Black Sea. Others say he was among the Varangians, the shamans of Siberia, or in the tundras of the far north. Most probably he headed eastward, to Afghanistan or India (perhaps like Jesus again?), Nepal or Tibet. But we must not conceal from ourselves the boldness of all these conjectures. True, it was admitted that Alexis's familiarity with the geography and languages and mysticism of the East suggested a lengthy stay in those fabulous and fascinating regions. But until quite recently that was the limit of our knowledge of this mysterious period in one of the most astonishing lives in history. And there matters would have remained had it not been for the emergence of a new factor: from 1952 and 1954 on, new sources and sensational revelations became available about this part of Alexis's life. We must go back a little to pick up the thread of what was to prove an exemplary discovery. Let us digress for a moment from Alexis to dwell briefly on the adventures of one who is perhaps the most curious figure in contemporary science.

Around the year 1890 there lived in Damascus a very gifted young man called Armand Bourdaille. He had been born in Saint-Gaudens of a Jewish mother, and was a great reader of Renan, Burnouf, ibn-Khaldun, and ibn-Batuta. From very early on he had been fascinated by Islam. His father was a vice-consul in Syria and a man of great learning and virtue; he was a friend of Maurice Barrès, Paul Claudel, and Victor Segalen, and had met Rimbaud when he was sent, a few years earlier, on a trade mission to Harar. Armand was brought up by his father in an atmosphere of learned poetry and mysticism. In 1892, when he was seventeen, Armand, stifling in Damascus among the soldiers and the diplomats and yearning for adventure and a life of freedom and purity, entered into an exalted friendship with a young Arab called Abed. Together the two young men left behind them the comforts of bourgeois family life, and joined a camel caravan which went across the Syrian and Arabian deserts to the Red Sea, Sinai, and Cairo. One after another Abed and Bourdaille saw the magic landscapes that had formed a background to the life of Jesus; the shores of Lake Tiberias; the monastery of Saint Catherine; the boundless wastes of sand and wind. And all the time they shared the harsh and slow existence of the Moslem nomads. Bourdaille was very struck by their piety, and the traditions of Judaism, Christianity, and Islam mingled in his mind and heart in a lofty, ardent faith in which all the strands converged to form an esoteric monotheism. After two years of this life of adventure, Bourdaille arrived in Cairo with Abed, whose charm and intelligence were equally outstanding. Unwilling to part from his companion or to go back and live in the shadow of consulates and business houses, he registered as a student at Al Azhar University, and for two or three years attended the traditional lectures on Islamic history and mysticism. At twenty-five Armand Bourdaille took his place with outstanding brilliance in the great line of French orientalists. It is difficult to decide whether the son of the former vice-consul in Damascus was the representative of French science in Islam, or the representative of Islamic culture in France.

Many years later, about 1948 or 1950, toward the end of his life, we find the elderly Armand Bourdaille a professor at the Collège de France and the École pratique des hautes études. He had become one of the most eminent specialists on the history of the Near East from the period of the supremacy of classical Egypt till the heyday of Islam. Throughout his life he had pursued the intellectual adventure of which he was the best embodiment. He had experienced a new mystical insight in Rome, on the eve of the First World War. One of his close friends, Alexandre de la Ferrière, a devout Catholic and godson of Albert de Mun, had made the acquaintance in Rome of a dazzlingly beautiful girl of Baltic origin. The young man had fallen madly in love with her, but the girl, who was a distant cousin of the Bourdailles and knew Armand well, was a Jewess. Alexandre de la Ferrière, barefoot and in a hair shirt, went around to all the basilicas in Rome offering God his life in exchange for the girl's conversion. Three months later she was converted and married Alexandre, who asked Bourdaille to act as witness. But after only a few months of rapturous happiness the young husband died suddenly.

The funeral was held in the little church of San Giovanni a Porta

Latina, just by the oratory of San Giovanni in Oleo, built on the spot where, according to legend, Saint John emerged unscathed from the ordeal of boiling oil. In front of the church, by a well, there was a tall cedar that shaded the whole square. Armand Bourdaille sat down on the lip of the well, worn out with grief and resentment, cursing in his heart the divine injustice that never hesitates to strike down innocence and happiness, and refusing to enter the church of a cruel and jealous God. The sun shone brightly, flooding with light the little square, the front of the church with the veil of shadow between its columns, the campanile, and the old cedar. Bourdaille, his eyes filled with tears, was staring unseeing at this beautiful view of desolation and of peace, when suddenly the sky seemed to grow dark, and all the light seemed to be concentrated on the cedar, which began to glow with a thousand fires. The organ inside the church seemed to have gone silent, but heavenly music poured from the tree, transfigured by some strange glory. An irresistible force threw Bourdaille on his knees with his face to the ground—the Virgin Mary had just appeared to him. The problem of evil, which had tortured his every moment for so many years, was now only a source of joy and faith— Bourdaille's spiritual destiny had taken yet another new turn.

He whose inspiration and life had been Islam now had only one wish, one dream—to become a priest of Christ and of the Roman Catholic Church. It is said that during one of the many private audiences granted him by the Pope, he described the continual progress made by Islam and said it was difficult to find one example of a Moslem converted to Christianity to oppose to the many examples of conversion in the other direction. The Pope smiled and said reproachfully, "Come, come, M. Bourdaille! What about you?" But conversion was not enough. Bourdaille wanted to be ordained. The difficulty was that he was married. But he didn't give up. He looked for a solution, and he found one. One morning early, his wife saw him dressed ready to go out. She asked him where he was going so early. He looked at her gravely, then, with tears in his eyes, fell at her feet, and asked forgiveness. He was going out to celebrate Mass. For the past two years, though she had not known it, Angèle Bourdaille had been married to a Uniate priest.

Though a Christian now and a priest, Bourdaille had sacrificed none of his fidelity to Islam. The Uniates, who, unlike the Orthodox Church, recognize the authority of Rome and the Pope, do not only have married priests. They also represent one of the essential links in the chain between the Roman Catholic Church and the world of Eastern faith and mysticism. Bourdaille now lived a pure life of the spirit in which religious ardor was based on learning. Until the end of his life his main preoccupation was a reconciliation of the three monotheistic religions. The conflict between Israel and Ishmael, Jews and Arabs, broke his heart. His Jewish origins, his familiarity with Islam, and his Christian faith are all closely bound up with his work, which can only be explained in terms of the loftiest inner life. Anecdote is here inseparable from faith and science—that is why we have chosen to dwell on it.

From 1950 on, Bourdaille spent several months every year in the Near East, to get on with his work but above all to try to compose people's differences. He was helped by a young Arab, Ahmed Badalwi, Abed's grandson. There was the warmest affection between them. Ahmed, though still young, was already a distinguished archeologist. A communist, brought up in Moscow, he had been converted to Christianity under the influence of Bourdaille, and he too had become a priest. Wearing an ancient Jesuit's cassock that was older than he was, and which soon became famous from Antioch to Tyre and Sinai, he directed the excavations in Jordan and Palestine and had contacts with many Arab shepherds, craftsmen, and truck drivers, who gave him information about the accidental finds thrown up here and there by plowing, building, local research, or mere chance. One evening when he was working at Petra a young herdsman asked to see him, in great secrecy and putting on airs of mystery. Ahmed saw him and asked what brought him there. The boy said that while searching for a lost sheep the day before, he had found himself in a deep, dark cave. Poking about after his charge, he had come upon a strange kind of parcel. He held it out, shyly. The priest undid the packet and glanced idly at some earth-covered scrolls that looked on the point of crumbling to dust. Then he looked more closely, and started. He turned to the boy, who was standing about, twiddling his fingers nervously, clapped him on the back, and gave him the biggest sum of money the boy had ever seen. Two hours later, though it was nighttime now, the Jesuit leaped into his jeep and set out for Jerusalem, where Professor Bourdaille had arrived a few days before.

I hope readers will forgive this long, not altogether irrelevant, digression. In the field of the human sciences, which in the last century has seen progress comparable to that made in the physical sciences, the discovery of the Petra manuscripts is an event of the same importance as the discovery of Hiram Bingham and Heinrich Schliemann of the ruins of Onessa. The Petra manuscripts have modified profoundly our knowledge of the history of Eastern mysticism. They have thrown new light on centuries of history. They have radically altered our ideas on the religious evolution of a large part of the world. Above all, they give us essential information about what was hitherto a practically unknown period in the life of Alexis. Thus, across the centuries, are indissolubly linked the lives of Armand Bourdaille, Jewish-Moslem scholar and Uniate priest, and Alexis, priest of the sun and Emperor.

It will be noted that the discovery of the Petra manuscripts dates from 1952, a certain number of additional texts having come to light at the end of 1954.[2] Furthermore, the Ritter manuscript, which has already been referred to in connection with Arsaphes and Simeon,[3] was found by the Berlin historian in the archives of the Sublime Porte in 1953. So around the middle of this century there was a complete renewal of historical knowledge concerning the origins of the Empire. Without the Petra manuscripts we should know nothing of Alexis's withdrawal. They enable us to arrive at at least a rough idea of the meaning and religious background of that withdrawal. All we shall say here about what has been called the "secret years" of Alexis is taken from the Petra manuscripts, from Armand Bourdaille's and Father Badalwi's interpretation of them, and from Sir Allan Carter-Bennett's and Robert Weill-Pichon's comments on that interpretation.

Alexis left Alexandria the day after the execution. With him went Philocrates, to whom he owed not only his life but also the constant moral support that he needed even more. He had two deaths on his conscience; he had committed a crime against religion; to degradation and debauchery he had added lying, dissimulation, and cowardice; he had brought about the murder of the priest who had initiated him into the cult of the sun; and he had delivered his mistress over to the most horrible torture. Seven (or twelve) years of renunciation and penitence would not be enough to erase the memory of these crimes from his mind and heart. Later on we shall see the attitude of the Catholic Church toward Alexis, and the honors it lavished on him. But at the same time the Church would also number him in the ranks of the criminals, and describe him as a "stinking goat" and "Antichrist." Dante, while weaving him immortal crowns, gives him a place in the Inferno, at the bottom of the Malebolge, between Archbishop Rugghieri, who betrayed Ugolino, who himself betrayed his country, and Bocca degli Abati, who betrayed the Guelphs.[4] Bossuet, Lacordaire, and Montalembert hold up to the opprobrium and execration of the ages the picture of Helen's son wallowing in the pleasures and follies of Alexandria. Only Armand Bourdaille forgives him everything and absolves him. For Alexis, the day when he left Alexandria for the wilderness and a new exile was the beginning of a second or even a third life, after the disaster of bastardy, after the tragedy of love and death. And, as Sir Allan Carter-Bennett puts it, "this second life opened upon a first death." For what Alexis would be seeking was the death of the flesh, the death of the mind.

It seems Philocrates stayed with his pupil a few months, and that Alexis then sent him away, in order to be alone with himself. Then, somewhere in the deserts of Arabia, he led the most wretched and retired of lives. According to the Petra manuscripts he at first took refuge in a cave, where he lived on goat's milk and dates. But soon even this existence no longer brought him peace—it was too easy, it left him too much time for memories and remorse. He needed to mortify and crush the flesh, to prevent the mind from thinking and the memory from functioning. Then he passed several months sitting motionless on top of a pillar, burned by the sun and whipped by the wind, tortured by insects and vermin, revived by the water and vinegar reached to him in a sponge on the end of a stick by pious women or passing caravaneers. Buñuel's unfinished film, *Alexis Stylites*, outlines in a few images, aesthetically very fine if sometimes historically debatable, this period in the life of the future emperor. But Vanessa's murderer had to look for and find something even worse than the torture of immobility, which at least left the body intact and upright and open to the sky. He had to descend under the earth, hide away from the sun, and break the limbs that had abandoned themselves to forbidden caresses.

One of the most valuable things the Petra manuscripts give us is information about certain mysterious sects, about which we knew almost nothing before, that were scattered over a vast area between the Red Sea and the Euphrates and that carried the religion and mysticism of the sun to sometimes terrifying extremes. Bourdaille has shown clearly the links between these sects and later phenomena connected with Islam, such as the practices of the Hachchachin (or Assassins, or Fidda'iyyun, Nizarites or Batinians) and of the howling and dancing dervishes. He also proved beyond all dispute, with the help of Professor von Grünefeld of the University of California, that the person referred to in the Petra manuscripts as Alachian or Alechia or Alaouis is none other than Alexis himself. During his years of penance and fasting, Alachian, Alechia, or Alaouis arrived at such mortifications and self-violence that the memory of them was consigned to secret documents kept safe from military expedition or religious inquisition. And these documents, hidden in the cave at Petra, were to be found centuries later by a shepherd searching for his lost sheep.

The sun worship of the sects Alexis went among consisted essentially of two complementary and opposite practices. The first, a kind of penance, consisted of hiding from the sun in the depths of the earth; the second consisted in exposing oneself to the sun until unconsciousness or sometimes even death ensued. To carry out this second practice, worshippers would lie on huge, flat stones, usually on a slight rise and in places where the air was driest and reflection most intense. There was a great risk of becoming totally blind, and these sects included a large number of people who had given their sight to the sun in exchange for the raptures of inner contemplation. Death from burns or dehydration was very frequent. Those who survived led a miserable life fleeing from persecution. Surrounded by popular fervor that could find little outlet in the extreme solitudes where they took refuge, they were pitilessly harassed and sometimes massacred both by the priests, who saw their excesses as heresy and provocation, and by the rulers and military chiefs, who regarded them as potentially subversive.

Probably even more painful than exposure to the sun were the practices connected with burial. The ascetics who did not deem themselves worthy of the violences of the sun voluntarily eschewed its rays and its other gifts and buried themselves underground for months and months, in tunnels, mostly hollowed out by hand, which often collapsed on top of them, and in which they led a vegetative life in solitude and darkness.

The two methods were often followed consecutively, and months underground would be succeeded by sudden exposure to the sun. In such cases death was rapid. Alexis first of all offered himself to the vengeance of the sun, but his youth and strength enabled him to survive. Then, since death would have none of him, he decided to bury himself alive.

Both Armand Bourdaille and Sir Allan Carter-Bennett stress the possible motives that may have led Alexis to submit himself for so long to this kind of suffering. It is very probable that at first he saw obedience to the strictest precepts of the sun cult as a reparation for the sins he had committed toward it, its laws, and its priests. But it is also possible, and even likely, that in the particular practice of burial he found a reminder and expiation of Vanessa's death. The Petra manuscripts give a rough and no doubt inaccurate location for the underground temples where Alexis interred himself. But they also give a comprehensive description of them that have been confirmed by various recent archeological discoveries, from the Red Sea to Yemen and even beyond the Tigris.

The temple or tomb—whichever one chooses to call it—opened outward on to a comparatively large kind of lobby, where worshippers and disciples would sometimes come to pray and leave offerings, food, and drink. Out of this atrium opened a sloping tunnel with niches in the walls that seem to have been filled with rough statuettes and other cult objects. The tunnel ended in a cul-de-sac formed by a slight widening in the form of an inverted cone. It was, of course, impossible to stand upright in the sacred chamber, and even though the occupant was immobile the slippery, uneven floor forced his body into the most painful contortions. Skeletons found on such sites confirm that the limbs and whole frames of the inmates became cruelly deformed. These constructions resemble in some respects the huge temples of the sun at Emesa and Edessa and Alexandria, where Alexis was initiated. Several of these tombs were quite large, and built not only by local craftsmen out of local materials but sometimes by quite famous architects using brick and wood to begin with, but later even such fine materials as stone and marble. Form, lighting, the slope of the tunnel were carefully calculated. At fixed dates—probably the summer and winter solstices—the rays of the sun at its zenith were made, by means of systems of movable mirrors, to reach the penitent in the depths of his cul-de-sac. But in addition to these impressively large and technically sophisticated edifices, the excavations conducted by Professor Bourdaille, from the time of the discovery of the Petra manuscripts until his death, have brought to light the almost vanished traces of many individual temples-*cum*-tombs, crudely constructed by hand and obviously doomed to rapid destruction. It seems Alexis first hid himself away in one of the large underground temples housing several ascetics, and afterward took refuge in a little vault hollowed out with his own hands in some deserted spot, where the death he yearned for would soon have over-taken him had an unforeseen circumstance not given his life yet another twist.

As if curiosity and admiration were fated to gather round him in renunciation as in pleasure, a fame remarkable in that place and time began to attach to his withdrawal, his wretched existence, and his attempt to achieve anonymity and secrecy. The Petra manuscripts mention the rumor that drew crowds of believers and sightseers and spread far and wide, in more and more modified forms, the name of Alechia or Alaouis. Among the documents discovered in 1954 by Armand Bourdaille and Father Badalwi is a mystical text known as the *Book of the Dead*, in which appears the mysterious and attractive figure of the "Teacher of Goodness." We have good reason to identify Alexis with this figure, the subject of some remarkable studies carried out by the Center for Oriental Studies at the University of California. For the present this can only be a hypothesis, but is is to be hoped that in the next few years new documents and new discoveries will enable us to resolve the problem and establish definite links between the Teacher of Goodness and Alexis. Hitherto we have kept strictly to our rule of putting forward only firmly established facts. It must be admitted that some people deny any connection between Alexis and the Teacher of Goodness; but although, of course, we do not wish to press too personal an interpretation, we are prepared to assert that we have no doubt about the matter. However that may be, how long did Alexis lead that gradually less and less secret life in the tombs of the sun? Three or four years, perhaps. We find traces of it beyond the Tigris and Euphrates, in Isfahan and Bamian, and on the banks of the Indus.

By a paradox, sun worship was linked with moon worship, its converse and complement. On nights of full moon the priests of the sun would emerge from their tombs at midnight and proceed, if not to worship the moon, at least to go through the motions of sacri-fices combining mystical elements with mockery, and with aspects both magic and erotic. Armand Bourdaille said this cult of the moon "was to the worship of the sun as the Black Mass is to the liturgical one." It was probably this cult of the moon that served as a link between the ascetics of the *Book of the Dead* and the schismatic seers and soothsayers farther east. These existed as powerful secret sects in Babylon, Seleucia, Dura-Europos, Zingara, Nineveh, and all over Persia; and through the ages their occult influence had helped to undermine the ancient religion of Zoroaster, Ormazd, and Ahriman, to which they ostensibly belonged. Within this inverted cult of darkness and the moon, light and the sun reappeared in the form of a flame destroying the darkness. This flame, in turn, was put out by the priests in solemn and still unknown circumstances, probably connected with the positions of the stars, the calendar, the weather, seed time, and harvest. Sun and moon, light and darkness, good and evil alternated with one another. And light was in darkness, evil in good.

Do the Petra manuscripts and the *Book of the Dead* actually mention Alexis's connections with the cult of the moon and the priests of Persia and Babylon? The question has given rise to endless discussion, but the obscurity and ambiguity of the texts themselves have so far prevented any definite answer. At any rate, there is no doubt that Alexis was in Persia and was familiar with the moon worshippers. These facts, like that of his secret life in the tombs of the sun, have only been established in the last twenty years. Before that it was only a matter of legends and conjectures, supported by texts, stone inscriptions, chronicles, and travelers' tales of which the true meaning has emerged only recently.

On the other hand, orientalists have been familiar for three or four hundred years with the figure of a mysterious pilgrim whose historical reality seemed sure enough, but whose origins, role, nationality, and even identity gave rise to many questions. Despite certain inconsistencies, most commentators saw him as a Chinaman who became a traveler for reasons of trade, religion, and curiosity. This nationality was attributed to him because he appeared in chronicles and inscriptions under the name of Ha Li-chien or Ha Lee-chiang. He was mentioned as having been in Isfahan, Samarkand, Bamian, on the banks of the Indus and the Ganges, and even on the way to Nepal and Tibet. His name figures in a Buddhistic reliquary discovered by Tavernier in 1661 and is described by Chardin in 1686 in his *Travels in Persia and the East Indies*. He is mentioned on a trilingual stele erected by a Buddhist ruler on the borders of Afghanistan and what is now Pakistan. His travels and trials are alluded to by Voltaire, Montesquieu, Maxime Du Camp, and Claudel, who was consul in China. Some accepted all the traditions and myths that lent his name a legendary halo; others rejected them all. Believers and unbelievers were equally mistaken.

This Chinese traveler attracted the attention of several scholars, including Armand Bourdaille, by reason of certain surprising physical descriptions, occasional allusions to his blue or green eyes, and especially the strange name he was known by in Isfahan and Samarkand, where he was called the Soul's Traveler or the Fool of God. Now the idea of the Fool of God is neither Buddhist nor Chinese, but obviously belongs, if not to monotheism or one of the other religions in which the term itself is frequently encountered, at least to some mystical or stellar cult. Bourdaille was struck by this, and toward the end of his life examined the whole matter in the light of the supposition that a Chinese or Chinese-sounding name might have been attributed to a traveler who really came from the West, from the regions that, either before or after the time of Alexis and sun worship, were the home first of Judaism, then of Christianity, then of Islam. This working hypothesis turned out to be fruitful, and soon led to a new discovery that rounded off beautifully those of the Petra manuscripts and the *Book of the Dead*. As the reader will have guessed, Ha Li-chien or Ha Lee-chiang, the Chinaman with green eyes, was none other than Alachian or Alechia or, in other words, Alexis.

It was then possible to reconstruct with reasonable probability the spiritual and geographical itinerary of the Teacher of Goodness. Sun worship had brought him into a symmetrical, contrasting relationship with the sects in Babylon and Persia which practiced the cult of the moon. The Middle East constituted what Sir Allan Carter-Bennett has called "a huge melting pot of religions and cultures," and in the midst of it Alexis, anxious for retirement and solitude but inveterately curious and open-minded, and in search also of peace and salvation, entered into contact with Persian sages, Indian mystics, Chinese pilgrims and merchants. He continued his flight toward the East. He went as far as India and joined caravans that, in exchange for spices and silk, brought to the outskirts of the Himalayas arms, objets d'art, and the produce of the vineyards of the Mediterranean. The Persian and Indian chronicles, and travelers in their accounts, accustomed to countless visits from sages and merchants come from a legendary China, and probably doing no more than the Chinese did themselves, bestowed on this other traveler a Chinese name. Experts on India and China take over at this point from Professor Bourdaille and Father Badalwi. They already knew much about the mysterious Ha Lee-chiang. The only thing they did not know was that he was Alexis. For us, who have been able to identify Alechia, Alaouis, Alachian, Ha Li-chien, Ha Lee-chiang, and Alexis as one, the whole life and destiny of the son of Helen and Fabrician the priest takes on new proportions and new meaning.

After the years in Arabia, and the quest for at least a spiritual suicide, our Chinese-dubbed traveler was profoundly affected by two other doctrines, Buddhism and Taoism. We learn from several different sources that a Tibetan traveler, whom he probably met in Isfahan or Bamian, opened the eyes of the so-called Ha Lee-chiang to a world of which he had hitherto known nothing. Within the limits of this historical biography it is impossible to set out even the main features of the metaphysical systems that have influenced all this part of the world for centuries. But we can imagine those evenings in Babylon, Isfahan, or on the banks of the Indus when, for him who had been one of the living dead, the doctrine of a transcendental power ruling the universe according to immutable principles was replaced by the idea of the void, of cosmic multiplicity and ontological unity. Today, for those who know and admire Alechia, Alaouis, or Ha Lee-chiang, it is certain that if Alexis had not become a leader of men he would have played a key role in the development of ideas and the history of religious doctrine. Resplendent proof of this is given by the poems of his which have come down to us and which date from about this period. The traveler from Tibet who had initiated him into the mysteries of Taoism and Buddhism made him relive in imagination the great myths of Asia so well calculated to confound a child of Greece and of the Empire: the four meetings of Sakyamuni or Siddhartha Gautama, later to become the Buddha, with the old man, the sick man, the corpse, and the monk; the birth of Lao-tzu, the Old Master, over whom his mother meditated in her womb for eighty years; the flight of the same into exile and retirement, and how the keeper of the pass to the West said, "Since you are going to live as a hermit, write a book to teach me what you know"—and the master wrote the *Tao Tê Ching*.[5] All these new visions were matter for wonderment and meditation. "Next, after Helen, Philocrates, and Vanessa, who taught him to live and love," writes Sir Allan Carter-Bennett, "Alexis's true teachers are the sages of the East—Buddha, Lao-tzu, and the Master K'ung whom we call Confucius. He did not follow them all the way, but they taught him to think." He was far from being converted by them, but they encouraged him to meditate, to look at the world, and to take in all at once the most ambitious systems, the most farfetched intellectual constructions, and the pitiable heart of man.

Edification, renunciation, profundity, pity, a vision at once deeper and higher of life and of humanity—such were the lessons Alexis learned from his exile in Asia. What a long way he had come from his boyhood expeditions in the distant forests of Balkh! And yet there was a continuity between the lad of those days and the man newly tempered by remorse and hardship. He who had been thoughtless and a dreamer was now indifferent to his own fate, and thirsted after a truth of universal dimensions. He had crushed in himself the love of pleasure and ease. He had kept a restless curiosity and that intoxication with the world that urged him, urged him ever onward and away. He had seen strange men, fabulous countries, curious manners, new religions: yet those years of wandering in Asia, mingled with suffering and remorse, had led him not to skepticism and disintegration, but to a conception of the universe, always to remain fundamental for him, in which diversity ended in unity. What remained in him, after his experiences in the East, of the sun worship to which he had been dedicated? It is difficult, of course, to answer with certainty. We may say that beneath the variety of doctrines and experiences he preserved a need for a unifying principle in which the contradictions of the universe are resolved and reconciled. The remarkable thing is that he resisted mysticism as he had resisted pleasure. Perhaps we should see here, and give credit to, the influence of Philocrates' teaching. Just as Alexis had not, finally, succumbed to sensual pleasure, so he emerged unscathed from the incomparable fascination of spiritual annihilation. Buddhism and Taoism would never make him lose his love of action, personal adventure, physical risk, creative courage—or even violence. Individual psychology is not in great favor these days, but what are these traits in Alexis to be attributed to if not to a specific character, temperament, or personal coefficient reacting to the situations in which it found itself, in which it seemed to be swallowed up, and yet which it surmounted in a way that constitutes, historically speaking, a destiny? There were also, of course, environment, the moment, chance, luck, circumstance. But he dominated and made use of them. He transformed them into fate.

We can now arrive at not too inaccurate a portrait of Alexis after those years of exile, eclipse, withdrawal. He was still handsome. The flame that had burned in the youth who threw himself into pleasure, debauchery, and folly was still there. It might be so well controlled that it seemed extinguished, but it still burned on, deep beneath the scars of remorse and sleepless nights. It was not that he wore a mask or tried to hide anything, but that his very feelings, nerves, and over-lively blood were ruled and mastered by a will whose strength might never be suspected in a body so elegant as to seem frail to a superficial eye. Nothing was left to impulse or caprice. Nor did Alexis, like Basil the Great, for example, fabricate endless plans and long-term plots. Ulterior motives were as foreign to his nature as acting on the spur of the moment. Much has been said of gifts, intuition, a mixture of genius and good fortune—but that tells us little. Perhaps the word "inspiration" is nearer the mark. One of the clues to Alexis is a long patience, comprehensive information, openness to everyone and every-thing, followed by irrevocable decision, with something dazzling as lightning in the execution and the victory. Then he seems really inspired by the gods, and to derive from some other dimension a wisdom and strength that in fact come from power of intellect and the very rare combination of concentration and dream. Some have said that Alexis brought the same qualities to the feasts in Alexandria, the temples of Arabia and Persia, the wars of conquest, and the exercise of power: patience combined with energy, friendship with violence, realism with imagination, soundest intellect with the promptest and even the most brutal action.

Neither the luxury of Alexandria, nor the rigor of the temples, nor the even more formidable doctrines of China and India had succeeded in destroying in Alexis the influence and memory of the great north-ern forests of the Empire. Though he passed whole nights with perverts and prostitutes; though he shared the life of priests and fanatics, submitting mind and body to the most extreme mortifica-tions; though with the sages of China and India, in silence and passion, he plumbed the depths of consciousness and annihilation— he never really forgot what he had learned in the forests of the north: action, the struggle for power, violence, ambition. By an astonishing combination that is the mark of his greatness, he united a respect for life derived from the Buddhists with an awareness of the harsh laws of the forest requiring that man should kill. The child was father to the man.

His eyes were green or blue, but so dark and, above all, so slitted that to anyone expecting to see a rather strange Chinaman that is what he may well have seemed. He had fair hair growing quite low on his brow, but probably dyed black all the time he was in Asia; a nose that was straight and slim and much more Greek than Chinese; strong but slender hands; and broad shoulders. Some have maintained that during some years of his life he suffered from attacks of epilepsy; but this may just be legend, the sources and significance of which have been extensively studied. The same theme recurs in inverted form later on in the life of Alexis, when he was credited with the power to heal certain diseases.[6] But all the reliable evidence concerning the Asian period shows an athletic figure with an iron constitution all the more surprising because it went with elegance and a misleading appearance of slimness and frailty. It was this basic robustness, probably inherited from Helen and the Porphyries, that ensured the survival of the debauchee, the ascetic, and the traveler. Suffering and hardship were rarely absent, from the frontiers of China to the Indus and the Euphrates. A man had to be made of steel to survive. Legend having naturally improved on fact, it is a hard task now to separate history from myth. The popular picture of the Fool of God and the Chinaman with Green Eyes doubtless owes more to Alexandre Dumas, Paul d'Ivoi, and Michel Zévaco than to Armand Bourdaille or Sir Allan Carter-Bennett. Nevertheless, the adventures of Ha Lee-chiang and the story of how he came to be identified with the son of Helen and Fabrician, and perhaps with the Teacher of Goodness, constitute one of the most vivid and lively pages both of past history and of modern historical science. And for the scholar, as for the writer of romantic fiction, Alexis's courage and energy, his whole stature, make him the equal of such real or fabulous heroes as Achilles, Alexander, Charles de Foucauld, and Lawrence of Arabia.

Seven years, or twelve, after the flight from Alexandria, Alexis emerged again into the light of day somewhere between Bamian, Samarkand, and Bukhara. He then proceeded to live a double life, trading in cereals and arms and at the same time surrounding himself with a crowd of young men whom he instructed in ethics, mathematics, poetry, and a mixture of astronomy and astrology. He was said to be skilled both in poisons and in their antidotes, and to be able to charm snakes, predict eclipses of the sun and moon, cure wounds and diseases, tame wild horses, and expound the Holy Books of the Jews, the teachings of Hermenides and Paraclitus, the Rig-Veda, the Upanishads, and the works of Master K'ung. He was himself the author of odes and hymns that ensure him a high position among the poets of his time. Some suspected him of practicing magic or witchcraft, and he was not immune from rivalry, resentment, mistrust, and jealousy. At the age of twenty-eight or twenty-nine, after so much privation and self-imposed suffering, he was still outstanding at wrestling, running, swimming, and every other exercise of strength or skill. It is as if there were different dimensions in him. Behind his elegance, behind what might even be called—despite his sufferings and ordeals—a certain nonchalance, there was power and strength. But, again, behind that strength, there was wisdom and generosity. And deeper still, behind that wisdom, a mystery, an expectation, a secret. Perhaps even a promise. But when, out of the darkness of the tombs and the caravans, Alexis reappeared in Asia, apparently with the intention of settling and spending the rest of his life there, he did not emerge into the dazzle of notoriety and pleasure that had surrounded him in Alexandria. He lived modestly, in retirement, struggling against the obstinate blessing, or curse, which was always winning him new popularity and new groups of admirers, always different, always the same, now attracted by his lavishness, now by his asceticism, now by austerity, now by prodigality, in any case won over by his incredible power to charm and please, persuade and convince. In Bamian, Samarkand, and Isfahan, rumors sprang up whenever he passed. Pilgrims, wandering minstrels, young admirers would recite his poems in the evening in encampment or village square. Did these good people know then what our scholars took centuries to learn, thanks to Armand Bourdaille, an Arab who became a Jesuit, and a shepherd boy from Petra—namely, that Alexis had buried himself under the earth for a sin against love and had traveled the roads of Asia to expiate the murders he had committed? Some say another woman came into his life at this point, a Yemenite,[7] tall and very beautiful, whose name is unknown,[8] as dark as Vanessa was fair. It is alleged that she became, almost despite himself, the exile's second great love, the subject of poems in praise of her form and hair and especially her very lovely arms. The authenticity of some of these poems is still hotly debated. Whether Alexis really wrote the original or not, this inspired rendering of one of them seems to capture something of the anguish and the power in the voice of the Fool of God, Vanessa's murderer.

So
I hold you in my grasp! I clasp your body
In my arms, and you offer no resistance, and I hear your heart
    beat within you!

True, you are but a woman. I am but a man.

And I can bear it no longer, I am like one dying of hunger
  who cannot hold back his tears at the sight of food!

O column, O strength of my beloved! Unjust that I should
  have met you!

What should you be called?—a mother,

So good it is to have you.

A sister, whose plump, womanly arm I hold between my
  fingers.

A prey, the smoke of whose life, breathed in, intoxicates me,
  and I tremble to feel you the weaker, like a quarry that
  shrinks as one holds it by the scruff!

I must away, I can bear no more, and you are in my arms like
  one who draws back,

Like one who sleeps, under the pressure of my hands. Tell me,
  power as of one who sleeps,

If you are her I love.

Too much, I can bear no more, I should not have met you, and
  yet you love me, you are mine, and my poor heart gives
  and breaks.

O, I am not strong! Who has said I am strong? But I was a
  man of desire,

Desperately toward happiness, desperately toward happiness
  yearning, and loving, and deep, and unsealed![9]

Who has said you are happiness? No, you are not happiness!
  You are that which takes the place of happiness!

I trembled when I recognized you; my whole soul crumbled.

I am like one who falls on his face, and I love you, and I say
  that I love you, and I can bear no more,

And I wed you with an impious love and a doomed promise,

Beloved thing which is not happiness.[10]

Is not this dark woman with rounded arms the double and converse
of the fair Vanessa; is not this ardor and fear, this tenderness and
violence, this happiness which is not happiness, the true voice of
Alexis? What matter the facts of history, chronology, documentation: let us leave attributions and sources, stylistics and arguments to
the exegesists and the erudite. For us, these words from the depths of
poetry and time are the words of Alexis—Alexis transformed into
himself for eternity by his passion and remorse. Ordeals over, Isolde

of the White Hands succeeds Isolde the Fair. The years in the wilderness are over at last.

It was in Samarkand or Bukhara that a Greek traveler already middle-aged, who also had seen many years and many sorrows, met one winter evening, in a modest booth, amidst a group of enthusiastic admirers, a poet who kept body and soul together by selling cereals and arms. The almost white-haired traveler was Philocrates, friend and teacher, who embraced with tears in his eyes his long-lost Alexis. He had crossed the world to tell Alexis of the great misfortunes come upon the Empire, once more beset by hatred, unrest, famine, torture, civil war. Once more, blood, fire, suffering; but once more hope. Isidore, his eyes put out, was appealing for help to those not afraid to die. Alexis was not afraid of death; it was what he was waiting for, what he was hoping for. He made Philocrates come over to the great log fire in a corner of the room, and the two men sat and talked about the Empire.

XIII

THE CALL, AND THE
END OF EXILE

ITH THE DEATH OF INGEBURGH AND THAUMAS, Basil and Gandolphus, a whole generation of power and glory disappeared from the scene of history, and the Empire entered again, and for years, into the pangs of decadence. History is never about anything but the folly of men. Peoples and states oscillate between peace and war, freedom and slavery, order and disorder. They tire easily. Even happiness soon grows wearisome. No sooner do they begin to enjoy the benefits of wise and just government than they demand more wisdom and a different kind of justice. Factions spring up. Everyone is on the lookout for new privileges. The equilibrium that was so hard to strike crumbles. Wild hopes are embraced. The system collapses. Everything has to be built up anew on the ruins of the past. But such an oversimplified political Manichaeanism never represents the real state of affairs. Peoples are fickle, but rulers are cruel. There is something intolerable about stability and order, something stimulating in the thrill of disorder. And the dignity of man consists in waiting and hoping and fighting for his hopes. Neglect, exploitation, denial of justice on the part of those in power drives those as yet powerless into revolt. The oppressed rise up, and to the thirst for novelty is added all the force of aspiration and legitimate resentment. Even just governments do not last—and governments are not often just. Perhaps it is impossible they should be—time passes and things change. Attrition and hope form the web of history, moving toward a happiness forever receding.

Basil the Great built his power on wickedness and guile, and provides one of the most perfect examples of political realism. But cleverness, too, can fail. Neither the priests nor the barbarians ever forgave him for the episode of the fox of Amphibolus. The supporters of the Porphyries only paid lip service to the descendant of the Eagle and the Venostae. The edifice he created was kept intact by his iron fist, Thaumas's prudence, Ingeburgh's popularity, and the artfulness of Gandolphus. But with the emperor dead, the empress dead, and the two rival ministers dead, one through the other and one after the other, the whole structure was thrown out of balance, and ferocity fought with discord among the wreckage.

Thaumas's predictions came true—the victory at Amphibolus was only apparent, the peace only a lull, and a tidal wave of barbarians flooded into the Empire, now largely defended by other barbarians. A few years after Basil's death the whole Empire was one vast chaos. Sir Allan Carter-Bennett aptly describes this period as "the Empire's third Middle Age." The first came between the (very dubiously) idyllic origins and the golden age of the City; the second came between the conquests of Arsaphes and Basil's period of power; the third came after Basil, and heralded the glory of Alexis.

The characteristic feature of the anarchy bequeathed by Basil was that there seemed no way out of it. The Venostae and the Porphyries were equally exhausted; the priests had been decimated by Basil; the barbarians were divided among themselves and soon came to be hated by the people. It will be remembered that the absence of a son was one of the reasons why Basil divorced Adelaide. Ingeburgh also gave the emperor nothing but daughters. Finally a son was born to Irene. He was now a poor infant of few years, without any influence, entirely under the control of advisers among whom it was impossible for him to choose, and who quarreled among themselves for power. The Empire was really ruled by a succession of rival sets of barbarians. But even their authority was illusory. Onessa, the City, Amphibolus, Evcharisto, Mezzopotamo, Parapoli, and all the other towns were each ruled over by some petty king or local or regional council that had seized power and had fought against the central government, which in theory still had its seat in Aquileus. The whole northern part of the Empire relapsed into anarchy pure and simple. In theory there were frontiers still in the east and the south, but they were broken through by armed bands that carved out spheres of influence where, as in the dark days between Arsaphes and Basil, they acknowledged no mastery but their own. Groups of twenty or thirty or several hundred, and sometimes even several thousand, families would fight among themselves; and the depleted armies of the emperor dared not venture farther than the edges of the forests and the mountains. Usually they ended by just staying in their cantonments. In the valleys of the Amphyses and the Nephta, on the plains at the foot of the volcanoes, and along the northwest coast, order was maintained after a fashion by detachments of barbarians who ignored one another when they were not fighting and got together only at the expense of the local farmers, shepherds and herdsmen, craftsmen, and fishermen. It was an order of things, a disorder, more heavy and cruel with every year. And there was no hope. Not a gleam anywhere in the darkness that covered the Empire.

The only possibility was to play the barbarians off against one another. It might have succeeded, but it failed. After the murder of Thaumas, the only ones left to combat those troubled times were a handful of isolated priests. They plotted together; they managed here and there to buy the support of a few troops; they tried to establish, now in Onessa, now in Amphibolus, now in some lesser place, a semblance of authority that might bring back law and security to town, country, and highway, and restore peace to people's minds. These miniature *coups d'état* sometimes met with a local success that kindled hearts and hope. But at once the rival groups of barbarians stationed in the other towns would bury their differences and unite against any sign of real power and all attempts to revive anything resembling imperial order. Thus there came fresh massacres and new divisions. All endeavors toward unification and peace ended in war and convulsions. Every man thought only of the immediate interest of his own tribe, his own group, himself. To foment the general disorder was to safeguard one's own privileges. These privileges were illusory and soon were swept away by the violence of fire or sword. But who saw that far? Who thought of the common good? Who thought even of his own, beyond today or tomorrow? The public interest, the common future, political strategy—none of these existed any longer. All that was left were the short-term ambitions of careerists looking for jobs, moneylenders seeking quick profits, and leaders of factions blinded by their own paltry illusions.

Want and famine spread daily farther over town and country. As corn and milk, fish and olives became scarce and more expensive, everyone grew more fiercely determined to seize at all costs what he needed to feed himself and his dependents. To survive soon meant to steal and kill. As well as the troops of the barbarians and the emperor, as well as the militia and the warring tribes, there soon arose bands of brigands and adventurers who reminded the less ignorant of the Empire's bloody beginnings and the fratricidal struggles of the Eagle and the Tiger. Now it was no longer a matter of Eagle and Tiger, but merely of eating. On the coasts the pirates reappeared; in the winter, the wolves. On the frontiers a fresh lot of barbarians from Scythia and Sogdiana, Arachosia and Sarmatia, Hyrcania and Gedrosia gathered in haste to pick up the crumbs of the spoils.

Blood. Fire. Rape. Murder. There was nothing left of the Empire. A few priests and philosophers hid themselves away to preserve the memory of past glories. They no longer aimed at spreading knowledge, wisdom, tolerance, liberty. Their only care was to try to save a few traces of them against some future resurrection. If no one knew how to lay out a garden, build a temple, write an ode, or minister to the gods, who would be able later to bring about the rebirth of culture, civilization, pleasure in living and learning? They cultivated but one flower—hope. They worked only for the children, the grandchildren, the great-grandchildren who perhaps would one day know what a past was and what a future might be.

Disorder and want called forth war with all its evils. There arose here and there a whole series of petty yet horrific tyrants, incapable of great designs but only too capable of murder and intrigue. They killed for nothing—out of madness, spite, revenge, vanity. Astakia in Parapoli, Mardoch in Mezzopotamo, Arrhideus in the north, and Kanishka in the south—nothing survives of them but the memory of injustice, torture, and slaughter, unredeemed by one palace, one statue, one feast, one poem. Abroad, neither Sicily, Pomposa, nor the great-grandsons of the Great Khan of the Oïghurs, who had extended their power from the borders of Scythia to the Alph and the Orontes, let slip the opportunities offered by the breakup of the Empire. Foreign ports on the northwest sea were closed one after the other to ships from the City or Onessa. Caravans avoided Aquileus and Amphibolus—their approaches were too dangerous. Coins of the Empire were refused at Syracuse, Pomposa, Maguelonne, and Xanadu. Looked at askance inside the Empire, the imperial currency was not even legal tender abroad.

Language and culture were not slow to follow the deterioration in maritime activity, the currency, and the trade in luxury goods. Civilization is weak without wealth and power. Greek ebbed far back from the shores where it had been carried by commerce, literature, works of art, and general admiration and esteem. It lost ground even within the Empire, where its place was gradually taken by the dialects of the mercenaries and barbarians. The theaters, the schools of grammar, music, and philosophy, the observatories had all been forced to close down long ago. Weapons were still made, and in large quantities, but of rough quality. Circuses were more popular than ever, but they had become only pretexts for obscenity and riot. The gods were forgotten, the shrines deserted, priests humbled, poets and philosophers mocked and persecuted. The Empire no longer had need of scholars, architects, geometricians, or historians. It no longer needed even sailors and craftsmen. The ships rotted in the ports; the water dried up in canals and reservoirs; houses crumbled away in gardens laid waste; roads and highways were overgrown with weeds. It was as if the gods were taking vengeance on man at last for his scorn and neglect. A new eruption of Mount Kora-Kora not only rekindled memories and legends, but also buried in ashes more than fourteen villages and thousands of men, women, and children. There were earth tremors along the Amphyses, and one winter's night a pack of starving wolves got into Aquileus, past the city walls, past the walls of the temples, and killed twenty-four priests as they slept. Bridges collapsed, statues of the gods broke out in sweat, and on the night of the autumnal equinox two pairs of albino twins were born, one in Evcharisto and one in Parapoli. A month later to the day, there was a three-sided battle halfway between the City and Cape Gildor, in which Scythians, Kirghizes, and Syrians engaged in a relatively small but utterly ruthless struggle that went on late into the night. The combatants were not many, but they practically wiped each other out with unexampled savagery. When the sun rose, three or four thousand corpses were strewn over the plain. All through the winter, internal struggles increased in the Empire. With the approach of spring, Astakia, Mardoch, and Kanishka tried once more to come to terms: they sealed their triple alliance with massacres and proscriptions. Sir Allan Carter-Bennett estimates the number of victims at one hundred fifty thousand at least: it was the worst slaughter since the banquet at Onessa, when Basil exterminated the supporters of the priests.

The priests that now remained no longer had any choice. Since, as before, they would be massacred whatever they did, they might as well fight. They set themselves at the head of a peasant uprising, which had only sticks and cudgels against arrows and spears. Toward the beginning of spring disaster struck again, and on the banks of the Nephta the priests' makeshift army was annihilated by a coalition of barbarians. The Nephta's waters flow red every spring, as we see in Théophile Gautier and Maurice Barrès. According to legend, this phenomenon goes back to that still unforgotten carnage.[1] What with murders, proscriptions, battles, and skirmishes, there was not a family in the Empire that did not mourn someone. But the blood already shed was not enough for the chiefs of the mercenaries and barbarians, who wished to strengthen their shaky authority with terror. All seers, soothsayers, and priests still left alive, their families and servants, all that remained in the Empire of memory or hope, were brought before summary courts for sham trials. Isidore was among the long lines of prisoners in chains waiting for the executioner under an already deadly sun.

It will be recalled that Isidore, who was Philocrates' friend when they were both students in Aquileus, had entered the priesthood.[2] During the time that Philocrates was in Balkh with Fabrician, traveling the roads of Europe and Asia with Alexis, and witnessing in Alexandria the close of the first part of his pupil's fabulous career, Isidore was experiencing from the inside the decline of the Empire, an appalled and helpless witness looking on from Aquileus, where he had lived all his life. After Basil's death he came out of retirement to support, in fiery speeches and in his writings, the priests' resistance to excesses not so much of power as of its absence. After the defeat on the Nephta he felt honor-bound to share the fate of all the rest before the barbarian courts. Sentence was not pronounced for many days. When the verdict was made known, it disposed of everyone in a few minutes, sending between ten and twelve thousand people to their death simultaneously. Those found guilty had their throats cut. One in a hundred escaped to tell in the towns and villages the tale of one of the most savage acts of repression in the history of man. Isidore was one of the one hundred or one hundred fifty the victors spared, whether out of clemency or ferocity, to serve as examples to the terror-stricken people. Even the survivors went through the hands of the executioners, who put out their eyes with long, red-hot needles or white-hot sabres.[3]

Blind, isolated, abandoned, Isidore was as determined as ever to oppose murder and anarchy. He tried to organize the few dozen men who had not been broken down by death, torture, or fear. His martyred body radiated power, the power of unimpaired conviction and fervor. He believed, hoped, and acted through words, and through the flame that still burned within him. In his suffering and darkness he often remembered Philocrates who was far away from the Empire and had escaped the troubles of the times. He sent his old friend via a lively, gay lad of about twelve or fifteen, so brave he was unaware of danger, always full of fun and mockery, the sad news of the Empire's agony, and the cry of anguish of a defenseless people. The boy, Jester, whose twin brother had been killed by the barbarians, managed to cross frontiers and track down Philocrates. When he found him he told him, laughing as was his custom, of the disasters, tortures, and massacres. Then Philocrates himself set out, accompanied by Jester, to scour the roads of Asia and find Alexis. Before the end of the winter, in a house far away in the East, two men and a boy dreamed of their future, and of the fate of an empire. They spoke in low voices. Whether the place was Samarkand or Bukhara, it was very cold outside.[4] Every so often they would throw a great log on the fire.

In a few hours Alexis had made his decision. It was the third time he had set forth: first from the forest, then from Alexandria, now from deepest Asia—and each time, suddenly, so many memories wiped out! He was able from one moment to the next to break all the links that bound him. Here, again, we see the staggering swiftness of choice and power to drop everything that were characteristic of him. But this was not due to insensitiveness or indifference. We have already referred to the disputed poem called "To the Yemenite," and to the apocryphal one on the blinding of Isidore. Now here is a poem from the East that we know to be by Alexis himself, which tells how he wrenched himself away from the past, and of the journey through Persia on the way back to the Empire. It is known under the various titles, "Exile," "Poem by Alexis," and "Persian Poem." It opens with the famous line:

Not for aye shall we dwell in beloved gold lands. . . .

It goes on to marvel at the poet's adventures, all he has lived through and learned, for there are

many things on earth to see and to hear.

It refers sadly to the work of literary creation (apparently called "Rain") that has had to be sacrificed to the exigencies of history:

The coolness running along the crest of language, the foam
still on the lips of the poem,

And man, pressed on all sides by new ideas, yields to the
surge, the great swell of the mind . . .
. . . O Rain, my poem that will never be written!

but it already foresees the fate of the warrior and statesman destined,
among dangers and triumphs, to have

> authority over all the insignia on earth.

As Sir Allan Carter-Bennett points out, Alexis here already presents himself as the heir not only of the Porphyries, but also of the
priests and of the Venostae, whose symbol he invokes much as a
Christian might invoke the Cross, a Moslem the Crescent, or a
Russian Marxist the hammer and sickle:

> Since yesterday two eagles hold the City in thrall.

He appeals at once to war and to the images of peace:

The City made bright with the flash of a thousand swords, the
sacred flight o'er the altars, the sky once more reflected in
the bowls of fountains.

He questions the future, with an allusion to his knowledge of many
different religions:

> Gods near and many, of what iron rose will you make our
> tomorrow?

And he turns once more to the present, and to the coming downfall of
the barbarians and mercenaries

Whose masters made off one night at a whiff of the graveyard![5]

Those were the last lines written in exile. The "Persian Poem" is
both a greeting to power, history, and the Empire, and a farewell to
distant Asia. Its author is midway between past and future, still half
poet and already half leader of men. Now, with Philocrates and
Jester, he set out for the burning Empire and for new adventures.
"The saint was dead," writes Sir Allan Carter-Bennett, "and there
could already be detected the hero, who was also, in due course, to
die."

Two men and a boy on horseback rode through steppes, deserts,
palm groves, rivers, mountains, and valleys. It took them weeks—
perhaps two or three months, according to Robert Weill-Pichon's
calculations—to reach the frontiers of the Empire. The sun was

already hot when they came to places where the light and the vegetation, the shape of the fields, the outline of hills and dells, the horizon, and the color of the sky were at last familiar. It was about twenty years since Alexis had left the northern forests of the Empire. Deep down, he did not feel that he belonged to the Empire. He came from the marches and had the attitude characteristic of the border dweller or assimilated foreigner, whose liking and admiration for the dominating civilization is all the more keen, and sometimes all the more conscientious, because he does not quite belong to it.[6] Nonetheless, even if he was half a foreigner, since being torn from the forest he had lived in still more distant countries, with strange dialects and weird customs, surrounded by men and women different from himself in blood and race. And as he crossed the dried-up river that in theory marked one of the limits of the Empire, Alexis's heart leaped within him as it had not done since his rides through the northeastern forests, since his initiation, and his passion for Vanessa. He stood still for a moment, looking around at the wild and arid hills stretching as far as the eye could see beneath a clear, almost cloudless sky. He stretched out his arms as if to measure the horizon and take immediate possession of all he surveyed. Then he knelt, scooped up in his hands the already sun-scorched soil of the Empire, mingled with sand and stones, and kissed it.

XIV

THE CONQUEST OF POWER

HE RIDE OF THE TWO MEN AND THE LAUGHING BOY across hostile territories, beckoned by the shades of the future, is one of the most fabulous adventures of all time. They were alone, strangers; before long, hunted. They had no help, no resources, no plan. They went at a venture, on the plea of a blind man, directed to him by fate, or history, or unconscious wisdom, or the gods.

Philocrates' and Alexis's first object was to find Isidore, and this they did without too much difficulty. The blind priest had taken refuge in a village at the foot of the mountains southwest of Aquileus, where there gathered secretly, after dark, those few, only a handful in all, who still nourished the hope of a rebellion. Now and then, disguised as beggars or peddlers, a priest who had survived the massacre, a former army captain, a poet or a philosopher, the owner of a fleet of ships or a herd of buffalo, a shepherd or a woodcutter would come to discuss wild projects with Isidore. Plans for killing Mardoch or Kanishka, for rallying an army of young men, for kidnaping the puppet emperor, for making an alliance with the new barbarians gathering impatiently on the borders, for appealing to Sicily or Pomposa or the descendants of the Great Khan—vague, fervent plans sketched out at night in the light of a meager flame, around a drop of rye brandy, only to disappear with the coming of morning. In all this fear and fatigue, one can imagine what a comfort Alexis's coming must have been. Hope suddenly sprang to life again. After so many years of wandering and exile, Helen's son had almost forgotten his imperial origins. But the others remembered for him, and greeted in Alexis the descendant of the Porphyries.

A Porphyry! We should try to imagine what the magic name of

the founders of the City must have meant at that time and in that place. The City was now no more than a memory, but it was the greatest and most noble memory the Empire possessed. Basil had built up imperial power, but only on treachery and guile. The order he embodied might be looked back on with regret in this new age of desolation, but in its time it had been oppressive and cruel, and the people had hated it. In a way it was the source of all the present troubles. Basil was a Venosta. Alexis was a Porphyry. The Porphyries had been feeble, extravagant, subject to foreign influence; but centuries had gone by, and what survived was the dazzling image of the City's greatness and prosperity. A Porphyry! The shade of Arsaphes and his victories already began to rise up before the vanquished.

Alexis was a Porphyry only on his mother's side. If not from his putative father, at least from the northern forests where he spent his childhood he derived the violence and the love of conquest that had been so absent from the pure race of the Porphyries. Arsaphes himself, who stood for the Porphyries in people's memories, had only belonged by marriage to that illustrious but ineffective line. Alexis, like Arsaphes, was connected through feminine links to the race of the Tiger—one more omen of good fortune and victory. In their present woes, the survivors of the defeat on the Nephta had nothing else to pin their hopes on but signs and portents.

The truth about Alexis's birth was a secret to everyone except Helen, Philocrates, probably Simeon, and perhaps a few others. It has been much debated whether even Alexis at this time regarded himself as the son of Fabrician the priest. But it seems rather unlikely that neither Philocrates nor Helen—or perhaps Simeon—should ever have spoken to him about it. Is not the answer to this question to be found in the conversation between mother and son that night, followed by the son's exile far from the forest? What is certain—and it shows Alexis's political maturity regardless of any preoccupation with his personal origins—is that he at once began to think and act less as a descendant of the Porphyries than as the unifier of the Empire. Sir Allan has expressed it well: "From the outset of his political career, Alexis is not so much the heir of the Tiger as the hero of the Empire. The banquet at Onessa is not so much avenged as forgotten. Alexis, flanked by Isidore and Philocrates, is nothing other than the Porphyries and Thaumas put together, the reconciliation in common misfortune of Onessa and the City, of the Eagle and the Tiger." From the depths of suffering, and from the wild hopes of Isidore, was first born the idea of an Empire that would be for the good of all.

The meetings, plans, and moves that then followed are known to history as "Isidore's Conspiracy." Isidore was its soul, Philocrates its counselor. Alexis was soon to become, if not the leader, the linchpin. He brought to the plot the calm, the inner force—yet also, in a sense, the humanity—the patience, ardor, imagination, and power of decision of which we have already seen such striking proofs, both in pleasure and in adversity. The plot was organized with absolute deliberation, as if there were no shortage of time or of money—and, it must be admitted, as if human life were of no account. Many writers have stressed the number not only of enemies slain, but also of voluntary victims, abandoned hostages, and innocent people caught up in the mesh of war and reprisal. One has to bear in mind the origins of the Empire and all the dead of recent years, and relate the sacrifice to all that was at stake. With the coming of Isidore and Alexis, blood continued to be shed. But now the blood was different—it was transfigured with hope.

Isidore's plan was to build up somehow a well-ordered secret force to fight disorder and oppression. Philocrates and Alexis adopted the main outline of this plan, but made it more flexible and practical. The whole conspiracy was based on cells ignorant of one another's existence that received their orders secretly, recruited independently, and developed like ever-spreading tentacles, so that before long it would become very hard for the enemy to destroy the whole system at a blow. Men might be knocked out here and there, but the system as a whole would be unaffected. Watertight compartments, secret messengers, missing links—even, where necessary, suicides or summary executions—made it impossible to trace anything back to its source. And at the source they were building up a small but powerful fighting force, which was to be responsible for the decisive action, and which would be supported, when the time came, by a whole network of partisans, pawns stationed to come to their support all over the chessboard. Philocrates believed the conspirators should be all over the Empire, in town, country, ports, and taverns, "like fish in the water."[1] Philocrates' special responsibility was organizing post horses and seeking out allies. Alexis reserved for himself the command of a group of young men, selected individually, which he called the Cohort of Death. At first they numbered twenty or so, then fifty, then one hundred and fifty, then three hundred. As we shall see, the total soon rose to five hundred, and remained at that figure for some time. But in the end it reached two thousand, and it was these two thousand who were to win the Empire, against an army who outnumbered them by a hundred to one. After the victory they formed the guard known as the Twelve Thousand, the elite and ultimate standby of the imperial army.

Henceforward Alexis is a historical character. Whereas before the problem has been to find documentation on his love affair with Vanessa and his secret life in Asia, from this point on the historian is overwhelmed with source material. But by one of history's paradoxes, Alexis's mounting fame is at first hidden. He was just one fighter among many, and he did his best to remain anonymous. As Robert Weill-Pichon puts it, "he enters clandestinely into glory." At first, it was a group of five or six people at most who knew his name. But despite his efforts his fame spread soon and rapidly. Then, in a characteristic gesture, Alexis reversed his attitude completely: instead of hiding his name, he proclaimed it and used it as a weapon. Alexis; Prince Porphyry; the Soldier of the Empire; the Beloved Bandit— these names were so many standards fluttering in the wind of revolt, spreading from one end of the Empire to the other the name of a mysterious, ubiquitous, legendary hero. People started to say he had been seen the same day at Mezzopotamo and Parapoli, at Onessa and Aquileus, that he flew through the air seeking out his enemies, and had made a pact with the eagles for them to carry him across the Empire. It is not impossible that two or three doubles, discovered by Philocrates, began to play, in widely separated areas, the part of the liberator.[2] According to a theory favored especially by English and Italian historians, the real Alexis was killed in the course of the struggle, and it is the memory of one of his doubles that we honor. It makes one think of the famous joke, "Shakespeare was not really Shakespeare but someone else who called himself Shakespeare." There is no need to invent such an imaginary Alexis. If an unknown did take over from Alexis at some point, he had the same kind of genius as Alexis, in fact the very same—a very improbable hypothesis. In all events, alone or with the help of his doubles, Alexis inspired enough passion and enthusiasm for Mardoch and Kanishka to put a price on his head. Twice he was taken prisoner, and twice set free by his own partisans. He had a few minor successes and several defeats. But the situation was now such that even setbacks usually turned to his advantage. His popularity grew, and his reputation spread. When luck is against you, everything fails—even success. When luck is with you, everything succeeds.

After his task of organizing the struggle, but connected with it, Alexis had two immediate preoccupations: to see his mother again, and to visit Arsaphes's tomb. His affection for his mother is sufficient explanation of his eagerness to find her. Helen, too, had been swept away in the upheaval of the Empire's decline. But it should also be made clear that both Alexis's desires here had also a political significance. Helen and Arsaphes both represented, for Alexis himself and especially for the people, his connection with the Porphyries. He wanted to affirm and exploit this connection.

The reader may recall the legend that grew up around Arsaphes's tomb: the conqueror's body was supposed to be put there by eagles and to come to life again in times of trouble.[3] The prophecies were not fulfilled to the letter. Seven times seventy-seven years had not yet gone by since Arsaphes's mysterious death. But the tradition, ceaselessly repeated, distorted, and modified, left plenty of room for different interpretations, and Alexis soon saw the use to be made of popular legend reinforced by the desire to believe and the need to hope. A vague suggestion that Alexis and Arsaphes were one and the same, a widespread rumor that the Bactrian captain had appeared in a new incarnation, whispers that swelled and traveled like lightning from one end of the Empire to the other—all this could only help a plan that depended at once on secrecy and rumor, mystery and revelation. Alexis or a new Arsaphes—the conspirators had no objection to such an identification. Alexis's link was with Arsaphes much more than with Basil. Or if with Basil, too, it was, as we have seen, in his repeatedly expressed desire to reconcile the Eagle and the Tiger, with the Basil of Thaumas rather than the Basil of Gandolphus. In any case, Arsaphes remained the legendary hero whose memory still lived in the imagination of the people of the Empire.

The pilgrimage to Arsaphes's tomb—a still empty tomb, it will be remembered—was an acute example of the sort of problem facing Alexis at the beginning. He had to act both in secret and in the broad light of day—in secret, because any open action would have been nipped in the bud by the barbarian armies; in the broad light of day, because the main object was to strike the popular imagination. It was not easy to combine the two, but Alexis succeeded. Over several days, small groups of his supporters trickled into the somnolent town of

Aquileus disguised as pilgrims or invalids, sellers of oil or rye brandy. They took up their positions at crossroads, in the streets of the town, in the open courtyards of taverns and gaming houses. They drank, gambled, slept, waited. A few hours before Alexis's arrival rumors began to circulate. It was whispered that the gods had taken pity on the Empire, that something was going to happen, that the fall of the tyrants was at hand. All eyes were turned upward hoping for thunderbolts or a chariot of fire. There was nothing in the sky but a blazing sun. Suddenly three eagles—released, no doubt, by Alexis's supporters—flew slowly over the city. At the same moment, with a stir felt simultaneously in all the streets, squares, and markets and along the sacred way that led to the temples, Alexis, preceded by trumpeters and standard-bearer, appeared. A few moments and he was before the steps of the great temple, then, while the priests looked on in stupefaction, entering it to the acclamations of the crowd. He withdrew, quite alone, to Arsaphes's tomb, and his meditation before the cenotaph in Aquileus, which later inspired a famous scene in Hugo's *Hernani*, soon became one of the main themes of historical mythology in all the then known world. When he reappeared in public he was no longer just Alexis and the descendant of the Porphyries, but Arsaphes himself, brought back from the dead for the salvation of the Empire. The incident created an enormous stir—Arsaphes had risen from the dead, and Isidore and Philocrates exploited the effect with extraordinary skill. A dozen messengers were dispatched to the four corners of the Empire to spread the marvelous news and the idea of the rebirth of the Empire. Of the twelve, more than half perished, crucified, tortured, or decapitated by the mercenaries. But in all the peoples of the Empire hope was suddenly reborn. Arsaphes had risen from the dead![4]

Several documents inform us that the Cohort of Death had for some time consisted of five hundred thirty-nine men divided into seven battalions. Historians have pondered a good deal over this curious figure, which corresponds neither to the sacred traditions nor to the military usage of the age and of the Empire as we know them. Robert Weill-Pichon, following the researches of Sir Allan Carter-Bennett, seems finally to have discovered the key to the enigma. Five hundred thirty-nine divided by seven is seventy-seven. So seven times seventy-seven was both the number of men in the Cohort in its finest hour, and the number of years that legend said were to elapse before the resurrection of Arsaphes. The prophecy did not come true in every detail, but this was a sort of magical homage made to it to win over fate, victory, and the gods.

The tyrants, mercenaries, and barbarians did not take long to learn that an enemy worthy of them had come into being, and a fight to the death began between them and Alexis. The alliance between Kanishka and Mardoch was strengthened, and Astakia was also brought into it. A manhunt was set on foot all over the Empire. Alexis, not content just to elude it with insolent ease, provoked his enemies and covered them with ridicule and humiliation. It was as if their efforts only amused him, and he turned to his own advantage their ineffectual power. And through the enemy detachments, despite danger and spies, he went to see his mother.

The meeting between Helen and her outlawed son was a scene full of emotion and color. Historians never tire of giving more or less fanciful accounts of it, poets have sung it, painters have recreated it in justly famous pictures.[5] The most famous representation of all is without a doubt the beautiful fresco by Piero della Francesca in the great hall of the municipal palace at Ascoli Piceno in central Italy. It shows Helen, in a flowing blue robe, opening her arms to raise up her son who has prostrated himself at her feet.[6] The fresco by Il Sodoma in the Farnesina in Rome[7] illustrates the same event in a very different style. The scene was destined to become one of the main subjects of Western art, and countless other works have created around it a wonderful frieze of colors and forms. But let us try first to discover, beneath the embroidery of legend, the perhaps more modest but still astonishing truth of the historical events, and then to describe briefly some of their most brilliant illustrations by pen or brush.

Helen had been separated from Alexis for some twenty years. She had had news of him, chiefly through Philocrates, until the time of his flight from Alexandria. After that there had been silence, and she like everyone else may have, probably must have, thought he was dead. But something inside her constantly clung, in spite of the evidence, to the hope that the child whose birth and whole existence had cost her so many tears would return. She never left the forests of the northeast. She lived there alone, abandoned by Simeon as well as by Alexis. She kept up a fairly regular correspondence with Philocrates and Isidore—she felt an affectionate friendship for both, mingled in the case of Philocrates with amused astonishment at his resourcefulness, and in the case of Isidore with admiration and respect. For Alexis, far away and probably lost to her forever, she always felt the passionate tenderness that began in Balkh, in the days and nights whose horror and delight were graven eternally in her flesh and in her heart. Absence could not alter this feeling, obstinate though silent. Simeon was enraged by it, and it was one more factor that drove the son of Roderick and Helen, dedicated to duplicity and perhaps to treason, into the camp of such as Mardoch and Arrhideus. Sir Allan Carter-Bennett remarks, perhaps not entirely without bias, that "Ambiguity and guile lay all with the legitimate son, fidelity and rectitude all with the bastard." The rumors circulating through the Empire had not failed to reach Helen's ears, but she had given them little attention and no credence. Justus Dion relates that she was one of those who believed in the existence of the doubles—to be precise, she believed that the doubles existed, but not their model. She thought they had usurped Alexis's name, reputation, and physical appearance, but that Alexis himself, far away and perhaps dead, had nothing to do with the activities rumor traced back to him. She who had never been able to bring herself to admit her son was dead began to doubt at the very moment when the repercussions of his return were rousing all the Empire. She felt a distant and slightly jealous sympathy for the doubles, whom she called "my children" or "my twins," but the mother's heart did not recognize the son in the already legendary adventures dinned into her ears by eager chambermaids and squires whose eyes shone with curiosity and excitement.

Justus Dion's account of the meeting between Helen and Alexis has been the point of departure for all the historians of the Empire, and still retains its freshness and naïve charm. It tells of how Helen was taking her usual evening walk in the forest, by a pool where she used to feed a pair of swans and their brood. She was accompanied by a few faithful retainers who had never left her. The sun was setting, and the little party was about to return, when the sound of galloping hoofs was heard in the distance. It was two horsemen; they were just visible through the leaves and branches. They rode up, halted, and the younger of the two—who in Piero della Francesca's fresco wears a blue page's costume and the famous little cap of yellow silk that so fascinated Proust and the thought of which haunted the dying Bergotte—approached Helen and knelt before her. He was a young lad with rosy cheeks and a laughing air—the faithful Jester.

In this world of culture and history with all its parallels between events and words, forms and colors, fiction and reality, the famous passage on the death of Bergotte in *À la Recherche du temps perdu* is so closely linked to the artistic heritage of Alexis and Helen and to Piero della Francesca's picture of their meeting in the northern forest that the reader who has been the witness of their vicissitudes will no doubt want to refer to it. Here, for his convenience, are the relevant lines from toward the end of the first half of Proust's *La Prisonnière*:

" . . . one of the critics having written somewhere that in Piero della Francesca's *Meeting Between Helen and Alexis*, a fresco that he adored and imagined that he knew by heart, a little cap of yellow silk (which he could not remember) was so well painted that it was, if one looked at it by itself, like some priceless specimen of Chinese art, of a beauty that was sufficient in itself, Bergotte set out for Ascoli Piceno and went to the municipal palace. At the first few steps that he had to climb he was overcome by giddiness. He passed in front of several pictures and was struck by the stiffness and futility of so artificial a school, nothing of which equaled the fresh air and sunshine of a Venetian palazzo, or of an ordinary house by the sea. At last he came to the Piero della Francesca which he remembered as more striking, more different from anything else he knew, but in which, thanks to the critic's article, he remarked for the first time Alexis's little page in blue, that the ground was pink, and finally the precious substance of the little cap of yellow silk. 'That is how I ought to have written,' he said. 'My last books are too dry, I ought to have gone over them with several coats of paint, made my language exquisite in itself, like this little cap of yellow silk.' Meanwhile he was not unconscious of the gravity of his condition. In a celestial balance there appeared to him, upon one of its scales, his own life, while the other contained the little cap of silk so beautifully painted in yellow. . . . He repeated to himself: 'Little cap of yellow silk with a blue suit, little cap of yellow silk.' While doing so he sank down upon a circular divan. He was dead."[8]

In the Piero della Francesca fresco the page in the blue suit with the little cap of yellow silk is a tiny figure at Helen's feet. Behind him rises the tall figure of Alexis, dressed as a Renaissance gentleman with a red cape over his shoulders. He has seen Helen and is restraining himself from throwing himself into her arms. Helen has not yet recognized him, but something in her look, her gesture, her whole attitude heralds her stifled cry and the spring she is about to make to her son's side. In the Il Sodoma fresco all is more suggestive, flexible, and passionate. It presents the scene in the form of a hymn to beauty, but just as plainly as the della Francesca it is based on the account in

Justus Dion. All three works, the two frescoes and the chronicle, express with the infinitely varied resources of talent and genius the faithfulness of memory, the keenness of surprise, at the very moment when sorrow and doubt are about to be swept away by the almost painful explosion of joy. "She had raised her eyes," writes Justus Dion, "to the lad who approached her. She lowered them now before the man, just sprung breathless from his horse, yet noble in mien and movement, who came up behind the boy. For a few seconds all stood motionless, Helen, the maids of honor, the squires, the knight, and his young companion, as if transfixed by surprise and the solemnity of the moment. Then there was a movement among the women, and Helen made a faint gesture as if about to retire. Then she looked up and saw him—disheveled, running with sweat, hardly able to stand, wild-eyed, and stretching his hands out toward her. Which of them cried out first? The horseman had already thrown himself at Helen's feet and embraced her knees. And Helen raised him up, took him in her arms like a child, stroked his face with trembling hands, and covered it with kisses and tears.

"The mother said in a low voice, 'My son, my son . . .'

"And the son said, 'Mother!' and kissed her hands."[9]

The meeting between Helen and Alexis was a turning point in the conquest of power. Helen had retained considerable influence over the warrior tribes of the northeast, though since the hope of finding her son had begun to wane she had ceased to exercise it. With Alexis's return, Helen immediately recovered her old energy and authority. She kept Jester with her, and in two or three months the two of them, the already elderly woman and the boy, had mustered a troop of soldiers from the backwoods, ardent for battle and blindly devoted to the cause of Helen and her son. Alexis now had what the rebellion and renaissance had hitherto lacked—a large body of troops trained and ready to fight. Already things were beginning to put on a different aspect, and the balance of forces was changing.

It will be remembered that the entire northern part of the Empire was more or less under the domination of a barbarian chief called Arrhideus. Repulsive-looking, fierce, always mounted on a little Barbary horse from which he was said to dismount only to sleep and make love, but not to eat or drink, Arrhideus was left out in the cold by the triple alliance concluded farther south by Kanishka, Mardoch, and Astakia. On his own, faced with the hostility not only of the tribes and the people, but also, most of the time, of rival barbarians,

Arrhideus had never managed to impose his rule and authority all over the north. Anarchy was the only undivided power there. Arrhideus did not bother. He would wipe out two or three villages from time to time to make everyone afraid of him, and apart from that was content with amassing gold and indulging in pleasures not of the most refined. After Alexis had gone south again to organize the revolt in Aquileus and the valley of the Amphyses, a struggle soon broke out in the north between Arrhideus and Helen. As soon as the news got about that Helen was going to take up the fight again, warriors and tribes flocked to her cause. Arrhideus was soon isolated, though he did not fully realize the precariousness of his position. Helen avoided a confrontation as long as she could. She extended her influence, continued to cut off her opponent, secured support even in the barbarian's personal bodyguard, improved her army's weaponry and supplies, and strengthened her communications with the rest of the Empire. Jester served as a link between mother and son. He was always on the road, over hill and dale, whistling and laughing and, with incredible gaiety, risking his life. Through all one spring and summer Jester traveled through the Empire like this, on foot or on horseback, a comical cap on his head to protect him from the sun, a song on his lips, and his head full of the names of villages and officers, figures, calculations, and messages. In the end he became famous throughout the Empire, which did not make his task any easier. Barbarians and mercenaries pursued him as fiercely as they did Alexis and Helen; there was a price on his head, too. His example, well calculated to inflame the enthusiasm of the young, caused first dozens, then hundreds of boys and girls to arise literally from nowhere, eager to give Helen and Alexis the help of their ardor and inexperience, and often even of their lives. It is on Germany and the Anglo-Saxon countries even more than on Italy and France that the laughing epic of Jester has left the deepest impression. He is the origin of countless tales and legends, from the young rogues of folklore beyond the Rhine and the heroes of Germanic *Wanderlust*, wandering across hills and forests with bundle or haversack on their shoulders, and on Midsummer Night faithfully celebrating the memory of Jester, easily recognized under various borrowed names—from these on the one hand to, on the other, the girls, the boys, and youths in Defoe, Schnabel, Johann Rudolf Wyss, the brothers Grimm, Hans Andersen, Dickens, Lewis Carroll, Selma Lägerlof, Robert Louis Stevenson, James Fenimore Cooper, and Kipling, all of whom are in some way or another in direct descent from Jester, imitating his exploits and deriving much of their reputation and success from him. Till Eulenspiegel is obviously one of Jester's avatars. In France, Fénelon's *Adventures of a Child of the Empire*, the Abbé Barthélemy's *Journey of the Young Jester*, Rousseau, Mme. de Genlis, Hector Malot, the Comtesse de Ségur, and Zénaïde Fleuriot all set him before the children of their time as an example. And everyone knows the fictional but famous representations of him left by Murillo (an inspired picture in the Prado in Madrid) and Luca della Robbia (the famous terracottas on the façade of the Spedale degli Innocenti (Foundlings' Hospital) in Pistoia, a stone's throw from the cathedral square.

But alas, the story was to end in blood. One autumn day on a bend of the Amphyses near Kora-Kora, Jester was suddenly surrounded by a detachment of Astakia's men. He went on laughing, defying, and making fun of them. They asked him for names, where he came from, whom he was going to see, if he had come across any of Alexis's supporters. His only answer was clowning; he threw his cap at their captain's head. He was hit in the side by a pike, and died gaily. The blood that poured from his mouth stifled his singing at last. Victor Hugo must have remembered Jester when he wrote *Les Misérables*. While the character of Enjolras is a portrait of Saint-Just, the death of Gavroche the Paris urchin is obviously inspired by that of Jester.[10] But the most extraordinary thing in the factual history of the Empire was that Jester lived on after his death. Alexis was genius enough to realize what the loss of Jester meant to his cause. So among the troop of children who had offered themselves to him he chose the bravest and gayest and named him Jester. This second Jester was to be killed in his turn, as was a third and a fourth. But in Alexis's shadow, innumerable new Jesters indefatigably arose. After the coming of victory and peace, we never find the Emperor without a boy called Jester at his side. His function is to amuse and provoke laughter, and he is permitted, and pardoned in advance for, any folly. This, as has been definitively established by the works of Robert Weill-Pichon and of the American ethnologist A. W. Grock, is the historical origin of the king's fool.[11] Hugo, in his old age, would have been surprised to learn that his Gavroche in *Les Misérables*, his Triboulet in *Le Roi s'amuse*, and Verdi's Rigoletto, were all one and the same character at different ages, all equally entitled to be called the heirs of Jester.

Meanwhile the struggle had broken out with great ferocity. While in the north Helen raised the forest tribes, in the south Isidore, Philocrates, and Alexis re-formed the instrument of the Empire's liberation and rebirth around the memory of the priests, the Porphyries, Arsaphes, Basil, and Thaumas. The nature and forms of this resurrection have caused much ink to flow. According to some it was a genuine national war before its time, while others see it as a popular revolt. Some believe it involved real pitched battles, though in that case they would have left less trace materially and in memory than the more ancient battles of Cape Gildor or Amphibolus, or even than obscure but almost contemporary massacres by such men as Astakia and Mardoch between the City and Gildor or on the banks of the Nephta. Others again, with apparently better reason, stress the subterranean methods of the conspiracy, and the gaining of imperial power from within.

But whether it was a real war or a popular revolt, the speed of operations was surprising. Less than two and a half years after Alexis's return, authority and peace were restored in the Empire. Compared to the long years of the flight into Asia and in the wilderness, these few months that changed the history of the world seem strangely short. Let us try to recount and to explain briefly the course of events.

Those who explain these events by secret action and those who maintain there was a violent confrontation all agree on one point: the operation set in motion by the conspirators is one of the most remarkable examples of a successful plot in the history of the world. Of course, we must be on our guard here against anachronism. Is there really any need to insist on the gulf that separates the Empire at that period from the tyrants who have organized modern states as we know them today? Not only demographically but also as regards communications, social and economic structure, and, above all, customs and ways of thinking, everything is completely different. There can be no question of comparison, or of drawing facile parallels and so-called lessons from the past. Yet perhaps some philosophers and historians have gone too far in the admittedly sound direction of specificity, differentiation, and the treatment of every historical epoch and outlook as separate. The Industrial Revolution and the evolution of religion since Alexis's day make his age and ambitions strange to us, romantic, almost fantastic. And yet his time and ours do have something in common. When he was alive there were already cities, men of ambition, mystics, the dangers of war, the longing for peace. Historians, too. Did the world really change so much between Alexis and the coming of the machine? Agriculture was already invented then; urban civilization, with all its allurements and all its tragedies, already born; the idea of empire already strong. There is not such a very enormous distance between Alexis and the Medicis or Peter the Great. As we have seen, it took Byron and Chateaubriand almost as long to get from Onessa to the City or Aquileus as it did Jester or Philocrates. We are scarcely emerging from an age in which Alexis was still our contemporary and resembled us like a brother. Probably the real cleavages come, on the one hand, in those far-off times when towns, writing, and agriculture came into being, and, on the other, in the present or the near future, when the intellectual and technological revolution ushers in a new world. Between these two extremes lies the age of the horse, the town, religious hierarchies, empires. Alexis's contemporaries are Hammurabi, Ramses II, Alexander, Asoka, Caesar, Julian the Apostate, Theodoric, Justinian, Charlemagne, Genghis Khan, Saladin, Julius II, Mohammed II, Lorenzo the Magnificent, Charles XII, and Napoleon. Yet we manage to understand all of them, despite the strangeness and the distance in time. To go further, there is something over and above the city and agriculture, the factory and the machine, which serves as a link between men, their hopes, and their passions. It is no longer the horse, nor the idea of empire, nor perhaps—perhaps—political ambition or religion. But there is always the love of laughter, the fear of suffering, the need to love, to have friends, or to keep up with the Joneses. Alexis, Tamerlane, Lawrence of Arabia—they are all the same man. Before Menes, Sargon, and Abraham, after Stalin or Henry Ford or Einstein, perhaps men were not and will not be the same as Alexis. But they were and will be men, men who fight and love. Already they give orders, still they make love, and on spring nights, after the struggle and often after injustice, they forever look up at new stars, as Alexis did in the forest at Balkh or from the depths of the temples in which he was buried.

It is this kinship between all men who belong to the age of empires and religions—and perhaps those before and after, too—that enabled a writer like Malaparte to draw on the experiences of Alexis, Lenin, and Mussolini in his famous study of *The Technique of The Coup d'État*. Obviously Alexis could not occupy power stations or telecommunications centers, but the art of manipulating men, of appealing to the passions, of maintaining a balance between promises and threats, all these remain more or less unchanged. What is striking in Alexis is the dual appeal to the past and the future. He handles it in a masterly fashion, and behind the eloquent voice of the conqueror one seems to detect the convincing, and no doubt convinced, murmur of his master Philocrates. How good life used to be under the Porphyries, in the great days of the City! How dark it was now, under injustice and oppression! How good it will become again soon in the new age of gold! It was with a chorus of "Long live Alexis! Long live the future!" that the poor peasants flocked behind the son of Helen, descendant of the Porphyries, heir of Arsaphes, and restorer of the Empire.

The poor peasants. Until his dying breath, they were to remain the closest to Alexis's heart. He knew them well. In the forests of the northeast, it was woodcutters, foresters, hunters of wolves and hares, small farmers, who had peopled a childhood far from the pomp and circumstance of the City's and the Porphyries' ruined palaces. Throughout his exile and the years spent out of the world, he had lived among the underprivileged, the wretched, the victims, the forgotten. It was they who had brought food to him on his column and, in the darkness of the tomb, they who had welcomed him on his return to the Empire. He had learned to love them, and seen the future that lay in them as against the mercenaries and praetorians. When, after so many years, the shade of Arsaphes began galloping once more across the plain, both past and future were embodied, for the poor peasants, in Alexis's silhouette against the horizon. It was a fabulous vision, and was to stay alive in the collective memory. In our own day, the poor peasants' revolt has inspired Abel Gance's *Alexis*, the first film to use a triple screen, and Eisenstein's masterpiece, *Thunder Over the Empire*. It gave André Malraux his first idea about the epic of history, always interrupted and always renewed, the dream of which he has pursued all his life under the lofty name of the "lyric illusion." It has been said that Alexis at the head of the poor peasants was invoked by the sailors at Kronstadt and the Black Sea mutineers. And Alexis was the only model Emiliano Zapata recognized for the Mexican revolution. Armed only with their ordinary tools, their poverty, and their wild hopes, the poor peasants thronged behind Alexis on his black horse. He spoke to them now from the top of a hill, now from a rampart, now from a palace window, now from the steps of a temple. He told them a tale of patience, unwearying hope, chains that would be struck off, a future of sunshine and happiness. They acclaimed him, followed him, were ready to die. Their endless winding columns covered the Empire, strung out over the fields and the hills. On they marched, through winter snow and the crushing heat of summer. Arsaphes, risen from the dead, galloped still over the plain.

There was another side to the glory and the passion. Behind legend and epic lay bloodshed. We are not concerned with propaganda or hagiography, and make no attempt to hide the fact that, according to many authors, the image of Alexis, purified by suffering and the desert, was tarnished again when he came to power. What pleasure and debauch had once done or undone, politics and the power to command could also do or undo. Disorder has its dispensations, order its demands. Alexis did not hesitate to condemn when in doubt, to execute without proof, or to massacre the innocent if they opposed him. He explained to Philocrates in a justly famous letter:

"It is a grave mistake to believe there can be justice in war or politics. All wars kill; every policy benefits some at the expense of others. The gods alone are just. And was it not you yourself, Philocrates, who taught me that they rarely intervene in earthly affairs? To try to be just is to believe that one is just, and to believe in the justice of one's own cause is to believe everyone else's cause is unjust. I do not believe I am the only just man. All I try to do is be the strongest—though I do try to avoid being the most unjust. I do not think any man is wicked deliberately, gratuitously, for no reason. True honesty consists in admitting that your enemy, too, has some sort of share in justice and truth. In any conflict, it is always two justices—and two injustices—that are at war, and what decides between them is force. Are we just, Philocrates? It was the others who killed Jester, but it was we who sent him to his death. Yet I killed the brothers of those who slew him. I have sentenced innocent people to death, Philocrates, and I shall do so again. The only way to have clean hands is not to have any hands. But we *have* hands, Philocrates, and arms to kill and heads to organize the struggle and the victory. May the gods give us a heart, too—but a heart to fight and win. A heart to hear the cries of the dying on the battlefield, and the weeping of mothers over the graves of their children—that must wait for peace. For victory."

Philocrates seems to have been more outraged than Isidore by what Léon Blum called Alexis's "cynicism," Georges Sorel his "profound honesty," and Lenin his "realism." Isidore had suffered too much to think of sparing the enemy. His first idea was to destroy him. Philocrates, on the other hand, found it difficult to accept the idea of truth and justice divided against themselves. For him who all these years had been so indulgent toward Alexis; who, from Aquileus and Alexandria on, had learned to know all of mankind's weaknesses; who was the incarnation of subtlety, resourcefulness, and, some say, guile —it was impossible for him to give way over what for him were life's chief and highest values: truth, justice, the same law for all, a refusal to admit the coexistence of incompatibles.

"If you abandon the idea of one justice for all and one truth for all," he wrote to his former pupil, "where will you stop? Tyrants believe in nothing but the gratification of their own wishes; they refuse to allow anything to anyone else, and injustice is their law. I grant that you are fighting for the return of peace and justice. But to remain pure that fight must respect laws and rules. Beware of force, Alexis! Do not be like Basil or Gandolphus! I will not ask what has become of my lessons, but what of the lessons of the gods and sages whose worshiper and disciple you once were? If there is not one justice and one alone, if there is not one truth and one alone, and if you do not respect and fight for them, where are you heading for but the abyss?"

Alexis answered Philocrates with the shortest letter he ever wrote: "You think, Philocrates, and I make war." Philocrates was bound to hear in these words the echo of his own teaching on thought and action, expounded so lucidly in his letters to Helen ten or twelve years before.[12] There is no doubt that what has been called Alexis's relativism derives directly from the precepts of Philocrates. It was Philocrates himself who enabled Alexis to overcome the allurements of sun worship and the mystics of Asia and proceed to life and action. But now Philocrates no longer recognized himself in his faithful, perhaps too faithful, disciple. As often happens, the pupil was bettering the instruction. "A superficial observer," writes Émile Bréhier, "might have expected Isidore to reject and Philocrates to approve Alexis's relativism. But by a seeming reversal, it is Isidore who agrees and Philocrates who disapproves."[13] The explanation is that Isidore's suffering made him deeply committed to fighting at Alexis's side, while Philocrates' skepticism was directed toward history rather than belief, circumstance rather than principle. The priest's main concern was victory, while for the philosopher victory was nothing without respect for something above victory. Each attitude has its greatness.

Throughout the struggle for power the difference of opinion between Alexis and Philocrates grew more and more pronounced. Philocrates carried on imperturbably with the task of organization and recruitment for the conspiracy. He went on covering the Empire with a network of fellow plotters. From the City to the source of the Amphyses, from Cape Gildor to Mezzopotamo, he raised two, three, four veritable armies. In the younger generation he kindled a wild, almost fanatical enthusiasm for Alexis's cause. But when Alexis made use of trickery or violence, when he killed hostages, or razed villages to the ground in order to isolate Mardoch, then something in Philocrates revolted. Did reviving the Empire mean having to go on torturing it just as cruelly as the torturers they were supposed to be fighting against? And if one applied their own methods to them, was it worth driving them out only to put in their place a justice and laws that were set at naught? It was better to die than deny one's principles! Perhaps the fundamental explanation was simply Philocrates' horror of blood and suffering. He had never gotten over the memory of the gruesome sacrifice in the temple at Mursa. He agreed with Alexis about their ends, but he refused to acquiesce about the means. Though he went on serving Alexis's cause as determinedly as before, Philocrates was on the brink of quarreling with him when events took it upon them to put an end to their differences.

Philocrates was on his way back to Aquileus after a secret mission to Amphibolus. As he was riding down one of the mountain tributaries of the Amphyses, a band of Kanishka's men surprised him, killed all his escort, and took him back captive to Amphibolus, where Kanishka lived. Kanishka was not a half-witted clod like Arrhideus. He lived with a certain lavishness, even luxury, and liked to give a cheerful turn even to murder. He went in for cruelty of a refined sort, and his victims perished amidst jesting and laughter. He soon realized how he could make use of his present prisoner. He had heard about Philocrates and how clever, subtle, yet inflexible he was, and he decided to employ him to negotiate with Alexis.

"I could have you put to death here and now," he said, "amidst torture and suffering. I prefer to send you to Alexis to propose peace, an alliance, and the division of power between us. Life is short, very short. Instead of fighting each other and wearing ourselves out, why should we not be rich and powerful together? I don't ask you to tell me any of the secrets, which, if I liked, I could get out of you by pain. All I ask you to do is remember I am setting you free expressly to take my message to Alexis, and that I shall be waiting here for you to bring me his answer."

"If you let me go," said Philocrates, "I shall advise Alexis to refuse your proposal and continue the war against you."

"Say what you like to him," answered Kanishka, laughing. "But you must come back here. If you bring peace I will lavish gold and honors upon you and you will be my adviser as you were once his. Perhaps you will be able to persuade and convert me. If you bring war, I shall treat you as an enemy. But in any case you must come back. I am told you love justice. Tell me if my proposals do not strike you as just."

"In the context of injustice," said Philocrates, "they strike me as just. I shall come back."

Philocrates left Amphibolus in chains and surrounded by men-at-arms. They returned him to where he had been taken prisoner, and set him free. Three days later he rejoined Alexis. For centuries their meeting has been an inexhaustible theme for dissertations and public speeches. From Pico della Mirandola to the Jesuit schools of the Third Republic, it was the pons asinorum of examinations and debate, a commonplace of both secular and religious culture. It is only a few years since, like Regulus and the cranes of Ibycus, it began to fade from the collective consciousness of schoolboys. Why should they remember Philocrates now when they don't remember anything at all? Alexis greeted Philocrates with emotion. He loved, respected, and admired him, and made him laugh by still addressing him as "master." It was unbearable to think of losing the teacher to whom he was bound by so much suffering and danger endured together. For two whole days and nights they went over and over the problem. Nothing remained of the differences that might have torn them apart. Alexis never suggested Philocrates should break his word, but offered to return to Kanishka in his stead. This Philocrates refused outright. Alexis was free to hand himself over to Kanishka if he liked. But in the first place it would be foolish, criminal, and in the second place it would not release Philocrates from his promise. Was there any sense in their both putting their heads in the lion's mouth? No, obviously the best thing was for Philocrates to go back and confront his fate alone. There still remained the question of Kanishka's proposals. Philocrates categorically advised Alexis to reject them. But Alexis was distraught and could not agree. "He suffered all the other's tortures in advance," wrote Justus Dion. For two whole days and nights, the decision was postponed from evening to morning, morning to evening. At dawn on the third day, Alexis's men came and told him Philocrates had disappeared. Alexis knew at once he had gone back to Amphibolus.

And now we come to one of the most painful pages in the story of Alexis. Unable to overcome his anxiety and sorrow, he leaped on his horse at once and set off with a very small escort after Philocrates. For hours, braving danger, ambush, the possibility of clashes with an enemy better armed, they galloped across hills and rivers. At sunset, in a narrow pass between two high cliffs, Alexis's horse stumbled over something lying on the path. It was Philocrates' body.

Alexis' despair brought him to the brink of madness. Destruction and death rained down on the Empire, and now, after so much fire and slaughter, after so many sorrows striking nearer and nearer, after the blinding of Isidore and the death of Jester, now came the loss of the oldest comrade of all, the one who had been with him always from the northern forest to Alexandria, and again from Samarkand to the borders of the Empire and to Aquileus. As his sad and silent escort stood by, Alexis wept long by the roadside over Philocrates' lifeless body. Doubt, discouragement, and despair swept over him. He asked himself whether peace and the welfare of men and women he didn't even know really had to be paid for with this loss and suffering, which stripped struggle and even victory of their meaning and value. The death of Philocrates was all the harder to bear because it came soon after disagreement between them. It left Alexis alone, lost, friendless. How futile and meaningless their quarrels and arguments suddenly seemed! Isidore had supported Alexis against Philocrates, but it was Philocrates who was his master and his friend, it was Philocrates he had loved. To fight without him . . . to win without him . . . was it worthwhile? Did the struggle have any meaning now? For several hours, perhaps several days, Alexis thought seriously of giving up the fight, going back to Samarkand or the borders of China and India, burying his sorrow, and forgetting the Empire. Fortunately he did not yet know about the rumors which were to be spread, the poisonous echo of which can still be heard today.

Philocrates' aversion to blood and violence made his courage all the more admirable. He had set out without hesitation, without a word, almost by force, on the path to torture and death. Nothing could have been more appalling in his eyes than the fate that awaited him. Nothing could illustrate more brightly his notion of trust and good faith, justice and truth, than this final act which placed his life in mortal peril. What a refutation of those who accused him of guile! Perhaps he was fortunate to be able to give, in the hour of his death, a silent answer, tinged with greatness and some disdain, to all who used his ingenuity and flexibility of mind to impugn his character. But envy and mediocrity were not to admit defeat. Because they could not square Philocrates' death with the image they had fabricated of him, they twisted it to suit their own arguments. The repugnance he felt for the death of others could only have been even greater in the case of his own. If one imagined him, they said, going to meet suffering and torture, one began to divine the hidden truth. He may have set out in good faith and full of courage; but he must have soon weakened and betrayed to Kanishka all the secrets of the conspiracy. The whole thing was then very simple: Alexis had seen through him and had him done away with. This explanation demonstrates very well the limitations of an abstract and superficial psychology, backed up, of course, by meanness of character, which simply makes deductions from appearances without going to the roots of people's motives. Alexis and Philocrates had quite violently opposed one another. Alexis had defended the use of violence and injustice in war. Since childhood Philocrates had had a horror of suffering and bloodshed. What more natural conclusion than that Alexis had secretly had Philocrates murdered because he disagreed with him and because, under torture, he had given away the vital secrets of the conspiracy?

The historian or chronicler must report facts and opinions impartially. But he is not precluded from expressing a preference and inclining to one side rather than another. I, for my part, do not believe for a moment in the base interpretation that accuses Alexis not only of murdering his master and friend, but also of treachery and cowardice. This explanation was, in fact, so arbitrary that other versions sprang up and multiplied. Why not? All they had in common was hatred or contempt either for Alexis or for Philocrates. Some had it that instead of a political murder it was a sordid killing carried out by acquaintances the philosopher had picked up and whose supposed tastes it is not difficult to guess. Some said it was a crime of passion organized by Alexis, suddenly overcome with jealousy. Others again said Philocrates killed himself because he was weak and a coward. I shall not even discuss the first two theories. But how could committing suicide before he got back to Amphibolus have solved the philosopher's moral problem? He had promised to return. Suicide was as much a breach of faith as defection. He might just have well have stayed with Alexis. Philocrates could have gone back to Kanishka and then committed suicide, before the torture and suffering began. He couldn't have done it before he had kept his promise. Moreover, his body was riddled with arrows and spear thrusts. Such wounds seem incompatible with suicide, to say the least. Instead of inventing a suicide that solves nothing or chance encounters that do not fit in with anything we know, instead of putting the blame for the murder on Alexis, why not accept Justus Dion's account, which seems perfectly logical and natural. It is well known that tyrants do not trust each other. What is more likely than that some of Astakia's or Mardoch's men came upon Philocrates on his way back to Amphibolus; that they stopped him, questioned him, and learned who he was and where he was going. Philocrates going to see Kanishka! The possibility of an alliance between Alexis and Kanishka already weighed like a threat on the tyrants. The fact that Alexis's adviser was on the way to Amphibolus was proof, and more, that the danger was real. Philocrates had offered his life to prevent Alexis from making an alliance with Kanishka, and the terrible irony of history caused him to succumb to the arrows of the other side, who also dreaded such an alliance above anything else. The black humor of war saw to it that the murderers of the philosopher who was against the alliance were those who were equally against it. Probably Philocrates was doomed anyway, whether at the hands of Astakia or of Kanishka. Nevertheless it was due to a mistake that he was pierced with spears and arrows.

This, in my opinion, is the simple truth—simple, yet devious and cruel, like the march of events. Philocrates died by mistake. But the mistake made sense in so far as it was enemies who killed him—stupid enemies who made an error, but enemies just the same. It may be objected that this is mere hypothesis. No doubt. But the explanation is probable, even convincing. Moreover it is a probability that brings, over and above the cruelty, peace and consolation. Perhaps it was a death the philosopher would have wished: at the same time as it spared him the suffering of torture, it spared him having to lie or perjure himself. He fell before the two adversaries he had hated and satirized all his life—violence and stupidity. All the inconsistencies involved in force were at last resolved. Philocrates' whole life was justified by his death.

The extremity of Alexis's despair had brought him near to throwing up everything, to going into exile again, to rejecting history and its tributes. Then suddenly he came down once more on the side of action. The influence of Helen is to be seen in this reversal. She had been as shattered by Jester's death as Alexis himself, perhaps even more. The death of Philocrates made her decide in favor of an immediate rising. If, after so much loss and suffering, all was lost, why wait any longer? Since Jester, Philocrates, so many hundreds and thousands of men, women, and children were dead, so many thousands of innocent people crucified, impaled, beheaded, blinded, let those who were left go out to meet the death that would reunite them with those they loved. Messages flew to and fro. Jester's successor went from Alexis to Helen, from Helen to Alexis. The flame of revolt spurted forth from one end of the Empire to the other. As Justus Dion puts it, "Alexis's laments propelled the Empire to freedom." The fighting redoubled in violence, breaking out everywhere at once. And it was not long before fate took a new turn and the miracle happened. To those who fought to die, the object of their sacrifice revealed its true face—it was the face of victory. There was really nothing surprising about it. It is fear that heralds defeat, and scorn for death that leads to every kind of triumph. Helen at last began to make open war against Arrhideus's bands. She seized Onessa, thrust as far as Evcharisto and Mezzopotamo. Arrhideus fled to the northern forests, deserted by all and accompanied by only two or three of his men. Helen took her success calmly, welcoming it with the same equanimity as she had welcomed sorrow. To the south there was discord between Astakia and Kanishka, discord that was evidently both cause and effect of Philocrates' death. Alexis took advantage of his enemies' disagreements, and in less than three weeks Parapoli, Aquileus, and Amphibolus had all fallen into his hands. For him it was all a complete surprise. He had expected despair; he had met with power and glory. Astakia and Kanishka were both killed within a few hours of each other. Only Mardoch was left. He was trapped between Helen's and Alexis's armies, and was still keeping up some resistance

south of Mezzopotamo, in a bend of the Amphyses among the foot-
hills, together with Astakia's son and some of Kanishka's lieutenants.
The fighting came to an end with the brief battle of Mezzopotamo,
known also as the Battle of the Princes or the Battle of the Empire.
Mardoch, surrounded, could only sell his now useless life dear. His
army was wiped out. He himself, disguised as an archer, managed to
get through the encircling steel, but was betrayed and murdered as he
was about to take ship near Cape Gildor. His murderers sent his head
to Alexis in the hope of a reward. But, perhaps in memory of Philocrates, he had them arrested, tried, and executed. "The day of the
murderers was over," writes Justus Dion. "The day of justice had
begun."

One fine autumn day in Aquileus, with the town given over to
rejoicing, Alexis was crowned emperor. Helen and Isidore together
placed the crown on his head. A rather undistinguished fresco by
Puvis de Chavannes in the main lecture-theater of the Sorbonne gives
a highly inaccurate picture of the splendor of the ceremony, with its
mixture of barbarity and sumptuousness so characteristic of the early
days of the Empire. Unfortunately the fresco was covered with
minium and Mercurochrome and badly damaged in May, 1968. It
shows a crowd of armed men and women in holiday dress with their
infants in their arms, in the great temple at Aquileus, the site of
Arsaphes's empty tomb and of Basil the Great's coronation in defiance
of the priests. The priests were dead. Philocrates was dead. Jester
was dead. And Isidore was blind. In the square before the temple,
priestesses in long white robes raised hymns to heaven, and amid the
din of rattles and drums waved red and black scarves toward the east
in memory of the victims, cursing the memory of their murderers for
generations to come. Alexis had had Vanessa's name joined to those
of Philocrates and Jester. There in the vast temple echoing with the
people's rejoicing, Alexis dreamed—of the forests of the northeast,
the feasts in Alexandria, the years in the wilderness, the silence of the
tomb, the Asian night, the words of the sages and their secret truth,
of death, of power. Some way off, scarcely visible among the worshippers and the companions-in-arms, a childish old man, almost an
idiot, had just, in the presence of the priests, renounced his hereditary
rights to the crown and the Empire in favor of Alexis. He was the last
of the Eagles, the son of Irene and the great Basil, the heir of the
Venostae. Perhaps he was dreaming, too—the dim, vague dreams
dreamed by the failures of history. A man still not yet past his youth

stood behind Alexis, in the shadow. His name was Bruince. He was a priest, the pupil of Isidore and Philocrates. How fascinating are the long chains of dreams, efforts, traditions, and revolts, of victories and defeats, death and renewal, renewal and death, which amidst faiths and empires make up the destiny of man.

XV

THE KHA-KHAN OF THE OÏGHURS

 HILE THE FOREGOING EVENTS WERE BESTOWING power on Alexis, the rest of the world did not stand still. None of the great powers involved through the years and the ages with the history of the Empire had escaped upheaval within or danger without. Since the time of King Regis, Sicily had been conquered three times and was still coveted far and wide for its fruit and corn, its fair blue sky and hills rising sheer from the sea, and its strategic position in the middle of the Mediterranean. Pomposa, rent by civil war and faction, still had succeeded in extending its maritime and commercial empire. Countering Sicily and its series of conquerors, it had occupied Rhodes and Crete, and continued to dominate all the eastern Mediterranean. But the most sweeping changes were those that affected the barbarians.

The reader may recall the large-scale migrations caused by the invasions of the Ainus and the Khmers in the time of Basil.[1] The great intermixing of populations that had forced toward the Empire hundreds of thousand of men, women, and children, horses, chariots, tents, sheep, and cattle—from those defeated at Amphibolus to rival tyrants driven out by Alexis—had gone on ceaselessly on the steppes and in the forests. The barbarians of Amphibolus, admirers of the Empire, whose religion and often customs they shared, and who had only fought against it in order to become part of it, had been submerged by a flood of much more primitive, dangerous, and bloodthirsty peoples from the depths of Asia. Dozens, hundreds of tribes, bands, and peoples fought among themselves and against the then great states of Persia, China, and India. There were scenes of revolting barbarity and cruelty. From the great ice-bound rivers to the deserts crossed by camel trains laden with spices and treasures for kings or gods, there was nothing but terror and suffering. Happy were those beheaded by the sword or transfixed with pike or arrow. The favorite amusement of the nomadic barbarians was to impale their victims, or to suspend them by the feet over live coals so that the bodies writhing with terror and pain gradually had their eyes, lips, and faces eaten away. We cannot attempt to give even a brief account of the confused and complicated history of the relations between the Hiung-Nus, Hu-Wuans, Khazars, Kaptchaks, Petchenegues, Comans, the Huns of the Caucasus and the Don, the Oïghurs, and the Hunigurs. The princes or chiefs bore the title of Kha-Khan, Chagan, or Tanju. They were named Mundzuk or Tchitchi, Ugek or Roïlas, Gadaric or Oktar, and massacred one another. The high plateaus, the limitless steppes, and the forests of the north provided them with almost inexhaustible supplies of horsemen and mounts. They galloped across the plain armed with bows and arrows that never missed their mark, and with long leather whips that whistled as they whirled them round their heads and inflicted dreadful wounds on the enemy and their horses. Like Arrhideus in the north of the Empire, they lived on horseback from childhood until they died. Legend had it that they were descendants of the centaurs, and according to tradition they were seen actually asleep on horseback, supported by their spears— whole armies of men and beasts, outlined, motionless, against the starry sky that hung above the endless steppes and fertile plains they laid waste to in their fury. They ate raw meat and drank fermented mare's milk—but they also drank the reeking blood of their dismembered enemies, out of their skulls. Winter and summer they wore leather and animal pelts flung carelessly over their shoulders. Variations of climate or temperature, from the stifling heat of the deserts or the damp of the river valleys and marshes to the icy solitudes of mountains, plateaus, and snowy peaks, seemed all one to them. Women were at once terrified and fascinated by their ugliness—their bodies deformed from a life in the saddle, their slit eyes and flat faces striped with scars. Nothing could stop them: rivers, mountains, mothers' prayers, fear of the gods, the stoutest ramparts—all gave way before the flood of their countless squadrons. They would swim rivers, lakes, and creeks, hanging on to their horse's tail or mane. Whole nations fled in terror before their approach.

They loved war. With only a few years between forays, they are to be found attacking the towers and fortifications built along the vast frontier of China by the emperor of the Middle Kingdom, invading the Caucasus, invading the valley of the Indus. As the wind raised the sand, they flew with it across the steppe, sacking, destroying, sowing death and destruction. They are not known to have had any gods to speak of. Religion, fear, morality, and pity were all equally unknown to them. Far from them the community of mind that existed between the Empire and the barbarians of old. They had nothing but scorn for the worship of sun, oak, or eagle. What they worshipped was a sword dripping with blood and driven into the sand among the chariots. To pull it out and parade it amid the war cries and acclamations of the tribes was the signal for fighting to begin. At the sight of it everyone armed and prepared for fresh exploits. In the wake of the warriors on their horses, safe from lances and pikes, herds of sheep and cattle and cartloads of women and children moved toward new loot. The barbarians were the scourge of men and gods, but they were also the youth of a world both brilliant and dark. They were ignorant of the charms of ease, luxury, indolence, avarice. For them, virtue was in the service of death.

For centuries the barbarians had lived divided into nations and tribes that fought among themselves. After many vicissitudes, reminiscent of tales of adventure but unfortunately too numerous to recount here,[2] they were finally united. This came about through such men as Bayan, Bleda, Theodomir, and Ertrogrul, but it was above all the work of Balamir, one of the most fascinating leaders of men in history. He was a descendant of the Great Khan of the Oïghurs who had met Basil at Famagusta, and the son of a petty princeling of the steppes. He had seen his family, and almost all his tribe, massacred: first it was the Chinese, then the Persians, then the Scythians, then the other barbarians. Naturally enough, this had imparted to Balamir himself a fearful violence, an insatiable thirst for cruelty, and an appetite for power, domination, and revenge. In darkness and silence he gradually won back, first from his own people, then from neighbors farther and farther away, the lands his father and grandfather had lost. He began patiently to forge the instruments of his power. At first he had only a handful of men, but they were subjected to a crushing discipline. Before being admitted into the group each warrior, on pain of death, had to stab and kill his wife or his son with an arrow or a dagger; bachelors who boasted of loving no one and nothing but glory in battle and loot afterward had to sacrifice their one attachment—their horses. When they had slain all they might have loved, all who might have weakened them, Balamir's men acclaimed him on a plain strewn with corpses. These five or six hundred warriors, stripped of everything, bound to their leader, drunk with blood, free, were ready now to conquer the world. And they did conquer a considerable part of it.

Then and thereafter, on the steppes and high plateaus, came long years of battle and negotiation. Allying himself with some against others, lavishing gifts on the strong and promises on the weak, pitiless toward any who dared resist, capable of magnanimity as well as of the most terrible crimes, Balamir not only carved out an immense empire based on the terror inspired by what were now hundreds of thousands of horsemen, but also succeeded in uniting under his sole authority all the barbarian tribes from Siberia to the Caspian and from the Danube to the Great Wall of China. Alexis was still an outlaw when Balamir had already been reigning for several months as absolute master over boundless plains, impenetrable forests, and the snowy summits of Caucasus and Altai. Always dressed in sable, at once rough and luxury-loving, greedy for gold and glory, Balamir was Tanju of the Hiung-Nus, Chagan of the Khazars and the Kaptchaks, Kha-Khan of all the Oïghurs; and he would say with pride that neither the sun nor the moon ever set on his territory.

One evening as he was sitting in his tent of felt decorated with silk and purple and gold, the floor covered with furs and rare carpets, his guards announced that a man of middle age, sumptuously clad and riding a magnificent but apparently exhausted black horse, was asking to speak with him. Since the stranger bore no weapon but a slender dagger inlaid with ivory and precious stones, the Kha-Khan ordered him to be brought in. The unknown horseman, who had been traveling day and night for nearly two weeks, bowed low before the prince and, following the custom, kissed the hem of his long robe of leather and sable. The Kha-Khan raised him up with all the courtesy due to strangers and, as was the habit then, asked after the health of his sons and the state of his horses, crops, and forests. The traveler answered that all this amounted to little compared to the vast wealth of the lord of the Oïghurs. Then the Kha-Khan asked the horseman to reveal his name and the reason for his visit, and learned with surprise that the stranger with the black horse who was drinking green tea in his felt and gold tent was none other than Simeon, brother of Alexis, come to offer Balamir his services against the Emperor.

A few months before, in a letter to Philocrates,[3] Alexis had said that in his opinion no one was ever deliberately wicked. Of course, Simeon knew nothing of this, but it applied very aptly to his own case. The elder son of Roderick and Helen was ambitious, of herculean build, an ardent hunter and warrior when it pleased or suited him, but incapable of understanding the motives or the success of "the mystical sensualist bastard," as he called his brother in private, and sometimes, when he was drunk, in public. The two brothers had nothing in common, and to Simeon the rise of Alexis had been unbearable. Historians are divided as to the explanation of this hostility. Some hold that Simeon was too ordinary and too jealous to be able to appreciate the vast sweep of Alexis's ideas or his mind, at once open and strong, rich and inflexible. The rivalry and emulation evident in their youth had intensified, first after the wolf hunt but especially after Alexis's return and rise to fame, into an unbridled hatred that also had something to do with Helen and her passion for the younger brother. Others, however, maintain that Simeon was moved by less disgraceful motives. According to this theory Simeon, passionately fond of his northeastern forests, had been disgusted to hear of the life Alexis was leading among the pleasures of Alexandria. Alexis's subsequent disappearance into deepest Asia only confirmed Simeon's view that his brother was unbalanced, oscillating between debauchery and asceticism. The younger son's elevation to the throne of the Empire appeared to Simeon not only a denial of justice, an insult to the memory of his father and of all the most sacred traditions, but also a threat to the Empire itself, which was now at the mercy of an unstable character perverted by Asia, foreign religion, orgies, and mysticism. It is certain that Simeon had been fascinated since childhood by treason, by the need to assert the worth that those around him failed to recognize, and by a curious mixture of puritanism derived from the traditions of the forest and the self-destructive violence that had once made him side with Gandolphus's army against Balkh and Fabrician and that now brought him to the Kha-Khan's tent. It is not impossible that his strange soul harbored all kinds of different and even contrasting motives, and with unconscious insincerity hid a twisted love of evil and hate behind a noble-seeming concern with justice, legitimacy, and the salvation of the Empire by fire and sword.

Balamir soon saw the advantage of having one of Helen's sons on his side in the fight against the other. It was plain now that war between the barbarians and the Empire could no longer be avoided.

In fact, for many long years, since the battle of Amphibolus and even before, the barbarians, ever fiercer, had been exerting a pressure ever-stronger on the frontiers of the Empire. Only the fact that they were divided among themselves stopped them from sweeping away all the defenses and establishing themselves permanently on the rich lands they coveted. Infiltration went on all the time, and the barbarians did succeed in getting a footing inside the Empire. But they operated only in independent groups, quite incapable of constructing and organizing a state. If Astakia and Kanishka, Arrhideus and Mardoch had made common cause instead of fighting one another, Alexis would never have mounted the throne of Aquileus. Balamir was bound to see the threat the Emperor now represented. All the things that might have been possible before were now impossible; and what if Alexis were to repeat the campaigns Arsaphes and Gandolphus had waged against the barbarians? If only Balamir had begun to imitate the Great Khan ten or fifteen years earlier so that his unification of the barbarians had proceeded further, events would have turned out very differently. But perhaps it was not too late. Perhaps if he acted quickly he could, with Simeon's help, nip Alexis's ambitions in the bud and topple an Empire still shaken by reconquest and civil strife. Such, in his tent of felt and gold, before the bushy-browed, black-bearded stranger, were the thoughts of the Kha-Khan of all the Oïghurs.

Meanwhile in Aquileus the thoughts of Alexis were taking quite a different turn. After his coronation, with the barbarians if not destroyed at least reduced to impotence, with peace and order restored, and the Empire reconquered and reunified, Alexis felt once more the temptation to forget the world and withdraw into himself. Every day he felt more keenly the loss of Philocrates and the original Jester, one of whom he had loved for a short time like a father, and the other for many years like a son. All through the struggle for the Empire he had developed so many plans depending on Philocrates that the latter's sudden absence left the Emperor lonely and lost. He was well aware, too, of the rumors that were beginning to circulate in the Empire, and that may have originated in Simeon's entourage, about his own supposed ambition and thirst for power. He would have thought it ridiculous, perhaps wicked, to give the lie to these rumors by weakness or compromise. If he was to rule he would rule with firmness, rigor, violence even. But was it worth ruling? Since he returned from exile all his thoughts had been filled with the risks of the conspiracy, the reek of conflict, the exaltation of the victorious captain. Now that the goal had been reached, he longed once more for silence and contemplation. Hardly had the imperial crown been conferred on him in the enthusiasm of victory than there awoke in him the memory and influence of the years of withdrawal and meditation. Fighting, that was fine—but ruling? Gold and purple oppressed him; the company of the stiff and self-important imperial officials seemed to him little improvement on that of the courtesans of Alexandria or the merchants of Samarkand and Bukhara. He was seized with a longing to leave aside the urgent material problems of administration and return to essentials. The essential and the urgent are never the same. For Alexis, the essential was the soul. And it was also the body and its happiness, the delight of cool springs at noon, of walks in the forest with disciples eager for knowledge and understanding, of frugal meals at evening, then love and dreamless sleep. It was the sun he no longer saw now because of the two Moors always sheltering him with silk parasols and ostrich feathers; it was the icy streams he no longer plunged in after strenuous exertion; it was the burning flagstones where he no longer lay before the steps of temples and other men's palaces. Now it was he who lived in palaces, to him the poor and needy addressed their prayers, and since it was he who gave it was forbidden for him to receive.

"Ah," he would say to Jester, the seventh or eighth of that name, a lad of ten or eleven, lively and mischievous as a monkey, "how different riches and honor look to those who possess them and those who seek them. I know it is unseemly for those who have gold and silk, and before whom others bow, to say they scorn fame and wealth. And I think it very possible that fame and wealth can bring happiness to the poor and wretched. But they cannot bring happiness to the rich and powerful. Fame and wealth govern everything, they send people to their death, and the dreams they inspire beckon to perseverance and crime, virtue and vileness. What incredible power they have when they go before like a mirage! And what poverty when you touch them and they vanish between your fingers! We thirst after everything— power, riches, and glory—and then nothing can slake that thirst. How big the world looks at night in the torchlight, to the lad who labors and dreams and thinks, I'll be rich and powerful, I'll have flocks and palaces, I'll lead armies. And how small the world is to the eyes of memory."

"My lord," Jester answered, "are not power and glory the means by which the Emperor may change people and things, and make his name and age remembered for centuries to come?"

"History . . . posterity . . . There are other kinds of eternity. I do not wish to be remembered. I wish for the eternal moment when sun and water, a soul empty and full, an ardor without object and a passionate indifference suddenly reveal to us the soul of the world. You will understand all this later," said the Emperor, stroking the child's hair as the boy gazed up at him. "All this, and many other truths that are great and beautiful and reveal something of the order of heaven and earth. Thaumas taught them to Fabrician, who taught them to Philocrates, who taught them to me, who have so often misunderstood. And in my turn, if you wish—" and the Emperor's voice grew almost humble, "—I will try to teach you what I know."

"Oh, my lord!" cried the boy. "We would all die for you!"[4]

Alexis was always amazed by people's readiness to give themselves to him body and soul. He often thought that the clue to his success lay not in his intelligence or will, nor even in chance, but in that rare response he aroused in others. He could feel a strong, immediate, and living bond come into being between him and the world around him. This sympathy included objects, nature, the trees in the forest, the water in the springs, and the orb of day whose son and servant he was. It was a grace he possessed, with marvelous power over men and women. Eloquence was not the whole explanation: even before he spoke he could feel the crowd taking him to their heart and offering themselves to him. And it was not power and prestige that drew them. Not only in Alexandria, where he was rich and brilliant, but also in the desert, on the caravan routes, and in Samarkand and Bukhara, where he was poor and unknown, everywhere all who saw and heard him wanted to follow and never leave him. No, it was not power. That universal willingness to serve, to give oneself to him, to die for him, was, rather, a burning sign of the passion of love.[5]

"You are young to talk of dying," said the Emperor, looking at Jester. "Learn rather to live, to enjoy the gifts lavished so prodigally by an unknown god: the heat of the sun, the cool of the sea at noon, the scent of the forest in the evening, horses galloping across the plain. You are rich because you are alive. Even unhappiness is still life. Learn to love and enjoy, and learn also to suffer. And, when the time comes, you will learn to die."

"My lord . . ." said the boy.

The Emperor stopped. They were walking in the huge garden that Justus Dion tells us stretched from the temple in Aquileus to the Emperor's palace. A stream meandered among trees and flowers; there were two or three rotundas in honor of the gods, and several villas of wood or stone, the residences of high officials, captains of the Emperor's guard, officers of the Cohort of Death.

"Speak," said the Emperor.

"If you leave us, my lord, and withdraw again from court and camp, what will become of all those who cry out your name, who love and need you? And what will become of the Empire if you are no longer there?"

The Empire! Not only the boy, but Helen, too, spoke of it. When Alexis went to tell her of his desire to renounce power as soon as unity and peace were really established, Helen reproached him for what she called spiritual egoism, and for being concerned, especially since Philocrates' death, with nothing but his own soul and fate.

"Just because the ambitious bring power into discredit, is that any reason," she said, "why those called to power by the decree of the gods or the trust of men should airily refuse? The soldier who runs away from the battle is executed; the schoolboy who gives his teacher the slip to go and idle in the fields is punished. Princes and emperors have their duties, too. And their duty is not to cultivate their soul, but to lessen the suffering of those whom birth or fate has entrusted to them. Do you think so much of your own peace and meditation that you put them before the good of your people and the peace of the Empire? You have no son; Philocrates is dead; Isidore is blind. To whom would you leave the Empire and those who live in it? Would you give it back to the barbarians, and leave it again at the mercy of their whims, their tortures?"

Neither Alexis nor Helen cared to speak Simeon's name, but the thought of him was there. The Emperor was already affected by the reference to the barbarians, and Simeon was to do the rest. His joining forces with the barbarians removed all Alexis's doubts and obliged him to remain in power. The news of Simeon's presence in Balamir's camp fell on Aquileus like a thunderbolt. The memory of the barbarians still inspired terror, and never, since the time of the battle of Amphibolus and the Great Khan whom for a while Basil had made his ally, had they been as strong as they were now. Balamir's reputation was beginning to spread. Everyone in the Empire had heard of his skill in war and his cruelty. Of Simeon, though he was a familiar enough figure to the people of the northeast, the inhabitants of Aquileus, Mezzopotamo, and Parapoli knew little. But they did know he was tough, brave, and violent, and above all they knew he was Helen's son. Simeon gone over to the barbarians! What might not come of this unnatural alliance? It could make available to the enemy much precious strategic and geographical information, and give them advance knowledge of all the characteristics and weaknesses of the Empire's troops. Simeon, of course, knew these better than anyone, having succeeded his father at the head of the auxiliary bands of the northeast, which, before they were decimated and disarmed by the barbarian tyrants, had been in time of war among the crack troops of the old imperial army. The wave of fear that swept through the land was intensified by rumors that Alexis was about to abdicate. Officers and men alike became demoralized; everywhere, even in the remotest corner, it seemed that the times of trouble were about to dawn anew.

Helen and the danger decided Alexis. Though, as we know, Helen had never concealed her preference for her younger son, for as long as possible she did her best to be impartial and to try to soothe the feelings of the elder. But his going over to Balamir seemed another proof of the instability, falseness, and love of betrayal he had shown so often since the affair of the dagger and the siege of Balkh. Helen declared herself openly against him, and after a few days' hesitation Alexis decided to stay on the throne and to muster against Balamir all the forces he could, still recovering as they were from the recent struggle. Messages went out from Aquileus ordering a census of men and arms throughout the Empire.

If the Emperor knew more or less what was going on in the camp of the barbarians, Balamir for his part had little difficulty in getting daily information, through Simeon's spies, of every decision, no matter how small, made in Aquileus. Every evening the barbarian received Simeon in the tent decked with precious objects and spoils, some of them the result of previous operations against the Empire. Helen's son was treated with great consideration, but of course he had to show his submission and respect for the Kha-Khan of all the Oïghurs by kissing his knee or the hem of his robe. It must have been a strange spectacle, this daily meeting between two men contrasting in every respect—geography, past, manner, habits, attitude, and way of thinking—but united by the irresistible forces of hope and hatred. Both wanted to rule over the Empire, the one for revenge, the other in order to give the nomads, weary of sand and steppe, the fertile plains of the Amphyses and the Nephta and the dilapidated palaces of the City, which in the rough imaginations of the barbarians still shone with an illusory glow across mountains and deserts. Both saw quite clearly that either defeat or victory would mean the end of their fragile alliance. But each thought that once they had prevailed together, he could get rid of the other either by trickery or force. Balamir counted on his victorious barbarians, Simeon on the conquered Empire, whose idol and champion against the invaders he would become. But the first thing for both of them was to conquer and kill Alexis.

The bloodstained sword was paraded from tribe to tribe, in makeshift camps, amid encircling carts and tents, in the light of fires and in sandstorms; and from the frontiers of China to Bactria and Paraponisada the call to war was greeted with savage joy. A sudden stir swept through the silent steppe. Felt tents were folded, harness and arms inspected, herds of sheep and cattle rounded up, and hordes of warriors, horses, and carts began to surge across the great plains of Central Asia toward the vast space between Lake Balkhash and the Aral Sea, the Jaxartes and the Oxus (the ancient Syr Darya and Amu Darya), the rendezvous for all the barbarian peoples on their way to conquer the Empire.

They came from everywhere, to the sound of drums and rattles, from Lake Baikal and the Yenisei, from the Kereke mountains and Lake Khantaïskoia, from the Patom heights and beyond the Lena, from the banks of the Orkhon and Selenga and the marches of China, from the passes of the Altai and the plains of Turfan. It has been said that two hundred twenty-four tribes each contributed some four or five thousand men. Once again Asia shook under the hoofs of steeds ridden by all the devils out of hell, with scar-seamed faces and heads and feet deformed from being bound in infancy. As the echo of the ride of the centaurs, with their infallible arrows, reached the Empire, distant at first, then nearer and nearer as the weeks and months went by, terror began to grip fields and villages and busy towns, surprised in the midst of money-making or pleasure. Even in the camps the anxiety of generals and officers spread uneasiness, mistrust, and sometimes disturbances among the men.

In the great battle that lay ahead Alexis could clearly see the inevitable aftermath of Amphibolus. What more eloquent proof could history give of the greatness of Thaumas and the rightness of his views? Now it was too late, and the Empire must drink to the dregs, perhaps to the point of disaster, the cup prepared by Basil and Gandolphus—and not by their defeats, but by their victories. In history as in other things, what cannot be forgiven is success. And by a bitter paradox, he who had betrayed Balkh and Fabrician and had gone over to Gandolphus's men was now again a traitor, and, by the unremembering irony of history, in the camp of those same barbarians whom Gandolphus had so hated and whose threat to the Empire all his guile had not, in the end, been able to avert. As he wandered through the courtyards of the palace at Aquileus, with a Jester suddenly grave, and surrounded by anxiety and the din of arms, Alexis reflected that civilization might have to pay dear for that night of love long ago in the besieged city of Balkh. Alexis could easily imagine, understand, and forgive the horror of the boy who came upon his mother swooning with joy in the arms of a young priest, in the midst of the flames and the groans of the dying. Simeon the traitor . . . and was Alexis so pure? Even before his birth he had been surrounded by bloodshed and crime, and it was in vain he had tried to wash out their stain in the long years of suffering and privation spent on caravan routes and in the tomb.

"Ah, well," said Alexis, taking Jester's hand. "It's not a question of being pure. The first thing is to conquer, and to live."

Outside the trumpets sounded. The sun shone. By the great temple of Aquileus, beneath the ramparts of the City, on the plain covered with helmets and horses as far as the eye could see, the army of the Empire awaited the Emperor.

XVI

THE DOUBLE DUEL

 ORE TIME WENT BY, AND NEW IMAGES CONSTANTLY appeared in the kaleidoscopes it slowly revolved before the eyes of history. A certain degree of peace returned to the Mediterranean. Sicily slept under a leaden sky. Pomposa was assimilating its conquests and consuming itself in carousal. For the merchant princes spring and autumn only meant long interludes of festivity in which minds and bodies were exclusively occupied with table or bed. Subtlety and intrigue, whether in love or politics, were carried to sometimes formidable extremes, and the procuresses, masks, spies, informers, ambassadors, and bravoes of Pomposa were all equally notorious. But at the same time it was the country of painters, musicians, poets, and sculptors, and life there was more agreeable and elegant than anywhere else in the world. It was a beautiful city, and the pleasures it offered were innumerable. The patricians enjoyed life, and war was left to soldiers come from Poland, Saxony, the Rhone, and the Alps. Cooks brought from Athens or Alexandria, pages brought from Africa almost always against their will (several painted wooden statues of them, inlaid with ivory and adamantine, have come down to us), spent all their time preparing the great balls that were held in the gardens, by the water, and on the wide lawns decorated with flowers, edifices of marble, masts with banners. Noblemen and courtesans danced there to the music of unseen orchestras. Hardly a month went by without ceremony, hardly a day without some concert. Sometimes the prince would sail forth on a sumptuous ship hung with brocade and velvet to celebrate the marriage of Pomposa with the sea and throw a gold ring set with emeralds into the waves; sometimes the streets would be full of the color and splendor of religious processions, aimed not so much at honoring the

gods—the Pomposans did not worry too much about them—as at giving painters special opportunity to make beauty out of reality.

Rome, far away on its arid Campagna and pestilential marshes, was crushed beneath the weight of its monuments and its past. It was a magnificent memory, perhaps the most magnificent ever, but it had fewer ships and soldiers than Syracuse or Palermo, both largely oriented toward the sea, and much less wealth and land than frivolous Pomposa, now at the peak of a power made glamorous by stolen mosaics and statues, by the reputation of its entertainments, and by the famous green invented by its painters. Rome had really only one resource left, though it was an important one: this was the high priest, at the same time ruler and prince, who bore the illustrious title of archpatriarch. A great builder of temples and bridges, he was the link between heaven and earth, the incarnation here below of the supernatural forces that made—and unmade—kingdoms. Everything in this world depended on him—wealth, fame, honors, advancement in the army, the future. He ruled not by force, but by trust, persuasion, reverential fear. He disposed of men and events not because he had an army, but because he knew words. He knew the words that console and strengthen, the words that fill with courage and hope, the words that make men live and survive, and he set against the cruel vanity of their destinies the peace and eternity of the gods. He was above kings and princes, even when they rebelled against his strange magnificence and his mysterious prestige. His reputation spread far and wide. He was the heir of the Eritrean and Cumaean sibyls, and amid the ruins of a once glorious city, which though only the shadow of its former self had preserved the treasure of its name, he continued to reign over the world and even over those who refused to recognize his powers. There had been terrible conflicts between Rome and Sicily, Sicily and Pomposa, Pomposa and Rome. The fighting had ceased, but the dust it had raised still cast its shadow, and the echo of the trumpets could still be heard. These reverberations of a struggle now over prevented a world deafened and blinded by its self-preoccupation from seeing that its fate was no longer being played out here, but elsewhere. Its future was not being decided between Como and Syracuse, Marseilles and Crete, but on the borders of the Empire, where the barbarians were gathering.

Balamir's envoys had now visited all the tribes. The bloodstained sword had been worshipped all over the land of the felt tents, and hundreds of thousands of warriors had poured into the wide valley where their assembly was to be held. We turn again to the colorful and, it must be admitted, imaginative pages in which Augustin Thierry describes this meeting at Székesfehérvár, a tiny village called Ki Lien-chan by the Chinese and Mugodjar-Aktiubinsk by the Russians. Not far from there, today, is the famous rocket base of Baikonur, well known to every school child. Alas, how many of them still remember the great assembly at Székesfehérvár?[1] How many could say more than a couple of words about it? And yet what was at stake there was the future of the world. But nowadays children are lucky to have heard of it from some conscientious teacher in one of the junior classes where they still deign to bother about the realities of history, before rushing into generative grammar or the theory of sets. People are not interested in the past any more. And yet it was the past that made us.

Let us close our eyes and imagine, across the centuries, that circular valley toward which surged hordes of warriors clad in furs and hides. Many of them knew nothing of Balamir's plans. But they realized war was in the air and there would be talk of conquest and loot. They were full of fierce joy, intoxicated already by the thought of great cities set on fire, the collapse of golden domes, fainting women thrown captive across their horses' backs. But in which direction would the nomad cavalry turn this time? Speculation was rife in the dozen or score of languages and dialects used by the barbarians. Some said it would be China, others Persia or India. Who cared? All that mattered was to fight, to loose arrows which never missed their mark, and to lay waste one or another of the coveted lands, whether east or south or in the fabulous west, which inspired the barbarians with mingled hatred and envy, made their narrow eyes gleam in their scarred faces, and sent them and their bloodcurdling cries, century after century, to the ends of the earth.

When Balamir told them what his plans were, there was a moment's stupefaction, followed by wild enthusiasm. Nothing could be more alien than the Empire to these barbarians of the steppes. With China and Persia they had long had close links of habit, familiarity, even camaraderie, born out of hatred and war. Barbarians had ruled China; trade between Persia and the high plateaus had never ceased; there was a certain interaction of religious and linguistic influence between the nomads and the great states of Asia. But the Empire simply stood for the mirages of the setting sun. True, the barbarians had sometimes thrust toward the west; but they had always been either destroyed or assimilated. The memory of Amphibolus was still green on the steppes, in the felt tents, in the shelter of the chariots ranged around the fire; and with the natural love of war and conquest there mingled a bitter thirst for revenge. As for men like Kanishka and Arrhideus, sensual upstarts out only for their own ends, the people of the Empire remembered them as tyrants and oppressors, but by the barbarians they were forgotten. The nomads of Altai and the Lena, however, had heard enough about the Empire to know that it was good to live there, that the streets of the City were paved with gold and silver, that there were many beautiful women, and that plump and gleaming cattle filled the pastures under the volcanoes where the hay and other crops grew much faster than anywhere else. Highly colored legends, martial chronicles, travelers' tales, and myths had among them created a picture of the Empire that was, with its suggestions of forbidden delights, at once fascinating and vaguely frightening. Balamir's speech to the barbarians played skillfully on their dreams and passions, heightening their rage, their love of war, their virtues, and their vices. When he stopped speaking there was a great silence. The wind of death seemed to sweep over the thousands of warriors standing motionless in the valley, still frozen with anticipation and restrained excitement. For a moment Balamir wondered if he had aimed too high, if, despite their numbers and their courage, the barbarians had been seized with holy terror at the thought of attacking the Empire. Then suddenly a cloud of swords and spears, standards and banners were brandished in the air, and a thunderous cheering broke against the steep-sided mountains, each with its lookout. Balamir and Simeon were swept off their feet and borne in triumph, shoulder-high, by a delirious crowd acclaiming war and drunk on thoughts of forthcoming victories and spoils. Under the last rays of the sun a flood of people stretched as far as the eye could see, shouting the names of the leaders who were to conquer the Empire and all the mirages of the City.

The weeks and months that followed saw two teeming armies advancing slowly toward one another. With the ordeal of civil war scarcely over, Alexis, Helen, Isidore, and Bruince mustered all their forces in defense of the Empire, appealing both to the spirit of tradition and to the new forces that had come into being during the liberation struggle. They hastily tried to re-create the famous regiments of Arsaphes, Basil the Great, and Gandolphus. The irony of history led Alexis to lavish favors on the crack battalions who had once fought for Gandolphus against Balkh, and the auxiliaries from the forests who had once threatened to support Simeon rather than Helen. The first thing to be done was to secure the allegiance of old enemies against the new. Alexis integrated these former adversaries into the army raised in the north against Arrhideus and in the south against the triple alliance of Kanishka, Astakia, and Mardoch. On these groups, once the license of rebellion was over, he imposed the strictest discipline. The Cohort of Death, ten thousand strong, was the kernel of the new army and the heart of Alexis's system of defense. But all these, together with the Syrian archers, the slingers from the Balearics, the Scythian mercenaries, and the troops from the northeast devoted body and soul to Helen, scarcely amounted to half or even a third of the barbarian hordes. Alexis sent ambassadors to Famagusta, Palermo, Syracuse, Alexandria, and Pomposa. Their mission was to explain that the struggle against Balamir did not concern the Empire alone. What the forests of the northeast and the deserts of the south were to the Empire, the Empire itself was to the Mediterranean and the common civilization that had slowly matured around its shores. The Empire had become the march land of all that western region now threatened by the unbridled ambitions of the Kha-Khan of the Oïghurs and his ally Simeon. Sicily and Pomposa were probably not sorry to see the Empire in trouble. The misfortune of a near rival is often even more agreeable than the defeat of a distant enemy. But the echo of the barbarians' hoofs was audible in Cyprus and Palermo, and even at the banquets in Pomposa; and Alexis obtained arms, ships, big supplies of corn, and a small amount of gold. Between thirty and forty thousand men from the countries he had appealed to landed at Onessa, in the harbor of the City, and at Cape Gildor, to be assimilated, alongside the mercenaries and foreign detachments, into the army of three hundred or three hundred fifty thousand men mustered by the Empire—in all, still less than four hundred thousand. The barbarians advancing against them were nearly one million, perhaps more.

It was at the end of autumn, under a still dazzling sky, some 300 miles southeast of Amphibolus, by a little, usually dried-up river that disappeared into the sand and that was called Illyssos by the Greek geographers, that the two armies first sighted each other and threw their advance guards into one of the bloodiest engagements in history. The barbarians, as was their wont, formed a shapeless mass spreading out to the horizon. At their head, bold, sumptuously accoutered, covered in furs, and surrounded by their guard, were Balamir and Simeon. In the middle, as far as the eye could see, stretched an endless column of carts drawn by oxen and buffaloes. Some were laden with women, victuals, weapons, tools, and felt tents; the rest were empty, menacingly awaiting their burden of booty. All around, in a whirl of seething movement and of colors lurid in the sun, companies of nomad horsemen wheeled and wove to and fro in all directions. They galloped in tight formations, maneuvering as one man. But each of these marvelously unified groups seemed to do as it pleased. It was like some wonderful and terrifying merry-go-round, where thousands upon thousands of horses and riders, divided up into threes or fours, dozens or scores, followed, overtook, intersected, and crisscrossed with one another. But this chaotic mass, scattering off in all directions, advanced inexorably. From it arose a tumult of cries, a cloud of dust raised by the horses' hoofs, and a gray shimmer that merged into the landscape, broken only by the red or yellow patches of standards.

The imperial army was terror-stricken by the barbarians' appearance and their vast, incalculable mass. Silent, ranged in perfect squares behind their colors and their officers, Alexis's men tensely watched the incoming flood from Asia. In a tent in the middle of the camp, the Emperor, Helen, Bruince, Jester, and a dozen generals consulted maps and plans and hastily prepared their orders. Blind Isidore was also there, listening and giving advice. In this extreme of danger, two men were at the heart of everything—Alexis and Bruince.

Bruince, whom we have already seen at the Emperor's side on the day of his coronation, was the successor of men like Thaumas, Gandolphus, Fabrician, and Isidore. Unlike them, he had not emerged from the class of the poor or the priests. He was the son of a southern nobleman, a wealthy proprietor of herds and vineyards who sent out ships laden with wool, cheese, and wine to Cyprus, Rhodes, and even Tyre and Pylos.[2] Bruince's father had frequented the court of Basil the Great, but though not a member of the priests' party he more than once found himself in opposition to the emperor, and he very wisely decided to retire to his estate rather than be entangled in the intrigues and power struggles that arose from the rivalry between Thaumas and Gandolphus at the end of Basil's reign. Bruince was an only son, and his father spared no effort to give him an education that for centuries was regarded as a model. Rabelais, Montaigne, Rousseau, Goethe, all the pedagogical treatises and *Bildungsromane* of the countries beyond the Rhine openly take their inspiration from it; many traits in both Pantagruel and Émile come in direct line from Bruince. His father arranged for him to awake in the morning to the sound of sweet music; a Greek tutor was engaged to teach him mathematics and philosophy; a Parthian horseman was his riding master; from the time he was five until he was thirteen his day was divided almost equally between training of the body and training of the mind. Bruince excelled at both. He was a champion swimmer, could recite Homer by heart, run faster than professional athletes, and calculate, by observing shadows, the position of the sun in the sky and the exact time in places as far away as Egypt, where it was scarcely dawn, and India or China, where it was already broad daylight. His father was very proud of him, and had great hopes of his winning success and distinction in trade, the army, or at the court of the emperor.

What strange process is it that takes place in the hearts of the young? When Bruince was just thirteen he told his father he loathed all his successes and saw no future for himself except in the rejection of the triumphs foretold for him. There is something astonishingly modern and at the same time comic in the descriptions that have come down to us of the father's despair at this catastrophe. "All that effort for nothing! All that money! If your poor mother were alive to see this! . . . Think of the future you're throwing away. Think what Glaucon and Philomena will say. Think of your Uncle Callicles who was so fond of you. Think of the old age you're storing up for yourself." But Bruince was not to be moved. He left behind riding masters and tutors, the fine house with its vineyards and its one hundred fifty servants, the horses from Syria, the robes of linen and silk, and the beds inlaid with ivory and tortoise shell, and set out as an ordinary sailor, beyond the Pillars of Hercules, along the coast of Africa, where life was at its toughest, whence many never returned. His father died of grief. He had thought to prolong his own life in the honors to be won by his beloved son, and now that life no longer had any meaning. Bruince was not there to hear the last words from lips that spoke only of him, nor was he present at the burial. He was already on some distant island—historians debate whether it was the Canaries, the Cape Verde Islands, or Madeira. But it is even more difficult for the fortunate of this world to escape their fate than it is for the unfortunate. Bruince's father had devoted what remained of his life to recovering his situation and influence at the emperor's court, so that, in spite of all that had happened, his son's future would be assured. The elderly nobleman, once so haughty, so scornful of intrigue, so contemptuous of compromise and accommodation, was now to be seen suing on behalf of his lost son for help the latter did not want and interference that had no effect. The old man seemed to have forgotten all family pride. The fops and climbers at court came to regard him as a rather ridiculous nobody, and openly made fun of him. But right at the end of his own career, one man was touched by the comedy behind which he divined the tragedy of a whole life, of two lives, and of a young man's ambition outsoaring tradition and aiming perhaps at the impossible. The man who took pity on the old noble was Thaumas. A few months later Thaumas was murdered. But he had had time to recommend to his friends a fifteen-year-old sailor of unknown whereabouts whose name was Bruince.

Many years later, after countless adventures, Bruince, still young, divested of all his wordly goods and entirely devoted to study, already well known for his learning and wisdom, was one of the priests of Aquileus. By a miracle he survived proscriptions, the fury of the barbarian tyrants, and all the other dangers. He hid, then followed Isidore, becoming his disciple and one of his most loyal soldiers. He met Philocrates, who recognized him as the boy Thaumas had told him of twenty or twenty-five years before, and introduced him into Alexis's personal entourage. There were plenty of things in common between the Fool of God and this Prodigal Son: in both, refusal and rebellion had been only the expression of an inflexible personality and a passionate expectation, the sign of a singular destiny. Alexis soon saw that Bruince possessed the rigor and magnanimity that marked him out as the successor of the former great servants of the State and of Philocrates himself. No sooner had Alexis come to the throne than he made Bruince procurator-general of the Empire, the highest official in the new hierarchy. On the Emperor's personal authority and that of Helen, with Isidore, followed by Jester, and helped by three or four officers directly responsible for troops, equipment, finance, and supplies, Bruince, the young man of good position, the ex-sailor, priest of Aquileus, heir to Thaumas and Philocrates, procurator-general of the Empire, was in charge of everything.

They were all there in the tent, confronting Balamir and the barbarian horde, and once again the fate of the Empire was in the balance. Work in the fields, peace in the craftsmen's shops, the learning of the priests, the singing and dancing of the children, the evening calm in the squares or in the valleys, all depended on the thousands of men whose tread, whose breath nearly, could be heard all around on the plain, and whose blood was about to be spilled. The numerical inferiority of the imperial army was obvious to all, and the old terror of the barbarians stirred in every heart. But even more than fear, they inspired hatred; and instead of fighting against each other, the two emotions combined and grew stronger—better to die than be subjected anew to caprice and injustice, cruelty and tyranny. Each man knew he was fighting for his home, the future of his sons, the resumption of feasts too long suspended, for his happiness, and for his gods. The barbarians dreamed of fertile lands, fields of wheat and rye, of treasure, and fine buildings in shining cities. Town and country had alike been ravaged by years of internal strife, but the nomads did not know this, and for them the Empire was still a beckoning vision. Lenin was right when he said:[3] "The class struggle is foreshadowed in the conflict between the Empire of those who had everything and the barbarians, who had nothing." The battle was on between those who stood only to lose and those who stood only to gain. So both sides had excellent reasons to conquer or die in the attempt.

The battle lasted six days and six nights—one of the longest, bloodiest, and most indecisive encounters in the whole of military history. "As rarely happens in war," writes Thiers, "the two opposing masses marched resolutely at one another, without flinching, until they came into contact." There was horrible slaughter. The barbarian squadrons broke against the imperial squares. But fresh waves of horsemen still came on from all quarters, and gradually began to penetrate the wall of pikes and spears that their arrows had already breached. The Balearic slingers wreaked havoc among the nomad horsemen. And against the barbarians' wild onslaughts Bruince, remembering perhaps the maddened horses used in the siege of Balkh, launched chariots armed with long scythes, or linked together by chains stuck with sharp blades, which mowed down whole ranks of the enemy like skittles, shattering the centaurs into their component parts and leaving them lying in their own blood. Puységur,[4] Guibert,[5] Clausewitz,[6] Hans Delbrück,[7] Shaposhnikov,[8] and Liddell Hart[9] have all made skilled, penetrating, sometimes inspired analyses of the maneuvers of both sides. But many as are the accounts of the battle, it is impossible to arrive at a very accurate idea of the tactics employed. According to some, Balamir's plan was to attempt a strong frontal breakthrough; according to others, it was a classic example of an encircling movement. As well as the authoritative works mentioned above, there have been numerous commentaries on and attempts to explain the action. There is something rather disturbing about the multiplicity of explanations offered for so many things nowadays, and this in every field, in literature and sociology as much as in strategy. In military as in all other matters, to comment is easy but not much to the purpose. Explanation is one of the curses of our age. Anybody is prepared to voice theories on books he didn't write and on victories he didn't win. In countless essays the maneuvers of Alexis and Balamir have been compared to the battles of Cannae, Austerlitz, the Marne, and Stalingrad, but the military historians, strategists, and polemologists have not been able to agree on any conclusions. Because of the inflation of theories and interpretations, anecdote is out of favor these days. Yet the only image popular tradition preserves of the six-day battle is of Balamir succeeding in galloping right up to the Emperor, who owed his life to Jester's intervention. Just as the barbarian prince was raising his sword against Alexis, the boy slipped under the Kha-Khan's white stallion and killed it with a dagger thrust. Balamir, unhorsed, managed with great difficulty to rejoin his men. By the evening of the sixth day, the barbarians had lost between two and three hundred thousand men, Alexis about fifty thousand. The two severely tried armies encamped on their positions.

It was during that night, in the very midst of the fray, that secret talks were held between Simeon and Bruince. They ended quite quickly in an agreement that both the Emperor and Balamir accepted, solemnly promising to observe its conditions under the supervision of a commission of priests and shamans chosen equally from both sides. At dawn on the seventh day, riders and trumpeters of both camps galloped through the lines and separated the combatants.[10] Fighting was suspended, and before each army heralds proclaimed the terms of the agreement. The war was ended, the dead were to be exchanged, and the quarrel between the barbarians and the Empire was to be settled by a double single combat between two barbarians and two warriors of the Empire.

The announcement created a huge sensation. Despite the general exhaustion, small groups gathered all over the battlefield, sometimes bringing together those who had fought against one another the previous day. A tense silence succeeded the tumult of battle. Excitement was greatest in the barbarian camp, for to them the agreement was a godsend. Single combat was held in honor among these rough and brutal people, and they all assumed victory was as good as theirs. Once the matter was settled, Alexis would have to submit to Balamir and the Empire would be open to the nomads. Those around Alexis were anxious, it is true, but everyone commended their cause to the gods, and all supported the Emperor's decision. Despite the unequal losses that had probably brought Balamir to agree to the settlement, the barbarians were still so numerous that another day's fighting might have seen the rout of the imperial army and the victory of the nomads. It was better to put oneself in the hands of fate.

On both sides a crowd of warriors pressed round their leaders asking to be nominated to take part in the combat. Balamir's choice was soon made. "I choose force and hatred," he said, "because it is those that bring victory." Force was represented by Dingizik, a man from the Urals whose size made him stand out among the rest of the nomad horsemen. He was a redheaded giant over 6 feet tall and broad to match, with a shaven head and two short braids. His massive, brutal body and cruel, scar-seamed face were so savage-looking they were enough in themselves to paralyze any adversary with terror. He boasted of having slain one hundred thirty-two men already with his own hand, raped more than one hundred women, left a trail of fire behind him everywhere he went, and of being the strongest of all the children of the steppe and the high plateaus. His name was known in every peasant's hut in the Empire, even as far away as Onessa and Gildor. By nominating him Balamir was not only choosing the best, most agile, and bravest of his warriors, he was also foreshadowing, as far as the means at his disposal allowed, psychological warfare, and the devastating effect of propaganda on a fear-stricken enemy. When the name of Dingizik began to pass from mouth to mouth among the imperial troops, a shudder ran through the camp. Dingizik! Who could possibly rival his skill and violence? The shadow of murder, extortion, and rape seemed to fall over the Empire again at the very sound of his name. So much for force. The barbarians' second champion—hatred—was to be Simeon.

Alexis took much longer to name the two men on whom the destiny of everyone in the Empire was to depend. He, too, thought at first of the strongest and most skillful. But when he heard the names of those who had been chosen on the other side, the fight seemed to him in any case unequal and lost in advance. He knew, as everyone did, the reputation of Dingizik. Above all he knew Simeon. Since boyhood Alexis's brother had been known as one of the most formidable warriors of the northeastern forests, a region that had given the Empire so many soldiers and so many leaders. Expert at all physical activity, passionately fond of war and arms, adroit and ingenious, of unparalleled courage when sustained by fury, Simeon had, above all, the most powerful motives for fighting for survival: ambition, revenge, and violent secret passions. Balamir had chosen well! Alexis accorded the Kha-Khan's subtlety an expert's admiration. It was while reflecting on Balamir's choice that Alexis came to the decision that plunged the army first into stupefaction, then great anxiety. Since it was not possible to pit force against force and brutality against brutality, recourse must be had to the passions of the soul—to the mind, the heart, the cardinal virtues, all the resources of character. To fight against the giant Dingizik and Simeon the traitor, Alexis named Isidore and Jester.

A blind man and a boy! It struck the imperial army like a thunderclap. "One could hear," wrote Justus Dion, "the silence of anguish and the tumult of beating hearts." A blind man, a boy! True, Isidore was strong and healthy and familiar, like many priests, with army life and military skills. He was unequaled at throwing a spear, and his courage had no rival. But his strength was not equal to that of Dingizik or Simeon, war was not his trade, and he was blind. A blind man and a boy—a great roar of laughter swept through the barbarian camp. Balamir alone was silent. There was something that made him uneasy in this choice. His uneasiness was visible, and before long had spread among the nomads, so that their scorn and arrogance became tinged with awe and vague uncertainty. Alexis, for his part, openly explained the reasons for his decision. "It was best they should entrust themselves to the will of heaven and the fate of the Empire. And these would speak more clearly through infirmity and innocence. It was to be the force of destiny against brute physical strength, it was to be gods against men." And he ordered prayers and sacrifices to be offered during the three days that were to precede the combat.

For these three days, Isidore and Jester vanished to prepare themselves for the fight. Dingizik and Simeon spent the time felling oxen with their fists and uprooting trees. And roaring with laughter.

On the day fixed for the double duel, when the sun had just broken through the clouds, the four men—the three men and the boy—presented themselves at the space that had been prepared for the combat. It was closed in by a light wooden fence, and all around it were gathered the soldiers of the two armies, intermingled. The site chosen was a hollow among gently sloping hills, so that the soldiers could spread themselves out in tiers and get a good view. In the middle of each of the long sides of the rectangle formed by the fence, a throne or dais had been hastily erected. Justus Dion uses the word for a dais; the barbarian historian Jornandez, whose account is based on tradition, says they were thrones. Alexis and Balamir had each taken their seat on one of these constructions, surrounded by their officers. Immediately around the fence, rather like referees in a modern contest, were the priests and the shamans. The audience took their places gesticulating and chattering. If it had not been for the momentous issues at stake, it might have been some popular holiday or carnival. Though by force of circumstance there grew up a kind of snarling fraternity between the members of this strange assembly, the attitudes of the two bodies of spectators were very different. The barbarians were distinguishable from the inhabitants of the Empire not only by physical type, demeanor, and clothes, all so characteristic and so different. It was also a matter of feeling, and of the spirit reflected in the men's faces. Some, joyful, arrogant, certain of victory despite a dim uneasiness, already spoke as victors. The others, consumed by doubt and anxiety, put all their trust in the gods and in the unexpected.

Dingizik and Simeon were the first to enter the enclosure, both emanating savage vigor and brutality. Stocky though strongly built, Simeon looked small beside the giant. Dingizik wore a roughly cured pelt, Simeon sumptuous furs and a kind of cap coming down over the eyes. Together they created a terrifying impression. The barbarians greeted them with a great ovation. The din had still not died down when Isidore and Jester appeared. Then a deep silence fell, which for different reasons neither the barbarians nor the imperial soldiers felt like breaking. The boy held the blind man by the hand, and they were dressed in white. Though Isidore was quite tall and strong, they seemed frailty itself as they confronted the giant with his two red braids and Simeon, standing hands on hips as if merely waiting for the kill.

Dingizik and Simeon were each armed with an axe and a bow. The barbarian also had a sword at his side, while Simeon had the inlaid dagger that never left him. At first glance Isidore and Jester looked completely unarmed, but closer inspection revealed a sling and a tiny dagger hung round Jester's neck, while over the priest's shoulder was a kind of long case or quiver, in which a keen eye could discern very thin wooden javelins, with tips of bone, ivory, or metal. The champions of the barbarians stood still and watched Jester lead the blind man along. A few laughs were heard, but they soon gave place to silence, tension, and perhaps a sudden shame at the sight of the cripple and the child. The four combatants ranged themselves in pairs on the short sides of the rectangle. Tens and hundreds of thousands of warriors froze and held their breath. All that could be heard in the silence descending from the hills were the slow footfalls of the four men. A trumpet and a gong were to sound simultaneously to indicate the start of the combat. Never had such an army been so still. To anyone looking down from above, they would have seemed like a petrified army of ants filling the narrow valley and covering the surrounding slopes. The trumpet blew and the gong rang out.

Then everything happened incredibly swiftly. Isidore and Jester appeared to be leaping in the air to avoid the arrows being fitted into the bows. But the boy, barehanded, landed all at once only a few paces away from the astonished barbarian, hampered by his cumbersome weapons, and wrenched the sculpted bow out of the giant's huge hands. Simeon aimed his arrow at the boy, but Jester swiftly dodged into the narrow space between Dingizik and the wooden fence, letting out a yell that echoed through the silence. As if guided by the sound, Isidore threw the javelin he was holding in his hand. The giant fell, and Jester drove his stiletto into his breast. Simeon loosed his arrow, but Jester had gone. He seemed to weave arabesques in the air around Simeon, shaken by the fall of his companion. The first act was over. Simeon was left alone against the blind man and the boy. A great roar rose up from the valley, hills, and plateaus.

Simeon soon recovered and sized up his own situation and the tactics of his opponents. There was no need to worry—he was only fighting against a cripple and a child. The first thing, obviously, was to see that Jester did not serve him, Simeon, as he had served the now expiring Dingizik. Simeon retired step by step until his back was to the fence. Once there, he breathed slowly, selected another arrow, bent his bow, and aimed at Isidore. Just as he was about to let fly he saw Jester aiming at him with his sling. The missile hit him as the arrow left the bow, making it fly aside and bury itself with a hiss in the fence a few yards away from Isidore, who kept moving so as not to present a standing target. Simeon staggered at the impact, but at once recovered himself and made to seize his ax. But Jester was already upon him, clutching his fur-clad form so tightly he could not get to his weapon. Simeon threw himself on the boy, who scarcely struggled, as if he wanted to be taken. Simeon picked him up and held him before him as a shield against Isidore's javelin, shouting in Greek that if he tried to strike Simeon he would hit Jester. The furious rhythm of the fight, which had lasted only a few minutes, perhaps seconds, since the gong and the trumpet, seemed to flag for a moment. Isidore appeared to hesitate. But Simeon himself could no longer use either bow or ax: he just hid behind Jester, trying to strangle him so that he should not cry out and guide the blind man on to his target.[11]

Simeon, still holding Jester in front of him for protection, now advanced slowly on Isidore, who stood with javelin poised in the air. Those nearest could see the tension and anxiety in the blind man's face as he strained for the least sound. But what happened next was too swift for the crowd of panting spectators to understand at the time. It emerged only later, in endless discussions at night around the campfire, amidst laughter and rye brandy and quarreling and mare's milk. Jester, who had kept both his sling and his dagger in his hand, managed to plunge the blade into Simeon's hip. It was only a slight flesh wound, but it made Simeon flinch with pain and lower for a moment his living shield. Jester uttered his cry. Isidore launched his weapon. It grazed the boy and struck Simeon in the eye. He fell. Plain, hills, and sky were filled with one immense roar. In the same way as he had finished off Dingizik, Jester, with his dagger, now slew the son of Helen and Roderick. On the imperial dais, rocking with the cheers that arose in wave after wave from the imperial army, while the horrified nomads were struck dumb, Alexis suddenly remembered the boy stabbing the huge wolf many years ago in the ancient forests of the northeast.[12]

Balamir and the barbarians submitted without complaint to the decree of fate. As soon as the combat was over the barbarian prince came and bowed before the Emperor and did him homage. Alexis arose, reached out, and made him rise. This encounter, this reconciliation between the Emperor and the Kha-Khan, brought a fresh burst of cheering, this time from both sides. Violent emotion can soon reverse the passions of the crowd. The barbarians, having lost a wager there was no question of going back on, had expected the worst. Alexis's courtesy to their leader transformed into enthusiasm the mixture of dejection and anxiety that had succeeded their former arrogance. As for the soldiers of the Empire, drunk with joy and with gratitude to the Emperor, they simply gave themselves up to trying to express their devotion. The festivities celebrated in the Empire lasted more than ten days, and marked something far more important than just another episode in the struggle against the barbarians. But the Emperor and Bruince were as yet the only ones to guess, and to foster, their future significance.

Successes are more difficult to surmount than reverses, but Alexis had never forgotten the lessons given by Thaumas and the high priest's attitude at the time of the battle of Amphibolus.[13] He had thought about it a great deal, and had come to the conclusion that he should make use of any victory he might win to come to a settlement with the barbarians. The hour of victory and reconciliation had arrived, and he was not going to let it slip through his fingers. The fact that it was Simeon's death that allowed the nomads to be reconciled at last with the Empire was not the least paradoxical thing about the situation. There was, and we shall see it developing further, an obscure, tortured, almost satanic side to Alexis's character. He was incomparably brilliant, radiant, but also surrounded with violence and darkness. His brother's death was a kind of sinister echo of the death of his mistress. "It was through one crime after another," writes Robert Weill-Pichon, "that Alexis rose to glory." To which Sir Allan Carter-Bennett replies: "Alexis had never wished for his brother's death. He accepted it, if not as an affliction at least as a necessity, and perhaps also as a sign." It was a sign that the childhood dreams in the forests of the northeast were over. The elegant prince and philanderer had died with Vanessa. With Simeon, the shade of Roderick and the great forest also disappeared. What the rejoicings of the Empire celebrated was really more than a victory—it was a revolution. The death of the brother and traitor who had gone over to the barbarians made possible at last, and in a strange way consecrated, the reconciliation, alliance, and union with the barbarians. The struggle against them had brought glory to Arsaphes, to Basil, and to Alexis himself. It was this struggle that had won Basil the title of Basil the Great. But it was to another title and another glory that Alexis, conqueror of the barbarians but also heir to Thaumas, now aspired. A new emperor was being born—Alexis, the Father of the Peoples.

XVII

DIREITO POR LINHAS TORTAS,

OR THE NEW ALLIANCE

HE TRIUMPH OF ALEXIS, ISIDORE, AND JESTER flashed around the Empire like lightning, stirring men's hearts and minds. Inscriptions in marble, poems, and legends sprang up everywhere to perpetuate the memory of it. Alexis did not wait to put Balamir to the test or to try his fidelity. On Bruince's advice he asked him to head, in the Emperor's name, all the imperial armies.

This was a bold and original stroke. Throughout history, from Vercingetorix and Caesar to Tamerlane and Bajazet, from Francis I and Charles V to Wilhelm I and Napoleon III or Hitler and Pétain, there have been encounters between victor and vanquished. They have often ended in the death of the vanquished, sometimes in reconciliation, real or apparent. But they have never led so swiftly to the unification of forces that a few days, even a few hours before were fighting each other to the death. The Kha-Khan asked for two days in which to consult his advisers and reflect. The next evening but one, he accepted Alexis's offer. One of the world's greatest empires had been brought into being through a six-day battle, a double duel, and the reconciliation of the adversaries.

From then on Balamir, though in command both of his own nomads and of the soldiers of the Empire, bore Alexis an affection that never wavered and was sometimes passionate. The Emperor had staked the Empire on a terrific wager—on the barbarian prince's loyalty. A stroke of genius had made him suspect that it was there, and he was not mistaken. All through his reign there were plots and conspiracies against Alexis, but the name of Balamir was never involved in any of them. The Kha-Khan was allowed to keep not only his freedom and his titles, but also his privileges and even his power. But he acted in the Emperor's name, and in consultation with him. The rapprochement between the Emperor and the Kha-Khan created an enormous stir throughout Europe and Asia, and even in distant Africa beyond the Nile and Carthage. Cyprus, Pomposa, and Sicily, all those who had helped the Empire against the barbarians, even the Middle Kingdom itself, were uneasy at the alliance between the two dangers that had for so long canceled one another out. They considered themselves tricked, perhaps betrayed. They seized every opportunity to try to stir up the old enmity between the two allies, to break up the union and the formidable power it conferred. It was immediately after the agreement between Alexis and Balamir, which was to go down in history as the famous New Alliance, that the first symptoms of future conflicts and their consequences manifested themselves.

The origin of these conflicts, which were to turn the world upside down and help to make it what it is today, has given rise to endless debate. Some blame Alexis's insatiable ambition, which they describe as one of those mystical ambitions that cause more harm and violence than the ordinary ambitions that aim merely at pleasure and power. Others see in the constant maneuvers of Pomposa, Cyprus, Sicily, and all the other great powers of the time who resented the success of the New Alliance, the true cause of the events that would be linked to Alexis's name as much as and even more than the rebirth of the Empire and the union with the barbarians. The difference on this point seems to correspond to two different mental attitudes, and by an escalation characteristic of contemporary culture the history of Alexis's conquests has become to a large extent the history of the different interpretations to which they have given rise and to the history of their historians.

But whether one is among Alexis's supporters or his detractors, one can only admire the boldness of his solution to the problem of the barbarians, so long a source of fear and trouble. The Empire was not strong enough to withstand their assaults indefinitely. As several documents show, Alexis and Bruince had at first considered the classical policy of channeling them back into Asia, and, by a series of treaties and other incitements, diverting their minds to the temptations offered by China, Persia, and India. But the New Alliance went far beyond that. It had the marvelous virtue of turning to the advantage of the Empire the greed which it was difficult if not impossible to stifle altogether. The Empire no longer drove the barbarians away: it made them its subjects, and used them to conquer the world. The simple audacity of the idea behind the New Alliance is astonishing. Sir Allan Carter-Bennett justly describes it as "a Copernican revolution in civilization and history."

This revolution was not accomplished without opposition and violence. The hostility of the great powers who had profited from the traditional conflict found support both in the Empire and among the barbarians. Many of the latter saw the New Alliance as the badge of servitude and shame. Immediately after the double duel not a single voice would have been raised to suggest continuing the struggle against the Empire—single combat was honored too much among the barbarians for anyone to question the outcome. But Balamir's subsequent policy of entente with the victor was more than many of the nomads could understand. Their new links with the Empire necessarily brought them into contact with the rich fields and cities they had so long dreamed of. These, as we have seen, were in a pitiable state after being exploited by the tyrants, then ravaged by civil war. But they were still a paradise to the barbarian nomads. Why shouldn't they attack them in force, take them by surprise, and thus wipe out the very memory of the defeat of the double duel? Balamir had great difficulty putting down five or six consecutive attempts to deprive him of power and destroy the New Alliance. The list of these revolts and putsches is as complex and tedious as the tangled history of the later Byzantine Empire. For two or three years Balamir galloped once again from Oxus to Lena, the Urals to the Altai. He won success after success against his rebellious subjects or his impatient allies. Alexis, in Aquileus, where he was reorganizing the Empire and its army, navy, trade, and priesthood, saw that he could trust in Balamir's fidelity. And, in the words of Justus Dion, "he rejoiced in his heart, dreaming of a new world and a peace born out of war."

The Emperor, too, had to deal with opposition that was often violent. Better organized, more patient, more subtle than the nomads' rash uprisings against Balamir, these attacks were also more dangerous. And they never ceased, whereas Balamir's only problem was to hold out during the three or four years that came before the great conquests: once the New Alliance had launched the nomads against the great plains of wheat and the gold-covered monuments, the barbarians were again behind Balamir as one man. But within the

Empire itself, military success and economic prosperity were never enough to reconcile everyone to the alliance with the barbarians. The hostility to the New Alliance—fostered, according to Robert Weill-Pichon, by Pomposan gold—came mainly from groups most deeply rooted in tradition: big ship and cattle owners, families where a naval or military career was handed down from father to son, merchants whose fortunes depended on good relations with Cyprus or Sicily, the ever-resurgent priesthood, resentful at seeing their recently revived power threatened by the New Alliance just as it had arisen out of its own ashes. All these different groups, once opposed to one another, now found themselves united in common hostility toward the barbarians and their influence on imperial policy. By a striking but easily explained paradox, many of those who thus opposed Alexis had been among his stoutest supporters at the time of the conspiracy against the barbarian tyrants. The reason was that they thought themselves more faithful than the Emperor to the lessons they owed to him. Had he not taught them to unite against the barbarians, to drive them from lands wrested from them by Arsaphes and Basil, to protect the customs, beliefs, and traditions of the Empire against the invader? And now here was the Emperor putting himself into the hands of the barbarians, receiving them at Aquileus, covering their leaders with honors, wealth, and marks of friendship, and entrusting Balamir, enemy of the gods and terror of the steppes, who had burned so many villages and murdered so many innocent people, with the command of the imperial armies! Many genuinely thought that the Emperor was deranged, that mysterious and sinister influences were affecting his mind and will, and that he was no longer responsible for his mad decisions and the perilous paths into which he was leading the Empire. They were filled with anger, and with real hatred against Alexis. One of the cleverest of his opponents found an explanation that worked very well—so well that all these centuries later it is found almost word for word in the accounts of some modern historians. According to this view, Alexis's policy after having beaten Balamir was exactly the same as Simeon would have imposed if he had beaten Alexis. The more subtle exponents of this theory added that Simeon would probably have had to be harsher toward his allies, and that it was unthinkable that he could have shown Balamir the same consideration and respect that Alexis now did. And so there spread through the Empire a kind of skepticism and even hostility that eventually came to threaten Alexis's authority. A year or two after the six-day battle, the Pomposan ambassador wrote to his merchant princes that the Emperor's position had never been more precarious, and that even many of his own supporters seemed to expect his fall.

The crisis was to be resolved by an event of considerable political importance, but above all indicative of the Emperor's moral and psychological evolution. Whether through conviction or self-interest, Jester, hero with Isidore of the double single combat, had secretly gone over to Alexis's enemies. Chosen by the Emperor to continue one illustrious line, the conqueror of Simeon and Dingizik had, like Bruince but unlike Thaumas, Philocrates, and most of the Jesters preceding him, come from another—from one of the greatest families in the Empire. He had been brought up to respect already ancient traditions, together with the military virtues to which the companions of Arsaphes and Basil had owed their fame. These traditions, these virtues, were cherished among all the old families whose origins were buried in the mists of time and had usually been employed in the service of one or another of the two dynasties that had fought for mastery of the Empire—the Porphyries and the Venostae. Jester's family had supported the Porphyries, and had only with reluctance acquiesced in Basil's domination and the triumph of Onessa. But in these ancient families the love of arms and glory was so strong that Jester's grandfathers and great-grandfathers had eventually performed wonders in the service of the hated Venostae. So excessive was the pride of these great nobles, so imbued were they with the idea of their own superior lineage, that they always considered the Porphyries themselves traitors to tradition and the purity of the race. Long before Basil's reign, Jester's ancestors had considered Arsaphes nothing more than a captain of mercenaries who had been raised to the top rank by his marriage to the Porphyries' heiress and by the fortune of war. They referred to him almost openly as a foreigner and an upstart. Through his mother, Alexis himself undoubtedly belonged to the great line of the Porphyries. But his birth, his escapades, his policy were all of just the kind to displease the great past-oriented families who had managed to survive the convulsions of the Empire, and in whom Robert Weill-Pichon with reason discerned the very type of the extreme conservative. The fight against the barbarians had temporarily reconciled them with the Emperor, but they meant to oblige him, and if necessary force him, to adopt their own policy. Jester's success had restored all their pride in their origins. They had begun to hope that the new order would restore tradition, privilege, ancestral ways, and the greatness of their houses. The New Alliance had been a great blow to these hopes, which soon turned into conspiracies. Jester, whom we have seen so devoted to the Emperor that he was ready to die for him and follow him to the ends of the earth, viewed the alliance with Balamir as a kind of betrayal. That he was influenced by the merchant princes, an explanation angrily advanced by Robert Weill-Pichon, seems to Sir Allan Carter-Bennett unlikely; and this is the view taken by most modern historians. On the other hand, the princes of Cyprus, who had various connections with Jester's family, do seem to have gotten to him, not so much by promises of advantage as by heaping on him flattery and honors. Passing through Famagusta, Jester had been received with delirious enthusiasm, and the lad, who accepted the affection and gratitude of his own people very naturally, had his head turned by the sight of a whole city, a foreign country, and strangely clad chiefs and princes acclaiming him and venerating him like a god. He was entering the difficult age between childhood and adolescence. By dint of always hearing that it was he who had saved the Empire and that Isidore had been merely the physical instrument wielded by his intelligence, he came to think he was charged with some special vocation with regard to the Empire, and began to see signs and hear voices. But two or three years after the double duel, Jester was still scarcely more than a very young man unconsciously conditioned by all sorts of influences. Those of the most traditionalist circles in the Empire joined with that of his family and friends, that of the priests, and that of the princes of Cyprus, to make him believe the barbarians he had overthrown all alone were still the enemy of the race, of tradition, and of all those to whom the Empire really belonged.

Alexis's victories had enabled the priests of Aquileus to recover the prosperity, influence, and power lost to them since the triumph of Basil. Through Fabrician, and also through Philocrates, who without being a priest himself had been very close to them, Alexis had too many links with the hierarchy not to follow Basil's later example and restore it to its former dignities and privileges. The priests had done much for the greatness of the Empire, in education, culture, the development of the arts, in bringing about a certain softening of manners, and in introducing a certain idea of the duties of life as well as of its beauty. They had had their faults. They had shown both boundless ambition and cowardice in the face of force. But such figures as Thaumas and Isidore—and Bruince, too—were enough, with the memory of their courage and magnanimity, to redeem and excuse the rest. And after all, in this Empire still filled with violence and uncouthness, Alexis felt quite close to the priests, despite their many differences. He liked to go and talk to them, not only about the affairs of the Empire, but, like his mother Helen, about man's place in the universe and his immortal destiny. But under these outward signs of friendship, a whole section of the priests of Aquileus were, in fact, fiercely opposed to him. They reproached him for his sun worship, his former life of debauchery, his mysterious links with the religions of Asia, which many regarded as mere magic and sorcery, and, above all, for being at once too harsh and too indulgent: they blamed him both for Simeon's death and for the alliance with Balamir. "What!" they would murmur, moving busily from group to group, "a man who murdered his brother and his mistress, who worships no god but the sun, who digs the grave of tradition, a debauchee, the friend of the barbarians—*he* the master of the Empire! Let us spring to the Empire's defense before the nomads rule in Aquileus, before the worship of the sun supplants that of the eagle and the oak, before all our old customs are destroyed."

Alexis's connection with sun worship might well have aroused the resentment of any who were profoundly attached to the religion of their ancestors. But in many cases this was only a pretext. The real motives were thirst for power, jealousy of newly recovered privileges, and the fear inspired by the New Alliance and a policy in which the influence of the barbarians was bound to counterbalance, if not threaten, that of the priests. Several times the priests of Aquileus offered Alexis plans for the elimination of the barbarians. All these schemes relied on trickery and on Balamir's trust in Alexis's friendship. It was suggested that on the pretext of some feast or entertainment the nomads should be lured into a narrow valley or pass, surrounded, and massacred. "Are you not ashamed," the Emperor answered the priests, "to use against the barbarians the same treachery that Basil once used against you? Are you, the victims of the banquet at Onessa, so anxious to become the executioners of the New Alliance? Treason and injustice are even more frail than violence and hatred, and they can never be sure of success. And even if they were, what you suggest would not be justified. It would be unworthy of you and of me to repay with baseness the loyalty of the barbarians, who probably think us more honorable than we are. If they should betray us, we shall retaliate. But if they are faithful, why should we betray?"

The Emperor also knew in his own mind that the power of the nomads could never be destroyed at a single blow. However many perished in a massacre, enough would still remain to overwhelm the Empire. And so, knowing himself responsible for all those who had set him at their head, Alexis resisted the priests and their mad schemes. It was then that they turned to Jester, who became in their hands an obedient instrument against the Emperor's prestige and the policy of the New Alliance.

The priests, backed by silver from Cyprus, paraded Jester from place to place as the living symbol of resistance to the barbarians. Each of his public appearances was accompanied by speeches paying equivocal tribute to the prestige of the Porphyries, uttering fiery incitements to the struggle against the barbarians, and lauding the example of the ancestral way of life. In a famous address to the college of priests at Aquileus, Isidore tried to point out to the younger among them, who were apt to talk airily about it, what life really had been like not only under the barbarian tyrants but, even before them, under Basil and Arsaphes. He recalled the daily threats, the fear of what the morrow might bring, the constant fear of invasion, the continual insecurity parried only by heroism and the efforts of genius. We all know, having translated them twenty times at school, the most famous passages of this inspired and eloquent address: "How long will courage be confused with temerity, and wisdom with cowardice? To save the Empire, men have to be bold, be bold, and everywhere be bold. The slightest stupidity or folly and all might be lost. . . . It is the magnanimity of the victor that gives its meaning to victory. It is the hope and image of peace that justify war. So let us learn to be strong without being unjust, and to bring out of conflict that friendship between men that is the secret of empires, that love of wisdom that is another name for virtue." Those priests who were hostile to the Emperor regarded this speech as a capitulation to the barbarians. Two days later, twenty-seven barbarian captains and over three hundred of their men were murdered near Amphibolus.

Balamir was at this time engaged in putting down a rebellion, far from the frontiers of the Empire. When he heard the news from two of the nomad messengers who used to bring information on their tiny, almost unbroken horses over unimaginable distances, the Kha-Khan was seized with fury. He was not familiar with the subtle intrigues of the priests inside the Empire, and from the messengers' account he was led to believe that Alexis was implicated. Of course, this was just what the priests had intended. They had calculated that Balamir's anger must bring about the rupture of the New Alliance and force the Emperor into the war he wanted to avoid. To make assurance double sure, the priests had left the nomads to die with refinements of cruelty more reminiscent of the worst excesses of the barbarians than of the fine ancestral customs they were always talking about. Instead of being crucified, the victims were riddled with barbed arrows ending in hooks that tore out lumps of flesh when the arrows were removed. The gaping, half-flayed bodies, still alive, were then buried in pits, with a covering of branches and stones that allowed some air to enter, so that death should be prolonged. These horrors, breathlessly recounted to Balamir by the messengers, fired the whole camp with a desire for revenge. Those among the barbarians who had been hoping for the destruction of the New Alliance also saw their opportunity, and urged Balamir not to leave such bloody insults unanswered. Balamir hesitated, spending almost a whole day shut up in his tent, pacing up and down and fingering the beads of amber, tortoise shell, and ivory that the emperor of the Middle Kingdom had given to him to appease the anger and anxiety that could make all Asia tremble. He reflected that the union of the barbarians with the Empire could lead to unparalleled successes; he shrank from attacking Alexis again; and he had a vague feeling that the matter was not as simple as was claimed by the more excitable and violent of his counselors, who wished for an immediate decision so that there could be no going back. But confronted with the determined, almost threatening attitude of those about him, who, bored with a long peace interrupted by only a few routine or police operations, howled for war and blood with perhaps an admixture of understandable indignation, the Kha-Khan decided to march against the Empire. Had he made any other decision he would have run the risk of being overridden by Alexis's enemies, and put both his own authority and his life in danger. Once again the earth shook beneath the hoofs of the wild horsemen, drunk with the thought of the fire and carnage they had been deprived of for so long. In them a strange new feeling that they were executing justice mingled with a familiar excitement at the approach to rape and plunder.

Alexis, in Aquileus, did not need the reports of spies and informers to tell him the grave, possibly irreparable, consequences of the mad act perpetrated by the party made up of the princes of Cyprus, the priests, and the great families of the Empire. All the work of reconciliation, the whole New Alliance, was threatened by this second massacre at Amphibolus—the very name of the place was full of sinister portents. Without hesitation, Alexis sent three messengers to the Kha-Khan of the Oïghurs, bearing messages of regret, promises of peace, and gifts. But, as he suspected how the nomads must be feeling, he had the messengers followed by secret agents with instructions to cover them and, if necessary, come to their aid. Before a fortnight was out, one of these men, disguised as a merchant, reappeared in Aquileus. He was gaunt, exhausted, scarcely recognizable. When he was brought before the Emperor, he barely had the strength to recount the horrors he had witnessed. The messengers, shadowed by the others who followed their movements secretly and from a distance, had ridden for nine days. On the evening of the ninth day, as they were crossing an almost dry river, a host of nomads had risen up from among the rocks and sparse vegetation overlooking the river, thrown themselves on the horsemen, and taken them prisoner. They had at once begun to torture them, first cutting off their hands and feet with refinements not so much of cruelty as of a real desire to avoid too rapid a death. The unhappy victims were revived after every stage and almost lovingly tended by a Chinaman with a long straggly beard who was both torturer and physician. By means of swords whose whetted edges had been tried first on grass and leaves, the Chinese had cut off, one after the other, their sexual organs, noses, and ears, and was about to disembowel them, when the secret envoys, no longer able to bear the awful sight, tried, under cover of dusk and of the spell cast on the barbarians by blood and torture, to make a surprise attack. Despite the unequal numbers they had already killed ten or a dozen when they in turn were overwhelmed and rendered helpless. Only the man now speaking to the Emperor had managed, during the struggle, to hide in a rocky hollow where the nomads could not find him, and where, after a long and unsuccessful search, they left him, to bury the thought of him in rye brandy and indifference.

Night had fallen. The man ventured to peer out over the rocks, and saw the barbarians lighting a fire. The prisoners were lying in front of it, tied together by their legs and arms. To the dreadful scene, the cries of pain, the drunkenness and the calm, precise, almost abstract gestures of the Chinaman who seemed to be officiating in some nightmare ceremonial, the dancing flames lent the appearance of a fantastic carnival in which flowers, music, and dancing were

replaced by blood, the moans of the dying, and the grotesque gesticu-
lations of executioners and victims. The three messengers finally died,
and the nomads seemed to have forgotten the prisoners thrown in
front of the fire. The barbarians shared out the gifts intended for the
Kha-Khan, perfumes, jewels, precious spirits in sealed jars; they
tossed the gold about in their hands, and unwound silks and velvets
so that they could be heard rustling through the darkness. From time
to time one of them would stagger to his feet and go over, with insults
and oaths, to thrust against a face or a body a burning brand or a
spear made red-hot in the fire. Then again, through the drunken
hiccupping, would come more groans of pain, and the light breeze
would carry the awful smell of charred flesh. Thus a part of the night
passed away. Then, just before dawn, the Chinaman, who had fallen
asleep, woke up. He stretched, rubbed his eyes, swallowed five or six
cups of rye brandy, threw more wood on the fire, and went over to the
prisoners. He tore off their nails, gouged out their eyes, and slit open
their stomachs, and stuffed into their mouths their eyes and genitals
and bowels. Some of the nomads were making love to one another in
the flickering firelight.

The Emperor ordered the survivor's story to be kept absolutely
secret. Two or three days later, the man died quite peacefully in the
palace at Aquileus, where he had been looked after carefully and even
sumptuously; rumor said he had been poisoned. The choice before
Alexis was simple, but difficult: either war to the death on the soil of
the Empire, with all the risks and suffering that that involved, or one
further step along the road of forgiveness and appeasement. The
Emperor closeted himself with Bruince. It was another of the most
painful crises of his life. "The Emperor," Justus Dion tells us, "cursed
the course of things, the concatenation of events, and the burden of
power. He saw that history was a cruel game, whether it was governed by the gods or merely grew out of itself. His mind was mazed
before this labyrinth of a world, pitched into space and time. But his
spirit was strong and his mind lucid. The time had gone by—or had
not yet arrived—for dreams of solitude, of withdrawal to the desert or
mountains or forest, of meditation on the soul and the divine. Action
was needed, to give the labyrinth some form for a while. He summoned Bruince and Jester and the chief priests, ministers, and generals, and decided . . ." The decision was to save the alliance and
put Jester to death.

The Emperor and Jester stayed alone together for almost a whole day. We know nothing about what happened during that time, only that they came out of the palace hand in hand and that Jester threw himself at the Emperor's feet before the assembled crowd. As with Balamir, the Emperor helped him to rise and took him in his arms. Those nearest could see tears streaming down the Emperor's cheeks as he embraced the boy. The executioner was ready. Alexis himself led to the red-draped platform surrounded with troops him who had saved his life, whom he called his son, and whom he loved above all. The trumpets sounded. Jester's head rolled from the scaffold.

His death brought countless consequences. The barbarian hordes had already advanced as far as the borders of the Empire. A few more days and they would inevitably clash with the main body of the army that Bruince had hastily mustered and massed along a line of defense some distance within the frontier. Meanwhile Alexis had made contact with the barbarian detachments stationed inside the Empire which had been encircled by the army after the massacre of the three hundred mercenaries and their officers near Amphibolus. These prisoners were already preparing for death when Alexis promised them they should live, and sent their leaders, under strong escort, to deliver a message to the Kha-Khan of the Oïghurs. The message consisted of a letter and Jester's head.

The letter has a curious history. It was supposed to be among the best and most expensive documents that the famous forger Vrain-Lucas succeeded in selling, between 1867 and 1868, to the too naïve Michel Chasles, of the Academy of Sciences, whose erudition did not save him from being hoaxed. In *Le Temps* of July 8, 1888, in an article on various historical studies of Alexis, Anatole France refers to some of the documents brought into being by the delirious imagination of Vrain-Lucas. The autograph letters include the famous message from Lazarus to Mary Magdalen announcing his resurrection; a letter from Cesarion, visiting Provence, to his mother, Cleopatra; letters written by Shakespeare, Charles V, Rabelais, Saint Theresa, Du Guesclin, Sidonius Apollinaris, and the emperor Hadrian; letters from Cleopatra to Cato, from Joan of Arc to her family, from Attila to a general among the Gauls, from Julius Caesar to Vercingetorix, Judas Iscariot to Mary Magdalen, Herod to Jesus Christ, Alexander the Great to Aristotle, Alcibiades to Pericles, and, of course, the fake letter from the Emperor to the Kha-Khan of the Oïghurs. "These letters," says Anatole France, "were written on paper, in French. But the paper was yellowed and the style archaic. Thus Mary Magdalen says to Lazarus: 'Mon très amé frère, ce que me mandez de Petrus, l'apostre de notre doux Jésus, me fait espérer que bientôt le verrons icy' [My dear brother, what you tell me of Peter, disciple of our beloved Jesus, makes me hope we shall soon see him here]. Vrain-Lucas was found guilty of fraud and sentenced to two years in prison, with a fifty-franc fine and costs." Alphonse Daudet, who made this affair the subject of one of his best-known novels, tells in *L'Immortel* how the supposed letter from Alexis to Balamir finally blew the gaff on the whole fraud when an expert discovered that the "antique" parchment bore the watermark "Papeteries d'Angoulême—1864."

But to turn to more serious matters, Marco Polo claims (though he was a great liar and his book, *The Million*, is, as we all know, full of inaccuracies and braggadocio) actually to have seen the genuine letter when he was at the court of Cambaluc, i.e., Peking. Was it he or some missionary who brought it back to Venice? In all events, by the beginning of the *quattrocento* it forms part of the treasures of Saint Mark's, together with the famous tiara of Saitaphernes, with a special note to the effect that it "is and remains" the personal property of the doge. It is not impossible that it was given as a congratulatory present by Yong-lo, emperor of China, on the election of Francesco Foscari as doge in 1423. Toward the end of the fifteenth century the letter passed, by obscure and perhaps sinister means, into the hands of the Medicis. Bernard Berenson liked to tell his visitors, half jokingly, that the *Virgin With the Letter* by Antonello da Messina, which for many years graced the walls of Berenson's beautiful villa, I Tatti, near Florence, and was purchased in 1959 by the Museum of Detroit, was really the portrait of a beautiful young nun who escaped from the convent at Fiesole and lived with the artist for two years before being poisoned by a Sicilian rival. Berenson would point out that in the picture Vanina Vanini (the nun, sometimes known also as La Pasticcierina, because she was the daughter of a pastry cook) was evidently reading a Renaissance copy of the Emperor's letter to the Kha-Khan of the Oïghurs before being interrupted by the crying of the child in her arms. And, indeed, one can decipher, on the parchment thrown carelessly onto the wooden table among some carpenter's tools, five or six Greek words—χαὶ τὴν χέφαλην τὴν τοῦ ἐμαυτου υἱοῦ—in which a benevolent interpreter might just see an echo of the last episode in the life of the unfortunate Jester.

What is certain is that the genuine letter reached France with Leonora Galigaï and her husband Concino Concini. After the murder of the maréchal d'Ancre by the future maréchal de Vitry, then still captain of the king's guards, the letter was seized by Charles, duc de Luynes. His widow Marie de Rohan-Montbazon, by then duchesse de Chevreuse, sold it to Finance Minister Fouquet, then at the height of his brilliance and prosperity. Saint-Simon tells how the sight of the letter in its casket of velvet and precious stones, during the famous reception at Vaux-le-Vicomte, was the last straw for Louis XIV. He coveted the treasure for himself, and Saint-Simon tells how, immediately after the reception, Fouquet was disgraced, tried, imprisoned, and most of his possessions confiscated. At that point trace is lost of the letter—or rather the traces are numerous, complicated, and contradictory. Some say d'Artagnan managed to secrete it at the time of Fouquet's arrest, and kept it for himself instead of handing it over to the king. The king is supposed to have heard about this when the captain of the musketeers was nearing his end, and according to this theory it was because of Louis's suspicions that the king's guard burst in on d'Artagnan as he lay on his deathbed at Maastricht in December, 1673. Not finding Alexis's letter, the guards impounded the manuscript of d'Artagnan's *Memoirs of My Life*, published for the first time in Amsterdam at the beginning of the eighteenth century. Having thus escaped confiscation twice, the letter was supposed to have remained in the possession of the Montesquiou-Fezensac family, of which d'Artagnan was a member. An express letter[1] from Gabriel Yturri, Robert de Montesquiou's secretary, inviting Marcel Proust to lunch at Neuilly and giving him some information he had asked for, states that the letter is still in the archives of the château de Marsan, near Auch, which had been in the possession of the Montesquiou family for centuries. Other accounts of the letter's history—and perhaps the author will be forgiven a momentary departure from proper historical objectivity, since the personal connection here lies at the very origin of the present work—other accounts maintain that the precious document was given by Fouquet to the counsel who defended him and saved his life in the face of the king's great wrath. The counsel's name was Olivier Le Fèvre d'Ormesson, and he was to deposit the letter in a place known only to Fouquet and himself. As we know, Fouquet and Lauzun, both victims of the king's envy, met in the fortress prison of Pinerolo, where the eternal seducer, Lauzun, abused the friendship of his companion in misfortune, and led astray his young daughter Marie-Madeleine Fouquet (future marquise de Monsalès and related to the Crussol d'Uzès family). The infatuated

girl, in her transports, is supposed to have told Lauzun the secret of
where Fouquet asked his defender to hide the letter. As soon as he
was let out of prison, Lauzun shamelessly went and found the letter,
which he then hid in the massive walls of the château of Saint-
Fargeau in Puisaye, now the department of the Yonne. The château
belonged to the Grande Mademoiselle, Lauzun's lawful but secret
wife, who was dying of love for him. But he is said to have stayed at
the château only long enough to carry out, with the utmost secrecy,
certain mysterious alterations. So Alexis's letter is still perhaps somewhere in the thickness of the tower walls at Saint-Fargeau, unless it
was destroyed in one of the two fires that ravaged the building in
1750 and again in 1852. Or unless—a last hypothesis—it was sold
for an unearthly price, as some claim, to an Italian-American, by the
hard-up and unscrupulous grandson of one of the recent owners, who
discovered it by chance. In that case the letter from the Emperor to the
Kha-Khan of all the Oïghurs would have gone to form part of the
loot of the Mafia, and is ending its long existence in the safe of some
bank in Palermo, Naples, Chicago, or Las Vegas.[2]

Alexis had judged well in entrusting to barbarians the task of
delivering his message to their prince. No one else would have been
able to escape the traps and ambushes laid along all the routes that
led to Balamir. Even the barbarian messengers themselves, known to
be from the Empire, were met with mistrust. But at last, after adventures that would fill a volume, they came to the Kha-Khan's tent,
where a barrier of the most dedicated enemies of the Empire watched
over Balamir, his fierce protectors as well as guard of honor. Their
captain came to meet the nomad horsemen and wanted to be told what
they had to say to the Kha-Khan. Then the leader of the horsemen,
without a word, leaned forward over the felt or horsehair blanket that
served him as a saddle, and drew out a round object wrapped in damp
rags steeped in spices. Slowly he undid the wrappings, still not
answering the captain. Then, with a powerful gesture, he sent
Jester's head rolling into the Kha-Khan's tent.

The Emperor's letter contained neither pleas nor apologies. It
simply related all that had happened, ending with the famous words:
"Every man sees things from one side only. Now you know the other
side. Do not let passion, impatience, or ambition put so swift an end to
all we have begun. Together we shall be impatient about many other
things, together we shall have many other ambitions. Do not turn

against the Empire. Remember, there is nothing that may not be ours if only we stay united. I send you this letter as a token, together with the head of my son—χαὶ τὴν χέφαλην τὴν τοῦ ἐμαυτοῦ υἱοῦ. Nothing was dearer to me. But your friendship is dearer to me, and that alliance between our peoples which will give us a whole world." It is said that when he read the letter Balamir shed the only tears he was ever seen to weep. But he did not waste a moment. He gathered the barbarians together, and spoke to them.

The Kha-Khan's eloquence must have been very persuasive. The rough, harsh men who listened to him had only one idea in their heads, only one hope in their hearts: to kill, loot, rape—make war. But he managed to persuade them to stay faithful to the alliance. What did he say to them? We know in part, not only from imperial texts, which are probably inaccurate and biased, but from Chinese and Persian chronicles that give similar accounts of Balamir's words. He held out to the nomads Jester's livid head, and went over all that had happened in the last month, putting all the blame on Jester. He read out the Emperor's letter, translating rather freely, with the help of two or three of his captains who were fluent in Greek. And then, knowing his men, he dwelt on the vast prospects opened by the Emperor's message. He spoke of the distant lands beyond the seas and beyond the Empire, far richer than the children of the steppe and the high plateaus could ever imagine, covered with fruit and wheat and towns in which the humblest cottage was finer than the tents of Mongol princes or the Persian houses which the nomads so admired. He spoke of ships laden with ivory and arms, of gold-roofed temples, of tall, languid women dressed in transparent silk among palace fountains and flowers and green and black marble, of horses from Arabia, of jewels hung around damsels' necks, of bronze vases, endless feasting, and the fruits of the vine through which everyone, on beds of silk and roses, under a sun that did not burn, could enter the gates of a paradise that knew no dusty heat or icy cold. He uttered names that the barbarians had never heard before, so that the sweet music of mystery and the unknown echoed in their ears: he spoke of Cyprus and Carthage, Pomposa and Rome. He said that beyond all these, where the sun sank into unfathomable depths, there was a great, storm-tossed sea, which made all other seas look like ponds for children to play in. But were the barbarian nomads, who had brought terror to China, Persia, and India, were they children? Instead of tearing themselves to pieces in unnecessary wars, let them join with the Empire and conquer the world as far as the sea where the sun disappeared!

When he stopped speaking there was, as always after his words, a silence of surprise and incredulity that lasted some time. And then cheering arose over the plain, and those who had been most hostile, those who had mistrusted him, those who had wanted to make war on the Empire and bring the Emperor back in chains, all threw themselves at his feet and begged his forgiveness. Once again Balamir had won the day. The pattern of history had shifted.

It had shifted in Aquileus, too. When the riders hurried back in triumph, bringing the Emperor a message of alliance and loyalty and bearing gifts, Alexis realized that the course of history had opened a new era in his life, and that in this era he would find his destiny. He was launched henceforth on a path from which he could not easily turn aside. The days of the struggle for liberation were already far behind. The Empire was saved. But there was the world to conquer. Not a day must be lost in getting ready the tools necessary for a task that only three or four years earlier the boldest spirit would never have dreamed of. The opposition to the Emperor had been stricken with terror at the execution of Jester. By a characteristic tactic, Alexis used the situation to meet some of the opposition's demands. He introduced various political and religious measures—at that time there was no real difference between the two spheres—designed to strengthen the army and navy, to revive respect for ancestral virtue, and to make the different peoples of the Empire more keenly conscious that they all belonged to one community.

Alexis's aims and their consequences have given rise to a new debate among the historians that recalls, on a much larger scale, the debate over Basil, prince of Onessa or unifier of the Empire.[3] Some, including Arnold Toynbee, consider that everything in the Emperor's behavior, his education, his past, the alliance with Balamir, the execution of Jester, points to the idea of a world empire. Others believe Alexis's sole aim was to prove the greatness of the peoples of the Empire, of those who had fought each other under the Porphyries and the Venostae, of whom he was the common heir, and who were reconciled in him. In this case, what distinguishes Alexis is the emergence, before its time, of a kind of national feeling which grew up slowly out of a struggle against feudalism. As Lucien Febvre points out, "feudalism" and "nationalism" are anachronisms here.

But already present is the mechanism that brings together the interests and traditions of great families with a military past, the rise of a national spirit, and the hope of a world empire. The antagonism between the two principles, nation and empire, is well brought out by Renan, who gives three examples: in the contemporary world, Germany and Italy, hampered in "their work of national concretion," the one by the weight of a Germanic Holy Roman Empire, the other by the papacy; the third example, from much earlier times, is the Empire at the time of Alexis. "The first condition for the existence of a national spirit," he writes, "is the renunciation of any claim to a universal role: a universal role is destructive of nationality."[4] Such is the confrontation between those who see Alexis, after Arsaphes and Basil before him, as the creator of a nation, and those who consider him the founder of the world empire.

Such rigid alternatives are not usually very helpful. What one has to do is accept the facts and see Alexis as both the pupil of the thinkers of Asia who resigns himself to sacrificing Jester to universal considerations, and the military leader who, within the New Alliance, devotes all his efforts to strengthening the State. It may even be that Alexis's whole policy consisted in maintaining an equal balance between opposing demands. No sooner was the alliance with the Kha-Khan of the Oïghurs confirmed—and at what a price!—than Alexis not only adopted some of the measures Jester had demanded, but also had spies and imperial captains in the barbarians' pay publicly executed. The Emperor explained these actions in another letter to the Kha-Khan. To adopt Renan's terms, the simplest way of putting it is that for Alexis the nation was now a step on the way toward a world empire, and that, as Sir Allan Carter-Bennett has it, "out of an assemblage of people who were not even a nation, Alexis made a state capable of conquering the world. And that is what we call the Empire." To attain this goal, every means was legitimate. Sometimes the emphasis would be on the universal and on peace, sometimes on racial purity and ancestral tradition. Jester was executed to save the New Alliance, but at the same time the lessons he taught and the example he set were not to be lost. Crime, contradiction, some would say duplicity were to have their place in the great design—as if the conqueror's fate were marked forever by the death of a mistress, a brother, and one who had almost been a son. Yet through all this deviousness, all these detours, through so many complications and reversals, Alexis's trajectory through the sky of history remains imperturbably direct. A late sixteenth-century Portuguese chronicle charmingly says: "Escreve Alexo, como Deus, direito por linhas tortas." "Por linhas tortas," indeed. They signify all the unjust deaths, the bloodshed, the fire in the night, the atrocities that have made Alexis, for many people, indistinguishable from such as the Mongol and Assyrian conquerors, Ashurbanipal, Genghis Khan, Tamerlane, Stalin, and Hitler, and for the Christians an Antichrist.[5] But "direito"—that signifies power. And glory.

The death of Jester was a great turning point even more in the mind and heart of the Emperor than in the foreign and internal policy of the Empire. Philocrates' teaching was not forgotten; it had simply turned out to be irrelevant. Jester had had to be killed to save the Empire from the barbarians. And now, in the name of the Empire, the barbarians would have to be sent forth to conquer the world. One thing followed another so naturally and inevitably that it sometimes seemed to Alexis he decided nothing at all—it was events that decided for him. But he was at the center of all events, and they revolved around him as if he were their master. And therefore he was their master. There was little question now of meditation or retreat. There were not enough hours in the day for the endless decisions to be made, the building of temples, the founding of towns, the raising of troops, the appointment of governors, prefects, generals. Sometimes, as dusk fell over Aquileus, the Emperor thought still of his letters to Philocrates or of his conversations with Jester. And he would dream, too, of the great forest, the nights in Alexandria, the temple at the gates of the city, the beach of fine white sand where they both used to lie, of the desert, and of the tombs where he had been imprisoned. How far away it all was! The debauchee, the saint, the Fool of God had been metamorphosed into the war chief, the emperor, the tyrant. Tomorrow he would conquer the world. And all this had come to pass because there is a game and the game has rules, because time passes and things change, because there are men and their dreams, and because every day the world advances a little and regresses a little.

Alexis had not wished for Vanessa's death—but he was responsible for it. He had not wished for Simeon's death—but he had been obliged to bring it about. He had not wished for Jester's death—but he had had, in despair, to decide upon it in order to save the Empire from the vengeance of the barbarians, which might have destroyed it altogether. That was the way things went. But they left traces of their terrible passing. Alexis was never the same after Jester's death. He was then in the prime of life. But all the evidence of those who knew him, chronicles, accounts by foreign ambassadors agree that after this crisis his character changed. A harsh, intractable element appeared in a temperament that had at first thought itself born for pleasure, then devoted itself to the gods, then been revealed to itself, before the final avatar, in war and the ruling of men. If Alexis had died during one of the orgies whose sinister reputation spread all over the Levant, he would have been remembered only as an obscure debauchee. If he had perished from his sufferings and fastings during the period of Asian religion and mysticism, he would have been revered for some generations as a saint and the Fool of God, then buried in hagiographies and forgotten. But all the products of space and time—the lands and peoples of the Empire, history, power, the memory of men—all seized upon him. He had seen people die around him, and he had sometimes been the cause of their deaths. He would never be the same again.

It was about this time that the process that historians and psychoanalysts have with some exaggeration dubbed "the break with the mother" began and was completed. Helen had been horror-struck by the execution of Jester. Alexis did everything he could to make her understand its significance and the motives behind it. Tradition, unconfirmed by any records, has it that Jester himself left Helen a letter in which he forgave the Emperor and asked Helen to do the same. But Helen never forgave. The Emperor always continued to show his mother the deepest respect and the most solicitous affection, but she took no further part in affairs. She withdrew more and more often into her ancient northeastern forest, where a stately mansion now arose in the place of the old fortified houses. And there, finally, she died. Alexis was in Sicily.

All that had been going on in the Empire had not left the rest of the world unmoved. Cyprus and Pomposa, which had helped Alexis against the barbarians, looked on uneasily at the setting up of the New Alliance (we have already seen the part Cyprus played in attempts to overthrow it). Its confirmation threw all the great powers of that time into consternation. From then on, for anyone who observed events closely and clearly, the future was already decided. Alexis was under no illusion. Even if he had felt able to advocate a different policy, he would in any case have been obliged to lay the foundations of a world empire. The princes of Cyprus saw the execution of Jester as an insult and a threat directed first and foremost at them. Alexis's attempts to appease them were of no avail. They wanted war. And they got it.

The eternal question of responsibility can in this case receive but a dusty answer. Cyprus, Pomposa, Sicily, and the others wanted to destroy the Emperor and the New Alliance. The Emperor wanted to build the Empire and defend it, and his victories and conquests led him ceaselessly on to other victories and other conquests. But history, alas, is not a matter of morals, as Alexis had learned from the life and death of Philocrates and of Jester. But is there any other morality than that of history? It is through history alone that the gods speak. Alexis felt as if he were becoming a god himself when he bore heavily on the human in order to obey the divine. What, for a time at least, became more important for Alexis than pleasure or meditation, and what made Goethe so admire him that he wrote one of his most beautiful poems about him, was action. Power and glory consisted in changing the world.

A year after the death of Jester and the Emperor's letter to Balamir, a solemn and momentous ceremony occupied all Aquileus. Holiday crowds filled the streets, which were strewn with rose petals, alive with murmur and song, decorated with bright hangings at every window, and full of the din and animation of soldiers in groups of five or six, merchants and peddlers in their booths, and crowds of wide-eyed sightseers come in from the country. Occasionally, bands of nomad horsemen would sweep by, riding from their quarters to the positions assigned to them. Arms were raised in salute as they passed, and the women might smile, though still only briefly and shyly. There had been no serious incident since the arrival, a month earlier, of the formidable warriors who had left so many memories of terror behind them here in the city of the priests and throughout the Empire. They had brought their sheep and cattle along in their wake, and roasted them whole over enormous fires in the fields outside the city where they had been quartered. The people of Aquileus brought them eggs, fruit, and rye brandy. The nomads had crucified a dozen or so of their own number for drunkenness, rape, or theft. Balamir himself, in his eternal white sable, had just arrived at the palace. In the morning the Emperor had appeared before the crowd with him, and now they were going up together into the great temple. Certain priests and representatives of great families had, of course, been indignant that the barbarian leader should visit the legendary tomb of Arsaphes and the most holy shrine in the Empire. They said: "What an insult to so many memories! For whom, for what did our fathers and brothers, our friends and our sons die? You notice Princess Helen is not here? She, at least, remembers Philocrates, and Jester, and the battles the Emperor has forgotten. All that is missing from the rejoicings is the five or six hundred thousand who were slain by the barbarians, and Simeon, resurrected, come at last to enjoy his triumph." Before the great temple at Aquileus, in the sacred meadow known first as the Field of Spring and then as the Field of the New Alliance, twenty thousand white bulls were sacrificed at once, and their blood gushed into the gridded channels and furrows that the priests drew on the ground. The bloody sword of the nomads stood upright in a block of rare wood at the very entrance to the temple. Alexis and Balamir together lit a sacred flame, the symbol of their alliance. The rejoicings were designed to include remembrance of all the dead, both those of the Empire and those of the barbarians. As at the Emperor's coronation, priestesses flourished red and black scarves toward the east. But now the list of those whose memory and death were linked to the Empire was longer: to Thaumas, Vanessa, Philocrates, Jester, and the many others was added the other Jester. The Emperor had expressly asked for his name to be included, and Balamir had agreed. The case of Simeon presented a problem. It was gotten round by invoking the memory of the victims of the double duel. Isidore and Bruince stood behind Alexis. Balamir was followed by his captains, clad in leather and hides. It was the beginning of a new age. Albert Mathiez used to compare the ceremony at Aquileus a year after the events connected with the death of Jester with the Feast of the Federation a year after the taking of the Bastille. In both cases, crisis and bloodshed were followed by reconciliation and consecration, sealed with unanimity and popular enthusiasm. And in both cases, alas, the bloodshed was not over. In exchange for his death, Jester had bequeathed the Empire a whole world to conquer.

XVIII

SCIENCE, CULTURE, AND EVERY-
DAY LIFE UNDER THE EMPIRE

URING THE FIFTY-FIVE YEARS OF HIS REIGN—ONE
of the longest in history—Alexis completely re-
organized the decaying Empire he had found when
he mounted the throne. This long-term task was
accomplished day by day, between military expeditions and the grand designs of foreign policy. Let us
pause for a while in our chronicle of the emperor's adventures, and
look at the inhabitants of the Empire and the kind of life they lived
at the time of Alexis.

The Empire had not changed very greatly since the far-off days of
Basil and Arsaphes. The centuries flowed by more slowly then than
now; it is only in the last hundred fifty or two hundred years that the
world has had a little more difficulty recognizing itself every morning.
Nature—the rivers and forests, wild animals and plants—was much
the same as ever. But year after year war had swept over cities and
fields, destroying ports, houses, flocks, herds, and harvests. Year after
year, fear had reigned over the Empire. For the peasant, the plow-
man, the shopkeeper, the fisherman, Alexis stood first and foremost—
and this is one of the clues to his success—for security and the end of
fear. After the successful reconquest, war never broke out over the
lands of the Empire again. True, the New Alliance meant a period of
intense military activity, but all these operations without exception
were carried out on foreign soil, farther and farther from the Empire's own borders. The war effort was considerable, and there were
few families that did not lose at least one of their members. But
people's homes were safe, and this levy on life itself seemed quite
natural. Men did not live to be very old in any case, and death on the

battlefield seemed more honorable than death from plague or famine.

These, together with war, were the great scourges of the age. But plague and famine greatly decreased under Alexis's reign. Bruince introduced vigorous long-term measures to ensure supplies, and brought about a vast expansion in the production of rice and cereals. And the Empire had only two epidemics of plague in the whole of Alexis's reign. The first was limited in extent, and the infection was brought in by detachments of nomads from Persia and India. The second, at the very end of the reign, wrought terrible havoc, and was started by a ship from a Scythian port that the Varangians had been besieging. Plague had broken out among the Varangians, and they were obliged to lift the siege. But before they withdrew, their leader, to revenge himself on fate, had the decomposing corpses of a dozen of the victims thrown over the walls into the city. This was enough to unleash the scourge there, too. The inhabitants, scarcely recovered from the rigors of war, were decimated by the plague. Some of the wealthier survivors got together secretly and chartered a ship to flee the stricken city. Several hundreds, with their wives and their gold, embarked they cared not whither.

After no more than a few days the plague rose grinning on the terrified vessel and struck one of the crew. They threw the man overboard, alive, using oars and boat hooks to avoid touching him. A couple more days went by. The more optimistic believed it might have been an isolated case, and hope was returning when, one after the other, a woman and one of the most important merchants of the town fell ill. The ship, on to which far too many refugees had crowded—by dint of money, pleading, or force—became a hell. Ashore, in the town, at least people had been able to isolate themselves, avoid suspected victims, or run away. At sea, on the ship, the hale and the sick were thrown together in a tiny space in which death alone could prosper. Some people took to the boats, in twos or threes, each anxiously examining his companions beforehand to make sure they still had their health and strength. A husband would abandon his wife because she looked rather pale; complete strangers trusted one another because their complexion was clear and they seemed sturdy. Meanwhile a storm had blown up, and from the deck those left on board watched with satisfaction as those who had escaped were swallowed by the waves. Some were stabbed and thrown overboard because they showed signs of fatigue, or even just because they were seasick. When the ship came in sight of the coast of the Empire, more than fifty passengers had already died—murdered, drowned, or carried off by the plague.

The survivors sailed into the port of Onessa. They were coming alongside, and a sailor had just leaped ashore to fasten the moorings, when he collapsed on the quay. The crowd of sightseers, which always gathered to watch the arrival of ships from distant parts laden with mysteries and dreams, sent someone to notify the port authorities. It did not take them long to establish the malady that had struck the sailor down—it was the plague. The fugitives were at once forbidden to land, and were ordered to put to sea again without delay. The officer in command of the port and his men had remained prudently on the quay, some distance from the ship. They saw the passengers hesitate, and little groups forming on deck, and though they could not hear what they were saying they could sense a kind of agitation forming and rapidly increasing, spreading uneasiness, almost dread, through the harbor and the big crowd now assembling there. Then suddenly the people on board the plague ship made a combined rush on to the quay, fanning out over the empty space fear had created around the ship.

The crowd of spectators fell back as one man before their approach, a sharp order rang out, and a shower of arrows rained down on the fugitives. About a dozen of them fell. The rest hesitated a moment, and then, with a shriek, men, women, and children resumed their mad rush forward. It was as if what they wanted to do now was not so much to escape as to touch and communicate to others the infection. The circle formed by the people of Onessa had widened still more to escape the plague carriers. Those who were trying to scatter had to make their way against the bolder spirits, who moved forward gripping axes, pikes, or cudgels. There was time for another hail of arrows; then came the clash. As they fell, the doomed newcomers clutched at their murderers, trying to clasp them in their arms and drag them with them into death. The port was strewn with corpses. But some had survived arrows, clubs, and pikes. Now was their chance, for no one would fight them hand to hand, and the crowd opened before them with cries of terror. Those of the passengers and crew who had not yet left the ship saw there was no hope of another mass rush on the shore, and they set sail as fast as they could, under the arrows and burning torches that fell down from all sides, threatening to add the perils of fire at sea to the ravages of the plague.

Messengers were sent at a gallop from Onessa to the City and all the ports along the coast to warn the troops to be on the alert for the plague-stricken ship. When it reached the entrance to the harbor of the City, three galleys barred its way. The condemned men sailed to and fro for days. They had started out with plenty of supplies, but now hunger and thirst began to slink in the shadow of the plague. Every night dozens of living and dead were thrown into the sea. One moonless night the survivors, now only about twenty strong, managed to elude the warships that had been following them at a distance all this time. They jumped off the ship and swam to the shore about a hundred miles north of Cape Gildor. Several were drowned, and fewer than ten of those who had escaped the Varangians' vengeance finally came ashore. But they were enough to finish what the earlier fugitives had begun at Onessa. In the last years of Alexis's reign, a terrible epidemic swept through the Empire, wiping out in a few weeks whole regions that had survived both war and the tyranny of the barbarians.

But the plague and the sufferings it brought were fortunately an exception in Alexis's long reign. For more than half a century, between conquests and other military expeditions, the Emperor devoted himself not only to the prosperity of all, but also to an idea that was then quite new—the prosperity of each. To meet the necessities of war and the hopes of peace as well, the administration of the Empire was entirely overhauled. Basil and Arsaphes had already set about the problems of roads and water supply,[1] but what would now be called the scientific and technical adjuncts of everyday life had been neglected in favor of more immediate worries, and often left in a state of chaos. Bruince, with a very modern sense of what government implies, considered it incumbent on the State to make its administration cover all the activities within the Empire and to introduce standards that would be observed as generally and as rigorously as possible. With the help of Bruince and a curious character called Logophilus, whom we shall come back to, Alexis concerned himself first and foremost with a radical reform of weights and measures, the calendar, and the coinage.

Caprice and confusion reigned in all these fields. Even more than vocabulary and language, the systems of calculating quantity, area, and the value of goods varied from one part of the Empire to another. Thirty-seven different ways have been noted of measuring liquid capacity and the volume of timber and grain; fifty-two of estimating the area of fields and forests; and a hundred and two different methods of payment in gold, silver, copper, or bronze coins. For all these units of measurement there were countless different names: each unit might have two or three or even more separate designations, depending on the area. And a coin bearing the same name everywhere often varied appreciably in weight. The difficulties entailed by this lack of uniformity hampered trade and held back prosperity. The coinage was so uncertain that many merchants preferred to stick to barter, which reduced both complications and the possibilities of fraud. Serious accounting was practically impossible; estimates, forecasts, budgeting, and the projection of sales was laborious and unreliable. And the calculation of time was no better. It was divided into moons, though no one was very clear whether these consisted of twenty-six, twenty-seven, twenty-eight, twenty-nine, or thirty days. And variations of five or six days per month, at different times and in different areas, produced considerable confusion as to the length of a year. The soothsayers and sages who were familiar with the motions of the planets disagreed over whether the year was made up of twelve moons or of thirteen. The whole matter ended up in total confusion, based as it was on calculations that mingled mystical and religious considerations with geographical observations on the dimensions of

Coin of the Empire depicting an elephant,
minted in commemoration of the battle of Adrianople.
Found at Pomposa.

tides and what the physicians of the time knew about menstruation. The priests had tried to introduce some sort of order into the problem, but the discussions they organized lasted so long—seven years, according to Justus Dion—that the scholars and the seers had been obliged to go their separate ways without having come to any agreement or put forward any suggestions.

Alexis, Bruince, and Logophilus also took as their basis the cycles of the moon and menstruation, the apparent trajectory of the sun, and all the great circular movements of nature. But instead of submitting to them blindly and trying to establish in detail how many fractions of each cycle could be fitted into the year, they turned the whole problem the other way up and subjected nature to the supreme authority of number. They thus took into account all the factors that had led the seers astray: moon, tides, menstruation, the magic of numbers, a mystical idea of the one and the many. But what the genius of these three men had discovered, or rediscovered, was the fertility of mathematics. It is impossible to establish with certainty to which of the three men the honor of this step belongs, though it must be remembered that it was facilitated by the earlier work of philosophers, especially Philontes' *Treatise Concerning the Worlds* and the famous Book VII of Aristo's *Metaphysics*. The most ancient magical and mystical traditions of the Empire held 2, 3, 7, and 12, and sometimes also 4, 5, and 9, as the sacred numbers par excellence. They were sometimes called "perfect numbers."[2] Now, because it came closest to the facts of nature, 12 was selected, and became the foundation of what Sir Allan Carter-Bennett calls "the administrative mathematics of the Empire."

The year was divided into twelve moons. Each moon consisted of twenty-eight days divided into four series of six days, with a holy day intercalated between each series and one day each moon dedicated to the Empire (on this day all activity was exclusively devoted to the community and the public welfare). This gave a total of three hundred forty-eight days, to which were added twelve movable days of feasts and games allotted by the Emperor each year among the different seasons, according to the course of events. So the year consisted of three hundred sixty days in all. The priests and scholars immediately pointed out the discrepancy between the religious year and the time it took the earth to make a complete revolution round the sun—or rather vice versa; this they knew all about. So to bring the two into line again, five or six days were added to the holy days, the feast days, and the days of the Empire. These extra days, known as "vague" or "embolismic" or "epagomenous" in the Empire computations of the calendar, were always regarded as erratic and irrational. They were shameful, almost accursed, and on them all kinds of folly and excess were allowed. Characterized by a strange combination of derangement and of laughter designed to exorcise it, these days were somewhat dangerous in their excitement. They had to be masked and squandered as fast as possible. They are the origin of our carnival.

The same principle that had governed the reform of the calendar was, of course, applied to measurement and money. The number 12 became the basis of calculation: 12 inches made a foot, 12 feet an imperial perch; 12 square feet made an imperial arpent; 12 scruples made a grain, 12 grains an ounce, 12 ounces an imperial pound weight. Similarly, 12 liards made an obole, 12 oboles a sou, 12 sous a stater, and 12 staters an imperial livre or lira.

But of all these reforms the most important by far was the adoption of a duodecimal numerical system, a system of what for those days were rather complex rules, later known to the history of science as positional mathematics. In Asia Alexis had been initiated into religions, mysteries, and cosmogonies that offered images of the world of varying degrees of subtlety and satisfactoriness, and that culminated in unspeakable intuitions where all the secrets of the universe might be had in exchange for the annihilation of consciousness and individuality. Minds that had not had a long familiarity with metaphysics found difficulty in accepting heady doctrines that suddenly reversed all the attitudes so familiar to the world and to mankind. As we know, Alexis himself had never followed the mystical experience right to its conclusion. The roughness of the forests of the northeast and the subtlety of Greece had accompanied him always in his descent into the abysses of Asia. Among the techniques and secrets revealed to him by the soothsayers, amidst the old wives' remedies, the herbs that cured snake bite, the breathing methods, the balms made from tigers' mustaches, the recipes for the raising of spirits, and the initiations into the void and the essence of the universe, he had been struck by one discovery in particular. He had long meditated on it, and the more he thought about it the more it seemed to him that this quite simple invention contained something of the secrets of nature, and at the same time offered infinite practical possibilities. This secret, this mystery, this revelation was quite trivial in itself. It was just a stroke: / or \ . Or, according to some schools, a square, □, or a circle, ○. The miracle resided in the use to which the sign was put: placed beside a figure it multiplied it by ten, twelve, or twenty, according to the convention employed. The reader will, of course, have recognized the sign as nought or zero—the sign royal of civilization.

It took centuries of reflection and genius to decide whether the sign should be placed to right or left of the figure it modified, and there was endless debate about what would be its best coefficient. Today a child of five knows that the system we are steeped in is the decimal system, based on ten characters—nine significant figures and zero. In this system ten characters are enough to represent any number whatsoever, zero having the dual function of multiplying by ten, a hundred, a thousand, and so on, and at the same time of indicating the absence of any unit in the column in which it stands. The decimal system is almost universal now, and nothing could be more elementary. But since the basis of any system is the number of units of a certain order that are necessary to form a unit in the order immediately above, it is obvious that any number of systems are possible. Contemporary electronic computers, for example, use the binary system foreshadowed by Leibnitz. The use of zero represented a fabulous step forward, and having adopted it Alexis came to the conclusion that the duodecimal system was better than the decimal. Why? Probably because the figure 12 corresponded to the religious and mystical traditions of the Empire; because it corresponded to the rhythms of nature as shown in lunation and menstruation; but also, no doubt, because 10 is only divisible by 2 and 5, and 12 is divisible by 2, 3, 4, and 6.[3] Many people still think the duodecimal system is better than the decimal and that Alexis is in the right, not we. And the twelve feet of the alexandrine, the dozen eggs or oysters, the division of the day into twice twelve hours, and up till quite recently the twelve pence in the British shilling, all odd but remarkable vestiges surviving in an otherwise decimal landscape, are probably a heritage from the Empire. The duodecimal system did not, of course, prevent Alexis from using the sign ╱ , ╲ , □, or ○, which corresponded to our zero. Only the sign royal, instead of multiplying by 10, multiplied by 12. So the order above 12 was $12 \times 12 = 144$, instead of $10 \times 10 = 100$; and so on. The Empire made use, therefore, of twelve characters: eleven characters signifying 1 to 11, and zero, which as well as multiplying by twelve also indicated, as in our own system, the absence of units in the column in which it appears.[4]

For the Empire the adoption of the duodecimal system marked the beginning of an era of incomparable prosperity. Calculation became ten times—twelve times—simpler, quicker, and easier. The progress made in trade, social and practical administration, architecture, navigation, in all the techniques and all the sciences was enormous. It would of course, be foolish to imagine that every shopkeeper and tradesman adapted himself to the duodecimal system overnight. But it was taught, a treasure buried among legendary beliefs and superstitions, among survivals of the cult of the oak and the eagle; it was taught to the priests and the soothsayers, who thus held in their hands a formidable tool of government. They were no longer just the priests of a tottering religion greatly threatened by the solar monotheism that the Emperor more or less openly favored. They became virtually the accountants of the State. Thus, by an unforeseeable twist in the history of science, their existence and the role they played were justified yet again; and a new light fell, in retrospect, on the inspired intuitions of Arsaphes and Basil, who had strengthened them and reinstated them in their powers and privileges. Now, thanks to the progress of culture and technology, these privileges made it possible to use the priests in the service of the Empire. "Alexis," as Sir Allan Carter-Bennett profoundly observes, "would have earned imperishable glory even if he had done no more than bring to the Empire the invention of the nought. . . . Alexis's genius consists in his conquests, and in nought."

In the field of scientific culture, as in several others, Alexis resembles Arsaphes rather than Basil. The Bactrian captain foresaw better, and earlier, than the prince of Onessa the importance of the role that science and technology would play in the future. If one considers Arsaphes's origins and the age in which he lived, one cannot help marveling at the immense accomplishment of the Emperor's predecessor, at his irrigation works and his preoccupation with communications in what was to become the Empire, and at the genius for organization which foreshadowed that of Alexis. But, as we have already said, it would be wrong to see Alexis's rule as a return to Arsaphes, an administrative or political revenge of the Porphyries against the Venostae. Despite the authoritarianism, violence, and sometimes cruelty of which Alexis gave so many examples in the second half of his reign, his title of Father of the Peoples was a rightful one. The reconciliation, that of the Porphyries and the Venostae as well as that of the Empire and the barbarians, was brought about with an iron hand. As Justus Dion naïvely put it, thus both shocking and delighting Sir Allan Carter-Bennett, "friendship between the peoples was imposed spear in hand, and sealed in blood." All the reforms we have just been considering served first of all to consecrate the unification of the Empire. The old division between the Eagle and the Tiger was completely abolished; the armies of the Empire marched under the double emblem of the Eagle on their helmets and the Tiger on their banners. This is the origin of a proverb still widespread in Macedonia, Epirus, and the greater part of the Balkans: to leave the eagle for the tiger means exactly the same as to escape from Charybdis only to be confronted with Scylla, or to jump out of the frying pan into the fire. The Empire was divided up regularly into provinces, with regional capitals that were the seats of the governors, high military and civil officials with extensive powers. First there were twelve of them, then twenty-seven, then thirty-six. At the very height of the Empire, there were a hundred and twenty-one provinces.[5] Army officers and priests were at their disposal to help them in their work. Each province had a tribunal. The most important matters might be brought before an Imperial Tribunal in the

Helmet surmounted with imperial eagle (Excavation at Adrianople by L'Ecole française d'archéologie).

capital, made up of priests, generals, and high officials. The Emperor himself, who might come whenever he wished and preside over the High Tribunal, always had the last word and the right of pardon.

Wise administration, stability lasting nearly half a century, and internal peace together with foreign conquest and, above all, with scientific and technical progress, gave the Empire a prosperity hitherto unknown. Less than ten years after Alexis had come to the throne, the Empire might have thought itself back in the legendary golden age of the City. The name of Bruince, indefatigable reformer and tireless worker, of whom it was said with a mixture of irony and admiration that for him a month was thirty-three days long, is linked to this renaissance. The study of the history of Pomposa and of the Phoenicians had taught Bruince that the great prerequisite of prosperity was a fleet able to ensure rapid and extensive communications. In ten years, Alexis had more ships than Pomposa and Sicily put together. Bruince had carpenters brought from the northeastern forests and settled them in the ports. They were master craftsmen whose skill had been wasted building miserable huts and making the same weapons over and over again in the backwoods. Under the supervision of defectors from Pomposa, they built high-decked ships that for centuries were the admiration of all the sailors in the world. Nelson said they were the masterpieces of a hand guided by the mind.[6] Bruince saw that a fleet was equally invaluable for both military and commercial purposes. In those days there was no distinction between navy and merchant navy. The military value of a navy was all the more evident because the barbarians, the Empire's allies, though they had an unrivaled army, possessed no ships. Thenceforward, in peace as in war, the ships of the Empire ruled the seas. The three almost simultaneous great naval battles against the Pomposan fleets—one off Cape Malea, another off the Cerbical Islands and the third off Patmos—were resounding victories. In this sense Alexis's links went back beyond Basil and even Arsaphes to a much older tradition: the glory of the Empire was heir to the ancient glory of the City. The explanation was that Alexis, freed by Balamir from having to worry about inland attack and protected by the New Alliance against any attack from Asia, could take over for his own purposes the old dreams of the City that the barbarians had once interrupted. To Sir Allan Carter-Bennett's classic equation that Alexis is Arsaphes plus Thaumas,[7] we should add another factor that is perhaps essential. Alexis in all his glory is the renaissance of the City whose beginnings had already dazzled the world.

The progress of trade, the creation of the navy, his concern both with tradition and, already, with a certain idea of the universal, all inclined Alexis to restore to the City its proper place—the first place. In the sixth year of his reign he himself came to live in the City, and there, too, he brought the government, the High Tribunal, the treasury, and the army headquarters. Only the college of priests remained in Aquileus. In an imposing ceremony in which for the third time all the imperial pomp and splendor were displayed—the first two occasions being the coronation in the great temple at Aquileus, and the second the confirmation of the New Alliance—the City was solemnly declared the capital of the Empire. Aquileus had never been more than a military and religious capital made important by its strategic position and the priests. This importance was now removed by the new orientation of imperial policy. And Alexis was not sorry to have an opportunity to shake up the old structures of the priestly caste a little, and reshape it according to his own ideas and for his own ends. The transfer of the seat of government from Aquileus to the City had everything to be said for it: it marked the return to a great tradition that the priests could scarcely oppose; it bore witness to the Empire's ambitions at sea and in the world, and to the universality of its intellectual and artistic mission; and it was a break with the exclusive domination of the priests, to whom Aquileus really belonged.

The rivalry between the Emperor and the priests was foreshadowed in the history of the Empire, yet the Empire could not be governed without the priests. Arsaphes and Basil had both learned by experience this double and indivisible truth; and Basil, having destroyed the priests' power on the night of the famous banquet at Onessa, had been obliged to restore it. The struggle between Alexis and the priests had been less hypocritical, less devious, but almost as violent. Jester's death, as well as changing the course of the Empire's foreign policy, also showed the priests who was master. But the priestly caste, still avid for power, still seethed with intrigues and plots and what the Marquis de Ségur, in *Alexis and the Priests*, once a standard work, called the "Frondes of the Empire." But Bruince held them in check even more vigorously than Thaumas had done. They had lost, and for a long while to come, their political independence; the policy of the Empire was now worked out in the City, and they, relegated to Aquileus, were only the Emperor's tool. But even with all the reforms and changes it had undergone, the tool remained a powerful one, and the technical progress that was being made rendered it more indispensable than ever. So religion was still, as before, one of the pillars of the Empire. Behind the negotiations of princes, the adventures of generals, the ups and downs of public life, the secret presence of the gods went on imparting its own rhythm to the inner life of shepherd, fisherman, and blacksmith.

We still do not know to what extent men like Alexis, Isidore, and Bruince, and such writers as Justus Dion and Valerius, shared these beliefs. Alexis had himself crowned by the priests, spiritual head of the hierarchy. Isidore and Bruince were priests themselves. But the religion of the Empire, with its multiplicity of gods and spirits, its countless legends, and its triple superstition of sun, eagle, and oak, had remained very primitive. It is hard to see how a mind as universal as Alexis's, initiate of a sun worship far removed from the crude polytheism of the priests of Aquileus and familiar with the mysticisms of Asia that represented one of the highest peaks of human thought, could have accommodated itself to beliefs already disparaged by the more advanced thinkers of the time. We know the reply of Feuerbach and the Marxists: Alexis believed in nothing but man; he did not even believe in sun worship, and his apparent acquiescence in the ritual and superstitions of the priests was pure politics. But not all historians of religion are so sweeping. Among the tendencies of current research, some, inspired by structuralism and such writers as Claude Lévi-Strauss and Michel Foucault, tell us we should not impose the values and criteria of our own culture on other cultures, which are all of equal dignity though organized differently. At that rate, the fundamental meaning of Alexis's religion would remain, if not inaccessible to us, at least very obscure. Others see each stage of history and religious thought as part of a continual growth toward maturity, the progress of morality and conscience toward an ever greater richness and universality. For example, Teilhard de Chardin writes: "Between the creative alpha and the christic omega are strung all the letters of the mystic alphabet. On the long road from the mineral to the society of the divine universal, the halts are called Abraham and Plato, Ikhnaton and Alexis, Augustine and Thomas Aquinas." And in an article that aroused the widest interest,[8] another Jesuit makes room for Alexis, together with Tamerlane, Peter the Great, and Lenin, among the helmeted prophets who bear, on ax, spear, or submachine gun, God's message to the peoples of their time.

We have said enough to demonstrate how impossible it is to speak of Alexis without attempting, as we have tried to do, to describe his predecessors, particularly Basil and Arsaphes, and even to give a brief account of what we have called "the Empire before the Empire." In his *Short History of the Empire Under Alexis for the Use of Milords of Trévoux,** Voltaire points out quite correctly that the idea of Alexis waking up one day and deciding to create everything in the Empire cannot be entertained. And he stresses the importance of the first golden age and the role played by Arsaphes and Basil. Chamfort, commenting on this passage in Voltaire, says: "Everything has its awaited moment of maturity. Happy the man who arrives, like Alexis, at the same time as the moment of maturity!"[9] Alexis appears to be the perfect embodiment of two opposite theories: that of the man of destiny, and that of the predominating influence of environment, cultural background, and the propitious moment. That Alexis was extraordinary there can be no doubt. But it is equally certain that he was served by circumstances of which he, in his turn, was the outstanding instrument. Sir Allan Carter-Bennett summarizes it very well: "Alexis is the conjunction of a man, a people, an age, and a civilization." The City was the symbol of that man, that people, that age, and that civilization. It was the incarnation of the Empire, and still bears witness today to Alexis's glory.

In Alexis's time the City had two centers. Its origin lay in trade, and one of the centers was the port. It had just replaced Aquileus as the capital of the Empire, and the other center, which contained the temples and the Emperor's palace, was called the "imperial city," or sometimes the "sacred precinct" or "holy city." To outdo in splendor the great temple at Aquileus, Alexis had called upon the greatest architects of his time. He summoned them from Greece, Egypt, Syria, and Samarkand, and under the supervision of two of the most famous among them, Sostratus and Metagenes, there had risen from the earth one of the most magnificent architectural ensembles of all time. Unfortunately all that remains today are ruins which convey little to the uninstructed traveler. But contemporary chronicles, the accounts given by ambassadors and travelers, and recent excavations by the French School of the City and the American and Italian archeological

---

* Trévoux was a center of Jesuit literary activity.—Trans.

missions combine to give a fairly accurate idea of how the City, its temples, and its port must once have appeared to a visitor.[10]

The port was entirely rebuilt by Alexis. As Petrarch says in his Latin poem on the Empire, it was "Omnium orbis terrae classium capax" (capable of sheltering all the fleets on Earth) and remained for a long time the largest in the known world. Ships passed into it under a huge allegorical representation of the sun in chryselephantine, which gave rise by contamination to the legend of the Colossus of Rhodes. In the third century B.C. Rhodes did have the famous giant statue that was counted as one of the seven wonders of the world, but, contrary to what the fable and the colored pictures of the souvenir merchants would have us believe, ships did not pass between its legs: it was at the entrance to the harbor of the City that galleys and triremes passed majestically, propelled by sail or oars, under the triumphal arch of the sun. The harbor itself was bordered with colonnades, warehouses, and markets, of which no trace remains. Only the northwest portico has been reconstructed by the Americans, under the name of Bruince's Portico; the documents on which the work was based are now in the Library of Congress. But of course this reconstruction is quite modern, and it has been the object of much criticism by specialists. Beyond the port a sacred way led to the imperial city; it was lined with statues said to have produced melodious sounds when touched by the sun, the morning dew, or the wind. At night the port and the sacred way were lit up with torches. The glow could be seen miles out to sea, heralding the splendors of the City to sailors making for the land. The fantastic imagination of Monsu Desiderio affords us a glimpse of this vision, amidst darkness and decay, in the famous picture in the Capodimonte Museum in Naples. The imperial city, on slightly higher ground, overlooked the port. It was surrounded by ramparts within which lay temples and palaces in profusion with gardens in between. The two most striking buildings were the great temple of the sun and the Emperor's palace. They have been considered the masterpieces of world architecture by Bramante, the three Sangalli, Vasari, Palladio, Ledoux, Wright, Mies van der Rohe, and Le Corbusier.

The vastness and majesty of the plan of the great temple give a somewhat extravagant impression, due no doubt to a mixture of influences, which made it impossible always to avoid the errors of taste involved in eclecticism and the monumental style. But the overall harmony together with the delicacy of the detail, the profusion of scenes in bas-relief, the elegance of capitals in which fabulous beasts from Persia and the East alternate with the geometrical simplicity of Greek motifs, the union of grandeur and gracefulness, rigor and imagination—all these, Justus Dion says, "evoked cries of wonder from astonished strangers." The subtlety of the general conception extended to details that have become famous in the history of architecture. These include a slight curvature in the masonry to facilitate drainage and to counteract the rigidity and starkness of perfectly straight lines; the inward slope of the vertical axis to avoid bulging and produce a pyramidal shape giving better resistance to earth tremors; and the placing of slightly thicker columns at the

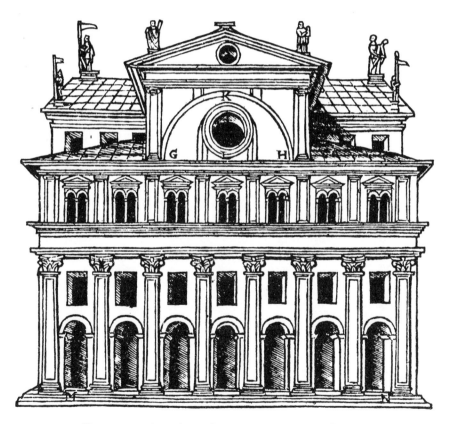

Reconstruction of northwest portico of the City,
known as Bruince's Portico
(American School of Classical and Oriental Studies).

corners to avoid the optical illusion by which columns uniform with the rest would look thinner because of being isolated against the sky.

The Emperor's palace was something entirely new in the architecture of its time. It was a huge edifice in the form of a pentagon, more like a medieval castle than a classical temple, and built entirely of brick and pink and green marble, with roofs of rare woods and pillared campaniles where priests trained in music and astronomy sounded, at various hours of the day and night, bells of bronze and silver brought from China and India. From the vast courtyard, said to be quite big enough to hold the Cohort of Twelve Thousand, a monumental staircase of Parian marble, lined with giants and fabulous beasts, led up to the throne room, where councils were held and where the emperor received high priests, generals, and foreign ambassadors. The view from the windows of the palace extended over the port and the City, part of the coast to the west, and to the east the valley of the Amphyses. Between the palace and the great temple lay a park planted with tall trees, meadows full of flowers, and fountains where water diverted from the Amphyses spouted from the mouths of Tritons and mermaids. Along the paths, in the gardens, inside the buildings, and above all in the Emperor's palace and the great temple of the sun, were statues, sculptured groups in pink stone or marble, high reliefs depicting work in the fields, myths, sieges, tiger or boar hunts. All were masterpieces; all, alas, are scattered, mutilated beyond repair, destroyed by nature, soldiers, scholars, and by time. A few undistinguished copies, quite unworthy of the originals, can still be seen in the British Museum, the Metropolitan Museum in New York, in the museums at Munich and Dresden, and especially in the fine Curators' Palace in the Capitol Square in Rome. Here is the most famous of all these reproductions, *Man Shooting an Arrow*, which was much admired by Winckelmann, Goethe, and Thorvaldsen. But all these copies give but a poor idea of that marvelous sculpture in which crudest realism mingled with wildest fantasy, and of which Focillon wrote: "It is the dream of the Creator before the creation, and it is God looking at all his creatures. . . . Both together, and in the same art, it is an encyclopedia of the imaginary and an encyclopedia of the real."[11] The paintings could not have been inferior to the architecture and sculpture, but it is difficult to know what it was like: canvases, paintings on wood, frescoes, all without exception have disappeared.[12]

Painting is not the only art in the Empire of which we know

nothing. We are almost completely ignorant, too, of its music, songs, and dances. The mind reels at the depths of our ignorance of a civilization as brilliant as that of the Empire. Innumerable trustworthy accounts tell us of its splendor, and yet we often seem to be confronted with a void. It is discouraging—it is as if that rich and powerful Empire had disappeared without trace. How can one help meditating, then, on the fragile destiny of all cultures? Valéry was thinking of the

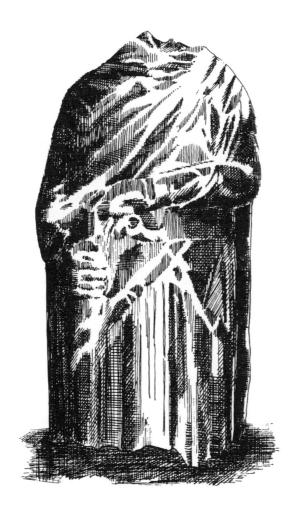

Torso of a mutilated marble figure.
Found in the ruins of the City.

Empire when he wrote the famous phrase that sounds like a knell for all history, including our own: "We civilizations know now that we are mortal."

The modern traveler arriving by boat at the site of the City does not experience any shock like that produced by the savage grandeur of Onessa's shores. But the sea is incomparably clear, and the hills, still green, stoop gently toward the jagged coast and what used to be the port. It was the sight of the bay, once lined with the glories of the City, that inspired one of Walt Whitman's finest poems:

O to have been brought up on bays, lagoons, creeks, or along
the coast . . .

The whole landscape has a unique charm, limpid and melancholy. Imagination sweeps both mind and heart into almost painful reverie, reconstructing, on the heights, the imperial city with its palace and its temples; bringing back to life the processions of priests and maidens singing hymns and waving palms and rose laurels all along the sacred way; filling with merchant ships, with heavy galleys, with triremes, with boats of all colors and sizes the pretty deserted cove that used to be the port. Here, on these now forgotten shores, which in their silence seem so far away from it all to tourists fleeing the noise and bustle of our metropolises, there once arose what for more than three centuries was the capital of the civilized world. The mind must conjure up the hum of activity, the prosperity, the luxury that then prevailed where now there is no stir save the swift flight of a goat, the roar of the waves on the beach, or the wind blowing in from the sea. Between this beach and those rocks, sailors, carpenters, potters, armorers, dyers, fullers, oil merchants, and bewildered shepherds down from the mountains used to rub shoulders with barbarian captains, priests, solemn magistrates, ambassadors borne in litters, and high palace officials accompanied by their guard. A sea bird flies slowly overhead; dusk is about to fall. You would swear all that never existed, that the fate of the world was never decided on those hills. How swiftly things fall from the heights of glory to the depths of oblivion! It was when visiting these haunts of terrifying silence that Chateaubriand, the Book of Ecclesiastes in his hand and borrowing from Bossuet, uttered the words that delighted Natalie de Noailles, and that many since have admired for their strength and simplicity: "We shall all die."

We shall all die. But we shall not die altogether. Something will be left behind us like a trail of light to transmit to succeeding generations all that is great in work and in the imagination. And more than crumbling palaces and mutilated statues, what shines forever in men's memories are the efforts of the mind to lift itself above everyday existence by laughter, terror, metaphysical thought, the beauty of the word, and the brilliance of ideas. By a strange paradox, iron and marble have been worn away by time; the jetties, wharves, and quays of the port have been flung into the sea or destroyed by fire; the temples and palaces of the imperial city have crumbled to dust. What remains, defying the ages, is what is most fragile, most intangible, barely existing in the form of murmurs, confidences, meditations, reveries: verses, speech, the words of poets and historians. The reader may recall the luster that philosophy and the theater had in the first golden age of the City. The Empire of Alexis seemed suddenly to remember all this vanished past. Comedy, tragedy, literature, art— the Empire, and above all the City, made them flower again and wore them to perfection.

Here, again, Alexis was well served by the age and by men. It was a time when talent and genius seemed to compete with and fertilize one another. But Alexis singled them out, honored them, helped them. He surrounded himself with poets as well as generals, and between wars would listen to readings from *The Onessiad*, or of Valerius's great poems on *The Creation of the World* and *The Birth of the Empire* (in the latter the poet goes so far as to refer, very discreetly it is true, to the affair between Alexis and Vanessa). In his palace in the City, Alexis attended performances of the tragedies of Polyphilus and Manalchas: *Arsaphes and Heloise*, *The Barbarians*, *The Tomb of Arsaphes*, *The Eagle and the Tiger*, *Basil the Great*, *The Banquet at Onessa*, *The Meaning of Death*, *The Four Before the Golden City*, *The Glory of Balamir*. With such lofty examples, writing soon became a fashion, an ambition, an honor, and the days were far away when literature had been despised. The Emperor Basil had sung coarse songs before ambassadors from foreign countries. Now refinement and good taste had conquered the court and the Empire. Various works on the literature of the Empire that differ in other things agree in this: that it was not uncommon, in great families, for the eldest son to adopt a military career, the second son to become a priest, and the youngest to go in for letters or philosophy. The Emperor encouraged them all. He remembered he himself had been a poet before becoming a military and political leader, and literature was still, in his eyes, one of the noblest of callings. He even admitted criticism, satire, including outright attacks, as long as their inspiration and form were worthy of respect. A very modern sense of the need for balanced values told him that freedom of thought makes countries great, and that by according honor to literature the Empire would add to its own another, reflected glory.

In Alexis's own entourage the history of his reign was recounted with minuteness, naïveté, and passion in the *Histories* and *Chronicles* of one of the greatest writers of all time, thanks to whom the people, manners, and happenings of his age live still before our eyes and to whom all succeeding historians of the Empire owe a debt of admiration and, in one way or another, of gratitude: he was called Justus Dion. He gives us a mass of colorful and lively information on the Empire at the time of Alexis and before. It is only natural we should want to know something about the mysterious Justus Dion. The historian gives us a history of the Emperor, and what we need now is a history of the historian. Who was Justus Dion? The question has been asked more insistently in the last couple of centuries, with the progress of historical criticism. Many still accept the traditional answer which, for a long while, was accepted by everyone—Justus Dion was a historian more or less contemporary with Alexis, who lived at the Emperor's court, and of whom the most important thing we know is that Alexis had complete confidence in him. But some people maintain nowadays that Justus Dion never existed. Of course, no one could deny the existence of the *Histories* and the *Chronicles*, the source of all we know about the Empire and the Emperor, to which such eminent yet different historians as Sir Allan Carter-Bennett, Robert Weill-Pichon, and Fulgence Tapir owe almost everything. What is in question is Justus Dion's personal existence and what he was like. As to this there have been the boldest hypotheses. According to Abel Lefranc, Justus Dion is none other than Valerius. For others, Justus Dion is a pseudonym for Bruince. But recent studies, including those of Jorge Luis Borges, Pauline Réage, and Roger Caillois, have gone further still. They say the name of Justus Dion was the pseudonym of the Emperor Alexis himself. We would thus have a Janus, one of whose faces is history as it is lived, the other history as it is written.

The poems of Alexis and the *Histories* and *Chronicles* of Justus Dion are now being subjected to structural analysis—in particular at

Trinity College, Oxford, and at the University of Besançon—in order to check this theory, which has left scholars deeply divided. Passionate arguments have been exchanged. Alexis a historian? It is easy enough to imagine the poet writing about the Empire. But when, among all his other duties, could the Emperor have found the time for so vast a body of work? The example of Caesar has, of course, been put forward. In the present state of research it is impossible to come down definitely on one side or the other; but it would certainly be astonishing if all we know about Alexis had come from Alexis himself. The history of the Empire would in that case be a closed circle. The jest of the German metaphysician and humorist Georg Christoph Lichtenberg would then be revealed as an inspired intuition, made as it was at a time when the problem of Justus Dion's identity had scarcely arisen: "History fabricates its own sources: it is from the *Histories* and *Chronicles* of Justius Dion that our idea of the Empire gets its life, and it is from our idea of the Empire that the *Histories* and *Chronicles* of Justus Dion get their life. Science, like the world itself, is the daughter of illusion."[13] Fortunately, whoever was their author—historian, poet, or emperor—we only have to reread the *Histories* and the *Chronicles* for the Empire to come to life again before our eyes, and for paradox and witticism to vanish before reality. The Emperor may perhaps have created Justus Dion, but it was not Justus Dion who created the Empire—it would take too much genius. One may perhaps, if driven to it, doubt that there was ever a Justus Dion. But who could doubt that there was ever an Empire?

Perhaps it was in philosophy more than anything else that the realities of the Empire were most splendidly reflected. It was descended, as we know, from Hermenides and Paraclites; it was encouraged, like the rest, by Alexis, who remembered with some regret his links with Asia, his conversations with the sages and saints of Persia and India, and all he owed to the lessons of Taoism and Master K'ung; and in a single generation, especially in the City, it recovered all its former splendor. It drew sustenance from the everyday life and the society of the time, it expressed and translated them, and, in its turn, it influenced and modified them. In addition to such distinguished masters as Philontes and Aristo, of whom Heidegger and Bertrand Russell both said, a few years back and in almost identical terms,[14] that they established what was to be the Western scale of values for centuries—and, indeed, they ruled unchalleged until

Bacon and Descartes[15]—philosophers from Greece, Syria, Persia, and China debated all day long, beneath the colonnades of the port and in the schools of grammar, the destiny of man and his last end, the meaning of truth and justice. The spirit of the age brought about a gradual neglect of those problems concerning the nature of things and their physical origin that had so much preoccupied Paraclites and Hermenides. Instead, interest was concentrated partly on medicine, which made enormous progress under the Empire, and partly on vast metaphysical and moral systems with mathematical references, which aroused passionate enthusiasm among the young. Aristo and Philontes built up majestic edifices that have justly been compared to the temples and palaces of the imperial city. Transposed into intellectual terms, they had the same overwhelming grandeur, together with something at once sublime and tinged with extravagance. These pyramids of entities in search of unity and salvation, these processions of hypostases solemnly advancing in the shelter of abstruseness, aroused in more modest spirits an admiration tinged with suspicion, and they went on trusting rather to common sense and to the racy vocabulary of the harbor's corn merchants and porters. But the rise of a culture is as rapid and contagious as its decline. The Emperor made it his business to be present in person at several of the great disputations in which philosophers and orators debated a prearranged subject. In his train came a crowd of courtiers, and soon after, to accommodate the debates of scholars and writers, Alexis built a portico halfway between the imperial city and the harbor, on a quiet, sheltered site with a little river that is often referred to in contemporary writings. It was there, in the course of public lectures or private meditation, that some of the most important works in the history of philosophy were conceived: the *Porphyrean Ethics*, the *Treatise on the Worlds*, and the *Confessions*, all by Philontes; the seventeen books of Aristo's *Metaphysics;* Martian's *Summa* and *Contemplations;* the *Book of Wisdom and Folly* by Aziri, a Bashkir from the Urals; the *Treatise on the Government of the Mind* by a curious character, a Jew from Albania or Italy, completely bald and vain as a peacock, the forerunner of Grotius and Pufendorf, a philosopher and jurist of genius, of whom we know little and who called himself Simon the Angel or the Polititian.

The Emperor's friendship and support gave both prestige and impetus to the work of the philosophers. A fashion for things intellectual and learned subtleties spread irresistibly, and behind the great names of metaphysics and ethics there crept in a whole herd of sophists, mountebanks, prophets more or less inspired, and sometimes mere imposters and cranks, who fell on the Empire like a plague of locusts. Perhaps the years of suffering and struggle had been too hard, and men's characters disintegrated, in reaction, with the return of prosperity and peace. Perhaps the progress of culture and civilization inevitably creates a sort of foam or froth in which the mediocre and the fanatic find their element. In all events, the reckless teaching of the sophists and rhetoricians brought the Empire to the very brink of destruction.

Martian and Aziri, both very profound minds, professed a theory that was to have a great future, and to which Péguy pays homage in his famous genealogy: "Martian qui genuit Aziri . . . qui genuit Kant, qui genuit Fichte, qui genuit Schelling, qui genuit Hegel, qui genuit Marx . . ." The originators of this doctrine or tradition—the point is disputed—called it sometimes substantial idealism and sometimes spiritual realism. It taught that the phenomena of everyday were insignificant, and that behind the appearances of things there was an ideal world much more real than the other. Hence the use of the two names, realism and idealism, for this school—a practice which gives so much trouble to beginners. It is clear that true reality is not that of the illusion of the senses, which merely offers the soul a deceptive show. True reality is in the intoxicating loftiness of a world beyond this one, doomed as it is to decay, change, and in fact nonexistence. The real world, i.e., the world of the soul, can only be reached, according to Martian and Aziri, through sanctity, ascesis, and death. It has often been pointed out how close all this is not only to German idealism but also to the most orthodox Christianity. And Saint Thomas did not hesitate to incorporate into the God of the Christians Martian's conception of a supreme spiritual reality or substantial idea. In such a doctrine, as in Christianity itself, death was the true recompense of life. Death was waited for, hoped for, wished for, because through it one passed from the illusion of appearances to reality. Aziri went slightly further than Martian. They both maintained that the ordinary world is a prison. But instead of being content, like Martian, to await the ineffable hour of deliverance, Aziri did not hesitate—covertly, it is true, and very cautiously—to recommend escape. The *Book of Wisdom and Folly* opens with the famous little phrase that Albert Camus so admired and that was to have such grave consequences for the Empire: "There is only one really serious philosophical problem, and that is suicide."

The great rebels, the prophets of violence and disaster, often die in their beds. Aziri died at the age of ninety-two of a burst blood vessel, after a banquet at which he had done too well by himself. But meanwhile all over the Empire there had been a great flood of mystical and esoteric teaching that claimed to follow on from the doctrines of Martian and Aziri and that culminated in an apology for suicide. It was the young men who most eagerly attended the lectures and sermons given in schools, on the steps of temples, in village squares, in the open fields, or in the shade of a tree. At the end of one such meeting, which usually ended in scenes of hysteria or possession, two or three fanatics went and threw themselves from the top of a cliff. The news spread rapidly, and by the end of a month there had been more than six hundred voluntary deaths in the Empire. From then on an out-and-out epidemic spread through town and country, lasting nearly three years. Justus Dion says the roads were strewn with the corpses of people who had cut their throats or dashed out their brains against a wall or tree. Brotherhoods were formed in which each member swore to help his fellows to die. Mothers slew their children before killing themselves. Revenge often sheltered under metaphysics, but it was difficult to know whether in fact death was not, for the victim, the most eagerly awaited blessing; the judges, unable to make out such obscure motives, would acquit the murderer and punish his friend at random. The madness spread to the army. Whole battalions marched shoulder to shoulder toward death, and if there was no enemy to give them what they wanted, they would throw themselves into the sea or on to spears and pikes fixed breast-high in the wall. The Empire was seized with a mortal folly. Wise and foolish vied with each other to see who would be first to leap into death. Suicide attracted the pious, the brave, the cowards, the philosophers, the unfortunate, the fashionable, the clever, and the stupid. It all mounted up. Anyone could foresee the moment when the Empire would be depopulated for the sake of that real world to which death gave access. Generals, governors, the Emperor himself grew uneasy at this strange and ominous malady. At the same time they realized it was almost impossible to struggle against it. One particularly thick-witted governor suggested applying the death penalty to any attempted suicides caught in the act. Another, more subtle, proposed carefully meted-out tortures. But it did not take long for everyone to discover how easy it is to die. Men and women who had been put in chains found the strength and the courage to hold their breath and die of asphyxiation.

The barbarians were untouched by the suicide epidemic. It attacked only those whose love of life had been undermined by metaphysics and civilization. The barbarians, who despised death but loved life, looked on curiously as these priests, merchants, peasants, and young people, seized with mystic frenzy, rushed toward extinction. Justus Dion declares that infatuation with the beyond cost the Empire as many lives as the struggle against the barbarian tyrants. It was at this point that Isidore, now aged eighty or so, wrote the masterpiece so admired by Saint Francis of Assisi, André Gide, and Francis Jammes—*The Joy of Living* or, according to other translators, *The Pleasures of Living* or *The Love of Life*. This charming book, too often forgotten now, once delighted whole generations. As late as the eighteenth century, the works most frequently found in great private libraries were *The Imitation of Christ*, Buffon's *Natural History*, the *Fables* of La Fontaine, Rousseau's *New Heloise*, the *Encyclopedia*, and *The Pleasures of Living*.

Isidore's book is a prose poem full of passion and delight. It looks on creation with curiosity, fervor, and humble submission. It does not reach for the heights of metaphysics but, rather, makes discreet fun of what it calls, long before Renan borrowed the expression, "the most tedious of the abstract sciences." The author goes on to ask himself, in minor mood and with an assumed naïveté:

> Must one then die in order to be peaceful and innocent?
> Take care: to die is to perform an act with incalculable consequences. . . . To say life is good or to say life is evil is to say something meaningless. We must say it is good and evil at once, for it is through life and life alone we derive the idea of good and evil. The truth is that life is delightful, horrible, charming, dreadful, sweet, bitter—that it is everything.

The poem is devoted to the exaltation of life. The tone rises gradually from the simplest reflections to lyric raptures. Streams, snow, gardens, pomegranates, palm trees and dates, the grass of the field, sunrises, books, war, east-bound caravans in search of sandalwood and pearls, south-bound caravans in search of amber and musk and gold dust and ostrich plumes, forests and cities, ardor and love—everything supplies the author with an occasion for happiness and amused wonder. The poem restores to a people exhausted by too rapid a rise the love of both adventure and peace. It sings of water and fruit, the alternation of day and night, the marvels of the earth and of existence, the paths that wind through the fields, and the cool freshness of fountains:

Springs delicate at evening, delicious at noon; icy waters of morning; gusts on the shore; spar-strewn bays, warmth of rhythmic shores . . .

Ah, if there are still roads to the plain; flush of noon; the fields' cool draughts, and for the night a hollow in the hay;

if there are roads to the East; waves on beloved seas; gardens in Samarkand; dances in Aquileus; poets' songs on the Amphyses;

if there are roads to the north; fairs at Onessa; sledges making snow spray; frozen lakes—Ah, then our desires shall not flag.

Boats sail into our ports with ripe fruit from unknown shores. Make haste and unload their cargoes that we may taste at last.

And elsewhere:

I am Isidore, watchman of the tower. The night had been long. From the top of the tower I cried out to you often, ye dawns! Never-too-radiant dawns!

Till the very end of the night I still hoped for a newness of light; I see nothing yet, but I hope; I know in what quarter the day will dawn.

A whole nation makes ready; from the height of the tower I hear a murmur in the streets. The day will break! Already the people go rejoicing to meet the sun.

"What of the night? Watchman, what of the night?"

I see a generation that rises, and a generation that descends. I see a great generation that rises, armed, armed with joy toward life.

"What do you see from the watchtower, Isidore, my brother?"

Alas, alas, let the other prophet weep! The day cometh, and the night also.

Their night cometh, and our day also. Let him who wishes to sleep slumber. Isidore, come down now from the watchtower.

Day is breaking. Come down to the plain. Look closer at each thing. Come, Isidore, come near! Day is come, and we believe in it.[16]

If ever a book played a role in human history, Isidore's *Pleasures of Living* has done so, just as much as Saint Augustine's *City of God* or Marx's *Capital*. But it is neither didactic nor revolutionary. It is a work of unconstrained delight and wonder at simple things, full of both enthusiasm and irony. It foreshadows Montaigne and Anatole France. Like the *Essays* it is shot through with tolerant skepticism; like *Penguin Island* and the *Garden of Epicurus* it combines good-natured raillery with human pity—but it is also full of religious and physical optimism. It sometimes reminds one distantly of Gide's *Fruits of the Earth*, with its lyric praise of life and all life's delights. *The Pleasures of Living* gave more to the Empire than a victory: it reconciled it to itself. "The Emperor," writes Justus Dion, "jested with Isidore, saying never had pleasure so well performed its duty."

The epidemic disappeared as rapidly as it had spread. But it had been a near thing. Alexis could understand better than anyone that distaste for life, that fascination with another world that he himself had once felt and that toward the end of his life, as we shall see, he was to feel again. But as Emperor he could not let death overcome life and depopulate the Empire. Those who had trusted themselves to him had to be saved from themselves. In this sense, to rule men is to oppose them. It was as if, by some malediction, each new event impelled Alexis further toward that absolute power and authority that before he had avoided and distrusted. Alexis saw this tendency quite clearly, and realized that others called it pride, madness, thirst for power, tyranny. But the time for hesitation was past. He had put his hand to the plow, and he must not look back. The suicide wave had shown how difficult it was to wield authority over those undeterred by death. So, since he could not govern effects, the Emperor attacked causes: education, speech, and writing were strictly controlled. Though counseled to do so by some of his advisers, he did not resort to such extremes as those Chinese emperors and Arab conquerors who burned all books, but, perhaps reluctantly, Alexis came to exercise an ever-closer supervision over all writing. He told Bruince of his astonishment at his own acts. If he had had a vision of the Emperor in the temple tombs or on the roads of Asia, he said, he would have been horrified. But time insinuates itself into us, men and events constrain and shape us, things change, and we change also. "Power corrupts," the Emperor said. "Absolute power corrupts absolutely. I knew that, and wanted to avoid it. But the gods decreed otherwise. It is no use complaining; all I can do is exercise worthily the power I could not set aside. Worthily means without weakness. It is not necessary to rule, any more than it is necessary to be a philosopher or write poems. But he who has chosen to rule, to lead men (who are not always good), to make peace and war, has chosen authority, brutality, violence, and blood, just as Philocrates chose justice and Justus Dion truth."[17]

It seemed to Alexis there was never enough rigor in people's thoughts and words. After, just as much as before, what Justus Dion with his usual naïveté calls "the epidemic of culture and philosophy," the Emperor still took great pleasure in literature and poetry. But now he liked them to be stricter, more difficult, more disciplined. The idea that anyone who liked the sound of his own voice should take himself for a Polyphilus or a Valerius amused and angered him. With age, he grew naturally less and less tolerant of novelty and ingenuity, and preferred the great works that had marked the heyday of his reign. He believed and perhaps he was right, they possessed a simplicity, a grandeur, a perfection of form and content that would never be surpassed. External circumstances, about which a few words must be said, encouraged Alexis toward purism in art and intransigence in everything.

The rules of language and of taste had been fixed toward the end of the first half of the reign by Logophilus, a long-obscure scholar whom we have already come across several times; half grammarian and half mathematician, he was possibly of Greco-Syrian origin. His *Plan for a Universal Calendar*, his *Treatise on Versification*, and above all his *Treasury of the Language of the Empire*, which was greatly admired by Malherbe and Boileau and sanctioned the assimilation into Greek of many Syrian and Mongol words, eventually won him eminence. Alexis made Logophilus not only literary legislator of the Empire, but veritable dictator of culture and the arts; and Logophilus, that great lover of language, strangely enough urged the Emperor to great rigor against the written and spoken word. Logophilus soon went far beyond the strict limits of his post, which was that of proveditor of the treasury and works, and had a great influence on the fate of the Empire. In the last years of Alexis's reign, power was in fact exercised by a triumvirate, which made all important decisions together. The triumvirate consisted of the Emperor himself,

Bruince, and Logophilus. The grammarian was not the most back-ward of the three in advocating authoritative and sometimes violent measures, even in fields that properly belonged to politics. The sack of Pomposa and Rome is attributed by several historians to his love of beautiful things. The famous bronze horses that decorated the great temple of the City, the two rows of chryselephantine statues at the entrance to the palace, and the fabulous collection of gold vases encrusted with emeralds which, according to Justus Dion, repre-sented a third of all the wealth in the world—all these splendors, and many more, were spoils of war, part of the loot amassed by the learned Logophilus, who after restoring the language of the Empire employed much vigor and not too many scruples to the task of beauti-fying its squares and palaces.

Language, the arts, drama, literature, philosophy, history: thus was made up the luster, frail yet immortal in men's memories, of a civilization. It is not inappropriate to speak of the age of Alexis as one speaks of the age of Pericles or of Louis XIV. Among the infinite combinations of men and events there sometimes suddenly appear such happy conjunctions that it seems as if everything conspired to produce their transient perfection. There is talent, peace at home, power abroad, prosperity, and even victories to lend a sense of great-ness and collective dignity. In every art, every science that for cen-turies has not produced a single great name, suddenly there are two or three or more. Great minds spur one another on, and their rivalry leads them to the heights. The triumph of arts and letters in the Empire, its military power, its wealth, the ships in the harbors, the buildings in the cities, the gardens and aqueducts, the steles con-tinuing right to the borders of the desert, the roads, the granaries, the statues in the temples, the columns hung with booty, and all the rest—all was no doubt due to some fortunate throw of the dice in the gamble of history. But it was also a heritage, the result of a long ripening process that went back to the first golden ages of the City, to Arsaphes and Thaumas, and to the endeavors of the priests, despite their many follies. All had their part in the flowering of the Empire: Isidore, Logophilus, Bruince, the philosophers and tragedians, poets and craftsmen, priests and architects, barbarian captains and sailors in the navy, and Alexis himself, who had willed and organized and created everything save the other people concerned, though he had discovered and singled out and honored them. But nothing of what Alexis had dreamed of came about exactly as he had hoped. It entailed much more harshness and cruelty than he had thought, but by dint of energy in the face of setbacks, strength of will, good luck, and genius, Alexis gave meaning and direction to what had been entrusted to him by fate, the gods, and history. There were some shadows across the light; there was a good deal of blood, mingled with just a little guile and with much greatness. There were faith, good will, trust, and sorrows. And all together, the dead and the living, those who wrote, those who carved in stone, those who took life also, those who brought back gold and silver from distant lands across the sea, those who gave orders, and those who obeyed—all combined, with Alexis, to produce the Empire and its glory. "Men," wrote Justus Dion with more modesty and moderation than might appear, "are capable of great things and many marvels. They have accomplished some already; they will accomplish more. But the Empire will remain through all ensuing time one of the symbols of man's greatness."

XIX

THE SPIRIT OF CONQUEST
AND THE MEANING OF DEATH

HE EMPEROR HAD GREATLY CHANGED WITH THE
passing of the years. He was no longer the young
man of legendary beauty and the Alexandrian
nights, nor the ascetic of the columns and the temple tombs, nor the hero of the battles of the princes
and of the six days. Physically, he had put on
weight and his features had thickened. He had grown a beard, which
was to turn white as time went by. Morally, power had taken hold
of him even more than he of it, and the love of authority, which he had
once so disliked, had come to him with age, with the exercise of
responsibility, with victory, and disappointment. Perhaps it had come
without his really wishing it; but now a whole mechanism of countless interconnected events was in motion all around him, and necessity was in command. But his inspired energy, breadth of conception, will power, and what Sir Allan Carter-Bennett calls "a cosmic
sense of history" were all still intact in him and more imperious than
ever. The Pomposan ambassador reported to the merchant princes
that "ordinary mortals saw the Emperor high on his throne in the
City as one hurling thunderbolts at history rather than as one ruling
men and things."

By then the conquest of the world was an established fact. We
have already referred several times to the insoluble problem of responsibility. It is certain that the fear and anger of the great powers,
especially Cyprus, when confronted with the New Alliance, were
influential in setting in motion a machinery that was to have far-
reaching consequences. But it is also true, and only apparently paradoxical, that the Emperor's whole training, his travels, his sojourn in

Asia, and even his metaphysical experiences, urged him irresistibly toward the conquest of the world. The acquisition of wisdom and knowledge only took on its full meaning for him in action and the handing on of all the treasures he had amassed. Robert Weill-Pichon hits it off well when he speaks of Alexis's conquests as a "metaphysical crusade." Like Hellenism and Rome, like the Catholic Church, like the French Revolution and Napoleon, like Lenin and communism, Alexis conquered the world to educate it and to make it share in the order, the revelation, and the civilization that he personified. This point has of course been much debated. But less general considerations—accidents of history—enter into the matter also. Let us dwell for a moment on two sets of causes which in their different ways, and among many others, were to play a part in bringing the future to birth.

After Helen, the courtesans of Alexandria, Vanessa, and the Yemenite, there had apparently been no woman in the Emperor's life. Bruince often reminded him[1] that the future of the Empire depended on his providing himself with descendants. The minister cited the Kha-Khan of the Oïghurs, who had married Zenobia, daughter of Helen and Roderick and sister of Alexis and Simeon, by whom he had had a son, Khubilai, whose dazzling career we shall see later. Several marriages were contemplated or even arranged for the Emperor: with a princess from Cyprus, with a princess from Sicily, with the heiress of one of the most important families in Pomposa, and even, in order to restore the balance between the families of the two princes, with Mesa, Balamir's sister, who finally—by way of demonstrating the barbarians' attachment to the New Alliance when this project, always rather vague, came to nothing—married Bruince. The Emperor always lacked time or inclination, until one day something happened that caused an upheaval in the Empire and was to echo through history right down to our own time.

The reader will recall the important role played by feasts, games, and combats in the period we are concerned with. The games, which often involved bloodshed, included chariot and horse races, the racing of bulls, wild-beast fights, contests of all kinds. One of the most popular is supposed to be the origin of the Japanese *sumo*, and the Afghan *bouzkachi* is thought to derive from a race, or rather free-for-all, in which no holds were barred and riders on tarpans or the little half-wild horses of Dzungaria or Mongolia tried to snatch a goat hide from their opponent. Polo, too, the horseman's sport par excellence, is said to have been transmitted from the Empire to Persia, whence, many centuries later, it spread to the Anglo-Saxon countries and to the Argentine. But of all the Empire's games the most famous and the most terrifying was that which historians, for want of specific documentation and exact knowledge, call simply the *ball game*. It was simultaneously a sport, an entertainment, a pantomime of war, and a religious ceremony. It is because of its sacred character that this popular sport, the rules of which we do not know, remains so much a mystery to us. Like everything that has to do with vanished religions, its spirit, general relevance, and real significance elude us. Here, too, there were two teams on horseback, and the game consisted in trying to put a ball made of light wood or stiffened cloth through a wooden or, more often, stone ring fixed to a wall; goals were scored with the aid of elbows, knees, and shoulders, or with a kind of long, curved mallet halfway between the Basque *chistera* and a baseball bat. *Sepak raga*, a kind of badminton played today in southeast Asia, where a cane ball is headed or kicked over a net, has close affinities with the ball game of the Empire. But during the period we are speaking of, victory by one or another of the sides in the ball game was followed by sensational events: the finest horse in the winning team and the captain of the losing side both had their throats slit on the ground where the game had been played and in the presence of the onlookers, and revolting scenes took place that were at once wild and chaotic yet ruled by a strict liturgy. Temple prostitutes crawled up to the two dead bodies, smeared themselves with blood, mimed the sexual act, and, following the preferences indicated by the crowd, proceeded, between themselves or with the priests, to excesses beyond description. The bodies of the man and the horse were then dismembered, and all the boys of the town or the surrounding district who were just twelve years old competed in ritual combat for possession of the heads.

These bloodthirsty games were enormously popular and watched by wildly excited crowds. Fighting and feasting, which had reached their heyday in the first golden age of the City and under Basil the Great, had declined for want of the necessary resources under the barbarian tyrants. But they had started up again more vigorously than before with the return of peace and prosperity. Alexis, largely in memory of Philocrates, who had often expressed his loathing of scenes that revived the memory of the sacrifice at Mursa, tried to suppress them, but had to yield before furious popular resentment. It was because of the social role of the games, the universal esteem in which they were held, their sacred nature, and the way they kept alive a love of arms and blood that Professor Bjöersenson said, in a felicitous phrase which we have met before:[2] "The Empire rested on three pillars. It had three preoccupations and three laws that were really one: war, feasting, and religion."

The fight among the boys for possession of the heads was only a prelude to a new development in this savage entertainment. When one or more of the boys, distinguishable from each other by the different bright colors they wore, had succeeded in getting hold of the heads, they had the honor of bringing them, still dripping with blood, to the priests and temple prostitutes. To the plaudits of the crowd they were given prizes of purple ribbons or fine robes, after which the head of the losing captain was shaved by the prostitutes and thrown by the priests back on to the ground between the two teams. Then the last phase of the game began, fierce and gory and more like a nightmare than an entertainment, accompanied by howls from the mob and scenes of hysteria and possession. Now it was the children, on foot, who imitated the game previously played by the horsemen, and tried to get the ball through the wood or stone ring. But the ball they used was the head of the vanquished captain. The boy who succeeded, with foot or knee, elbow or shoulder, or with the curved mallet but never with the hand, in getting the head through that monstrous empty eye, that symbol of the gateway to death, was received with great solemnities by the priests. He underwent rites of purification and lustration in the temples, he offered sacrifices to the sun and the tutelary deities of the Empire, the priests crowned him with laurel and oak leaves mixed, temple prostitutes initiated him into love, and he was equipped as a warrior, with choice weapons, a shield of wood or leather, and a helmet surmounted by an eagle. Often he would enter upon a religious or military career. But that career was likely to be short—the captains of the adult teams in the ball game were often chosen from among the young men who had won their laurels in it as boys.

The temple prostitutes who entered the arena after the double massacre of the man and the horse, between the game proper and its gory simulacrum, enjoyed a very special status in the Empire. They were part of the sacred world of the priests, but were excluded from the society of the Empire's ancient families, of high officials, and even of the priests themselves, who collaborated with them in religious ceremonies and often enjoyed their bodies, but in private life treated them with disdain and sometimes contempt. They obeyed no rule comparable to that which restricted the activities of priestesses of the temple of the sun, like Vanessa. They were bound by no vow. All they did was make love before everyone during the games. They occupied their place in the sacred liturgy by offering themselves to the gods by way of the priests, the boys who conquered in the ball game, and the pilgrims. In his journal, translated by Henri Estienne and quoted by Montaigne,[3] one of these pilgrims, speaking of the prostitutes, remarks with naïve enthusiasm: "And I assure you there are so many of them for the use of those passing through and of pious and fortunate travelers that it is a wonder and great delight." In theory they were available to anyone for a price in accordance with their age, beauty, fame, and speciality, but they were not obliged to give themselves if they did not choose, and jokes were often made about immensely wealthy merchants and even governors who had met with refusal and been turned away. They were, in fact, rather like the great Italian courtesans who delighted, one after the other or simultaneously, the cardinals and monklings at the courts of the Italian Renaissance, and who appear in Boccaccio, Brantôme, and later in Balzac's *Contes drolatiques* (Ribald Tales). The picture was even completed by farcical intrigues, with the women playing off powerful protectors against younger sweethearts. But the nature of their functions, at once sacred, bloody, and public, made them, even for that day and age, more frightening, and lent them something at once more awe-inspiring and more coarse. It was not unusual for one of them to give up her profession out of lassitude or love or having made her fortune. A few, though with difficulty and usually after a hard struggle, managed by intelligence and energy to attain quite a high position in imperial society. Menalchas the dramatist is said to have begun his career as the protégé of one former temple prostitute. Another, who became extremely rich, is supposed to have contributed to the costs of building the great temple of the City.

Despite the repugnance he had always shown for cruel games, the Emperor's position and his concern for his own popularity obliged him to attend at least once a year. In those days the preparations for feasts and combats created as much rumor and excitement as *corridas* in Spain or horse racing in England nowadays. In the year with which we are concerned, no one in the City talked of anything but the beauty and majestic elegance of a temple prostitute whose successes had made her extremely proud despite her youth. The rumor reached the

Emperor, who decided to attend the games. The young woman, as depicted in mosaics in the City and Pomposa, one of which is preserved in the Brera in Milan and the other in the Metropolitan Museum in New York, was indeed very beautiful—slim, wide-shouldered, with a fair, pale complexion and a face and bearing of peerless nobility. Her long, black hair came down to her shoulders. Her abstractedness amounted to insolence, yet when she raised her dark eyes toward the spectators, there glowed in them, according to contemporary accounts, a flame that seemed to speak of passion held in check by scorn or indifference. The games took their usual course. Yet it was amidst a silence unbroken by any of the usual shouts, perhaps frozen in men's throats at the sight of such rare beauty, that the temple prostitute crawled through the blood to the two corpses, and, following a ritual handed down through generations from antiquity, mimed the act of love with the dead man and the animal still twitching from its death agony. Justus Dion takes care not to mention the incident, but contemporary chronicles relate that the courtesan, perhaps knowing of the Emperor's presence, performed her office with such loftiness and dignity that "the crowd was seized with a frenzy from on high which was the voice of the gods." At all events, the Emperor cannot have been indifferent to the ceremony, nor to the satisfaction of the gods, nor to the officiant who inspired it, because we know that the same evening a messenger was sent from the palace to fetch her. Scarcely one moon later she abandoned her office to live there, and before the year was out Alexis married her. To the scornful yet furious smiles of the patricians, male and female, the temple prostitute put on the great imperial azure robe. She was not yet twenty. The Emperor was forty-nine. Her name was Theodora.

The sensation caused in the City and throughout the Empire can easily be imagined. The Emperor's marriage widened still further the gap created between Helen and her son by Jester's execution, and Alexis's mother never met Theodora. There had been attempts to dissuade the Emperor, and the chief priests and old families even brought pressure to bear to try to make him renounce his passion, or his vagary—both words are to be found in contemporary texts—and bring him around to the advantageous marriages long put forward by various ambassadors. But apparently he had made up his mind the very first day, perhaps the very first instant, and he never wavered. Alexis's will was not in the habit of yielding. But also Theodora was a very exceptional woman. The future proved that the Emperor was right, and Theodora left posterity a great name worthy to be coupled with that of Alexis. Forceful women famous for one reason or another are not rare in history, from the Queen of Sheba, Cleopatra, and Zenobia of Palmyra to Catherine Sforza, Isabella d'Este, Elizabeth of England, Catherine of Russia, Maria Theresa of Austria, and Queen Victoria. And love between man and woman is not as unknown as people like to pretend. But rare in any age are couples in which the man and the woman both collaborate, with equal happiness, in the same great design. The two most illustrious examples are the Emperor Alexis and the Empress Theodora, and Justinian, emperor of the Eastern Roman Empire, and the other Theodora. There has often been some confusion between the two Theodoras, encouraged by the fact that they share the same name, though it is one quite frequent in history, and perhaps also by some slight similarity between their lives. Both women were geniuses, of humble origin and unyielding character. But it also seems that by contamination many of the traits belonging to our Theodora were attributed to the empress of Byzantium, and that the latter's place in history is largely due to the name she had in common with her predecessor. Many historians, and more especially essayists, writers of melodrama and would-be historical plays, and novelists given to the lamentable genre of historical fiction, bear the heavy responsibility of having contributed to what amounts almost to a fusion of the two Theodoras. The best known of the culprits is probably Victorien Sardou. As is well known, his play *Theodora*, performed with enormous success in 1884 and typical of the historical melodrama then in fashion, was based on the personality and experiences of Alexis's wife. But the situations and atmosphere owe a great deal to the history of Byzantium, which was more familiar to Sardou than that of the Empire. Even today, when our knowledge of Alexis and his time has been expanded by many excellent books on the subject, the confusion is still often met with. But it cannot be overemphasized: historical accuracy requires that most of the anecdotes and enterprises ascribed to the Byzantine empress should be restored to the former temple prostitute. And, of course, when we use the name Theodora hereafter we refer only to the wife of Alexis.

It was not long before Theodora showed her mettle. Two years after she married Alexis there was a violent uprising in the City, in which the priests most hostile to the Emperor joined with barbarian mercenaries from the Tigris and Euphrates. The rebels invoked a new and unpopular tax on the orange trade to gain the support of a large section of the population of the City: hence the rising became known to history as the Orange Rebellion. In only a few hours the situation became grave. At the end of two days, things looked desperate for the Emperor and his party. The priests and great landowners who had not forgiven Alexis for the execution of Jester and did not accept the New Alliance had joined in an unnatural coalition with a large body of barbarians who demurred at Balamir's submission to and friendship with the Emperor. It is clear that this coalition, if it had been successful, was bound to disintegrate after a few weeks, but meanwhile it would have drawn down countless catastrophes on the Empire. The City, weary perhaps of prosperity and peace, was seized with a kind of madness, and it seemed that the inhabitants—backed by the riffraff often found hanging around seaports, come from none knows where, unconcerned with the people's real interests but eager for looting and arson—were gaining the upper hand. There was a wave of panic. Bruince and Logophilus themselves seemed on the point of giving in. The Emperor hesitated. It looked as though a last effort on the part of those known as the "Oranges" might throw down the whole patiently constructed edifice of the Empire. Then Theodora calmly announced that the Emperor and his ministers might leave, but rather than yield she would die on the spot amongst a faithful few. "If you choose to run away, Alexis, very well. You have money, your ships are ready, the sea is open. But I shall stay. I like the old proverb that says the sky makes a good shroud." This calm and unshakable determination changed the situation at a blow, and the revolt was crushed. "A dozen words," writes Sir Allan, "had changed the destiny of the world." It was a lesson the great recalcitrants of history were not to forget.

After her resistance to the Orange Rebellion, Theodora exercised a great influence on the policy of the Empire. Although Alexis was not really ambitious, the Empress was. Alexis has been described as a metaphysician in power, eager to persuade and to spread his teaching—if necessary by fire and sword, for how else could princes and captains act upon the world?—guided by a deep faith, and perhaps a terrific love of humanity, rather than by ambition. But Theodora *was* ambitious. She wanted the lands over which the Emperor ruled to grow; she wanted Alexis's glory to fly from one city to another; she desired with all her strength—and that was saying a good deal—that the Emperor should leave behind a dazzling name, and that the historians of the future should make him come to life again after he was dead. In almost diametrically opposed forms, Alexis and Theodora were each a prey to the most consuming of passions, the passion a contemporary philosopher has eloquently named the desire for eternity. They understood this desire very differently. For the Emperor, it was a desire for the eternity of revelation taught to him by the sages and seers of Asia, of which he had spoken to Jester long ago.[4] Theodora's concern was with the eternity of history. For Alexis, time everlasting in the blaze of a moment. For Theodora, the indelible trace left in passing time. It is not hard to see the brilliance that might result from the coming together of these two contrasting minds, these two equally strong wills.

No serious attempt to understand the foreign policy of the Empire can afford to neglect one final element—the financial aspect of things. Reforms, administration, the upkeep of the army, temples, and palaces, the Emperor's love of beauty and fine buildings—all these were expensive. The Empire was rich again, but its resources were not inexhaustible. Cyprus and Pomposa, on the other hand, were overflowing with gold, ships, and objets d'art siphoned all year round toward the capital by countless merchants scattered in colonies and factories all over the world. The temptation to seize such treasures, within arm's reach, was irresistible; and the Emperor, pressed by Theodora, bound by his engagements to Balamir, forced to war by the provocations offered by the princes of Cyprus, yielded, though his thoughts were still full of dreams of humanity and universal brotherhood.

Cyprus was the first stage on the long road of the wars of conquest. Its rulers' rashness had passed all bounds. Terrified by the New Alliance and the threat of the barbarians, against whom they had long hoped to persuade Alexis to fight, disappointed by the failure of Jester and the priests in their pay, and perhaps disappointed that the Orange revolt, in which some historians see once again the influence of Pomposan and Cyprian gold, had been crushed, they launched themselves into a sort of escalation of violence. While still active within the Empire through their agents and spies, they attacked the barbarians on the maritime frontiers of their power, in Syria, at Byblos, and all along the coast between Tyre and Sidon. For several years in succession they launched spring and autumn campaigns that were at first quite successful—for a while Cypriot troops were on the Euphrates. Emboldened by success, the princes of

Cyprus then attacked the Empire directly. History never repeats itself, but geographical conditions and natural imperatives, the capes and bays, the passes and fords essential to military strategy constantly impose themselves on the plans of armies and their captains. One spring morning, at dawn, the Cyprian army suddenly appeared in an area we know well. They disembarked at Cape Gildor.

It was quite a well-planned operation. Most of the barbarian troops that might have been called in to help were engaged in a large-scale campaign on the frontiers of Persia and India. At the time of the debarkation, the Kha-Khan of the Oïghurs was in fact just crossing the Khyber Pass and descending on the rich plains around Peshawar. As for the army corps permanently stationed in the Empire, it had been detailed to cover the Euphrates, and had just arrived there. But the Cyprian generals could not hope to hold out for long against the forces of the Empire even when these were obliged to depend entirely on themselves. They did, however, succeed in laying waste to the whole area around Gildor, in taking a large number of prisoners, and in loading their ships with an impressive amount of booty. The princes of Cyprus had only resolved on such an attack because they thought themselves safe, on their island, from reprisal by Alexis. The Emperor saw at once that negotiations, fortification of the coasts, and keeping the army on permanent alert was of no use so long as Cyprus's attitude remained unchanged. No precaution could stop them from repeating the operation, making a surprise landing, laying waste to the crops, and sacking the villages. But Cyprus showed no sign of changing either its policy or its tactics. So no other solution remained but confrontation on an altogether different scale.

There were two factors that Cyprus overlooked, two ways in which its princes underestimated what Alexis and, above all, Bruince had achieved: the construction, or rather reconstruction, of a mighty imperial fleet,[5] and the continuation of Thaumas's policy of maintaining good terms with the pirates.[6] The latter had become scarcer and less of a threat since Basil's day, but they had never entirely disappeared and could still be an appreciable factor. Bruince had just won their alliance, and they were delighted at the idea of joining with the troops of the Empire to throw themselves on Cyprus. The Empire's navy alone was becoming a formidable force, and, backed by the pirates, it need fear nothing but the warships of Pomposa. When the Kha-Khan of the Oïghurs returned from Peshawar and Samarkand, a council of war was held in the palace of the City, attended by the

Emperor, Theodora, Bruince, Balamir, and Logophilus, together with some generals and other officers. They decided to launch a naval attack against Cyprus.

There were many advantages to this operation, not least the fact that it offered a sop to the impatience of the barbarians. For years now Balamir had been promising them possession of the world, and for years he had been using them for routine operations against Persia and China. Cyprus with its palaces and temples and treasure would shine for them like a golden gate to the West of which they had dreamed as they raided the dusty steppes. But the choice of Cyprus as the first objective gave Balamir and the barbarians another and even greater reason for satisfaction. The barbarians possessed irresistible power, but they had no ships, and in deciding to attack an island the Emperor put within their reach a prey that they could never have grasped alone and unaided. Belatedly, but indisputably, Alexis was proving his sincerity; those supporters of Balamir who had struggled so long against the impatience of his opponents within the barbarian army itself were at last rewarded; and the New Alliance emerged stronger than ever from a decision that was momentous not only for the future of Cyprus, but for the future of the whole Mediterranean, that ancient basin that the history of the world had chosen as its center.

Famagusta, where Basil the Great had met the king of Sicily and the khan of the Oïghurs, Balamir's distant ancestor, was impregnable by land. So instead of trying to disembark troops at some point that might have been comparatively lightly defended, the combined imperial and pirate fleet, under the command of the famous Carradine of the flaming red beard, made straight for the port itself, the approaches to which were defended by the great citadel. The sentries looking out over the sea from the watchtowers were so delighted to see the coming of the enemy ships so evidently doomed to destruction that "the sound of their laughter," according to Justus Dion, "could be heard by the officers and men massed on the decks of the galleys." But their amusement was to be short-lived. Among the detachments of barbarian soldiers on the ships, some of whom were seeing the Mediterranean for the first time and were, incidentally, suffering acutely from seasickness, Alexis and Bruince had seen to it that there were also those same carpenters from the northeastern forests who had worked at the construction of the fleet. Under the astonished eyes of the defenders of Famagusta the ships of the Empire anchored under the very walls of the citadel and, protected by huge shields, the carpenters set to work raising wooden siege-engines, towers, and great battering-rams resting partly on the decks of the ships and partly on the ramparts of the citadel. The Cypriot troops tried to hinder them with showers of arrows, pitch, and boiling oil, but the men from the forests of the north, sheltered by the leather tents and wooden awnings they had rigged up before they started, got on with their work without turning a hair.

After some days, perhaps weeks, a wind arose from the northwest, a variant of the famous melteme still familiar to sailors and tourists in this part of the Mediterranean, especially in the Aegean, round about the Cyclades and Northern Sporades. The leaders of the besieged city gathered on the ramparts to look at the attacking ships, on the point of foundering. That evening there was a thunderstorm, and soon lightning flashes were illuminating the battered vessels hurled against one another by the waves. The men of Cyprus rejoiced at the baleful sounds that rose up out of the darkness. The storm lasted three days. The oarsmen, sailors, barbarians, pirates, and carpenters had all lashed themselves to seats, masts, and stanchions. Two ships sank. But the fleet was not scattered. On the fourth day the sun reappeared over a calm sea. The noise of hammering arose once more; it sounded like a knell to those within the besieged city.

The princes of Cyprus still had one hope left. One galley had managed to break through the blockade that the imperial navy maintained all around the island. It was manned by a reliable crew who were to carry the alarm to the merchant princes of Pomposa and invoke the help of their fleet. It was a race against time. As they watched the forest of scaffolding rising all around them out of the sea, the princes of Cyprus anxiously calculated how long it would take their messengers to reach Pomposa, and then how long it would take the Pomposan fleet to row and sail to the help of the besieged island. As the days and nights went by, hope began to revive in the city. Two attempted attacks had already been repulsed. It was almost four moons now since the siege had begun. Every morning the lookouts scanned the horizon for the great black and white sails of the merchant warriors. The princes were always sending some officer or page to ask the sentries:

"Well, Semias?"

"Nothing yet."

"We must just wait. They can't be long now."

The sun would set.

"Well, Comazon?"

"Still nothing."

"They'll be here tomorrow then. Courage!"

Cyprus did not lack courage. But the black and white sails still did not come, and meanwhile the towers grew ever taller and more numerous by the ramparts and the posterns. One morning before daybreak, Alexis and Balamir launched the attack. It was a staggering sight: "All the devils of hell," says Justus Dion, "seemed to be rising out of the sea and materializing out of the air." Clusters of barbarians and pirates dropped on the defenders from the wooden frames and engines now overhanging the ramparts. In this first assault nearly all the attackers were killed, but enough survived to open breaches through which the rest of the army could pour in. The barbarians swept through the town. Alexis had been violently opposed to massacring women and children, but he was only partly obeyed, and the siege of Famagusta survives in history as a stain on his memory. Justus Dion declares that fire broke out by accident, but at all events, when the victors at last turned from killing off the survivors to fighting the flames, it was already too late, and Famagusta was destroyed.

Five days later the Pomposan fleet appeared before the ruins of one of the strongest cities in the Mediterranean. The lookouts were astonished, as they approached, at not being able to make out the towers, walls, and lofty mansions of Famagusta overhanging the sea. The reason they could not see them was that they no longer existed. Carradine's fleet lay in ambush on the other side of the island. With great difficulty Alexis restrained the barbarians from throwing themselves on the Pomposan ships just as they had done on Famagusta: but the time was not yet ripe. He sent out a large carrack to the black-and white-sailed fleet; the admirals and men of Pomposa were amazed to see it issue forth alone from the port, which gave no other sign of life. When it was within earshot of the most stately of the Pomposan ships, on which sumptuously clad nobles sat at table before rare dishes and Greek wines, wondering at the strange welcome Famagusta was giving the reinforcements come to save her, the men on the carrack leaped up and threw the bloody heads of the princes of Cyprus onto the flagship's deck. According to chronicle and legend, it was on this occasion that Alexis murmured one of those phrases constantly held against him by historians, especially Christian historians: "Now they will all know the meaning of death."

It is not impossible such words were actually uttered. What is surprising is that succeeding historians have seen them as nothing but savagery. No doubt, as we have seen, Alexis was by now very different from the ascetic visionary nursing his remorse along the roads of Asia. Not only had he returned to the instinctive violence that was bound up with his childhood and formed the basis of his character, but the inexorable march of history and events had swept him still further into a headlong course in which to rule was to use violence whether one liked it or not. All this is evident and indisputable. But in Alexis violence and blood always coexisted not only with what Sir Allan Carter-Bennett has called his "cosmic sense of history," but also with a real metaphysical nostalgia and an inextinguishable love of meditation on the destiny of man. How can one fail to hear in the famous phrase an echo of despair at the human condition? Perhaps it is going too far to follow Heidegger, and see the Emperor's terrible deed as "a metaphysical experiment in action, a lesson on the anguish of death, a tragic unveiling of the totality of the void at the heart of which is that which exists."[7] Let us merely say that Alexis gives a helpless and disillusioned acknowledgment of the equivocal relation between thought and action, a ferocious reminder of the mystery of which man is both object and prey. Alexis was no longer just a repository of truth: now he wished to transmit it to the world. He took on the supremely dangerous role of "instructor in the universal."[8] It was an office that could scarcely be exercised but in blood. The Emperor resigned himself. He had unleashed the barbarian horde on Cyprus, and the machinery was now in motion that would lead him, with his Twelve Thousand, the army of the Empire, and all the squadrons of the nomads, to that Western ocean on which Balamir had fed his barbarians' dreams.

Through this prodigious enterprise, probably unique in the annals of history, Alexis did his best to remain what a manuscript preserved first in the Irish monastery of Glendalough, then in that of Cuchulain, calls "li reis e li empereres de grant vertus e merci." Countless acts of generosity and mercy—we ourselves shall meet with more than one of them—are attributed to him by contemporary chronicles, in the midst of brutality and sometimes savagery; and apparently this does not seem to be due merely to the propaganda that other rulers in other times and places (for example, the Emperor Augustus in Rome) were to raise to the level of an institution. Alexis, though responsible for so many deaths, did not love violence for its own sake. But he was making war; he had written as much to Philocrates many years before, and he repeated it throughout the years of conquest. He made war in order to establish the reign of the universal on earth. Diversity, contradiction, and difference seem to have caused Alexis actual physical suffering. The claims of unity and necessity expressed themselves in him with astounding force. The history of the Empire, the vicissitudes of his own life and the lessons of Asia all taught him the perils of division and the beauties of harmony. The avarice of the rich, the greed of the poor, want, fear were all the result of division; security and happiness were born of a world that was unified. War was a necessary transition from the reign of diversity to that of unity and necessity. And Alexis waged that war at the head of the barbarians—in other words, of those who for the civilized world represented the element of contradiction and the destruction of every kind of harmony and happiness. Many cities had to be burned to bring about peace. Léon Daudet, who has a certain sympathy for Alexis and sees clearly the desire for unity that drives him, is nevertheless surprised at the alliance with Balamir, and curiously dubs the Emperor the "maniac universalist" and the "devotee of difference." The truth of the matter is that Alexis stands at an intersection between a phase of history of which the battle of Amphibolus is the key event, and a religious and mystical experience in which human life is much less important than the advent of the universal. This dual pressure, translated into terms of ordinary politics, meant that the constant threat of invasion by the barbarians was intolerable, and that it was absolutely necessary to remove it by bringing the barbarians into close association with the life of the Empire and making them partners in the task of unifying the world. Thus and thus alone can one explain the New Alliance, the entente with Balamir, and the collaboration with the barbarians in world conquest.

Balamir, who was a man of powerful intelligence, realized sooner and better than anyone else what the Emperor's offer might mean to the barbarians and to himself. He accepted that offer sincerely, and was to remain faithful to it all his life. And as violence ineluctably penetrated and permeated Alexis, so the Kha-Khan of the Oïghurs was won over by the insidious charms of culture and civilization. It is very interesting for the historian to trace the dual movement precipitating the Emperor into all the rigors of power and the Kha-Khan into all the delights of ease. Balamir the barbarian becomes a disciplined prince whose chief pleasure is in the tragedies of Menalchas and Polyphilus and the poems of Valerius. And Alexis the sage and poet, who spent years of suffering expiating two deaths and the excesses of his youth, ravages the world at the head of his armies. The fact is that it is impossible to rule without violence. As Hegel well puts it in his *Phenomenology of the Mind:* "The stone is innocent and Alexis is guilty. But he is absolved, because he represents the necessary work of universal history and the very form of the new world."

XX

THE SACK OF ROME

OMPOSA, WHOSE DAZZLING AND FRIVOLOUS HIStory was from the beginning inseparable from that of the Empire, heard with consternation the terrible news brought back from Cyprus by its admirals. The city of painters and processions, sailors and procuresses, immediately began to prepare for war. It was unlikely it could be fought out on land, where the New Alliance obviously enjoyed a crushing superiority. Fortunately Pomposa could contemplate much more hopefully a struggle at sea. The Empire's fleet, swelled by that of the pirates, was comparatively new. Pomposa had the advantage of experience and of numerous factories scattered all around the shores of the Mediterranean. Preparations for war at sea were pushed forward as fast as possible. Whole forests were cut down in Dalmatia and Carinthia to supply the naval dockyards with wood for galleys and warships. Negotiations were resumed more vigorously than before with Sicily, Rome, and the Dalmatic republics in which Pomposan influence prevailed. A year or two after the fall of Cyprus, Pomposa's power in the western Mediterranean was once more at its height.

But meanwhile the situation in the eastern Mediterranean had not improved—Rhodes, too, had fallen. Unlike Cyprus, it had offered little resistance to Alexis's ultimatums. As soon as his fleet was sighted approaching the harbor, Rhodes opened its gates to the Emperor. Only the citadel of Lindos on the east coast of the island attempted any defense. Lindos held out for a fortnight, and saw its courage rewarded by being made an example of. Its ramparts and palaces were reduced to the ruins the tourist still admires today. The Pomposan ships charged with defending the interests of the merchant princes in the various parts of the Mediterranean were taken by surprise and defeated first in sight of Cape Malea, then near the Cerbical Islands, and above all off Patmos. It was too much. The High Council of Pomposa decided not to yield one inch more and to strengthen all its naval and military forces. The whole of Crete, recently conquered, was transformed into a vast fortress. A fleet cruised around it, charged with preventing the imperial navy from repeating its exploits against Cyprus and Patmos. A second fleet protected Pomposa itself, and a third, the strongest of all, was kept in reserve in the huge triangle between Sicily, Crete, and Dalmatia. But all these precautions were soon shown to be useless. At the very moment when after its first reverses Pomposa was recovering its position at sea and seemed at last able to resist the attacks of the imperial and pirate fleets, astonishing news reached Pomposa: The battalions of the Empire and the squadrons of the barbarians were on the move on land. They had already crossed the straits between the Black Sea and the Aegean by means of a pontoon bridge and were approaching Macedonia and threatening both Greece and the Danube.

The magnitude of the danger was apparent at once to the High Council's military and political advisers: the Emperor could now descend at will upon Athens and Corinth where Pomposa had important interests, or else continue toward the valley of the Danube, the Pomposan factories on the Black Sea, and perhaps toward Niš and Dalmatia. He must be stopped at once, thrown back into the sea, prevented from pursuing a strategy that might open wide to him the gates of southeast Europe. Pomposa drummed up its allies and clients. Again gold started to flow like water. The pay of mercenaries and sailors was doubled. The unprecedented decision was made to conscript the sons of patricians into the army. In less than two months an army was got together that included side by side, in dazzling disorder, the powerful forces of Kings Stephen and Sigismund, the Transylvanians of Jean Hunyadi and Stephen Báthory, King Ladislas and his militia, the Teutonic legions of Count Varus, the knights of Rhodes and Cyprus summoned back from the Euphrates,[1] the troops of the grand master of Jerusalem, five or six generals from Burgundy and the Rhine, the constable of Provence, the count of Nevers, Marshal Boucicault, the legate of the patriarch of Rome, the formidable Spanish infantry under Captain Jules Branciforte, the Lusitanians under Don Pedro of Alfarubeira, together with his famous dromedaries, and General Hernani Bragmardo whose memory is celebrated by Rabelais, the Pontic mercenaries, the one hundred thousand nephelibate knights dressed all in black and led by the Prince of the Entommeures, bold, dashing, tall, and thin, with his fabulous nose and ruffian's face, the hundred and fifty thousand Arismapian infantry, the Poldevian detachments led by King Mieszko, Prince Hegesippus, and Prince Simon, and lastly the Pomposan army and the Moldovalacks commanded by their voivode Mircea.

Against the coalition raised by Pomposa, Alexis and Balamir ranged the serried masses of their Tcherkesses, Petchenegues, Comans, Bactrians, Sogdians, Tokhars, Syrians, troops from Khorasan, Khwarizm, Kabulistan, Fergana, Kandahar, Orkhon and Kerulen, Transoxiana and Djagatai, Cossacks, Massagetan archers, Balearic slingsmen who had served the Empire for years as mercenaries, Circassians, Siberians, and Samoyeds. The two wings consisted of mounted squadrons of nomads divided into four corps according to whether their mounts were black, white, bay, or dappled. In the center were Balamir's two massive *corps d'élite*, the Sipahis or "men-at-arms" and the Yeni-tcheri or "new troops," on either side of the Twelve Thousand with Alexis at their head. But what above all was to amaze and alarm the armies of the coalition with surprise and terror was a marvelous innovation they had never heard of save in old tales recounted by their nurses—the front line was composed of three hundred war elephants carrying towers of archers, intended both to terrify the enemy and, having borne the brunt of his attack, to penetrate his lines.[2]

The two armies came face to face outside the walls of Adrianople. The battle of Adrianople, one of the few dates every schoolboy still knows, was yet another frightful massacre. It decided the history of the world for several centuries. A Persian chronicler reports:[3] "The two armies, both fanatically sure of victory, fell on each other with such frenzy that the sun was hidden by clouds of dust, and the storm of wild, whirling, foaming, howling horsemen made it seem the earth had opened and the vapors of hell were licking at the sky." The knights of the Pomposan army, oblivious of order and discipline, displayed quite heedless daring. Each one aimed not so much at common victory over the enemy as at outdoing his own companions-at-arms in dash and boldness. The sons of the Pomposan patricians and, even more, the knights of the generals of Burgundy, the constable of Provence, and Marshal Boucicault managed to get the better of the advance guards and outflank the elephants. King Stephen and the voivode Mircea ordered them to halt, to wait for the massive infantry support of the Transylvanians from the mountains and the Arismapians. But, carried away by their success, they would not listen, and continued to advance until the ribbon of mounted skirmishers suddenly fell back and they came face to face with the serried mass of Balamir's Yeni-tcheris, a wall of leather cuirasses and bronze helmets. The first ranks of the "new troops" were kneeling, their long pikes thrust forward, and the men of Burgundy and Provence, unable to halt, were literally spitted. Uccello's polyptych, *The Battle of Adrianople*, divided up among the Louvre, the National Gallery of London, and the Uffizi, has fixed forever in a motionless splendor, a geometric poetry of colors and volumes, the instant of tumult in which, from one end of the canvas to the other, flashing pikes are raised and fall, and pink or gray-blue horses with vast cruppers and silver bridles rear or are laid low. Behind the men with pikes the archers loose their arrows. There was a few moments' hesitation. The onslaught of the attackers slackened, faltered, broke, and began to fall back here and there in disorder. And then all at once the attack turned into a rout involving the entire huge army of the coalition. Throughout the rest of the day until nightfall, Alexis's and Balamir's horsemen pursued the survivors across the battlefield. Some succeeded in escaping westward and getting back to Dalmatia, others managed to reach the Pomposan ships cruising far away off the coast of Macedonia; but most of them were taken prisoner. They expected to be killed, perhaps tortured, but Alexis gave orders for them to be fed and treated kindly. The distribution of goods and weapons abandoned on the battlefield did much to keep the victors obedient and well disposed. The survivors were spared and the wounded properly tended. Many eventually served in the imperial army. Alexis's reputation for mercy and humanity even in the midst of violence, which was to do so much to embellish his legend, dates from the battle of Adrianople.

The imperial troops and the nomads wintered in Thrace and Macedonia, where once more Alexis's genius for organization was seen. But at the beginning of spring the army was on the move again. For elephants and men it was a sort of long walkover, the stages of which are too well known to need going into. Alexis had decided that whenever the citizens of a town or the defenders of a fortress threw open their gates to the imperial troops their lives would be spared, they would be treated with all the honors of war and retain their former offices and privileges. Towns and citadels that resisted would be delivered over to the barbarians. Thus were destroyed Sirmium, Spalato, Pola, Aquileus on the Adriatic, and Grado. It was not yet autumn when Alexis's and Balamir's elephants entered the Po valley.

Pomposa had raised a new army made up this time of Romans, Sicilians, Moors, Irishmen, and more troops from Spain and Provence, from the Rhine, the Loire, and the Seine. It was led by the four Della Scala brothers, Cangrande, Bartolomeo, Alboino, and Cansignorio, and it met Alexis on the plain of Verona. For a large part of the day the battle was indecisive; then suddenly, through fear, revenge, or self-interest, the contingents from the south of Italy went over to Alexis and the Pomposan army was crushed. There was now no further obstacle before the Emperor, and he entered Pomposa on the day of the summer solstice.

Let us pause a moment in the great square in Pomposa, full of standards and banners, where the High Council of the merchant princes came to give ceremonial welcome to the victor of Verona and Adrianople. Pomposa, city of painters and masks, bride of the sea, ruler by virtue of gold and intrigue, was in mourning. But for Pomposa even mourning had to be decked in the accustomed splendor. Like those women who even at the point of death put on a last, superfluous beauty, so the city glittered to captivate its conqueror. The square had never looked more beautiful. Everyone was there: velvet-clad pages with long trumpets like angels in frescoes; cavaliers with gold and brocade trappings; stern magistrates in the modest white collars and severe black gowns that had made the City tremble in the days of the Porphyries; courtesans with long trains, sparkling jewels, fringes on their brows, and heavy necklaces, and followed by great mastiffs; sailors carrying their oars over their shoulders as soldiers did their pikes; priests; men-at-arms and men of the law; eager painters scribbling sketches in the palms of their hands; lovers, uneasy as always; thieves watching their opportunity; scullions; physicians in their tall hats; the ambassadors of Sicily and of the Grand Mogul; the legate of the patriarch of Rome; excited chambermaids; usurers; Moors; financiers; porters; idlers. Accompanied by Theodora, Balamir, Bruince, Logophilus, red-bearded Carradine (now an admiral), the leaders of the barbarians, his generals, and his priests, the Emperor Alexis moved forward slowly on his white horse.

Benozzo Gozzoli's *Magi* in the Medicis chapel of the Riccardi Palace in Florence shows us how the Italian Renaissance imagined the scene. The first rider, on whom is concentrated all the attention of the crowd, all its hopes and fears, is Alexis the demigod. The second is Bruince. The third, a Moor representing Balthazar, is in fact Balamir the Oïghur, the nomad, the barbarian, the Asiatic, transformed by popular imagination into an Ethiopian. The procession advances slowly, through a terrifying silence. The High Council, motionless, is at last tasting defeat. What Alexis is feeling the merchant princes know well. They often experienced it themselves when they received the submission of peoples reduced by Pomposan ships or gold. What is new to them is the fear that grips them, a fear loftily hidden under the patrician's impassivity before a suddenly hostile fate. They have no idea what awaits them—perhaps, this evening, they will be crucified or hanged. Motionless they watch the three fair-haired pages clad in black, mere dots in comparison to the vast crowd, as they go alone across the square to meet the Emperor, to present to the victor on cushions of purple, azure, and gold the salt of welcome, the keys of the city, and the gold ring set with emeralds that for centuries had symbolized Pomposa's invincible sovereignty over the sea. Alexis is swept by a wave of pride. Once again his past rises up, and instead of moving through the silent trembling crowd he is amid the oaks and birches of the great forest of Balkh; Vanessa is near him, moving lightly in her white robe and smiling through her tears; the ancient mansions become temple tombs; dusty roads suddenly covered with ice stretch as far as the eye can see from the high mountains of China to the frontiers of the Empire; Helen, Jester, Philocrates, and Isidore, old and ill, are all with him, looking on as he takes possession of Pomposa. He rides on. There is nothing to be read in his face—neither revenge nor ambition nor weariness nor contempt. He rides on. He leans down from his white horse to the pages. He tastes the salt, picks up the keys and lays them down, puts on his gloved finger the golden ring of Pomposa.

At such a moment, when history was in the balance, when one of the most formidable conquests of patience and genius was being engraved in time and men's memories, it was impossible not to think of the now distant days when Pomposa reigned over the City. Then in fear and trembling the Porphyries received the orders of the High Council; then the mercenaries in the pay of the merchant princes galloped arrogantly through the terrified streets of the city of the Tiger. Now the Eagle and the Tiger had Pomposa in their power. How much time and suffering, how many setbacks and ordeals had

had to be gone through before victory was won? Alexis rode on toward the High Council of the merchant princes, reflecting that henceforth the world was his. How long it takes to conquer a world! How easy it is! It takes only a few hundred thousand dead, perhaps a million, perhaps a little more; they will not have seen the Emperor take possession of Pomposa, but their sacrifice will not have been in vain, for it will have made possible man's historic dream of a world empire. Alexis rode on. He thought how the dead must be honored, have steles and altars raised to them, rituals and ceremonies devoted to them, so that their sons would be encouraged to give their lives as they had. He knew his task was written in the firmament of history and that it was not yet finished. It could be finished only at the end of the journey—when the sun never set on the Empire, its seas and forests and deserts and plains and rivers and mountains.

Alexis rode on. The sun shone over the city, upon victors and vanquished. Henceforth let them be one people; let peace and justice reign! Let ships leisurely sail over the oceans, laden with gold, ivory, rare vases, precious woods, and spices; let crops no longer be laid waste by armies on the march; let roads be safe and nights peaceful in the sleepy towns; let palaces and temples arise more numerous than the trees in the forest; painting and music become like dreams come true; philosophers and historians leave to future generations the memory of noble sufferings and triumphs that will form the basis of other victories. He rode on. The great square of which they were so proud suddenly seemed interminable to the quailing merchant princes. Would the Emperor never finish riding slowly, silently across it on his white horse? At last he drew near the High Council, who waited pale with dread but concealing their fear. The merchant princes bowed. He gazed at them. Then he leaned forward and said: "So, we shall build the world empire together."

Night fell for the first time on conquered Pomposa. The City, capital of the Empire, was beautiful, with countless sites admired by travelers and geographers. But it was new. Everything in Pomposa, on the other hand, had the fragile dignity of that which already belongs to the past. The old houses of the patricians were painted red, ocher, or yellow. Their roofs were eaten with moss, their stone columns crumbling. Some were in a state of collapse, others had crumbled already or would soon do so. Death as well as beauty lurked everywhere. But from the dilapidated walls rose up the memories of the greedy merchants and proud painters, the cruel and unjust judges, the seductive and shameless women, all of whose hidden virtues had made the sovereign of the seas a masterpiece forever. In the falling dusk, everything looked lovely and unreal. Alexis had never visited Pomposa during his travels with Philocrates, but he had often dreamed of it. And now here it was, the place that wore time like a jewel, whose very vices added to its beauty. Alexis felt no hatred and took no vengeance. He was simply bringing together the scattered members of a larger empire. Gaiety was absent now but certain vague signs—the stifled sound of women's laughter, the curiosity of people in the streets, the bustling activity of the shops—showed it was ready to revive at the first opportunity. Alexis already knew he would not destroy Pomposa. Beauty, too, can be the weapon of power. He would absorb it into the Empire: Pomposa with its inexhaustible treasures, the barbarians drunk with blood and gold, and the City itself would all, in Alexis's Empire, merge into one.

The Emperor dismounted. There was business to attend to. Troops had to be assembled; supplies organized; land distributed among the nomads, governors, and magistrates installed in their new offices. He convened a meeting for the following day of the High Council, who were already half reassured. They went home to their palaces, where amid untold wealth and swarms of little black pages their wives waited, in heavy gowns of brocade and velvet ornamented with lace and oriental pearl, together with their children attended by fencing and philosophy masters or wily duennas. The masters of all this, speaking as experienced politicians, said the worst was over, a fresh start must be made, and perhaps there was still some way of creating a future that did not consist entirely of rubble and ruins. Of course, something would have to be sacrificed—a few ships, much gold, statues, and precious stones, perhaps a certain number of heads would have to roll. Pomposa would no longer be free. It would have a directory, consul, senate, or something of the sort, worked out by Logophilus, supervised by Bruince, and at the orders of the Emperor. But at least the city of the sea would not be destroyed or handed over to the dreaded barbarians; it would be allowed to keep its painters and its courtesans for new masterpieces and new pleasures.

The capture of Pomposa lent the Empire a splendor nothing else could have conferred, and gave it the reflected glory of antiquity and decadence. Alexis often went to Pomposa to rest between campaigns, mixing with the painters, engravers, sculptors, and poets of whom he had dreamed so much. Many of its artists were invited, with argu-

ments ranging from persuasion to constraint, to settle in the Empire
and especially in the City, which owed them much of its reputation as
a capital of literature and the arts. The others remained in Pomposa,
surrounding the Emperor with flattery sometimes rather forced, but
also with beauty. Equestrian statues of Alexis were set up in the
squares; he was depicted as general, saint, prophet, donor, Solomon,
King David, crowned with halo or laurels, in the great religious and
military paintings in the temples and palaces. A Pomposan poet
whose name is unfortunately unknown wrote a Latin poem, "Hymn to
the Emperor Alexis," which is in effect a plea for the conquered city.

Only a handful of artists paid no heed to laws, war, the Emperor,
or their own careers, and modern commentators as different as Albert
Camus and André Breton have agreed with one another and disagreed with Giraudoux and Claudel in thinking them the best.[4] The
Emperor was always indulgent toward all artists. So much so, indeed,
that when arrested, highway robbers and conspirators often tried to
pass themselves off as artists, in order to save their necks. Thus, in the
city of the merchant princes, Alexis, having served his apprenticeships to pleasure, saintliness, and force, now served his apprenticeship to beauty.

But Pomposa was to bequeath to Alexis memories of something
other than happiness—or perhaps it was indeed an obscure and
terrifying kind of happiness. For it was there amid the feasting and
the gold that death, which would have none of him in the wilderness
or on the battlefield, brushed him with its wing. When he was in
Pomposa the Emperor liked to stroll through the narrow streets
almost or even entirely alone. He would look at the sunlight falling on
the old houses, the statues standing out against the sky on their
bronze or marble columns, the color of the stone in the dusk. Sometimes there was so much beauty he could scarcely breathe. Then he
would think he used to breathe more freely in the desert. And he
would be seized with a kind of fury against painters, sculptors,
architects, engravers, and metal founders, and would talk of getting
the barbarians to destroy all the treasures born of sin and greed,
themselves begetters of frivolity and effeminacy. Balamir even had to
defend against the Emperor the gilded temples, marble lions, and
votive columns. The fact was that the barbarians, settled on estates
taken from the High Council and the wealthiest merchant princes,
laden with jewels, stuffed with meat and wine, dazzled by the splendor of the squares, streets, palaces, and even the simplest houses, had

been conquered by their own conquest. They felt they now shared in it, and they were glad. Unlike the Emperor, they felt no revulsion. They had dreamed of wealth and luxury too much, and now they too began to love money, to dress in silk and purple, to look down on their clumsy weapons, and to wear chains of precious metal and chased daggers. But something irresistible rose up in Alexis at all this ornate superfluity, these vain treasures, these images of wonderfully camouflaged nothingness. He wanted to burn and destroy. It was a thirst for purity, a desire for simplicity and nakedness, for a void, for a reduction. And then he would look once more at the city at his feet. It was beautiful. And he was conquered by its beauty.

One day as he was walking in Pomposa, just before an expedition beyond the Alps toward the Rhone and the Rhine, he was dreaming as usual of the world empire where peace would reign with the same rules for everyone, where there would be no more question of barbarians and patricians, within and without, or the dreadful gap between laws and men—where the Empire would be the world itself, and he, the Emperor, his long task accomplished, would at last be free to withdraw. Suddenly he caught sight of a street with pink- and yellow-painted houses, and in the distance a stone bridge over a river, a little square with a tree in flower, a column, a sculptured wellhead, and a young woman at her window, laughing in the sun. He just had time to think how pleasant it must be to live there, free from care and ambition, taking life as it came and waiting for death without puzzling one's head about the world, when a divine hand was laid on his heart and threw him to the ground. He was given up for dead. For five days, physicians worked desperately at his bedside to save him. The question of the succession to the immense Empire began to stir hopes and ambitions. And then, on the sixth day, he arose, cured. All he would say was that beauty is that which is closest to death, and that there are mysterious links between them.[5]

Power, like love, cannot be halted. No sooner had Pomposa fallen than Rome and Sicily rose, with their threats and temptations over the horizon of the Empire. Alexis only needed an excuse for tearing himself away from Pomposa's formidable charm, and he threw himself into conquest as if it were a liberation. The army moved off again, going southward with the slingers and the elephants. The archpatriarch of Rome and the king of Sicily did not have time to raise an army. The whole of Italy lay open to whoever wanted to take it, and the Emperor, attracted in spite of himself, could do no other than be drawn into this political and military vacuum: he had always been drawn to go over the hills and far away. And there was a new phenomenon, too, though it scarcely surprised Alexis: voices were beginning to call on him and sing his praises, in Rome itself and in Sicily, just as other voices had done years before in the deserts of Arabia and the public places of Samarkand. There had been stirrings in the Eternal City; agitators and fanatics had announced from the Capitoline Hill the advent of a new age and the reign of Alexis; the name of the Emperor had been acclaimed by the mob on the Janiculum slopes, beyond the Tiber, and in the Palatine gardens. The archpatriarch summoned the college of priests with whose aid he ruled Rome and where there had already been differences of opinion, and he soon realized it would be impossible to resist the alliance between the Empire and the barbarians that had already conquered Pomposa and the army of the coalition. At first he thought of just awaiting the attack and dying at the gates of Rome. But the danger of looting and slaughter made him change his mind. He decided to go to meet the Emperor and beg him to spare the city which, more than Pomposa or Onessa or Aquileus, perhaps even more than the City itself, had played so dazzling a part in history that many saw it as the center of the world.

The archpatriarch was an old man, worn out by fever and suffering. But he mounted his horse and rode out of Rome by the great bridge over the Tiber which gave on the road to the north. He was followed by an army that reflected exactly the spirit of a Rome that today, after the passage of so many centuries and so many different civilizations, is so difficult to imagine or understand. Nothing could be weaker than the archpatriarch, yet nothing could be stronger. When, a few years earlier, Balamir had asked Alexis how many horsemen the patriarch of Rome could put in the field, the Emperor had had to reply that the power of Rome rested not upon horsemen but upon virtue, faith, the strength of the soul. The Kha-Khan of the Oïghurs had laughed heartily. Nothing could be nobler or more elevated than the archpatriarch's teaching—sometimes it got lost in metaphysical speculations impossible to describe—and yet nothing in all the Mediterranean and beyond had drawn down on itself more hatred and scorn. Rome had inspired the most profound philosophers, the most exquisite poets, the sublimest artists, and it had been called infamous and obscure. The reason was that Rome was ruled by paradox. Minds were governed not by violence and fear but by charity and love, yet countless pyres had been lit to burn not merely books but men and women condemned, out of love, to suffering and fire. For some, Rome and its patriarch were nothing more than a hangover from primitive mentalities—fraud more or less tainted with sorcery, derived perhaps from Ikhnaton or Mithras. For others it was the light of the world and its only hope. The patriarch was the seventh to be called Hadrian. Among his escort were to be seen the faces of saints and ascetics, mingled with those of sensualists and torturers. Some were wearing cloth so thin and coarse the skin could be seen between the strands, while others were clad in red or blue velvet, with gold thread and precious stones that sometimes called forth exclamations from the plowmen or peddlers of fruit and fish who flocked by the roadside to see the procession go by. At its head the archpatriarch, all in white, his scepter in his hand, wearing a tall white cap derived perhaps from the bull's horns in Mesopotamian folklore, with his long beard and face covered in wrinkles and worn with prayer and fasting, seemed to be dreaming of the other world he believed in despite his own unworthiness, a world linked to our own, despite the gulfs that separate them, by hope and faith.

During his descent on Rome Alexis had settled his barbarians on various excellent sites where time and human genius would create cities destined to become famous. He founded Siena, Borgo Pace, Vallombrosa, Impruneta, Monteriggioni (mentioned by Dante), Monte Oliveto Maggiore, San Gimignano, Pienza, Gubbio, Montepulciano, Spoleto, Urbino, and Todi. He was on the shores of Lake Bolsena, between Bolsena and Viterbo, almost on the spot where the town of Montefiascone stands today, when he saw advancing toward the imperial army the strange cortege led by the archpatriarch. The barbarian squadrons were just getting ready to launch their arrows and charge when the Emperor noticed something—the approaching troop was surrounded by lighted torches, whose pale flame was scarcely visible in the bright sun shining out of a sky quite clear but for a few thin white clouds. It was a surprising spectacle, this band riding along in white robes, dazzling dalmatics, wretched habits, but not a single suit of armor, preceded by candles and cressets burning in broad daylight, as if they had to make their way through the shadows of darkness. The truth was that for them this world was indistinguishable from night. Alexis rode his horse a little nearer and looked at them intently—these men riding at foot pace seemed unarmed, without even the short daggers every traveler then wore to defend himself against robbers. He listened. The wind carried the strains of hymns sung at the tops of their voices by the riders and the men who accompanied them on foot. The thought went through his mind that this was the power that scorned swords and acted upon men's souls. He ordered his troops to halt, and went forward alone. The archpatriarch Hadrian saw this sumptuously clad captain or general, whom all his companions seemed to obey, ride out from among the host that filled the fields and woods, the hills and the shores of the lake. Hadrian ordered his attendants to stay where they were, and he too rode forward alone. From afar the imperial army and the patriarch's little band both saw the two men watching one another as their horses approached at a walking pace; they saw them draw level, stop, bow, and, without dismounting, begin to talk.

Of all the encounters of which history is so prodigal, that between the Emperor Alexis and the archpatriarch on the then delightful shores of Lake Bolsena is certainly one of the best known. Like Alexis's reunion with Helen it has inspired many poets and painters. Dante describes it with a majesty that made both Flaubert and President de Brosses yawn.[6] It inspired one of Raphael's most famous frescoes—*The Miracle at Bolsena*, in the Heliodorus Room in the Vatican Museum. (Only a few yards away is the equally famous *School of the City*, which shows Aristo, Philontes, Marcian, Aziri, Polyphilus, Menalchas, Bruince, Logophilus, Isidore, and the Politian grouped around Alexis; nearby lurk the anachronistic shades of Hermenides and Paraclitus.) Earthly fear can be seen in the pontiff's fine features, but also faith in another world more powerful and more pure. The Emperor's attitude registers the surprise and respect of a conqueror face to face with the spiritual dignity and power that overcome mere force. Goethe used to declare he would have given half his lifetime to know what the two men said to each other. But it is one of the best-kept secrets in history, and science has never penetrated it. We can only imagine the words of flame that must have been exchanged when two visions of the world at once so alike and so unlike confronted, opposed, and joined with one another. They were alike in that both claimed to apply to all men and offer them a happy future in which contradictions would disappear. They were unlike for the same reason: neither Alexis nor Hadrian accepted any limit to their power. Certainly the calm audacity of the pontiff, which nothing in this world could intimidate, impressed the Emperor. But though Raphael does not depict it, Hadrian's surprise must have been considerable when he saw the conqueror amidst the barbarians, full of violence and anguish, yet obviously inspired, like himself, less by the savage fires of conquest and destruction than by the flame of history bent on cooperation and unification. What they said to each other, Heaven only knows—man does not. But there are plenty of theories. Some are convinced that the Emperor's amazing power of persuasion, which Gurdjieff and Swami Sri Sarabhavanamuktenandāmanayagaṁ, otherwise known as Babaji, call his "magnetism," "initiatory power," and "inner force," affected Hadrian in the same way it affected everyone else. Others believe, on the contrary, that in the Roman patriarch Alexis suddenly saw written in letters of fire what he had been seeking all his life. Some authors go even further and attribute to this first meeting between Alexis and Hadrian the beginnings of a system that was to play a tremendous part in the history of the world, and the official origins and formidable consequences of which we shall come to later. This system was, quite simply, the dividing up of world rule between Rome and the Emperor. But that a tacit—some say an explicit—agreement was discussed and arrived at on the occasion of the encounter at Bolsena, there is of course, here again, no proof; there can be no more than a risky and romantic working hypothesis, more proper to the novel of adventure or fictionalized history than to science. The one definite fact—and this we know with certainty—is that after the miracle at Bolsena the Emperor Alexis, following a nationalist and reactionary tradition, far from repulsing Hadrian as Raphael suggests, made a ceremonial entry into the Eternal City by the side of the pontiff, to the acclamations of the Roman crowd, at the head of the two rival forces, the immense imperial army and the patriarch's slender following, joined into one.

What Rome was like then all kinds of evidence vie to tell us—inscriptions, texts, ambassadors' reports, travelers' tales. It was a city sumptuous but poor, the empty shell of former splendor. The rise of Pomposa and of the City had dealt a death blow to the military and commercial power of the sovereign city of the world. It was still full of temples, baths, triumphal arches, columns, and statues, but it belonged to the past and now exercised only a spiritual prestige. Yet the brilliance of the setting survived the city's decline, and the barbarians' entry into Rome struck contemporaries like a thunderbolt. The capture of the Eternal City without a blow being struck marked the final collapse of a world long undermined, and the triumph of Balamir in the eyes of his nomads. He had brought them where he had promised to bring them—in the fall of Rome the Kha-Khan's speech after Jester's execution found its epilogue.[7] Even more than Pomposa, the refinement of whose civilization filled them with a sort of shyness and fear, the quiet grandeur, nobility, and majestic simplicity of Rome and its treasures dazzled and fascinated these rough, wild men. It is very probable the Emperor had promised the arch-patriarch he himself would be responsible for the safety of the Eternal City and the discipline of the nomads. And for the first few days they did in fact camp without causing too much disturbance in the Field of Mars and around the Janiculum. But one sweltering summer night[8] with a storm threatening, a series of obscure incidents, due no doubt to drinking, led to an outburst, and the barbarians, too long without women and crazed with wine and gold, fell upon the unarmed city. The murder, rape, and looting lasted two whole days and three nights, and only began to abate at dawn on the fourth day. Even today the people of Rome still remember the hours of terror, dubbed "le tre notti dolenti."

In the course of the ages, five great waves of invasion have broken over Rome: in 390 B.C., despite the geese of the Capitol, it was the Gauls, with the long swords they tossed scornfully into the scales in which the vanquished weighed out the gold for ransom; in the fifth and sixth centuries it was Alaric's Visigoths, Geiseric's Vandals, Ricimer's Suevians, Odoacer's Heruli, and the Ostrogoths of Totila; in 1084, the Normans of Robert Guiscard; in 1527 the imperial troops of Charles V and the constable de Bourbon. But the most terrible of all was the work of the barbarians of Balamir and Alexis. In three nights—"le tre notti dolenti"—the great circus was destroyed, the amphitheater burned, the baths laid waste, the triumphal arches knocked down, the hanging gardens ruined, the noble pine-bordered road among the tombs dug up in search of gold. The ground was strewn with rubble. As Amédée Thierry writes in his *Stories from Roman History*, "In a single conflagration Rome was completely buried in its own ashes. . . . The inhabitants rushed forth pell-mell, men, women, children, slaves, and masters, calling each other by name, dragging at and colliding with one another, and those who escaped the flames did so only to fall on the barbarians' swords in the streets. At the height of the fire the threatening storm burst with indescribable violence, drowning all other noises; repeated claps of thunder and flashes of lightning pierced the darkness. It was as if heaven were joining with man to wipe out the unhappy city.

Several big buildings were struck; in particular, temples and other edifices in honor of the gods. . . . Wherever the eye turned it saw bronze shafts projecting from walls, shattered roofs, broken pediments, felled columns, blackened and melted statues. . . . Wherever fire did not rage, murder, rape, and looting spread like another scourge from one quarter to another. No woman was safe from outrage; neither rank, age, nor religion offered any protection. Several sacred virgins were victims of the utmost violence. In the ferocious barbarians the attraction of debauchery was reinforced by natural cruelty, familiarity with bloodshed, a love of torture, and above all a passion for money; and the golden palaces of the patricians were the scenes of the most lamentable tragedies. . . . As a contemporary vividly put it, fire and the sword divided between them the fate of the world's sovereign city. For Rome it was a time of weeping, and in three nights Balamir won the terrible name of 'destroyer of the Eternal City.' " A few days after the sack of the city, Hadrian VII exclaimed, in a famous tirade: "There is none like thee, Rome, though thou art now little more than a ruin. . . . But the rubble of three nights shows what thou wert when whole. . . . On thee thy leaders lavished treasures, fate its favor, artists their genius, and the whole world its wealth. And now the city is fallen, of which, if I wish to say something worthy, I can only say: it was Rome."

The modern tourist can still find traces all over Rome of those terrible three nights. It was centuries before the people's resentment abated. The famous corbel traditionally known as the *Bocca della Verità* in the church of Santa Maria in Cosmedino, long considered an Etruscan remain, is really a caricature of Balamir in the form of a grinning mask with a vast mouth into which children are afraid to put their hand. Stendhal, in his *Walks in Rome*, tells how right up to the beginning of the nineteenth century the *pasquinades*—scraps of satirical verse placed by anonymous authors in the mutilated statue of Maestro Pasquino, at the corner of the Braschi Palace, beyond the Piazza Navona—still sometimes took the Kha-Khan of the Oïghurs as their target.

At the news of the sack of Rome the Emperor, who was then in the Alban Hills on the way to Anagni, Capua, Pompeii, Beneventum, and the Basilicata, gave vent to an anger as terrible as the deed that inspired it. The barbarians were duodecimated—i.e., one out of every twelve was beheaded. The rest were divided into two groups, of which the first, with Balamir, went via Provence and Marseilles to conquer Spain, while the others were dispatched to continue the war on the borders of China. So the consequences of the sack of Rome constituted a new stage in the growth of the Empire and the completion of the conquest of the world. In less than five years Balamir, anxious to redeem himself in the eyes of the Emperor, after annexing in passing Provence, Languedoc, and Aquitaine, and having led his men to the shores of the ocean he had made them dream of, had crossed the Pyrenees and had taken Spain. He in his turn founded León, Salamanca, Guadalajara, Toledo, Aranjuez, Mérida, Cuidad Real in honor of Alexis, Las Navas de Tolosa, Málaga, Medina-Sidonia, Granada, and Córdoba. Then, beyond the Strait of Gibraltar, he joined up with part of the imperial army which had set out from Antioch and Tyre. The junction was made on the east bank of the greater Syrte[9] between Cyrene and Barka, not far from the site of the present town of Benghazi. The whole of the Mediterranean basin now belonged to the Empire. The Kha-Khan entered Alexandria more than half a century after the death of Vanessa. Some say he had been asked by the Emperor to destroy such traces as still survived of Alexis's early adventures there.[10] Once North Africa was pacified, Balamir joined the army fighting against the Chinese, after an immense journey that inspired Rabelais's war of Picrochole. It was in this last, oriental campaign that Balamir met his death.

Operations began with a great victory at Ki Liu-chan over the Chinese general Ho K'iu-ping, who thought the Kha-Khan was still five or six days' ride away. Fighting had been going on for several hours before the Chinese leader realized he was faced with something more than a minor advance guard. When he saw his mistake and that the whole barbarian army was massed against him, the battle was already lost. Balamir's mobility won a new nickname for the destroyer of the Eternal City: the Chinese called him "the flying general."[11] For over six months the flying general sowed terror throughout the Far Eastern marches of the Empire, as once he had sown terror along the Amphyses and the Nephta, in Dalmatia and in Rome. He won success after success, commemorated in the great winged horse of stone that was put up on the arid heights of Shensi, between Yen-ngang and the bend of the Hwang Ho, the very place where, centuries later, Mao Tse-tung stayed after the Long March—and afterward preserved in the imperial palace in Peking, in the heart of the Forbidden City. While the Chinese expected an attack on Cambaluc (now Peking), which would have meant the loss of the north of the

Middle Kingdom, Balamir swerved aside to the region then called Kao Keou-li (now Korea). His object was to seize all the ships and barges in the Korean ports and make a surprise landing in Japan.

Balamir took up his position on a height to watch over the preparation of his makeshift fleet. Below, warships, fishing boats, canoes, galleys, junks, and sampans jostled one another. A huge army of porters and traders had loaded weapons and provisions in the holds and on deck, and the expedition was about to sail for Hondo and Kyushu when a violent storm—which some superstitious historians have seen as a kind of reprisal for the summer storm that had broken over Rome—tore up the moorings and scattered the ships, destroying most of them and throwing the rest up on the coast. From his tent on the hill the Kha-Khan of the Oïghurs watched in silence the disaster that was overtaking him. It was the barbarian army's first reverse. Nature had got the better of history.[12]

The emperor Jimmu Tenno, then reigning in Japan, saw the providential typhoon as a sign of the protection afforded him by the god Izanagi and the goddess Amaterasu, born from Izanagi's left eye. The emperor built a temple at Naiku in Ise province, and dedicated it to Amaterasu, goddess of the sun, ancestor of the mikados, and to her brother Susanoo. We still do not fully understand the worship accorded there to certain mysterious objects, one of them a concave mirror the edge of which has eight indentations—*yatano kagami*—and in which is reflected a black sword—*kusanagino tsurugi*. It is not impossible that this veneration for the reflection of the sword symbolizes the overthrow by the planetary gods of Japan of the bloody sword of the Oïghurs.

The Korean disaster plunged Balamir into despair. He had hoped to reach one after the other the two extremities of the then known world—the great ocean in the west, and the islands and sea of Japan in the east—and so give the Emperor, to whom he was still passionately attached, supremacy over the whole world. But now, after the years of triumph, he had met with a setback. "Every man," he wrote to Alexis, "has seen the wall that limits his destiny." His was ending in Korea. Although he was impervious to remorse he was riddled with superstition, and could not help thinking this was retribution for his involuntary disobedience in Rome when he had been unable to keep his barbarians from disobeying the Emperor's express instructions. His nights were haunted by the ghost of Rome crying out for justice, and telling him that till the end of time he would be an object of reprobation to all poets, artists, believers, and travelers. Sometimes his agitation was so great he would wake up, seize his sword, and rush from his tent, trying to drown in blood the visions that made him experience for the first time the mysterious emotion that had once so intrigued him. Balamir, covered with sweat and roaring in frenzy, was finding out what it was to be afraid. The storm prevented him from trying to forget by venting his blind fury on the islands of Japan —all he could do was remember. He wrote a last letter to Alexis, asking forgiveness both for having let Rome burn and for having failed to conquer Japan. Then he retired to his tent and gave himself up to the malady from which even princes and victorious generals and the powerful ones of this world are not always exempt. The Kha-Khan of the Oïghurs died of grief in his tent on a Korean hillside, on the shores of the sea of Japan, five years and nine moons after the sack of Rome.

The barbarians did not want to leave behind in some insubstantial grave that might be violated the remains of one who had laid waste to so much of the earth. At first they thought of taking the body with them in their retreat, and then, considering the perils of a long journey across vast spaces filled with enemies, they changed their minds and tried to honor his memory with a tomb that would be worthy both of him and of themselves. They began to hollow out the side of a hill, after the fashion of the cave tombs of Xanthus and Telmessos,[13] but still this did not seem safe enough. So then they decided to divert the course of a river and build their prince's tomb in the river bed. They chose the river Naktong or Naktonggang, on which the United Nations forces took their stand in 1950, during the Korean War. By means of dams and canals they deflected the water for a stretch along which a hundred or so Chinese prisoners, strictly guarded, were made to work. After four or five days a wide deep grave had been dug in the river bed. The body of the Kha-Khan was carried there at night, by torchlight, while bronze drums beat out a funeral chant to the accompaniment of muted cymbals and the whine of a Chinese organ with twelve bells and twelve pipes. In accordance with their ancestral traditions, the assembled barbarians had cut their faces with daggers and knives, so that their tears, as they flowed, were mingled with blood. It must have been an astonishing scene, all these crooked warriors, their fearsome countenances covered with scars and open wounds, weeping in the warm night, to the sound of savage music, for their dead leader.

Balamir's treasures were buried with him, and the wildest stories have always circulated about them ever since. Some writers have maintained that during his passage through Egypt the Kha-Khan managed to get hold of the treasure of Tutankhamen. As is well known, when Howard Carter and Lord Carnarvon discovered Tutankhamen's tomb in 1922, they realized at once that tomb robbers had been there before them.[14] Certain bold spirits have concluded that the thief was none other than Balamir. In the present state of historical and archeological research this hypothesis cannot be completely dismissed, but neither can it be regarded as established. Other historians have suggested that the bold Kha-Khan also annexed the treasures of Delos, Halicarnassus, Ezion-geber,[15] Babylon, and Ophir. None of these theories is based on adequate proof. But in such murmurs of history not everything is false, and here, as often, truth is stranger than fiction.

A fabulous treasure did indeed fall into Balamir's hands. It was Solomon's treasure. But it did not happen in Jerusalem, where Balamir, on his way back from Spain and Mauretania, paused on his journey to Persia and China. It happened in Rome. The Romans had seized several priceless works of art from Solomon's Temple as war booty, and taken them to Rome: jewelry; Solomon's gold plate; religious objects, including the "sea of bronze," a huge engraved bowl designed to serve for ritual ablutions before worshippers entered the temple; and, above all, subject of the highest veneration for the Jews, the seven-branched candelabrum that the traveler can still see depicted in bas-relief on the Arch of Titus in the Forum. Balamir had seized this treasure during the sack of the Eternal City, and throughout his journeyings, first around the Mediterranean, then across Asia, he had never let the seven-branched candlestick or the sea of bronze out of his possession. And the twists of history have decreed that Solomon's fabulous treasure should rest today by the side of the Kha-Khan of the Oïghurs in the bed of the Naktonggang in the Land of the Quiet Morning.[16]

One black, one white, one bay, and one dappled horse were slain over the grave and buried beside the prince and his treasures. Dawn was breaking when all these lengthy preparations were at last concluded. Then the Kha-Khan's Mongolian and Chinese concubines came to mourn over the tomb, tearing out their hair, waving rattles, uttering ritual sobs and funeral chants over the corpse, and scratching their faces and bare breasts with their orange nails. The three youngest and prettiest, who for the last few months had usually shared his nights and his ravings of Rome and slaughter, were put to death like the horses, and their blood flowed down over the prince's body, the seven-branched candelabrum, and the rest of Solomon's treasure. When all was over, the bronze drums gave one last salute to the Kha-Khan of the Oïghurs as he lay surrounded by his wealth, his women, and his horses, and the waters of the Naktong were released to follow their natural course once more. They rushed back foaming into their bed, covering forever the remains of the barbarian chief who had destroyed Rome and shaken the world. To make sure the site of the tomb should remain secret, all the prisoners who had taken part in the work were murdered on the spot and their bodies thrown into the river. Then, under the rising sun, the leaderless barbarians mounted their horses and set off westward, toward the steppes and the high plateaus.

The news of Balamir's death reached Alexis on the Rhine. Sardinia, Corsica, the Balearics, and Crete had been conquered almost without a fight. Only Sicily had attempted to resist, but it did not take Carradine's fleet long to organize a veritable pontoon between Regium and Messina and force the straits. Syracuse held out for three months, Segesta and Selinus were destroyed and razed to the ground. Only half a dozen temples were spared by Logophilus to bear witness to Sicily's glory and, in their present ruined state, to fill the modern traveler with wonder. Alexis ascended the throne of Palermo less than six months after his triumphal entry into Rome at the side of Hadrian VII.

From the Mediterranean the Emperor went to the valleys of the Tigris and the Euphrates to inspect the imperial troops there. He went through Edessa, Samosata, Dura-Europos, and Ctesiphon about eighteen months before Balamir passed there on his way to Bactria and China. The Emperor himself went on as far as Gedrosia, Arachosia, and Paraponisus; he, too, crossed the Khyber Pass and went down into the plain of Peshawar, watered his horse in the Indus and the Hyphasis, and took Lahore. Two separate series of negotiations were begun, with Prince Kuchan in the northwest and King Maurya in the southeast. It would obviously be difficult, not to say impossible, to go into the details of these talks. Their result was to extend the supremacy of the Empire almost to the Ganges valley, to Pamir, Lake Balkhash, the Aral Sea and the Urals. Farther east, up to the Altai and Lake Baikal, the New Alliance maintained the domination of the Empire indirectly. And thus was formed, between the taking of Rome and the death of Balamir, the greatest empire in history. During the few years of its greatest, though fragile, expansion, the Empire stretched from Spain to China. In Europe its limits were the Rhine and the Danube. When Balamir was breathing his last in Korea, Alexis had already left the Indus and the Ganges, had spent a few months in the City, and was making for the Rhine and Danube frontiers, where the people were restive. It was here he was overtaken yet again by one of the fateful messengers who pursued him all his life. This one had just crossed the whole Empire to bring the Emperor the news of the Kha-Khan's death.

The alliance with Balamir had been the keystone of Alexis's policy. It had replaced the barren, exhausting, potentially fatal struggle against the barbarians with the fertile, stimulating notion of a world empire in which everyone, including the barbarians, had their function and their place. In the realization of this great design the wild Kha-Khan had always shown both intelligence and loyalty. He too—and here his merit was perhaps as remarkable as the Emperor's genius—had seen all that the New Alliance had to offer his people: culture, civilization, a world to conquer. Alexis had had to fight against the patricians, the priests, the tradition of hostility toward the barbarians. Balamir had had to resist the nomads' savagery, their love of bloodshed and pillage, their thirst for adventure, their hatred of constraint and institutions. But both Balamir and Alexis had overcome the obstacles confronting them, and had managed to install the horsemen of the steppes in Toledo and Siena, Guadalajara and Montepulciano. The construction of the Empire would never have been possible but for the coexistence at the same time of the Kha-Khan of the Oïghurs and the Emperor Alexis. Separate, these two powers canceled one another out, each closing to the other the way that led to universal power. Together they were capable of conquering the world; and conquer it they did. In the West, the only areas not within the Empire were unknown Africa beyond the Sahara, that was then a kind of world's end, and the impenetrable forests of northern Europe, bordering on the icy lands of Thule. Among the great powers of the Orient, only the kingdoms of eastern India, southeast Asia, the Middle Kingdom, and Japan, whose princes bore the mysterious titles of *tenno* and *sumera no mikoto*,[17] escaped Alexis's domination. And no doubt even these would have fallen if Balamir had lived. The death of the barbarian general marks the apogee of the world Empire, and foreshadows its decline.

When he learned of the death of the Kha-Khan the Emperor decided that in Nîmes, Trier, Vienne on the Rhone and Vienna on the Danube, Verona, the two Aquileuses, Carthage, Timgad, Alexandria in Egypt, Tyre, Palmyra, Antioch, Ctesiphon, Samarkand, Bactria, Onessa, Pomposa, and the City, solemn funerals should be celebrated by the men of the Empire and the barbarians together, for the hero whose body lay buried on the other side of the world under the waters of the Naktong. It was the first time ever that a single celebration was held simultaneously in so many different places. Balamir died in the spring, probably about the middle of May. The Emperor had learned of his death in the middle of summer. The Kha-Khan's memory was honored in the autumn. Some maintain that this was the origin of All Souls' Day, November 2 in the calendar of the Roman Catholic Church.

Balamir's end was remembered throughout the latter part of the Middle Ages and the whole of the Renaissance. Imaginary portraits of the Kha-Khan appear—in many a *Danse Macabre* and *Triumph of Death*—from the monastery of Saint Benedict at Subiaco to the Campo Santo in Pisa and the catacombs of the Capuchin convent in Palermo.[18] Andrea Orcagna's great fresco in Santa Croce in Florence, of which unfortunately nothing survives but a few heads, striking both for their exaltation and their brutality, was entirely built up around the terrible countenance of the barbarian prince. He is there again in Dürer's *Knight, Death and the Devil*, Holbein's *Simulacra of Death*, Füseli's *Satan, Sin and Death*, and Valdés Leal's *Finis Gloria Mundi* in Seville, where the half-submerged corpse beside that of the bishop is the body of the Kha-Khan. He is clearly among the *Death's Heads* sculpted by Picasso in 1943, and one of the motorcyclists of death in Cocteau's *Orphée* is called Balamir. The fact is that the universal and imaginary funeral for the Kha-Khan of the Oïghurs struck the world with wonder. Alexis had forbidden any human sacrifice, but in every town a hundred and forty-four white horses, solemnly consecrated to the memory of the barbarian prince, were sacrificed on the same day, before the assembled priests and soldiers at the moment when the sun was highest in the sky. The crowd sang funeral hymns, the children waved palms or reeds or young oak branches, and horse races or mock combats went on late into the night, by the light of torches that the priests extinguished at dawn by plunging them into the blood of the slain horses.

The Emperor himself felt Balamir's death cruelly, and wondered yet again at the frivolity of history. Some thirty or thirty-five years earlier the death of the Kha-Khan of the Oïghurs would have been greeted with outbursts of joy by the peoples of the Empire. But how rapidly things change! Now the death of the barbarian captain struck dismay even into the patricians of Pomposa, even into the priests of Aquileus, even into the ancient families of the City and Onessa. The patriarch of Rome himself wrote to the Emperor in praise of the Kha-Khan. He said that the role of the archpatriarch was to forgive, just as the role of the barbarian general had been to conquer and perhaps to destroy. And he, the archpatriarch, forgave.

All his life Alexis, like everyone else, had been surrounded by death. But until now it had seemed to him an accident. Vanessa, Simeon, Philocrates, all the Jesters, thousands of soldiers and innocent victims had died one after the other in the long tempest of glory that had been his life. What was tragic about their deaths was that they might have lived. But Balamir, in the Land of the Quiet Morning, at the other end of the earth, opposite the islands of Japan, had come to the end of the road. Helen, too, whom he had never seen again and who had died during the siege of Syracuse—she also had fulfilled her destiny. The truth was that time passed, and empires, like men, hastened toward their death. For Alexis there had always been something pointless about war, about the maneuvers of politics, about ruling men, about the Empire itself: and this sense of the vanity of things indeed finally led toward complete self-effacement.

The most surprising thing about Alexis's career is that he was brought in spite of himself to power, conquest, and domination. He scorned ambition, success, and violence; and he hated bloodshed. But man and the world had organized themselves around him, and genius, good fortune, and a passion for unity had taken care of the rest. But now, suddenly, he was overcome by a great weariness. Everything seemed to lead to attrition and decay. For years he had sacrificed what was essential—the color of water, the sun, the brief moment of twilight, the soul—to useless struggle. The struggle had always been victorious, but it had always been useless. It was a fight lost before it began. The only victor was time.

XXI

THE PEACE OF THE EMPIRE

 ALAMIR'S DEATH ON THE OTHER SIDE OF ASIA opened up the longest period of peace any empire has ever known. The peace for which Alexis had waited and hoped for so long extended from the Atlantic to China, sending forth ships laden with corn and wine, black pepper, nutmeg, ginger, cinnamon, cubeb, cloves and other spices; sellers of scents and silks; astronomers and physicians; caravans bearing pearls, amber, and diamonds, stuff for banners and pennants, camacas and brocades, samites and tartairs, atabi and gold dust. The threads of history that had seemed to be broken were knitted together again in a web of sparkling colors; the blind alleys of fate suddenly opened into the crossroads of trade, fine arts, power, and glory. The Eagle and the Tiger were reconciled in Alexis. The priests were reassigned the place Arsaphes had given to them: a mixture of science, prestige, and submission. The prosperity of the City during its first golden age was but the anticipation, precursor, and promise of the unparalleled splendor it now attained. It took its place beside Babylon and Nineveh, Peking, Rome and Byzantium, Baghdad and Damascus, Memphis and Thebes, Susa and Persepolis, Jerusalem and Athens, among those edifices of marble, brick, and mire destined for magnificence and destruction, in which, between trivial incident and masterpiece, the history of the world takes on a new aspect. It was for the Empire of Alexis that there had been hatred between the two sons of the first prince of Onessa; it was for the Empire of Alexis that Archimandrite had invented the probability calculus and that Hermenides and Paraclites had each conceived their view of the universe; that Arsaphes and Basil the Great had fought against the barbarians, Aquileus, Onessa, and the High Council of the merchants of Pomposa; that

the ships of the City had first been defeated off the Arginous Islands, and then beaten the pirates at Cape Pantama and the fleet with black and white sails at the Cerbical Islands and off Patmos. The whole history of the Empire, and of the Empire before it became the Empire, was like some great riddle to which the answer was suddenly given, some dark labyrinth suddenly filled with light. Alexis, dominant figure of a whole age, not only fashioned the face of the future, but also gave meaning at last to the past. None of the efforts, the victories, the suffering, the setbacks had been wasted. The humblest soldier who fell in the dust of the steppes or in the snow of the Alps or Caucasus took his place in the litanies of the priests and in the inscriptions set up everywhere—by rivers, in mountain passes, where valleys opened into the plain, in the heart of conquered cities. No one had died in vain. Whether crucified by the merchant princes at the gates of the City, impaled by the Oïghurs in the deserts of the southeast, thrown alive to lions or tigers, flayed, blinded, the dead, though its destiny was hidden from them, were the prophets and martyrs of the Empire.

Three times—once before the golden age of the City, once between Arsaphes and Basil, once under the barbarian tyrants between Basil and Alexis—there had been nothing but desert, without sculptors or gardens, without feasting or hope. The only prospect was exile, torture, suffering. But now anyone who killed was immediately brought before judges appointed by the Emperor. Everyone knew what the morrow would bring. The codes drawn up by Bruince and Logophilus and the treatises of the Polititian set out what was allowed and what was forbidden, laid down rules, distinguished between different cases, prescribed penalties. There was a Georgian saying to the effect that the Empire was so safe under Alexis that a beautiful maiden of fifteen carrying a platter of gold coins on her head could cross it alone by night from end to end without running the slightest risk.[1] Roads were built one after another, always with an invocation to the gods carved on marble steles, and the traditional reminder: "I, Alexis, built this road for the protection of men and beasts . . ." Post stages were organized. One traveler, Odoric Pordenone, wrote: "Couriers gallop at top speed on the swiftest steeds or, in the arid regions, on racing camels. When they come in sight of the stages they sound a horn to announce their approach, and the men in charge of the posts get ready another rider with a fresh mount. He in turn seizes the dispatches, leaps into the saddle, and gallops to the next post, where the procedure is repeated. Thus within twenty-four hours the Emperor receives news from places normally three days' ride away." Fire-fighting brigades were set up in each large town. Alexis and Theodora founded more than four hundred almshouses, hospitals, public refectories, and veterans' homes all over the Empire. New harbors were dug. Spaniards, Syrians, and Persians raised thoroughbred horses, fighting elephants, bulls, and hunting falcons. Libraries were built up in the City, Aquileus, and Onessa that held books and manuscripts in thirty different languages together with commentaries upon them. Schools of painting and sculpture were patronized by the sons of merchants or officers converted to beauty by a tutor from Greece or Sicily. As in the first golden age of the City, the theaters were full, as were circuses, gardens, gymnasiums, and the porticos, where sophists and teachers of rhetoric told of the origins of the world and speculated about man, destiny, and death.

Four or five special classes or castes were organized and developed: the army, the priests, the merchants, the teachers and artists, and the officials in charge of weights and measures, justice, and supplies. Civilization, prosperity, and the vast size of the Empire entailed the development of public services and the extension of state authority over every kind of activity. The organization of the police and of taxation assumed a completely new importance—both institutions were destined to have a considerable future. The pursuit of criminals, the arrest of the guilty—all maintenance of law and order —had long alternated between arbitrariness and anarchy, usually indistinguishable one from the other. Sometimes summary justice would be executed by groups of individuals setting themselves up as tribunals; sometimes, especially in the time of Basil and of the barbarian tyrants, the armed forces themselves would spread a reign of terror over town and country. Alexis gave Logophilus the task of creating militia bands, which alone had the right to intervene on behalf of the State, whether on land or sea, in the private lives of citizens of the Empire. This was the origin of one of the Empire's most celebrated institutions—the famous black galley of Onessa, whose responsibility it was to pursue escaping criminals into the most distant regions. Logophilus' officials, whose position in the Empire was somewhere midway between that of an army and that of a civil service, also performed the no less important task of helping the priests levy the taxes that supplied the treasury. One of the most obvious motives for Alexis's conquests was the need for resources with which to maintain the army, to improve the City, Onessa, and

Aquileus, to build roads and bridges, to develop ports and markets, and to help the needy and sick. Once the Empire had been built up, taxation became Bruince's and Logophilus' most important preoccupation. The reform of the coinage and of the system of weights and measures[2] had been an important stage in the improvement of methods of taxation. All over the Empire uniform standards had been adopted, based on land area and the value of goods, with quite sophisticated weightings according to the abundance of harvests and the prosperity of the various regions. Only the priests were capable of the complicated calculations involved in such large-scale administration, so the collection of taxes was naturally entrusted to them, with the help of the police in cases of refusal or dispute. The army had to intervene in more than one instance in countries that lay farthest away, or where there was fierce opposition to the mere idea of taxation—for instance in Palestine and Armenia, in the regions of the Rhone and the Loire, and in Corsica, where the suggestion of taxes caused a rebellion.

The system obviously called for uniform training of officials, and especially the priests who fulfilled the function of accountants. Here to a certain extent the opposition between Thaumas and Gandolphus cropped up again, under Alexis, in a conflict between Bruince and Logophilus. Bruince wanted to make the privileges and duties of the priesthood available to anyone, from Provence to the Persian Gulf and from the Danube to the Atlas. Logophilus maintained that the priesthood should remain exclusive. He argued that the territories of the original Empire, between the forests of the northeast and the southern steppes, were quite large enough to supply all the priests that were necessary, and that their main task was to perpetuate the domination of the victors over the vanquished. Alexis had to intervene in person before Bruince's views prevailed. But then there arose a new series of difficulties. The teaching of the priests was hampered, in the distant parts of the Empire, by the many different faiths that were current. The rise of the priests, their propaganda, and often their arrogance, or at least their sense of superiority (frequently justified), led to severe tension and sometimes serious problems in such places as Palestine, Syria, and Persia, where the followers of Zoroaster still held out; farther east still, where Buddhism, once dear to the Emperor himself, continued strong; and in Rome, where the patriarch was ready to yield in anything except the doctrine of which he was the repository. All this led the Emperor to adopt a mixture of tolerance and syncretism: tolerance for religious and metaphysical doctrines and ideas; syncretism in the teaching of mathematics, social morality, and methods of government and administration. Here, again, was manifested the great design of the Empire, the unification of minds. Thus, little by little, there came into being, midway between the priests and the lower officials entrusted with duties concerning police, justice, or administration, a class of sages and scholars who continued to bear the name of priests but had nothing in common with them but a vague belief in the divine forces that existed in varied and indefinable incarnations. The patriarch of Rome was almost alone in steadfastly opposing the dropping of specific beliefs and the merging—or even coexistence—of different religions: he was God's messenger upon earth, His spokesman and His legate, and he alone had the power to choose the way that led man to the gods. Between Alexis and Hadrian VII there existed mutual esteem—admiration even—and affection, and the ways of the pontiff were not the ways of violence. But over what was essential the patriarch would never give way. And Alexis was to respect his faith right to the end. As we shall see later, he even went somewhat beyond respect.

Thanks to the priests a vast operation of surveying and systematization was carried out all over the Empire. Fields, forests, estates, cattle, ships, and fortunes were counted and entered on rolls kept in provincial archives to serve as a basis for taxation. There grew up, one superimposed upon the other, three or four bureaucratic hierarchies, often rivals, in the hands, respectively, of soldiers, priests, provincial governors, and envoys from the Emperor. All came together in the City and the imperial palace, where decisions were made and from which Bruince and Logophilus sent out instructions to the Emperor's troops and couriers, in Spain and Sogdiana, on the Danube and the Euphrates, in Sicily and Egypt. The system soon grew stiflingly complicated. In the host of officials bustling about the offices at the palace—spathaires and protospathaires, heteriarchs and hypogrammateurs, silentiaries and protovestiaries, curopalates and logothetes of the drome—an experienced eye could have detected the symptoms of future decadence. But in Alexis's time everything was still alive with the flame of enthusiasm and novelty. The leaders' loyalty and large-mindedness, the rich resources available, and the people's support made it possible to deal with problems as they arose. The future was not yet menacing, but full of hope.

In the center of the Empire the City, whose splendor and marvelous expansion we have already seen,[3] was the symbol of the Empire's greatness. It was from this complex that Alexis and Theodora, Bruince and Logophilus governed the Empire.

Alexis held Bruince in affection and respect, but his feelings for Logophilus were more mixed. He admired the grammarian's rigor and business ability, his zeal and his real devotion to the public good, but considered he was prevented from participating in the grandest notions of the Empire by a certain lowness of mind and a tendency to concentrate on enriching the City rather than on conquest. Alexis employed him as a highly skilled comptroller and steward. He entrusted him with the organizational tasks at which he excelled: the provisioning of troops in the field; the commissariat; the gathering of taxes; the drawing up of treaties and legal texts; and, of course, the arts. He appointed him proveditor of the treasury and of works. But it was Bruince who was always directly involved, with the Emperor, in general policy, and who corresponded with the provincial governors, from Brittany to the Arabian Ocean and the frontiers of China. Alexis and Bruince—and Balamir up to his death in Korea—had little time to spare for Aquileus or Onessa, and in general the territories united under Arsaphes and Basil the Great, as distinct from the conquests of Alexis, were ruled over by the Empress. After the putting down of the Orange revolt, Theodora, who rarely left the City, reigned there supreme. Her courage, energy, intelligence, and unfailing loyalty had won Alexis's entire confidence, and he used to say that the Empress was the greatest man in the Empire. The Kha-Khan's death led the Emperor to entrust even more responsibility to Theodora and Bruince. One senses in Alexis a new and acute temptation to divest himself of power.

The fact was that the Emperor was in a way alien to the Empire. Even in conquest and victory itself, his triumphal advance never ceased to astonish him. He was, of course, passionately devoted to the idea of unity and universality of which the Empire was the expression; but the means to success soon wearied and often angered him. Not only bloodshed and war but every kind of dependence, servitude, or submission to any human order had always been hateful to him. And now he was the embodiment of human order and even of violence. All this had come about both through him and in spite of him, and he himself was that Empire of which so many aspects horrified him. Theodora, Bruince, and Logophilus were very familiar with the fits of dejection he was subject to,[4] which made the burden of authority and its consequences intolerable. Several times—after his coronation, just before Simeon revived the danger of barbarian invasion, during the Orange uprising—he seemed to be seeking an excuse, almost an alibi, for abandoning the throne, withdrawing, and giving up everything. Some have seen these crises as evidence of a lack of courage or resolution. But the truth seems to be just the opposite. Whenever the Emperor showed a wish to retire, it was when people and events could get along without him—when the barbarian tyrants had been driven out, when the Empire had been freed, when the priests and patricians were ready to take over the management of affairs themselves. But as soon as an event like Philocrates' arrival in Samarkand, or Simeon's arrival in Balamir's camp, or Theodora's stand against the Orange revolt gave the signal for a fight, then the love of struggle and risk, which coexisted so strangely in him with the desire for withdrawal and meditation, laid hold of him once more and threw him into the fray until yet again victory was won. The Empress and Bruince had come to understand his depressions, but Logophilus viewed them with scorn as weakness and dereliction of duty. He thus foreshadowed two schools of thought, one of the extreme right and the other of the extreme left, that have always denounced the Emperor as a hypocrite or false mystic, and, indeed, have almost gone so far as to call him an idiot.[5]

In one sense, though not that of Logophilus and his successors, this appraisal is not entirely wrong. Beneath the Emperor's genius was hidden one who was indeed backward in the eyes of the world, one of those the Beatitudes call the poor in spirit. Nothing could be more complex than Alexis's personality, at once direct and ambiguous, wild and dreamy, always unpredictable. When Philocrates imagined that the war for the liberation of the Empire could be waged by compromise and circumspection, he found himself confronted with a captain devoid of scruples. But when Logophilus wanted to see the Emperor dominate the world, it was a metaphysician he encountered, and a moralist. Is this so surprising in a philanderer who disappeared into the desert, a poet who was metamorphosed into a war leader? It sometimes seems as if the Emperor, with his dazzling career, with that apparently clear trajectory across the sky of history, really only groped his way through the darkness of circumstances and events. "Humanity knows not what it does. The meaning of its days and nights is in the lap of the gods." According to Justus Dion, this was a favorite saying of Alexis's. It applies not only to human history in general but to the Emperor in particular.

All these considerations help to explain the varied and even conflicting opinions held through the ages by the very people who admire Alexis, from Saint Thomas Aquinas to Lenin and Gobineau. Some, whose view I cannot share, see him as the type of the ambitious man, who worked out in advance all the stages of his career; others see him as the instrument of a historic destiny to which he yielded himself up blindly; others, again, as an improviser of genius who could adapt himself immediately to all men and every circumstance. None of these interpretations, which are all based solely on the Emperor's public career, gives an adequate account of Alexis's life as a whole. He cannot be explained merely in terms of ambition, submission to history, or empiricism. Ambition—he did not desire power. Submission—he was always asserting that to rule was to dominate the power both of history and of men. Empiricism—all his life he was the personification of fidelity and rigor, the very opposite of guile and subtlety. It is easy to see why followers of Nietzsche,[6] Bossuet, historical materialism, and Machiavelli try to claim him for their own. But how can any impartial observer fail to be dazzled by the flame that burns in Alexis's life? He possesses, above all, passion— passion for unity through diversity, for the universal; a thirst for beauty, knowledge, happiness; a quest for a key, a secret, a system, a society of souls. So much fervor or even folly cannot be without inconsistencies, and inconsistencies are not lacking in Alexis. But they are parts of himself and his personality rather than external accidents, weaknesses, or betrayals. For him, everything was grist to the mill of unity.

Thus the greatness and the peace of the Empire are inseparable from the personal aspect that Logophilus found so irritating. From the beginning to the end of his career the Emperor was always hesitating between the world and salvation. For years he probably thought the two objectives could be pursued simultaneously; and during this time the Empire represented for him peace and happiness, the salvation of the world. He threw himself into the struggle. Ruins, fires, widows and orphans, the sick and the dead were merely the price of peace and universal happiness. But he soon realized that in fact he was not prepared to pay that price. The old quarrel of ends and means preyed on him and was to end by overcoming him. He no longer recognized himself in the phrase he had once written to his master and friend: "You think, Philocrates, and I make war." It was a post-humous triumph for the philosopher. Now Logophilus could, if he dared, have addressed the Emperor in what were once Alexis's own words. Alexis was then engaged in one of the most amazing exploits in history, in a conquest of the world that made him the equal of men like Rameses II, Assurbanipal, Hannibal, Alexander, Asoka, and Tamerlane; and he rejected his triumph. Alexis has been called "a conqueror outstripped by his conquest," but it is not certain that the opposite is not the case. Perhaps it was the conquest that was out-stripped by the conqueror.

"Humanity knows not what it does. The meaning of its days and nights is in the lap of the gods." Peace had necessitated war; happi-ness had required battles and sieges. The world Empire was built upon conquest. Alexis's opponents have said he might well have murmured, on nights of slaughter or battlefields strewn with the dying, the famous "That was not what I meant" characteristic of the failures of history. The difference in his case—and it is an important one—is that the confession was wrung from him not by defeat, but by victory. It was his own triumph and glory that the Emperor, to the scorn of Logophilus, hesitated to accept. He had once set himself at the head of poor peasants; he had embodied the hope of the down-trodden and the needy; he had fought for justice and peace. Was it not the most natural thing, to fight? But the Empire of the world is a much heavier burden than that.

XXII

THE LEPER PRINCE

HE END OF A REIGN IS OFTEN MAGNIFICENT, BUT sad. The accumulated glory of a man blessed with all the gifts of the gods—power, success, victory, loftiness of ambition and ideas, and, above all, length of years, the time without which all the rest is nothing—that glory which gradually takes the place, till they are almost forgotten, of the burning passions of youth, bathes the world in its light. There is a beauty about the end of things. Ceremonies in temples filled with priests and ambassadors in gorgeous uniforms, with buckles of agate and precious stones, silk sashes and plumes from rare birds; reviews of victorious troops marching behind their trumpeters and standard-bearers; nocturnal banquets with fountains playing in moonlit gardens full of laughing girls in robes of muslin and velvet, eager to dazzle and please; the wisdom of old men; the formality of immutable rites and traditions; the prestige of literature and the arts; order; civilization—all contribute to a picture of a world that is stable at last and in which everyone has his place marked out by the gods. But across the walls of the edifice that took so long to build runs the little crack, tiny, insidious, eager to spread and destroy all, the almost invisible fissure in which the bitter eye of the prophet sees the flames and ruins, the collapses and catastrophes to come. Already, beyond the great rivers, a savage tribe is making ready to attack. Or plague. Or famine. Or rebellion by a forgotten nephew or the governor of a distant province. Or else some young man has been born on the frontiers, in a hovel near the marshes, or at the foot of a volcano, in a forge or behind a baker's shop. He has already chosen his arrow or his dagger, he revolves his plans feverishly every evening. The old king, weary, pensive, sees in the curly-headed rebel, described at that morning's

council meeting, the impression he himself used to make on the powers of this world in the days when he, too, was eaten up with the ambition to destroy those powers and take their place. Thus begins and develops the only, the eternal moral of every human history— the inexorable genealogy of hope and struggle, victory, power and glory, decline and fall.

Alexis realized better than anyone that history was full of such ups and downs.[1] Robert Weill-Pichon writes that all through the last part of his reign the Emperor was expecting failures and setbacks that never came. At one moment, in the City, in Rome, in Aquileus and Pomposa, everyone thought defeat was at hand—on the frontiers of the recently pacified Empire the Ibos, the Alans, the Samoyeds, the Ainus, and the Khmers were growing restive again. Parthian and Mongol battalions had to be sent to defend the Empire on the Yalu, the Ganges, at the foot of the Atlas and the Anti-Atlas, on the Dnieper, and the Don. But still, everywhere and all the time, victory clung indefatigably to the imperial standard. The Emperor was tired of fighting and bloodshed; above all he was tired of winning. He had a profound sense of what was fine in struggle and what was hateful in success. Almost his only pleasure now was in the company of poets and writers, and once again he surrounded himself with the priests and seers with whom his life, through all its vicissitudes, had been so closely bound up. Justus Dion tells how, during a conversation with Logophilus in which the grammarian made his usual apology for the peace of the Empire and the restoration of order and justice, Alexis interrupted him impatiently with the phrase Simone Weil so much admired: "Justice, Logophilus, justice! A fugitive from the camp of the victors." Through all the last years of his public life Alexis seems to have been caught in what Sir Allan Carter-Bennett calls "a metaphysical dilemma": he was fighting to maintain the glories of the Empire, and he was longing for obscurity. The epilogue of the story is already there in that dual pursuit. There is some truth in Logophilus' comment, again reported by Justus Dion: "At the height of his power, with the barbarians subdued, the priests loyal, the whole world conquered, the universe at his feet, the Emperor had but one enemy—himself."

Some months after their marriage the Empress Theodora had given Alexis a son, whom she named Manfred. To continue is perhaps even more difficult than to begin, and it was this Manfred whose adventures and misfortunes were to tempt Lord Byron and Schumann, among many others, to give his fate a dramatic form, the first in a poem, the second in an oratorio. Weary of injustice and victory, Alexis transferred to his son all the hopes that had been such a disappointment to him—not because they were not fulfilled, but because they were. "There are two misfortunes in life," he used to say. "One is to fail. The other is the same, only worse—to succeed." Manfred was handsome and intelligent, everyone liked him, the gods had lavished their gifts on him, and he was anxious to give something in return. He seemed eminently worthy of his father's lofty ambitions for him. The Emperor entrusted to Bruince personally the role Thaumas had played with Fabrician, Fabrician with Philocrates, and Philocrates with himself. The procurator of the Empire devoted fifteen years of his life preparing Manfred to become the model of what an emperor should be. And Alexis continued in his son the design of his whole life, and the idea of a world Empire with which he had linked his name. He saw to it that even while still a child Manfred was not limited in his outlook to the City and the old part of the Empire. He spent whole years in Rome, where Bruince, who spent most of his time there, initiated him into history, philosophy, and the government of men and things. Then the Emperor sent him to the East, where Manfred followed in his father's footsteps, drinking from the sources of Asian philosophy and mysticism with a fervor that began to worry those who knew him. When he was fifteen or sixteen, in Isfahan or Lahore, he began to dress and eat like the local people and adopt their ways of behavior and thought. In order not to seem like a foreigner among them, he even changed his name. He was known as Akbar.

Akbar's reputation soon spread like wildfire through Asia, but as a sage rather than as a prince. Before he was eighteen he was venerated as Akbar the Blessed from the Erythrean Sea to the steppes. The Emperor recognized in his son the same flame that had consumed him; and he was glad, but uneasy. Alexis had had behind him the roughness of the northeastern forests and Greek subtlety. Manfred had behind him only the weight of an enormous Empire, the veneration of countless followers, all the facility of triumph, and all the servitude of power. At his son's age all that lay before Alexis was danger, hopeless struggle, and the omnipresent threat of death. Manfred had before him the legacy of the Empire, power, and yet more power. Luck was becoming a risk, and happiness a danger. Alexis had once said, "All power corrupts, absolute power corrupts absolutely." Manfred refused to let himself be corrupted. He struggled against others and against himself; he threw himself into study, privation, charity, and self-mastery. The Emperor, vaguely conscious of danger, had given orders for his own past life to be concealed from the boy. The reader may recall the missions sent, through Balamir and on other occasions, to eliminate any traces of the liaison between Alexis and Vanessa, and the other escapades of a young man fascinated at once by debauchery and asceticism. Historians have often seen this as a sign of hypocrisy or of a concern with his own dignity very uncharacteristic of the Emperor. Sir Allan Carter-Bennett interprets it, more subtly, as a desire to avoid provoking Manfred to further extremes. The future was to demonstrate the wisdom of these precautions, though they were, **alas,** futile. During one of his visits to the Land of the Two Rivers (Mesopotamia) or to Persia, Akbar heard by chance, from a priest of the moon who was probably unhinged—himself a figure well worth further study[2]—of the ordeals Alexis had submitted himself to at the time of his exile. The revelation overwhelmed Manfred. The young man had always felt unworthy of the Emperor and the legendary figures around him—of the memory of Helen, Thaumas, and Philocrates, Bruince's great stature, all the glories of the Empire, its martyrs, and its heroes. Even his mother seemed to the child like some terrifying divinity. Time, among all its other works, had transfigured Theodora. We first encountered her as a temple prostitute whose beauty and courage made men tremble. But she also had died to be born again, and, through the inner alchemy that changes people and the world, had become a reincarnation of Helen and of the supreme greatness of the Empire. Her beauty remained, but it had taken on another aspect. Instead of the disturbing beauty that held whole amphitheaters breathless, hers was now a beauty of strength and serenity. She had become the very symbol of the Empire, of its permanence, its dignity, and its authority. Manfred did not rebel against the crushing weight of all these great examples; he merely wanted to be worthy of them, to be able to climb, himself, to heights where the air was purer, more rarefied. Especially after the revelations of the priest of the moon, he found the life marked out for him impossible. It was his turn now to fast and mortify the flesh; he would have nothing to do with luxury and magnificence; he tore himself away from the worldly goods with which he was laden; he visited the lepers. A saint was in the making for the Empire.

No accurate portrait of Manfred survives, and there is something poignant about this absence of evidence. The prince always refused to let himself be represented in any statue, painting, carving, or coin. Later, in obedience to this wish, Alexis had all existing likenesses of his son destroyed, together with all documents referring to the forbidden name. And so we know comparatively little of Manfred's fate. But we do have Justus Dion's account of the terrible day when the Emperor, in Rome, received from one of the messengers who had punctuated his whole life with tidings of victory the news of the obscure disaster he had so long expected. It was the anniversary of Balamir's death, when, each year, wherever the Emperor happened to be—the City, Samarkand, Ctesiphon, or Vienna—a great religious and military feast was held, in the presence of the chief officials of the Empire, the army, the priests, the imperial family, and a huge crowd of spectators. That year Alexis had just arrived in Rome, and the ceremony took place on the most venerable hill of the Eternal City, still only just emerged from its own ashes—it took place on the Capitol, covered with statues draped in mourning and buildings some of which were not yet finished. The Emperor and Empress were there, attended by Hadrian VII, Bruince, Logophilus, the Polititian, and numerous generals and high priests. The ritual prayers were being said in memory of the barbarian leader now lying in the bed of the river Naktonggang. The archpatriarch had insisted on presiding personally over the celebration in honor of the man who had laid waste to his city. Hadrian was now an old man of ninety-two or ninety-three, but he still stood erect and his voice was still firm. Alexis no longer tried to stifle the secret admiration he had always felt for him. Beside the emptiness of military triumph and the voids of mysticism, the patriarch's forgiveness of wrongs and belief in universal love were like a cool, refreshing spring, restoring value and color to an empty world. Many in the Emperor's entourage, especially some of the priests of Aquileus, whispered that the pontiff was a hypocrite motivated only by ambition, and accused him almost openly. But the Emperor looked on with secret envy at the old man praying fervently for the salvation of the destroyer of the Eternal City. Others prayed for their friends and families, for success, for victory; he alone prayed for others, for his enemies, for his own defeat, for a universal love that was the opposite of victory and yet was perhaps the only victory that did not end in defeat.

All around the square Balearic slingers, Scythian archers, Syrian horsemen, Bengal lancers, and detachments from Sogdiana, Mauretania, Provence, and the Don, formed a magic circle of color and strength in which, as in a dream, the Emperor saw pass before him all the bloody and triumphant stages of his long life as world conqueror. There was something unreal in this splendor, something fleeting in this force, something horribly bitter in this accumulation of victories.[3] The archpatriarch lifted up his hands and implored his gods to bestow eternal life on the Kha-Khan of all the Oïghurs. The varied robes of the priests stood out smooth against the metallic glitter of cuirasses and helmets. Some of them were in black, others in white, some, from the farthermost parts of Asia, in saffron yellow or orange. Many hated each other because their beliefs were mutually exclusive and their gods unknown to one another. Only the iron hand of the Emperor, Theodora, Bruince, and Logophilus had made them live together in apparent peace, in the service of the Empire. They sang. Valerius, Philontes, Menalchas, and Logophilus himself had composed hymns that could offend no one's superstition. The archpatriarch was still praying. Alexis did not pray. There was an emptiness within him, a withdrawal, an impulse toward repose, a longing for the void that had long been torturing him. His whole life was now spread before him, in the leather uniforms of the Numidian horsemen and the long silk or woolen robes of the priests of Zoroaster. There arose before his eyes the wolves on the snow in the great forest. The lotteries in Alexandria. The pale shadow at the end of the garden. The body half buried beneath stones and mud. The columns in the desert and the temple tombs. The wood fire in Samarkand. Aquileus rejoicing after a night of riot. Jester's head rolling on the scaffold. Famagusta burning and invaded by the pirates. The little bridge in Pomposa. All the lights that burned at night in the City now restored to life . . . How he had loved power, the triumphal entry into conquered cities, the palms and roses strewn along his path, the peace and justice imposed by his invincible battalions! But nothing fails like success. This rich, full world suddenly seemed to him more arid than the sands of the desert in which he had once taken refuge. He heard himself once more talking to Jester in the gardens at Aquileus, Jester the beloved son whom he was to send to his death as he had sent so many others, but this time with his own hand: "You are young to talk of dying . . ." But Jester was dead, and it was he, Alexis, who had caused his death.

Death was all around him. He was like an island lashed at on every side by the waves. Death was attacking, the island still stood out for a few moments above the seething breakers, then was overwhelmed by them and disappeared forever. He was the emperor of nothingness. These sumptuous colors and shapes, all this magnificence, the hymns of the priests, the swords and lances, the plumed helmets, the palaces around the square, the standards stamped with the Tiger and the ensigns surmounted by the Eagle, the thirst for power and the thirst for gold, even the beauty of the gardens and the sky, even the happiness he felt within him on spring mornings, all, the impatience of youth, the friendship of men, ambition, anguish, all, including the pomp and circumstance of history, was nothing but illusion, nothing but the mask covering gulfs that held only silence. Never had Alexis felt so strongly the emptiness of the world that he had conquered. Even his own ideal of what the Empire should be was no longer enough to keep him afloat on the ocean of vanity. It was at this moment, in the midst of the great ceremony in memory of the Kha-Khan, when the entire crowd of soldiers and priests turned to the Emperor to acclaim and do him homage, that the messenger from Asia appeared on the Capitoline Hill.

This messenger had traveled for months, on foot, on horseback, by boat, by elephant and camel, to bring the Emperor news of Manfred. No, the prince was not dead. Yes, he knew everything about Alexis and his escapades now: the life in Alexandria, the passion for Vanessa, the exile in the desert. But Manfred's almost painful admiration for his father was only the greater, and each day he was more desperately afraid of proving an unworthy heir. He, too, dreamed now of repentance, of battles, and the intensity of his emotion might make him seem unbalanced. The violence and fervor with which he, in his turn, was now abasing himself and seeking to calm his passions in poverty and charity, was making him immensely popular not only within the Empire, but also in China and all of southeast Asia. Here, Akbar the Blessed was more and more venerated as a prophet and saint by the lowly people among whom he lived, tending the sick, visiting those in prison, giving his goods to the poor. The fact was that Akbar the Blessed, Prince Manfred, heir to the Empire, had carried to their logical conclusion the dreams of greatness and humility that Alexis, but with ambiguity and inconsistency, had dreamed before him. He had finally become one of the wretched whose glory both father and son had envied—Prince Manfred was a leper.

The terrible news spread like wildfire through Rome and all over the Empire. Logophilus tried once more to protect his own ideal of the Empire. The messenger died in mysterious circumstances, though nothing but vague suspicions could be alleged against the grammarian. But Alexis himself did not try to conceal the truth for long. And less than three months after the ceremony on the Capitol in honor of Balamir, the Empress Theodora died of grief.[4] Manfred also died, doing all he could to wipe out any trace of his passage here below. But despite all his efforts to achieve oblivion, his memory was to remain alive all over southeast Asia. Akbar had asked that no statue should transmit to posterity the likeness of a perishable body unworthy of immortality. Without flouting this wish, the Khmer king Jayavarman VII made a place for the shade of Alexis's son in one of the finest monuments ever raised by human genius. It was thus that the glory of the Empire came to extend as far as Angkor, and the traveler arriving from Siemréap is moved to discover in the middle of the ancient *enceinte* of Angkor Thom, almost hidden under the encroachments of the jungle, amid the huge Bayon sculptures in which the mystic architecture of the divine universe is reflected in stone, the almost disembodied smile of the leper prince, the famous "smile of Angkor."

It seemed to the Emperor as if his whole life had been nothing but a waiting for disaster. Everything was crumbling away. This tiny world the immensity of which he had had such dreams, which he had crossed on his horse and held in his hand, this world was now changing and slipping between his fingers. Peace, justice, unity, happiness were only a dream, a folly, imagined by idiots who tried to make time stand still in a universe ever-elusive. Power was melting away—nothing was left but suffering. For more than three moons the Emperor shut himself up and abandoned himself to grief. He was old, he was alone, and the Empire, now meaningless, was without an heir.

It was then that the Emperor turned to Hadrian. The archpatriarch did not receive him as conqueror, statesman, invincible captain now vanquished by arms or by fate. He received him as a man who had always been engaged in a lengthy struggle against destiny and the world, and who had been finally overcome only by time and the gods. The archpatriarch was old and ill, his city had been entirely destroyed, his priests were divided among themselves, and the very doctrine of which he himself was the symbol and guarantee was being attacked on all sides. In the eyes of the world, despite what remained of his wealth and his palaces, the archpatriarch, too, was one of history's vanquished. But the pontiff was custodian of a secret, and the secret was that defeat and poverty were the same as salvation, that it was the vanquished who were victorious. He said, "O Death, where is thy victory?" and he envied the happiness of the poor, the sick, the feeble-minded, and all the rest of life's victims. It was not only death he hoped for, like Aziri and Marcian, but suffering and pain. Strangely, he saw in them the image of heaven on earth, and he thanked his gods for sorrows, torture, the thorns on the rose, the wild beasts, and the tears shed by mothers over the corpses of their children. He did not envy the rich, the victors, the powerful, the happy of this world—he pitied them. Many people, especially the most fortunate, often laughed at him and his foolishness. But his charity and concern included even those who mocked. He believed that in failure, illness, in evil itself, even among thieves and prostitutes, there was a divine spark unknown to the happy. He also believed, unlike anyone else, that it was for the poor and sick to help the rich and healthy merely by thinking of them, remembering that men's sacrifices and sufferings were more pleasing to the gods than milk and honey and the blood of bulls. In the leprosy that had fallen on Akbar he saw a sign from the gods and a blessing for Alexis.

A mind like that of Logophilus could only hate Hadrian's doctrine fiercely. Logophilus did not love the poor, the sick, and the vanquished; but at least he did not ask them to cherish their misery. He respected power, and distrusted this pontiff according to whom the weakest were more powerful than the strongest. He often declared he would not be proud to be vanquished, and he was not ashamed to be victor. If he were poor, he would try to get rich; since he was rich, he declined to become poor. In either case, Hadrian's teaching and his cult of pain were detestable to Logophilus, who saw in them a hatred and scorn of life, its beauty, and its pleasures.

But Alexis had found in Hadrian's words a distant echo of the Asian saints and sages. There were many differences between the doctrines of Rome and the illuminations of Horeb, the Arabian deserts and the banks of the Indus. But they all turned away from a world of appearances in which happiness and unhappiness were equally precarious, they all aspired after something else, a new life, a liberation from evil, salvation. The archpatriarch was very gentle and good, but his was a gentleness of steel, an intransigent goodness, and he, too, was not without a certain form of pride. For he alone was entrusted with the keys to all the secrets of the world, and, as we have already seen, in his view truth could neither be divided nor discussed. Just as the Eagle and the Tiger were the arms of the Empire, and the ring signifying the marriage with the sea the symbol of Pomposa, so the archpatriarch's emblem was a key, called Hadrian's key, the only one that could open the gates into the other world. Hadrian often said he was the way, the truth, and the life, and that no man came to salvation but by him. Unlike the monks of India and China, more concerned with their own salvation than with that of the world, Hadrian only wished, as he said, to rule over men so as to be better able to help them—though Logophilus claimed that he wanted to save them whether they liked it or not, and that the humility of love was strangely like the pride of power. According to him the cult of failure had never been such a success, nor had the love of poverty ever known such luxury and wealth.

Hadrian's religion had a very precisely worked-out liturgy and ritual from which blood was banished and replaced by salt, fish, water, grapes, wheat, and unleavened bread. Instead of the eagle of the priests of the Empire, there was a lamb, symbol of innocence and of the rejection of all violence. To underline even more strongly the reversal of values in favor of the other world, and the replacing of the otherwise universal appeal to the rich and powerful by love of the poor and the prisoner, Hadrian's religion set up as objects of worship, instead of the sun and oak of the Empire, instruments of torture—the stake, the whip, the pillory. Virginity was the object of special veneration, in which there seem to be traces of cruelty and even sadism;[5] but, as in earlier days in the Empire, there seems to have been at the same time a somewhat ambiguous cult of the courtesan and the prostitute, whose suffering was presumably sufficient to redeem her impurity. Iconography informs us that religious painters often represented such women with long, fair hair down to their ankles and carrying jars of the perfumes of Arabia. As we have seen, humility and charity did not preclude the pomp and magnificence that provoked Logophilus' sarcasm and mistrust. Several of the Roman patriarchs who embodied this mystique of gentleness, humility, love, and poverty were proud and violent warrior chiefs, dreaded by adversaries whom they did not shrink from putting to death, avid for gold and women and sometimes for boys. In purely religious matters as well as in customs and thought, the historical improbabilities, contradictions, and variations of the Roman faith seem to us today so many and so obvious, especially in comparison with the relative simplicity and internal consistency of the Empire, that we find it hard to form a clear and accurate idea of them. Some authors, following Couchoud, have even gone so far as to attack first the historical role, and then the very reality of the Roman moral and social teaching. For them the archpatriarch, his love of failure and poverty, yet at the same time his magnificent temples and palaces, the dual cult of the virgin and the prostitute, and the adoration of the stake and the whip are all nothing but myth. And they, of course, deny that Hadrian VII ever really existed, and relegate him among the figments of the historical imagination, along with Prester John and Pope Joan. Nonetheless it does seem that the Roman religion really did exist, and moreover that it played a comparatively important part in history. The real existence of founders of religion, popular leaders, and great statesmen and generals has always been called in question: skepticism, like naïveté, can be carried too far. The existence of Abraham, Solomon, Christ, Charlemagne, Joan of Arc, and even Napoleon[6] has been challenged in the same way as that of the archpatriarch, Alexis, and the Empire. But the reality of Rome and its pontiff can no more be doubted than that of the City, the Empire, and the Emperor. In the two cases the sources, texts, and other historical evidence are equally numerous and decisive.[7]

The archpatriarch pressed Alexis, who had found in Hadrian's religion at least a partial answer to the questions he had always asked himself, to renounce the gods of the Empire and adopt those of Rome. But Alexis was kept from a real conversion by the continuing influence of Philocrates' relativism, his experiences in Asia, and the mixture in his own character of nihilism and ardent curiosity. The Emperor had known too many different religions and revelations, he had meditated on the truth in too many forms and incarnations, and had perhaps too much faith in man and his powers to adopt any new belief and new rites. So he remained faithful to the gods whose legends and myths had surrounded his childhood, and above all to the sun, which for him was the symbol not so much of multifaceted truth or good as of unity and universality; for there were many gods, but there is only one sun, and it shines on everyone. The Emperor lavished privileges and wealth on the archpatriarch. He gave the priests of Rome schools and temples, sent them to spread their teaching in all the different parts of the Empire. But it seems he never himself adopted Hadrian's beliefs. Despite all the opinions to the contrary, particularly numerous in Spain and Italy at the end of the nineteenth century, Alexis's formal conversion to Hadrian's religion remains to say the least improbable. Some authors have fallen back, for want of anything better, on the somewhat flimsy theory of a secret conversion, but all the most recent studies contradict this hypothesis. Alexis told the archpatriarch that all the various gods in heaven must be under some unknown god—ἄγνωστος θεός τις—who ruled over them all, and that this God, if He existed and if He looked down from the sky and was amused by men and their antics, must in the end take pity on all that effort and all that suffering, and recognize His own. Soon after Theodora's death the Emperor wrote the short treatise known as *The Banquet of the Soul*, in which occurs the famous tirade plagiarized by Voltaire in his *Essay on Tolerance*, which begins with an invocation to the unknown God: "It is no longer to men that I speak, but to Thee, God of all beings, all worlds, and all time. . . ." Its closing words reflect the dream of universality which always haunted Alexis: "May all men remember they are brothers . . . and let us use the fleeting moment of our existence to bless in a thousand different tongues, from the Naktonggang to the Atlantic, Thy goodness which has given us that moment."[8]

Although the Emperor seems never to have yielded to the pontiff's urgings, the archpatriarch did have one dazzling success: the procurator general of the Empire, Bruince himself, publicly embraced Hadrian's faith. Bruince's conversion marks a new turning point in the history of the world. It caused an enormous stir in the Empire, and its consequences influence all of us still. It is never too difficult to explain what is past, but in this case the event fits in naturally enough with all we know of Bruince. To put it baldly, Bruince stood halfway between the Emperor and Logophilus. He was in charge of the Empire of this world; he was concerned with both justice and efficiency; he was as far from Logophilus' rough cynicism as from Alexis's self-torments. He wanted order, peace, equity, strong and stable institutions, laws for the powerful, hope for the downtrodden, and Rome gave him all these. One autumn morning on the other side of the Tiber, at the foot of the Janiculum Hill, Bruince received from Hadrian's hands the bread, wine, salt, and fish that opened the doors of the kingdom of which the archpatriarch was the earthly guardian.

The ceremony reflected the two aspects of Hadrian's religion: magnificence and humility. Bruince, clad in a pink and green dalmatic interwoven with gold thread and embroidered with sapphires, lapis lazuli, and emeralds, covered his head with ashes and lay in the dust at the feet of the archpatriarch. He vowed to defend the poor, the sick, and the fatherless against the rich and powerful; then he reviewed the archpatriarch's meager battalions. There were probably not very many of them, but they were mixed with barbarian detachments and imperial troops arrayed in an imposing mass along the river bank. The Emperor was present at the ceremony, thus lending the procurator general the sanction of supreme authority. This was not unnecessary, in view of the hostility shown by the priests of Aquileus and, above all, by Logophilus, who made no attempt to hide his disapproval at seeing the highest person in the Empire, after the Emperor, abandon the traditions of his ancestors. The conversion of Bruince contained the seeds not only of his own tragic end—which Georg Büchner, after many others, dramatized in 1835 in *The Death of Bruince*—but also of all the future troubles within the Empire, its convulsions, and its decline.

In order to understand the events that are the main concern of this book it was necessary to give an account of the Empire before Alexis. The Empire was to survive for some time after the Emperor, the procurator general, and the proveditor of the treasury, but it is, of course, impossible, within the limits of this brief historical and biographical essay, to do more than allude to the future.[9] But to put it in a nutshell, the new face worn by the Empire after Alexis dates from the conversion of Bruince, which represented yet another step toward the manners, values, and society of our own time. We cannot do more here than express the hope that there will be many studies made in the future of Bruince and his religious and political thought, of Alexis's successors, and of the later development of the Empire, thus throwing on our own condition the light that only the past can throw upon the present.

Hadrian VII died less than two years after the conversion of the procurator general. His remains were interred in what was known as Hadrian's Mausoleum, which later, as the result of events we shall deal with in due course, became first the Castel Sant'Angelo and then a fortress. Bruince succeeded Hadrian on the archpatriarchal throne, which he was to occupy for fourteen glorious years, preparing the way for the Peters, Gregorys, Sixtuses, Juliuses, and Leos to whom more than anyone we still owe the image of the world we live in.

Meanwhile, on the other side of the Empire, in Samarkand, Bukhara, Karakoram, the Altai mountains, in the steppes, and on the high plateaus, a young man of about twenty, whom the reader may remember, was beginning, in his turn, to have extraordinary adventures. He was the son of Balamir and Zenobia, the Kubla Khan of Coleridge's poem, later to build his famous capital of Xanadu on the river Alph—the future conqueror of the Chinese, of Peking, of the valley of the Yangtze Kiang, and all the Indochinese peninsula: Khubilai.[10] This is not the place to retrace the stages of his rise, but we may just recall that Zenobia was the daughter of Helen and Roderick, and so Simeon's sister and Alexis's sister or half-sister. In Khubilai the Emperor found an echo of his own turbulent youth, a reminder of Manfred, a kind of composite image of all that had gone to make up his own life, from his rides in the northeastern forests with Simeon to his military expeditions at the side of Balamir. Deepest Asia, which had left an indelible mark on Alexis, revived again in the ardent and ambitious youth, then in the violent conqueror so attached to Buddhism that he prized his Buddhist titles of *ktuktu* (venerable, divine) and *chakravartin* (universal monarch) above all his innumerable others.[11] Marco Polo, who many centuries later was to exercise his gifts as geographer, historian, and observer as far afield as China, tells that when he became emperor, Khubilai welcomed with great pomp the relics of the Buddha sent to him by the rajah of Ceylon, and that he always had the support of the lamas of Tibet. But Khubilai's passion for universality, inherited no doubt from Alexis by those mysterious processes which owe less to blood than to kinship of mind and heart, made him sympathetic, despite his preference for Buddhism, to all other religions—to Nestorian pilgrims, to the priests of the Alans, to the clergy of the Greek rite, whose holy books he would kiss when they were sprinkled with incense before him. Like Alexis, Khubilai practiced at one and the same time the fiercest war, religion, the arts, and trade. He exploited the coal mines in north China ("Black stones extracted from a kind of vein in the mountains, which burn like logs and so well that no one burns anything else in all Cathay"[12]); he made the Yangtze Kiang the main artery of the Chinese economy ("There came and went on this river more ships and more rich merchandise than on all the ships and all the rivers of the West. Every year two hundred thousand boats went up the river, not to mention those that went down"[13]); he developed trade guilds worthy even of Pomposa and the City ("There were so many merchants, and they so rich, and they carried on so great a trade, that no man could measure it. And you must know that neither the masters of each trade nor their wives ever soiled their hands, but lived a life so rich and elegant it was fit for a king"[14]); he went further even than Alexis and Bruince, and introduced the general use of paper money (*ch'ao*), which Marco Polo amusingly called the real philosopher's stone ("And I assure you everyone willingly took these notes, because wherever anyone went in the lands of the Great Khan they could use it to buy and sell with just as if it were fine gold"[15]). The Arab traveler ibn-Batuta confirms in every detail the marvels remembered by Marco Polo. The genius of Alexis foresaw the genius and achievements of the son of Balamir. The Emperor thought that the first and last duty of those to whom nations were entrusted was to ensure, over and above their own concerns, the prosperity, greatness, and peace of the countries in their charge. "The Emperor," wrote Justus Dion, "looked around him. He saw Bruince on the throne of Hadrian, burning with a passion for justice, and Khubilai Khan in Asia, panting to make war in order to impose a great peace." How could Alexis fail to recognize himself in these two men, the old man he had loved for half a century, the other, still almost a child and whom he had scarcely seen, but in whom he saw again his own dreams of universality contained in laws, his own contradictions, his own dual temptation by both tolerance and violence?

The last years of the reign show an Emperor already far away, in whom the spectacle of time passing and never ending has gradually changed anguish and self-torment into a quest for serenity. Few lives in the whole history of the world have been so rich in fulfillment— and even the failures are exemplary. When, toward the end, the Emperor looked back on his past, he felt as if it belonged to someone else. Successes seemed hardly more important than sorrows and weaknesses; the great designs grew dim; everything was reduced to the same level before the mysteries that once enchanted his youth and of which he now sensed the approach and perhaps the solution. He was filled, then, with what Robert Weill-Pichon calls "a metaphysical indifference in which the passion to understand finally gets the better of the thrill of action." The Empire was at its height; the justice and peace he had promised to the nations reigned from Brittany to Korea, from the forests of Saxony to the deserts of Arabia; the same laws governed everyone; and as far as he could see the conquest of the world was not in danger. But he was not quite sure he did not find it pointless.

He told Justus Dion that history itself seemed to him no more than a tale, a show, the symbol of all vanity. To make history! What was the good? Pomposa had made history, and Pomposa had collapsed beneath Alexis's blows. The Empire, too, would collapse. The Emperor asked to be told about Khubilai's ambitions and his first successes. He could already see in his mind's eye the future conflicts, the peace that follows conflict, prosperity, happiness, and then once more the limits of fate and ruins again and the end of the great dream. He used to say history was an imaginary rock of glory and mud, dragged by torrents of blood to where no shores were. He was no longer quite sure that the way to the universal really lay through history. Perhaps he had been wrong. He had been torn away from meditation by the sufferings of the Empire, by injustice, by cruelty. And then, crushed by the rock he had tried to topple, he in his turn had been the embodiment of cruelty, injustice, and all the violence in the world. That was what was called history. Men and events formed a great infernal wheel where the only choice was between being victim or victimizer. The best moment in history was when the victim slowly arose and struck down the victimizer. Then he became the victimizer himself, and there was nothing left but to await new victims who would strike him down in their turn. But the Emperor had had enough of conquering and condemning.

In Logophilus' opinion, the Emperor's attitude was due simply to age, fatigue, and illness. Contrary to Alexis, the grammarian believed in history alone. It is only fair to add that he did not cultivate history for reasons of vanity or ambition. He believed in an anonymous history in which violence was justified by success, and the march of events brought the reign of happiness and truth nearer every day. More: Truth and happiness were history itself. History was held back by a siege that was too long, a battle that was lost, by regulations that were too mild. It was pushed forward by the entry of troops into exhausted cities, by victorious navies, by roads across the mountains and post stages with fresh horses. Logophilus said history had no conscience, but it knew the way it had to go, and the only mistakes it made were those men made when they tried, in vain, to oppose its course. Many historians have depicted Logophilus as a repulsive character. But he was not even cruel. All he wanted was to see the system work. Massacres did not matter. History must triumph. Logophilus' three sons were killed, one at the siege of Lindos, one at Adrianople, one at Verona. History is expensive. He believed courage was needed to make it advance, to make it gradually reveal to all its justice and truth, and for them it was but cowardice and treason to refuse to accept passing time and its pitiless demands. Justus Dion had a profound insight when he said that the Emperor and Logophilus happened to collaborate in making the history of their time, but that the Emperor fought against history while Logophilus worshipped it.[16]

In the last book of his *Chronicles*, Justus Dion tells of a stroll he is supposed to have taken one evening in Rome with the Emperor, through the great garden which then extended over the Palatine Hill. The whole city, risen at last from its ashes, lay stretched before them. Minute in the distance, soldiers could be seen carrying out maneuvers; priests offering sacrifice to the gods; passers-by strolling from one portico to the next; fruiterers, cobblers, weighers of gold, and prostitutes plying their trade—the noise from the streets and the squares rose to the palaces looking out over the hill. The Emperor looked down on it all, and Justus Dion remarked that it was to him that the peoples of the Empire, in Samarkand, Antioch, Pomposa, Toledo, and Tyre, owed the peace and quiet they enjoyed. Alexis answered that he had never made war except to ensure peace and justice. Then after a moment's silence he said in a changed voice that the time had come for him to hand over to others the burden of the Empire. Justus Dion realized that this time the decision was final. But still he struggled against it. He tried to point out how necessary Alexis was to the Empire, to convince him it was his duty to rule. It was then Alexis made his famous answer, that to force men to do things was never a duty. He repeated what he had always said—that no one *had* to rule, but that it was impossible to rule without violence. In this sense Logophilus was right. And if one declined to worship history as he did, perhaps one would be led to withdraw forever from government and public affairs. Justus Dion asked if the Emperor had lost all interest in history, if it really seemed just the pointless vanity he spoke of so often. Alexis thought for a moment and then said history was something at once so dreadful and so marvelous that from then on he would try to understand and explain it in the light of humility, like the philosophers, rather than create it as conquerors and legislators do, in the darkness of fame, on battlefields and in assemblies. It is this equivocal passage that has led so many commentators to think that Alexis and Justus Dion were one and the same person, talking to himself.[17]

Enough has been said to throw some inner light on a decision that, coming from the master of the greatest empire in the world, was to provoke, at the time and throughout history, uneasy and sometimes angry amazement. Once he had made up his mind to leave the stage of history—a decision that must, in spite of everything, have been a painful one—Alexis's first thought was for the future of the Empire. If misfortune had not struck, there is no doubt that the imperial power in its entirety would have passed to Manfred. The only chance for the idea of universality to survive lay in resisting at all costs the forces of dispersion and disintegration. Theodora would probably have been given important responsibilities enabling her to remain for a while by her son's side and help him with her counsels. But with Theodora and Manfred both gone, we know the Emperor's first idea was to make Khubilai sole master of the Empire. Logophilus urged this course, but the Emperor hesitated. The youth, the violence, the very ardor of Balamir's son made Alexis fear for the future. He feared endless war, an oriental despotism intermingled with mysticism and ignorant of the facts in the West and the Mediterranean basin he himself so loved. Alexis spent almost another two years in self-interrogation and consultation. Then he summoned the Great Assembly of the peoples of the Empire to meet in the palace of the City and hear of his decision. The assembly consisted of priests from Aquileus, Rome, Antioch and Alexandria, Edessa and Ctesiphon; army leaders; the chief magistrates and representatives of the guilds and corporations; all the princes of allied or conquered countries; and all the provincial governors, from the Great or Atlantic Ocean to the Land of the Quiet Morning, from the snow-covered forests of the north to the burning deserts of Africa and Arabia. Half a century after the nomads' assembly at Székesfehérvár, which decided on the invasion of the Empire, the barbarian generals were mingling with the Pomposan nobles, the great landowners of Evcharisto and Parapoli, the priests of Aquileus and the archpatriarchal legates. Among the crowd were Moors, men with fair hair and long mustaches from the bank of the Rhine, slit-eyed Koreans, Indians with shaven heads, voluble Sicilians, Scythians, Lusitanians, Libyans, and Persians. Every possible language was spoken, but, as at Famagusta so long ago, at the time of Basil and King Regis, Greek was predominant and served as a link. The Emperor sat between Bruince and Khubilai. Behind him, the well-informed recognized Admiral Carradine, his beard now almost white; old Valerius, nearly in his dotage; Menalchas; the

Polititian; Aziri, now over ninety but still gay and lively after having driven so many young men to despair; and, of course, Logophilus. Isidore, Polyphilus, Philontes, Aristo, and Martian were dead.

The assembly lasted twelve days. There were magnificent celebrations, games, banquets, tournaments, horse races, and theatrical entertainments. These included the first performance—in the great auditorium in the palace (which was to inspire Palladio's Olympic Theater in Vicenza) of Menalchas's last tragedy, *The Glory of Balamir*. The splendor of the Empire was then at its height. Gifts were lavished on the princes and generals; the magnificent buildings, the flowers, the tinkling fountains in courtyards and gardens, the splendid tents erected by the nomad chiefs at the City gates, the silk standards and rare carpets, the rose petals strewn in the streets, the brilliance of the clothes and ornaments, the exotic food and the great dishes of pure gold left lasting traces in the mind, both of those present at the ceremonies and of the millions of men and women who see traces today in dance, folklore, and popular song. The theater of Clara Gazul, the Chinese and Sicilian marionettes, the shadow theater of Karagoz, the songs and dances of Albania, the Japanese *kabuki*, the Indonesian *wajang*, the great Georgian epics of Rusthaveli and Chakhrukhadze are all full of allusions to the Great Assembly in the City, the huge meeting of peoples recorded by both Christian and Buddhist tradition and invoked, as they undertook their own great enterprises, by Urban II, Peter the Hermit, Frederick II of Hohenstaufen, and al-Malik al-Nāsir Salāh-al-Dīn Yūsuf, whom we call Saladin. The assembly heard speeches by Bruince, Logophilus, Carradine, Khubilai, and lastly the Emperor, to whom it renewed its homage and obedience on the evening of the sixth day.

On the morning of the last day of the assembly, the Emperor appeared in public dressed in a long mauve silk robe, without helmet or armor, without any kind of weapon, but scepter in hand and with the crown of iron and oak on his head. His air was grave, and he was accompanied as usual by the archpatriarch and the son of Balamir. In his right hand the pontiff held Hadrian's key, the symbol of his authority in this world and the next. Khubilai, radiant with youthful beauty in the hides and furs traditional among his people, carried the legendary sword of the Oïghurs. The assembly, risen to its feet in a tense silence, realized at once that something very important was about to happen. Alexis spoke, and thanked all those who had come from the ends of the earth in order to strengthen the rule of peace and justice everywhere. One after the other he addressed in their own language the people of Tyre and Samarkand, Pomposa and Ctesiphon, Granada and Ephesus. He reminded them that they, too, were the Empire. Then he turned to those of the ancient Empire, those from Onessa and Aquileus, Evcharisto and Parapoli, Amphibolus and Mezzopotamo, Gildor and the City, those from the great forests and those from the plains at the foot of the volcanoes. It was with them it had all begun. They had fought against hatred, injustice, servitude, against the lawlessness that put the weak at the mercy of the strong. He called on them not to repeat the sufferings they had known for four centuries, not to inflict on others what they themselves had hated. He asked all of them, from one ocean to the other, from the eternal ice to the desert sands, to look on one another as brothers, to preserve the unity of the Empire as their most sacred possession, and to remain just as well as strong. For force without justice was rightly hated, and justice without force feeble and ridiculous.

These words were to echo down the centuries, from Saint Thomas Aquinas to Pascal and Hegel, and the assembly listened to them with passionate attention. Everyone felt that something even more important was to come, perhaps something terrible. There was an atmosphere of dread. Now Alexis spoke of Helen, Philocrates, Isidore, the great forest of Balkh, and the memory of Hadrian. For more than half a century, he said, he had been surrounded by great minds and great souls to whom he owed everything. Many had died helping him. Mankind as a whole lives forever, with the gods' help, in the continuity of empires and institutions; but the individual lives only to die. The Empire extended over the world, yet the Emperor, too, was just a man alone facing death. And now he, Alexis, wanted to devote all his thoughts to the death that had for so long spared him. He renounced supreme authority over all the peoples of the Empire and the world. He was ceasing to be Emperor in order to try to be a man. Not to learn to live—it was too late for that—but to learn to die.

There was an amazed and terrified silence. Everyone looked at his neighbors, whispered, wondered if he had heard aright. Then suddenly the Emperor raised a hand for silence. His decision was irrevocable, he said, and he had taken all necessary steps to ensure peace and the continuity of the Empire. Then each one knew his fate was about to be pronounced. Once again uproar was succeeded by silence, and Alexis announced that he was handing over the world Empire to Khubilai and the archpatriarch. To Balamir's son went land and sea, the armies, the navies, trade, the treasury, and the title of Emperor; to the archpatriarch went nothing but the peoples' souls and whatever there might be of the divine in the justice of men. And the pontiff, without power, without wealth of his own, without soldiers, and without a palace, was given supremacy over the master of the Empire—the archpatriarch, chosen by the priests and seers, stripped of all worldly wealth, would nominate the Emperor from among the families of the Porphyries and the princes of the Oïghurs. He would crown the Emperor, he would remove him from office if he proved unworthy, he would act as the sacred link between men and the gods. Thus for the second time, by laws and texts instead of fire and sword, was founded the vast community of peoples known to historians and to tradition as the Holy Altaic Roman Empire,[18] or the Holy Mediterranean and Asiatic Roman Empire,[19] which was to fill the centuries with the clamor of its renown and of its decay.

It is here, on the morning of the last day of the assembly of the Empire that the modest task of the Emperor's historian ends. Some words must be added about the man and what happened after his death, but that great convocation marked the close of the public career and the political and military achievements of the Emperor. Of course, great men survive in the influence of their work, the institutions they created, the historical or intellectual movements they set in motion. Alexis is much more than just Alexis. Still hardly a week goes by without our being reminded by some piece of research or sociological survey, or even in the newspapers or on television, of the New Alliance, the sack of Rome, the conversion of Bruince, the assembly of the City, the Holy Mediterranean and Asiatic Roman Empire, and their consequences through the ages. To follow the legend of Alexis in the minds of men would merely be to write world history over again from a slightly different angle, an onerous task that we shall leave to younger pens. All we need say here is that the Empire could not resist time: it disintegrated, it fell. This was the City's second decline, and this time it was irremediable. Constantinople had already been captured twice, once in 1204 by the Crusaders and once in 1453 by the Turks, America had been discovered, Protestantism had been born, and still the City persisted in its rites and memories, continuing to crown, in what had become a pitiful and poignant farce, the degenerate princes of the line of Alexis and Balamir. These were the famous Porphyrogenetes, descendants of the Porphyries, of whom the last, Constantine, was to die at dawn one

morning toward the end of the summer of 1925, dead drunk, out-
rageously made up, with a bullet through his head and a woman's boa
around his neck, among the moth-eaten palm trees of Monte Carlo, a
victim of *trente-et-quarante* or *chemin de fer.*

Thus empires are born, and shine forth, and die. When Alexis
ceased speaking, after determining the history of three continents for
hundreds of years, and when the tumult had somewhat died away, a
voice broken with age was heard in the assembly. It was Valerius.
The old poet suggested the Emperor be given the title of Alexis the
Great. Even before he had finished, a storm of cheering drowned his
words. Then the Emperor arose once more and asked for silence. He
seemed to have aged twenty years in the few moments since he last
spoke. The man, worn by suffering and life, by time and by power,
was beginning to emerge from the demigod. He said how moved he
was by the homage of all the nations of the Empire. But he declined
to accept it. He wanted history to speak of him only as the Father of
the Peoples, the title that had given him most happiness. Some had to
renounce and retire, others had to fight and go on fighting. He turned
to Bruince and Khubilai. He said again he was entrusting the Empire
to them, which was nothing, and its peoples, which was everything.
He went over to them and embraced them. All three, standing, wept.
As for himself, he no longer believed in the crowns bestowed by men
and was setting out for an unknown realm "where neither friends nor
treasure nor thrones are of any avail."[20] Tears ran down the rough
faces burned by the sun and winds, by dreams, by the dust of the
steppes and the salt of the sea. Logophilus said, of course, that there
had never been such pride. But Justus Dion, without actually con-
tradicting him, presents the matter differently, more moderately, and
probably more justly. He writes that the rejection of glory and the
rejection of the Empire only added more luster to both the glory of
Alexis and the glory of the Empire.

XXIII

LOSER TAKE ALL, OR

THE OTHER LIFE

 HE EMPEROR WAS NO LONGER EMPEROR. HE HAD BE-
come Alexis again. But it was impossible to escape
immediately. Every province and city in the Empire
pleaded for a visit and everywhere he was met with
enthusiasm. There are many vivid accounts of all
the celebrations in Alexis's honor, but history has
preserved above all the memory of the welcome given to him by the
Eternal City. *The Triumph of Alexis* was the theme of the fine series
of twelve Flemish tapestries commissioned in Bruges by Leo X for
his Chamber of the Sibyls in the Borgia apartments, beneath the
Raphael rooms; and now in the Vatican Museum. The fifteenth-
century idea of the Age of Alexis and of his apotheosis on the Capitol
is illustrated in naïve detail by the miniatures in the *Très Riches
Heures de l'Empereur Alexis*, a very rare work of collaboration by the
then elderly Jean Fouquet and the still young Attavante degli Attavanti, a gift from Mathias Corvin to Louis XI, preserved in the
château of Chantilly. Reading contemporary accounts, it is easy to see
why artists were tempted by the appeal to the sensuous imagination
contained in this incredible display of color and pomp. Although
Alexis had already laid power aside, he still appeared, in the words of
Justus Dion, "the most powerful man in followers, lands, and treasures who ever lived, from the time of Adam until today."[1]

It was autumn. For nearly five moons the sun had shone down on
the Eternal City and on all of Italy out of a clear sky. It was as if the
protecting planet also wanted to render a last homage to the intractable son who may have betrayed him but had also done so much for
his worship, and been inspired by him to impose on the world the idea

of a single law and one universal good. The whole population of Rome had gathered round the sacred hill where once the messenger from Asia had interrupted another ceremony.

Entering the square the Emperor was confronted with an astonishing spectacle. One hundred twenty elephants of state or war had been brought to Rome, and the moment Alexis appeared on the Capitol "they all knelt and bowed their heads before him, trumpeting as if in homage."[2] Every region and city in the Empire had sent six men and a woman to represent them. Some wore long red or blue robes, others togas or cuirasses, others hides or furs, others again colored trousers caught in around the ankles, or dalmatics of silk and purple and sparkling with precious stones. Some carried birds of prey on their wrists, or led bears or leopards, giraffes or ostriches. Treasures from temples and palaces had been escorted to the Capitol by archers and men-at-arms: the sun glinted on jewels out of Persian and Indian legend, sprays of emeralds, diadems of diamonds, fans of ivory and gold, staffs and parasols of precious wood inlaid with tortoise shell and silver, carved and jeweled weapons, rare ornaments that teams of craftsmen had spent years embellishing. All around this splendor was the brute force that protected it from ambush and envy. Every troop in the Empire had sent twelve soldiers for the Emperor's last guard of honor.

All the great dignitaries of the Empire who had taken part in the Great Assembly of the City were also there on the Capitol, come once again, one last time, to bow down before Alexis. Children sang, flowers rained down on all sides, bulls and horses were slain by the priests, blood streamed over the ground and was drunk up by the thirsty earth through the cracks the heat had made between the flagstones. The souls of the people all merged into one in the golden light, as if to tell Alexis that the dream of a whole lifetime was at last fulfilled. Just as the sun sank below the horizon, twelve imperial eagles were released into the pink and purple sky, and a great roar rose up on the hill. Then the Emperor bade farewell to his people of Rome as he had bidden farewell to his peoples of Asia and Africa, of the City and Samarkand, of Toledo and Pomposa. Alexis had decreed there should be no speeches. Words no longer meant anything; it was a celebration of silence. The Emperor just went over to an old captain of the Twelve Thousand who, many years earlier, had been one of the first to join Isidore's Conspiracy and now could not hold back his tears. Alexis put his arms around him, and it was all the peoples of the Empire that he clasped to his heart. When he went back and seated himself for the last time on his throne among the dignitaries of the Empire, he heard Logophilus murmur:

"The real sacrifice would have been to stay."

Without looking at him Alexis replied: "There is something higher than power."

"But how is one to be sure it is not oneself?"

Alexis turned toward Logophilus. The grammarian had suddenly reminded him of the very words with which Helen had once reproached him, just before the confrontation with Balamir and Simeon, when he was already thinking of relinquishing power and putting his love of meditation and repose before the good of the people and the peace of the Empire. He looked around him. Rome lay at his feet in the falling dusk. Lights were coming on one by one in the darkness. In the distance one could still just distinguish the river, the hills heavy with memories and hopes, the palaces and temples rebuilt by Hadrian, some obelisk or triumphal arch which had miraculously escaped disaster and the *tre notti dolenti*, hundreds, thousands of humble dwellings. Farther away still, beyond the horizon and the eye's reach, lay the roads of the Empire, the navies, the ports, the countless cities, the armies and merchants, villages perched on mountains or hidden among trees, all the force, all the heady murmurs of life. He was renouncing not merely power, but this whole teeming world, so rich and inexhaustible. All around him he could hear the crowd chanting his name, still hoping to dissuade him; "Alexis! Alexis!" The motionless troops only waited for one word from him to march to the ends of the earth again. One word, and Khubilai would do him homage. One word, and Logophilus would make over to him all the complicated machinery on which the destiny of the world depended. But what was the good? It was all the same—all alike and all a matter of indifference. He did not even care, as Logophilus imagined, about his own salvation.

Many writers have, of course, pointed out what a strange combination is made by Alexis's charismatic gift and this passion for silence and humility which the most famous contemporary psychoanalyst has called "the irresistible need to disappear."[3] The ceremonies on the Capitol and the second disappearance only repeat in a different key the feasts in Alexandria and the first disappearance. It is hard to avoid talking, in both cases, of a "life neurosis." This is not the place to enter into the subtle details of the various interpretations that have been put forward, historical, metaphysical, psychological, materialist, and religious. Some see here an interiorization, perhaps pathological, of the problem of time; others the presence of God; others again the interaction of social and economic forces of which Alexis was merely the plaything. Some see the phenomenon as a plain manifestation of a kind of sexual behavior dominated by withdrawal, interruption, and flight.[4] How is one to choose among so many theories? All we have attempted here is a modest essay in historical phenomenology. All it allows us to do is observe the emperor's wish to relinquish power. We can also discern the ostensible causes of his decision: his personality, the year he spent in Asia in his youth, the influence of Hadrian, the deaths of Manfred and Theodora. But the search for the underlying causes lies outside the scope of this book, which aims simply at an objective exposition of events and facts. We may just remark in passing, however, with Sir Allan Carter-Bennett, that the entire public career of the Emperor is like a brilliant interlude between two withdrawals—the first exile, and the last great rejection.

At the end of the assembly of the City Valerius had proposed in vain that the Emperor be given the title of Alexis the Great. At the very close of the ceremony on the Capitol, Bruince, Khubilai, Logophilus, and the other dignitaries of the Empire came to Alexis and implored him one last time to remain at the head of the Empire. It was then that he made his famous reply, sometimes ascribed to Saint Gregory the Great:

"I am the servant of the servants of the Empire, the humblest of the humble, of all the despicable the most to be despised."

The Emperor had had brought up to the Capitol a blind deafmute, a leper, a man condemned to death for parricide, a lame prostitute with goiter, an epileptic visionary, and a Jewish beggar called Ahasuerus, who had known every humiliation and outrage and whose travels through the world were to make him famous.[5] Alexis now gathered them around him, knelt before them, and washed their feet.[6]

Coming down from the hill after nightfall, Logophilus begged Alexis to let him at least have monuments put up in memory of the Father of the Peoples. But Alexis refused again. He remembered his son, and, apart from the masterpieces that had been dedicated to him here and there and which it was not in his power to destroy or deny, he wished for no temple, palace, marble inscription, or statue, and for no poems to his glory besides those already written by Valerius, Menalchas, and Polyphilus. This is why evidence about the Emperor is now so rare and precious. The cameo at Dresden, the three great statues in the Louvre, and the sculptures in Munich and the Metropolitan Museum in New York are almost unique.[7] But Bruince and Logophilus did not entirely give way over this. They had a fine equestrian statue of gilded bronze put up on the Capitoline Hill, a work which later inspired Donatello's monument in the Piazza del Santo in Padua to the Venetian *condottiere* Erasmo di Narni, better known as Gattamelata, and Verrocchio's statue of Bartolomeo Colleoni, in the Campo dei SS. Giovanni e Paolo in Venice. Alexis's statue now stands on a plinth after Michelangelo, between the Senator's Palace, the Capitoline Museum, the Curators' Palace, and the huge figures of the Dioscuri, at the top of a great ramp also designed by Michelangelo and ornamented with black granite tigers. But the statue of the Father of the Peoples has undergone many changes and vicissitudes. Perhaps because the collective unconscious secretly obeyed the Emperor's wish and concealed from itself the origin and meaning of the work, it was taken to be a statue of Constantine throughout the Middle Ages, and then, more recently, regarded as a representation of Marcus Aurelius. In several books the same thesis is still maintained, but there can no longer be any doubt. The grave countenance full of inner peace clearly recalls all the known likenesses of Alexis, and unmistakably expresses all we know of him. If further proof were needed, it is supplied by Valerius's last work, *The Ceremonies on the Capitol*, left unfinished at the poet's death and often quoted by Justus Dion. It contains an indirect but clear enough allusion to the equestrian statue on the Capitol, and its failure to respect the Emperor's last wishes. The content and tone of the passages in which Justus Dion refers to Valerius's poem contribute greatly to solving two of the historical riddles linked to the life of Alexis and the subject of much discussion: the statue on the Capitol, and the identity of Justus Dion. For the historian not only testifies to the erection of an equestrian statue of the Emperor, but also condemns it angrily, which might not have been surprising in Alexis himself, the author of the prohibition, but is so in the chronicler and apologist, who like Valerius, Bruince, and Logophilus, might have been expected to regard disobedience in this matter as a pious tribute and a pardonable offense. Like the evening walk in the gardens on the

Palatine Hill,[8] Justus Dion's vehemence on the subject of the statue on the Capitol has always been used as an argument by those who see the shape of Alexis himself lurking in the shade of Justus Dion.

Alexis left Rome two days after the apotheosis on the Capitol. He had taken leave of Bruince, Khubilai, Logophilus, and the rest. He passed for the last time by Hadrian's mausoleum—an enormous building, at the same time round and square, that lay by the river, opposite a bridge lined with ornamental statues; above it shone a golden sun, with a key of bronze and marble and a stake of silver. Alexis halted his little procession to meditate for a moment on what he had called "the Empire's most sacred monument." Many years later the city was visited by a dreadful plague. The pope, Saint Gregory the Great, organized prayers and other ceremonies of intercession. He himself was crossing the bridge that Alexis had ridden over when suddenly there appeared on top of the mausoleum an angel putting a flaming sword back in its scabbard. At the same moment

Medieval tapestry depicting Alexis washing feet in the Capitol (Vatican Museum).

the pontiff heard a thunderous yet kind voice saying, "Be not afraid, Gregory. I am Alexis." This vision foreshadowed the end of the plague, and the people of Rome, in their enthusiasm, renamed Hadrian's mausoleum the Castel Sant'Angelo Alessio.

The little group that accompanied Alexis left Rome by the same gate through which the Emperor and the archpatriarch had once made their solemn entry to the accompaniment of cheering crowds. Then they set out toward the north. The historian follows them a few days more, across the Sabine Hills, amidst the silence of vineyards and olive groves. They crossed the foaming waters of the Nera by the Narni bridge, with its picturesque arcades later painted by Corot. They went through Spoleto, Assisi, and Gubbio, entering the Arno valley east of Florence, to pass through the Casentino, with its beech and chestnut forests and innumerable streams, the *fiumicelli* sung by Dante. It is against this storied and bloodstained yet smiling background that the poet describes the old Emperor riding, lost in dream, among

> Li ruscelleti che de'verdi colli
> Del Casentin discendon giu' in Arno,
> Facendo i lor canali e freddi e molli.[9]

The Emperor probably spent a night either at Vallombrosa, as Milton says in *Paradise Lost*, or at Poppi, Camaldoli, or Verna, near Bibiena—Dante's "Alevernia d'Alessio"—in steep limestone country, wild and lonely, between the source of the Arno and the source of the Tiber:

> Nel crudo sasso tra Trevere ed Arno.[10]

Farther north the Apennines hung over rich Emilia, with its corn and vines and flat, monotonous landscape. At a gallop, on the fresh horses that awaited him at each staging post to speed his flight to the realms of absence, Alexis crossed the Po, avoided Pomposa, went through the sugar-loaf Euganean Hills with their orchards of apple, pear, peach, orange, and lemon. He went by Vicenza and the cypresses of Verona, all pink and red in the distance, and hastened, either by the Cadore, the Passo del Pordoï, or the Passo di Sella into the Dolomites and the Alps. A summer sun still shone over the plain. But already, in the mountains, it was winter and icy cold. Snow fell on the little band of travelers, fewer every day, for each evening Alexis would send three or four men back to Rome, Pomposa, Verona, Milan, or Como. When he reached the high peaks of the Alps he was alone with Justus Dion—or perhaps with himself, if the supposed companion was really only his double. Be that as it may, the historian describes, in the last pages of his *Chronicles*, how the two men went forward, their horses now moving at a walking pace, over the magnificent white landscape. They did not speak. Justus Dion tried to hold back his tears. Alexis had already entered that other life he had so long been waiting for. One evening before sunset the two riders came to a somber blue lake reflecting tall trees and snow-covered mountains. Alexis reined in his horse and dismounted. Justus Dion did likewise. The Emperor put his hand on his companion's shoulder and said:

"We have come to the place and the moment where our fates divide. I vanish from the world where all fades and passes away. Do you stay, to tell future generations what were our struggles and our dreams. Every man has but one life—a few years, much suffering, much sorrow, which all end in death. Tell those who come after us to believe and hope, and to do something with their brief passage on earth and among men. We have done some fine things. Let them do others, finer. Do not tell them how to act, how to think, or how to love; just tell them what we were and what we did. The others will be different and act differently. Everything about the earth is good— happiness and tears, war and peace, sun and water, indifference and passion, suffering and death. We have to believe all is well. I am not going out of scorn for life, but to live more and better. I am going because we die. Others remain—may they be blessed. Some will hate and despise me—may they be blessed. Many will think the best thing is to laugh at the world and be amused by it—may they be blessed. Some will overcome them and bend them to their law—may they be blessed. Others will arise and lay these low—may they be blessed also. May the world, and life, be blessed, and suffering and death. Just tell the world what we were and what we did. And add a little beauty to beauty, a little history to history, a little world to the world, and a little life to life."[11]

These are the last words of the Fool of God and the victor of Adrianople. Justus Dion tells us how, at the last moment, he could not restrain his tears. He wanted to follow Alexis, to go with him to the ends of the earth, to abandon him to none but death. The Emperor forbade it; the historian resigned himself. He obeyed once again, and fell on his knees on the frozen ground. The Emperor raised him up and embraced him. Then he mounted his horse and rode away without looking back. And Justus Dion, standing there motionless, watched him disappear alone into the snow and darkness, the man who for so many years, amidst pomp and splendor, had been the master of the world. Thus ended, in the eyes of men, the earthly adventures of the Emperor Alexis.

There is no text or other testimony to tell us anything more about the Emperor's life after his parting, real or imaginary, with the faithful Justus Dion. And we know nothing of his death. Several places have claimed the privilege of having sheltered him. The Black Forest; the Bavarian Alps, from the Königssee to the Tegernsee and the Starnberger See; the islands of Krk, Rab, Hvar, Korčula, and Mljet on the Dalmatian coast; Cappadocia and the Northern Sporades; the little island of Symē near Rhodes; Patmos; Bodrum (or Halicarnassus); the Cnidus peninsula, and Ephesus—all these claim, with the aid of dubious archeological evidence, to have seen him die. In a letter to Richard Wagner,[12] Louis II of Bavaria, the mad king, refers to a note of October 20, 1847, sent by his grandfather Louis I to the dancer Lola Montez. The note, which has not survived, alludes to the site of Alexis's grave as a family secret of the house of Wittelsbach. According to tradition, it stood exactly halfway between the two nightmare castles of Hohenschwangau and Neuschwanstein. But the historically minded tourist is not let off so lightly. A letter from the Bishop Juvenal to the Empress Pulcheria gives him reasons for seeking out, this time near Ephesus, another last resting place ascribed to Alexis—*Iskanderdjik kapulu*.[13] This site, too, has its allusions and arguments to support it, especially since the revelations of a German visionary, Emma Katharina Emmerich, who at the beginning of the last century said she had seen the Emperor Alexis in a dream, breathing his last in a little wooded valley and in a house unknown to her, but which more or less corresponded, as far as her halting account could convey, with the building at Ephesus.

But the best-known legend gives yet another version. According to this, the Emperor never died. He is still alive in an old deserted castle in the forest, on a high mountain surrounded by glaciers. There he sleeps, his elbow leaning on a stone table around which sit, clad in velvet and gold and transfigured by love and faith into great noblemen and a beautiful lady, the six unfortunates whose feet he bathed on the Capitoline Hill. They are all there, the blind man, the leper, the parricide, the prostitute, the epileptic, and the wandering Jew, redeemed and cured by the powers of the Emperor, deep in a splendid dream until the universal Empire returns. By that time the Emperor Alexis's white beard will be so long it will encircle the table three times. And then the Emperor will awake from his enchanted slumber and rouse his companions. Ahasuerus, the wandering Jew, will set off again over hill and dale, but changed now into a radiant archangel, riding on a tiger with the wings and beak of an eagle, to spread the good tidings of the Emperor's resurrection.

This jumble of legends and rival myths shows the marvelous power of survival of Alexis's glory. His disappearance from the sight of the crowd merely makes him present everywhere in men's hearts and imaginations. There are few great events in history in which he does not play his part. William, Harold, and swan-necked Edith all saw him on the battlefield at Hastings, lamenting that he himself had not conquered Britain.[14] He was reported as having been on the ramparts at Constantinople both times it was taken, in 1204 and 1453. He told Benvenuto Cellini to kill the constable de Bourbon outside the walls of Rome in 1527.[15] Cervantes recognized him on October 7, 1571, during the battle of Lepanto, just as the volley was fired that cost the future author of *Don Quixote* his left hand. He appeared to many of those present at the battles of Kosovo, Tannenberg, and Marignano—wherever the fate of the Old World was at stake. Often both sides laid equal claim to him. In the course of the Russo-Japanese War he appeared first to Admiral Alexeev, viceroy of Manchuria, then, during the disaster at Mukden, to Generalissimo Aleksei Nikolaevich Kuropatkin.[16] And on the eve of his encounter with Admiral Rodzhestvensky off Tsushima island, Admiral Togo, who had gone up on deck for a breath of night air, saw through the darkness the shade of Alexis walking toward him over the waves.

Not content with intervening from beyond the grave in the government of men and their destiny, Alexis also interests himself in the forces of nature. Every German child knows that when it snows it is because Frau Holle, housekeeper to the gods and goddesses, is shaking the Emperor Alexis's eiderdown out of the window. At the same time, for the Italians, he is the companion of the dreaded but beneficent witch Befana, who gives children presents to herald the return of spring. On the other side of the Latin world, the orthodox inhabitants of the Carpathians, Bucovina, and Transylvania, when they break their gaily colored eggs, painted with flowers, crosses, and diamonds and signifying the Easter resurrection, not only cry

Christos a înviat!
Adevarat a înviat!

but also invoke Alexis as symbol and immortal image of cosmic renewal: "Taiasca Capitanul Alexie!" (Long live Captain Alexis).[17] The Father of the Peoples is still present all over the surface of the globe, where countless towns, capes, mountains, villages, and hamlets derive their names from that of the Emperor: The small town of Alexain, for example, near Laval in Mayenne; Alixan, near Romanssur-Isère in the Drôme; perhaps even Alès in the Gard, though the origin of this name is disputed; anyhow, Aleksin, between Kaluga and Tula on the outskirts of Moscow; Alexikovo, between Saratov, Voronezh, and Stalingrad; Aleksine, on the Moreva; the great Aletsch glacier, in the Valais; the Ala-chan plateau on the left bank of the Hwang Ho in China; Alexandria in Piedmont, which despite the claims of those who know no better has nothing to do with the Macedonian conqueror; and finally, among many others too numerous to mention, Alassio on the Italian Riviera, between Bordighera and Finale Ligure. But above all Alexis reigns above us, in the majesty of cloudless and moonless nights. For the people of Turkey, Syria, all the Near East, and Iran, the star Alpha in the constellation of the Eagle, eleventh among the twenty brightest stars in the heavens, is "the star of Alexis."

The Holy See could not long remain indifferent to the cries of love and trust that went up everywhere to the Father of the Peoples. In a brief of 1077, the same year as Canossa, Gregory VII, perhaps one of the two or three greatest Roman pontiffs, who had admired Alexis when he was still only monk Hildebrand, pronounced the beatification of the Emperor. In 1498, Pope Alexander VI, at the entreaty of his daughter Lucrezia Borgia, performed the solemn ceremony transforming the beatification into sanctification. It was an event unheard of in the annals of the Church, the only example of a non-Christian being worshipped as a saint. Nine years later Julius II della Rovere issued a decree confirming his predecessor's decision and fixing July 17 as the feast day of Saint Alexis. And now it is to be seen in any post-office calendar on any kitchen wall.

For several centuries the people had already revered Alexis's humility and detachment from the goods of this world, and they welcomed his sanctification with rapture. One work of piety followed another, gradually exalting and finally fixing the Emperor's image. After the twenty-eight lines of the *Cantilène de sainte Eulalie* and the two hundred forty verses of the *Vie de saint Léger*, the *Vie de saint Alexis*, written in the eleventh century, is one of the oldest and most priceless treasures of French literature. It consists of one hundred twenty-five regular stanzas of five ten-syllable lines linked by assonance. The reworkings of this poem in the twelfth, thirteenth, and fourteenth centuries constitute a history of language and taste in that period. The work inspired Henri Ghéon's long-famous miracle play, *The Poor Man Under the Stairs*, in which he imagines Alexis living as a beggar after his abdication. In Byzantium at the beginning of the twelfth century, Anna Comnena's *Alexiad* ('Αλεξιάς, or rather 'Ιστορικὸν πόνημα περὶ τοῦ Αλεξίου), a historical work of fifteen volumes, in prose, is one of the soundest sources for the epic of the Emperor. From then on there sprang up innumerable versions of the "golden legend" in every country and in every language, both classical and modern. The twelfth and thirteenth centuries produced versions of the works cited above and the Greek and Latin writings of Callisthenes, Clitarchus, and Aristobulus, transcribed into Low Latin, Persian, Turkish, Arabic, the Indian languages, the dialect of Picardy, High German, the Slavic languages, Spanish, Portuguese, and Italian. And always the stress is not so much on power and glory as on the vanity of all things human. In *Das Lied des Alexis* (The Song of Alexis), by the priest Lambrecht, the Emperor makes a Jew weigh a magic jewel in the form of an eye, the gift of a sage from the Euphrates. However much gold the Jew puts in the other scale, the stone is always the heavier. Then the Jew replaces the heap of gold with a little handful of earth, and the scale with the magic eye in it immediately flies upward. The Jew explains to the Emperor the hidden meaning of the miracle. The precious stone is Alexis himself, who will never be content with all the gold in the world, but whose body, after his death, will be covered by a handful of earth. The Emperor, revolted by his own foolish ambitions, at once reforms.

Other examples: the *Historiae Alexii Magni; Alexis's Expeditions* (Αναζασις 'Αλεξίου), an imitation of Xenophon's *Anabasis;* the *Res gestae Alexii Magni e graeco translatae;* Lampidus' *Le Dict d'Alexis;* the *Iskanderkjik Nâmeh;* Firdussi's *Shâh Nâmeh*, with its many Koranic references, dedicated to Alexis; the *Sharaf Nâmeh* of Nizami, who makes Alexis a descendant of Abraham, brought up by the sage, Wilaquwratus (Philocrates?); the eighty thousand Picard alexandrines that make up the five or six versions, chiefly by Lambert Le Tors and Alexandre de Bernay, of *Li Romans d'Alexis;* the supposed *Letters of Alexis;* the *Alexii Magni iter ad Paradisum; El Libro de Alejo*, a Spanish poem of over ten thousand lines divided into two halves of seven syllables each and arranged in monorhymed quatrains on the *cuaderna via* system, in which Alexis longs to mount into the highest heaven "por veer todo el mondo como yaz o en qua manera" (to see all the earth in its disposition and order); the German romances of Rudolf von Ems and Berthold von Herbolzheim; the poem by Ulrich von Eschenbach in which, through Alexis, the author eulogizes King Ottokar, the father of his protector King Wenceslaus II of Bohemia; Master Babiloth's *Cronica Alexii des Grossen Königs* and the humanist Johannes Hartlieb's *Chronicle of Alexis;* the *Historia Alexii* by Quilico da Spoleto; and *I Nobili Fatti di Alessio Magno*, an anonymous work wrongly ascribed to Simon the Clerk. All these writings all over the world continually repeat the inexhaustible themes of Alexis's glory, embellishing them with descriptions of feasts and tourneys, scenes of love and chivalry, moral and metaphysical reflections, and sentimental digressions featuring Circe, Roxana, or the Queen of Sheba. Sometimes the Emperor is shown capturing Troy with the help of Oberon the dwarf, king of the elves, son of Julius Caesar, and twin brother of Saint George; sometimes he is seen dying of poison; meditating on Achilles' tomb; conversing with the Almighty, and on His orders going to pull out four teeth and the beard of the admiral of Babylon; descending in a glass barrel to the bottom of the sea; or flying up to heaven on an airy bark drawn by griffins. Many years later Victor Hugo referred to this last episode in *The Death of Satan.*

The Emperor's companions in these works—Sudanese, animals with the gift of speech, enchanters, and magicians—are as extravagant as the adventures and fabulous countries themselves, and are usually just the product of unbridled imagination. But here and there one suddenly catches a glimpse, in distorted and almost unrecognizable form, of Philocrates or Helen, Carradine or Bruince. And for having refused to take part in the Emperor's act on the Capitol, with words that always clung to his memory—"Sire, said he, never shall I wash the feet of these rogues"[18]—Logophilus was for centuries bracketed with figures like Ganelon and Judas. All this jumble of truth and invention is intermingled with philosophical discussions, scientific dissertations, travels to the land of Gog and Magog, Egyptian or Islamic legends, and recipes for the elixir of life. There are even parodies. The Emperor, once the associate of angels, is seen among brigands, a highway robber, and cutpurse. In 1493, just before his canonization, a comedy was performed in Lübeck entitled *Alexis Attempts to Conquer Heaven*. The dawn of the Renaissance, the end of the fourteenth and the beginning of the fifteenth centuries, saw the decline and deterioration of mysticism and the epic. But at the height of the Middle Ages the poems and romances concerning the Emperor were held in at least as high repute as the *Chanson de Roland* or the *Matière de la Bretagne*, and the *Quest of the Holy Grail* borrows several details from the legend of the Fool of God. Alexis is of the same stature as Charlemagne, Roland, King Arthur, Tristan, or Lancelot of the Lake. One of these great works in honor of the Emperor, Gauthier de Châtillon's *Alexeid*, which no one would think of reading nowadays, called forth from an enthusiastic admirer the exclamation that something had been born that was greater than the *Aeneid*: "Nescio quid maius nascitur Aeneide."

These works culminated in mystery plays, of which the most famous is *Le Vray mistère de la prise de Balkh*, and is the precursor of the tragedies of Hans Sachs, Jacques de la Taille, Alexandre Hardy, John Lyly, and, above all, of Racine's *Alexis the Great* and Metastasio's *Alexis in India*, set to music by, among others, Paisiello, Cimarosa, and Cherubini. But taken all together the works on Alexis constitute a unity in themselves that is known as the "gestae of Alexis" or the "Empire cycle." The romances that make it up copy one another, proliferate indefinitely, and stretch from Italy to Iceland, Spain to Norway, Brittany to Persia and India, Holy Russia to Damascus, Baghdad, and Isfahan. Ariosto, Rabelais, and Cervantes, who mark the end of an age, testify, by their very jests on the subject of Alexis, to the late survival of this universal popularity. Marlowe's *Alexis the Great*,[19] derived from Ruy González de Clavijo's *Vida del Gran Alejo*, transforms the Emperor into a titan of the Renaissance. Later still, Goethe's *Faust* is just another avatar of the omnipresent Emperor, the symbol at once of love and good and violence and evil, though doubled in the latter role by Balamir, transformed into Mephistopheles. The whole work is a long paraphrase, sometimes far from faithful, of Alexis's destiny. The old myth of the magician and necromancer, as told in the *Volksbuch* of Johann Spiesz, is inextricably intermingled with the memory of the Emperor, who finally becomes identified, after the most richly symbolical transmutation in world literature, with all the longings of modern man for action and salvation:

> Wer immer strebend sich bemüht,
> Den können wir erlösen.

One ought to go into more detail about the musical works inspired by the figure of Alexis, which include ballets, two great operas by Handel and Vivaldi, sonatas and concertos by Corelli, Scarlatti, and Boccherini, and the satirical verses by Heine set to music by Debussy and Reynaldo Hahn. And there is also the cinema.[20] But perhaps enough has been said to bring out the main point. Through the halo of legend and divine honors rendered to the master of the world, through the alternations of magnanimity and violence which so struck the popular imagination, through the epic of adventure and repentance, and through all the naïveté and credulity, what emerges most forcibly everywhere is the moral reflection on the vanity of vanities, on the inevitable failure of all ambition, the futility of this world, the frailty of man, repentance after wickedness, the yearning of all creatures for a supreme good always beyond the here and now, and on the fear of a God named in every tongue.

But we have not yet paid homage to the most important contributor to Alexis's glory—the greatest poet of the already declining Middle Ages and perhaps of all the Christian West between Virgil and Shakespeare. The reader will recall that Dante plunges Alexis into the deepest circle of Hell, in the well of the Malebolgi.[21] There, in a clap of thunder that shakes the universe, the archangel Michael and Virgil come at the Almighty's express command to snatch the fortunate sinner from eternal torment and bring him, together with Trajan, Justinian, and Saint Benedict, to the Paradise of Thrones and Dominations. Thus Dante also, though more magnificently than any other, gives a definitive form and perfect number to the image of Alexis that for centuries has haunted men's memories and imaginations, this golden legend of the Emperor and saint. Dante immortalizes not only Alexis's greatness and power, but also and above all his humility and renunciation, the negation of the triumphs of this world. *The Divine Comedy* sums it all up in *il gran rifiuto*—the great refusal. Power ends in rebellion against power, sin in a thirst for justice, and grandeur in dust, ashes, and a passion for the void. And this void constitutes the Emperor's other glory, the more dazzling one perhaps, and perhaps the more real.

XXIV

THE POWER AND THE GLORY

～～～～～～～～～～～～～～～～～～～～～～～～～～

WHAT SURVIVES FOR US TODAY OF THE POWER AND glory embodied in Alexis?

History is accidental necessity. It is made up entirely of hazards, coincidences that hang by a thread, armies suddenly held up by storm or snow, negligent or ingenious generals, unlooked-for conversations, unexpected encounters or deaths, plots successful or foiled, outlaws who escape and runaways who are caught, temperaments and inspirations that miraculously correspond to the needs and hopes of a place or age. But once history is inscribed on the unfolding hours, days, years, and centuries, it is more immutable than the course of rivers or the outline of volcanoes. Transparent and shifting as liberty, it becomes, as it unfolds, more immovable than nature. God himself can do nothing to change it. Yet the future will uncover now one face of it, now another. Thus, as Justus Dion points out, the historian's work makes him more powerful than God. For God is master of the future only. History is a second creation, and it is the work of man, who alone can play with the past and revive it by his art: "The future belongs to God, but the past belongs to history."

Each of us carries within him all the world's past, and we find there only what we put in it. We create our own history according to our class and tastes, our education and heredity, our time and the circles we move in. Especially since Marx and Freud, it is clear that objectivity in history is a mirage that the traveler over the deserts of bygone ages, thirsty for truth and certainty, can never reach. The crisis over historical objectivity is but one of many aspects of the crisis over truth. It is not history that makes the historian, but the reverse, and no historian does anything but give birth to his own universe. It is in this sense that the greatest of the historians of the

Empire has presented the legend of Alexis as first and foremost the symbol and reflection of our own hopes and dreams.[1] Each culture, each age, and each different mind will modify the slant and the interpretation, putting the stress on Thaumas or Gandolphus, Bruince or Logophilus, violence or saintliness, continuity or renewal, imperial order or the rejection of greatness.

The historian who has devoted his life to the glory of the Empire finds the image of the Emperor gradually merging with all men and things. Little by little he makes his way into men's minds and hearts, slips into their houses, between the pages of books, and suddenly appears in our inmost depths. World history is marked forever by the flashing trajectory, from the forest of Balkh and the brothels of Alexandria to the Capitol and the Dolomites, of the Fool of God and the victor of Adrianople. But in the world that actually surrounds us, it is impossible not to see and feel, behind each tree and each dwelling, in squalor and in beauty, the invisible presence of the captain and saint. There is no need to try to make him come alive again, however clumsily. One has only to turn one's gaze away from the turmoil of vanity and look around one and in oneself to discover, still living, clear but hidden, like the rabbit in the children's puzzle, hidden among the cabbages, the radiant yet ambiguous image of the Emperor Alexis.

Accompanied as usual by his brilliant train, with his trumpeters and pages, priests and warriors, poets and courtiers, the bits and bridles and helmets goldly gleaming, the purple cloaks floating in the wind, the foam-flecked horses, the castle in the distance between the cypresses and hills already blue with evening, his greyhounds and Moors lost in the crowd among the halberds and the masts of ships themselves only guessed at, the Emperor rides on one last time through the splendors of memory and imagination. A glory, a dim halo, an almost imperceptible radiance floats about his head. If you stand on tiptoe you can see on his right, above an angel-musician, Hadrian, all in white, and the Empress Theodora, like a haughty madonna. And there is Helen[2] calm and gentle as ever, between Isidore and Philocrates, a Jester with his cap, the mighty Logophilus, and, incomparable in his majesty, slightly larger than those about him, who obviously revere him, Bruince, the future pontiff. Nor is Carradine far to seek, with his red beard beginning to turn white, less at ease on horseback than on the deck of a galley. Oh, and there is Valerius, between Menalchas and the Polititian, the latter swelling, as usual, with the vast projects seething in his bald head. Behind, Polyphilus, Philontes, Aristo, Martian, and all the rest, with their strange coiffures and one hand on a book or raised heavenward. The procession has almost disappeared. It is about to turn the corner of the wall where the fresco ends. But wait! Up there, on the winding path, under the threatening clouds, one can just make out Arsaphes, Basil the Great, Thaumas, and Gandolphus, risen from the shades. And there—no, there, lower down, right at the bottom, on two fiery prancing steeds, side by side, wild and somber, are the Kha-Khan of all the Oïghurs and the boy Khubilai. The one great shade that is absent is that of Justus Dion. The historian effaces himself behind the history he tells. For a few moments longer the faint noise of the hoofs and the voices, the faint glow of the colors, hangs lingering in the air. Then it fades and vanishes into the darkness falling slowly over the path, the hills, the deer pursued by hounds, the strayed peacocks, and the cypresses. The stage is empty. It is as if the whole story, with its din, its characters, its familiar memories, had gone to join all other vanished kingdoms. . . . Where have they gone, where are they, crushed by the insatiable present, the kingdoms lost forever, the Ninevehs and Babylons, the Memphises and Lagashes, Uruks and Urs, Elams and Larsas, Sumers and Agades, Kadeshes and Karkemishes? They live in our dreams and memories, our trips into the forest, our long swords, our childish passions and paradises, our vanished hopes. Life has passed over them as it passed over the Empire. Where are they, all those delights, our expectations, our mad passions, our wild ambitions? Life has swept them away as it swept away the Emperor, as it swept away the Empire. But we keep them all in our hearts. Art, religion, culture, history raise a frail barrier in the minds of the living against the abysms of death, passing time, oblivion. The dead have no life but in us. There would be nothing left of Alexander and Caesar, Virgil and Dante, if we ceased to think of them. All that power and genius, all that knowledge and glory would disappear at a blow. And if we stopped thinking of and loving Alexis, there would be nothing left of him. It would be as if the vast Empire that ruled the world had never existed.

ONESSA—THE CITY—AQUILEUS—ROME
1967–1971

NOTES

BIBLIOGRAPHY

INDEXES

NOTES

Chapter II

1. Gibbon's *Rise of the Empire* remains the best study of the Empire's origins. Also to be read with pleasure, especially on the Hiram Bingham and Heinrich Schliemann expeditions, is C. W. Ceram's amusing *Des dieux, des tombeaux, des savants* [Gods, Graves and Scholars] (Plon, 1952), a history of vanished civilizations presented in terms of those who discovered them.

2. See the excellent article by Max and Moritz Struwwelpeter in *Zeitschrift für Geschichtswissenschaft und historische Forschung* (Berlin), vol. XXII, pp. 722–791.

3. The best introduction to the earliest philosophies of the Empire is Bertrand Russell's now slightly outmoded but still classic study, *Hermenides and Paraclitus* (Oxford University Press, 1936).

4. See *Histoire de la Philosophie*, vol. I of *L'Encyclopédie de la Pléiade*, ed. Raymond Queneau, pp. 117–118 and 123–126.

5. *L'Empire de l'Aigle et du Tigre* has just appeared in the series *Les Grandes Oeuvres de l'histoire*, which already includes volumes on Greece and the *Iliad*, on the India of the Mahabharata and the Ramayana, on the Slavs and the story of Igor's campaign, on Sumer and Gilgamesh, and on Persia and the Shah Nameh.

Chapter III

1. See the Marquis de Custine's letters and René Grousset on travelers from the East in the Empire before Basil the Great.

2. Justus Dion, *Histories*, I, 176.

3. Various modern travelers have said this custom still exists in the area between Dyushambe (formerly Stalinabad) and Mazar-i-Sharif. (See *The New Yorker*, Jan. 22, 1967.)

4. Corneille, *Arsaphes and Heloise*, act 5, scene 3. For the interest of scholars it is interesting to note Dryden's famous rephrasing of these great lines.

    HELOISE

    I begged, sir, that you'd speak with me no more.
    Your presence mines a courage weak before.
    That converse which should be the soul's delight
    Can only worsen Eloisa's plight.
    And if she suffers, how is it with you?

What pain's the less for being one of two?
Be satisfied you've lived to see my shame.
I own your power, own you a conqueror's name
Which bids you quench, not feed, an inauspicious flame.

ARSAPHES
Full well I knew the woe you'd work my heart,
But who seeks death must seek the fatal dart.
Since Eloisa's everlasting hate
Shows me my fate scorns me, I scorn my fate.
Yet, if death's pangs may any mortal move,
Take, with my latest breath, immortal love.

HELOISE
Nay, sir, to end your days you are not free.
My forebears and your own posterity
Alike the same severe commandment give.
The City claims you: Arsaphes must live.

ARSAPHES
Let all die with me, madam. What care I
Whose footsteps tread the earth wherein I lie?
Your fathers cannot rise from out the grave,
And, resurrected, who knows but they'd have
Reason to curse the offspring of my race
Unfit to do meet honor to their place?
No, love's sun set, all else is vanity.
One brief, warm touch of live felicity
Is more than icy aeons of proud eternity.

Chapter IV

1. On religious prostitution in the time of Arsaphes and Basil the Great see an interesting chapter (VII) in *Les Courtisanes dans la société*, by H. Baer and P. Faure (Ch. Bourgeois, 1967).
2. See Montesquieu, *Cahiers*, CXXI, and *L'Esprit des Lois*, ch. VII; Voltaire, Letters LXXII and DXXI; and Stendhal's famous allusion—referring also to papal Rome—in his letter to Balzac, Oct. 30, 1840.
3. See especially "Routes, paysages, économie," *Diogène*, 208 (summer, 1963), and "Politique des communications: un exemple . . .," *Diogène*, 229 (fall, 1968).

Chapter V

1. For details see Otto Rank, *Der Mythus des Todes des Helden* (Munich and Vienna, 1909), ch. VI; Oskar Adler, *Glück und Ende des Feldherren Arsaphos* (Leipzig, 1932); and *Ucheniye zapiski Leningradskogo gosudarstvennogo ordena Lenina Universiteta* (ser. istor. nauk), CXI.

2. *Zeitschrift für Geschichtswissenschaft und historische Forschung*, vol. X, pp. 9–37.
3. Valerius, *Amores*, Book III.
4. Justus Dion, *Histories*, III, 27.
5. Justus Dion, *Histories*, IV, 54.

Chapter VI

1. The theory that there was some emotional, and even homosexual, relationship between Basil and Thaumas has been vigorously maintained, especially in England and the United States. See Algernon Queen, *The Sexual Background of a Historic Friendship* (Oxford University Press, 1954), and note to p. 64 below.
2. The theory of a homosexual relationship between the emperor and the high priest is paralleled by the myth, for which no conclusive proof has been offered, of a love affair between Thaumas and Ingeburgh. The latest research seems to effectively dispose of this gratuitous suggestion.

Chapter VII

1. See René Grousset, *Les Barbares* (Payot, 1952).

Chapter VIII

1. See the Comte de Saint-Amarante, "Lettres d'amour et d'affaires: Ingeburgh, Thaumas, Hélène," *La Revue des Deux Mondes* (April, 1879), and Nico Epistolos, *Thaumas's Political Correspondence*, vol. II of *Annals of the Faculty of Letters of the University of Athens*, pp. 87–89.
2. Justus Dion, *Histories*, XXXII, 21.
3. For a more or less complete bibliography see Igor Fedorovsky, *The Hero and the Traitor*. See also an undeservedly neglected play by Villiers de L'Isle-Adam, *Le Procès de Siméon* [The Trial of Simeon].
4. By J.-J. Pauvert (Paris, 1969).
5. This work, though full of violent invective, contains some of the finest writing on love in French literature. Many attribute it to Louis Aragon, but this has not been proved.
6. Justus Dion, *Histories*, XLIX, 71.

Chapter IX

1. The whole aspect of this area has been altered by the recent construction of a hydroelectric dam at Novokarkaralinsk. There is an interesting series of articles that mention the ancient forest of Balkh, with many references to Alexis, in *Le Monde*, Feb. 2–9, 1968 (Michel Hubert-Michel, "Histoire, milieu, développement").

2. Sigmund Freud, *Psychopathologie des historischen Daseins* (Vienna, 1902). This work is almost unknown, and a translation would be welcome.

3. *True Mystery* . . . , c. 1211–1283.

Chapter X

1. The port of Mursa in Asia Minor is not to be confused with a town of the same name on the Drava on the borders of Illyria and Pannonia, famous for the victory of Constantius II over the usurper Magnentius in A.D. 351.

2. True, the Greeks occupied a rather special position. Although they were foreigners, the fact that Greek was the Empire's official language gave them something of a privileged status.

3. *Letters from Philocrates to Isidore*, XXI, 7.

4. Victor Delbos compares the character of Alexis with that of Spinoza. Both suffered from *fluctatio animi*, both summoned up against it the ideas of necessity and unity (see *Les Spinozistes*, ch. III, p. 132).

5. Professor Weill-Pichon puts his age at twenty-eight; Sir Allan Carter-Bennett puts it at twenty-four or even twenty-three.

6. They appear as "Alexis Positions I, II, III, IV, V, and VI" in the famous classifications of erotic positions established by Krafft-Ebing, Havelock Ellis, and Kinsey.

7. Several authors categorically deny that Alexis was initiated into the cult of the sun, and regard the various texts used in support of that theory as apocryphal. Their strongest argument is that sun worship had died out by Alexis's time. A good deal has been written, much of it polemical, on whether it might have survived in various religious centers. Jacques Benoist-Méchin, who has already published many remarkable biographies in the series "The Longest Dream in History," is working at present on a volume to be called *Alexis ou le rêve couronné* [Alexis or the Dream Crowned], in which he hopes to resolve the problem once and for all.

Chapter XI

1. *Letters from Philocrates to Helen*, XI, 3.

2. Among those who see Philocrates as an agent of Basil and Gandolphus are Taine, in his *Études d'histoire et de littérature;* Renan, *La Réforme intellectuelle et morale;* Maurice Barrès, *Le Roman de l'énergie nationale.*

3. See *Letters from Philocrates to Helen*, XI, 7, 8, and 13, and XII, 2.

4. Lampidus, *The Story of Alexis*, trans. G. Lewes, 1847.

5. Barbey d'Aurevilly: *Alcibiade, Alexis, Lauzun, Brummell, ou du Dandysme dans l'histoire.*

6. Writers as different as Bustos Domecq, Gervasio Montenegro, Macedonio Fernandez, and Don Isidro Parodi maintain that one of Jorge Luis Borges's most famous short stories, "The Lottery of Babylon," is based on the lotteries organized by Alexis in Alexandria.

7. The first is classical Arabic, the second vernacular. Some think our word *macabre* comes from the Arabic *qabr* (tomb).

Chapter XII

1. Roger Caillois, in *Le Mythe et l'homme* [Myth and Man] (Gallimard, 1938), speaks of the period of "occultation" or eclipse that the hero always goes through prior to his time of trial and eventual triumph (p. 199). As examples he gives Dionysus at Nysa, Apollo when he was shepherd to Admetus, Oedipus before he met the Sphinx, Achilles among the women of Skyros, Vautrin in prison, and, in real life, Alexis's retirement to the East. Other examples readily occur to one, from Julian the Apostate, Buddha, and Jesus to Joan of Arc and General de Gaulle.
2. The Petra manuscripts were acquired in 1962 by the Robert Garrett Oriental Collection, Princeton University Library.
3. See above, ch. III, p. 28, and ch. IX, p. 94.
4. *La Divina Commedia, Inferno,* Canto XXXIII.
5. There is a vast but often superficial body of work on this fundamental element of Tao philosophy. The reader should consult the works of J. J. L. Duyvendak and Paul Demiéville; *L'Esprit du Tao*, by Jean Grenier; and Liu Kia-huai's translation of the Tao Tê Ching itself, with a preface by Etiemble. There are various allusions to Alexis in Karl Sigmund von Seckendorff's novel, *Das Rad des Schicksals oder die Geschichte Dschuang Dsïs*. As an introduction to Buddhism, see Alexandra David-Neel, *The Buddhism of Buddha;* F. Huang, *Buddhism from India to China;* A. K. Coomaraswamy, *Hinduism and Buddhism.*
6. See Marc Bloch, *Les Rois thaumaturges, passim,* and especially the chapter on "Alexis and the Development of the Supernatural Character Attributed to Royalty," pp. 51–76, 170–176, and 418–419.
7. Some texts say she was a Circassian.
8. It has been suggested, but only on the basis of doubtful evidence, that her name was Tamar.
9. Sir Allan Carter-Bennett sees in "deep and unsealed" a reference to the temple tombs.
10. Trans. R. Graves.

Chapter XIII

1. A recent analysis of the water of the Nephta showed a high iron content. See *Bulletin de la Société d'histoire et de géographie de l'Empire,* III (1969), pp. 227–244.
2. See above, ch. X, p. 106.
3. There is a poem on the collapse of the Empire and the blinding of Isidore that is often attributed to Alexis, but the text, which exists only in a French version, has been revealed through an anachronism as the work

of the Franco-American poet and diplomat Saint-Léger Léger, author of
Éloges and *Vents*.
4. The extreme cold referred to by Justus Dion and other extant sources
has cast doubt on whether Alexis and Philocrates really met in Samarkand
or Bukhara, where the climate is quite mild, or farther to the south, where
it is more rigorous. The Hindu Kush, Pamir, Karakoram, or even, farther
east, the Altai mountains have all been suggested, but the problem is so
far unresolved. See *Trudy Instituta, istorii, arkheologii i etnografii Aka-
demii Nauk Kazakh., Tadzhik., Azerb., Turkim. i Uzkm. S. S. R.*, XXIII
(1969), pp. 27–61.
5. For the complete text see N. R. F., Paris, 1953.
6. Regnar Soszla-Sczimonovski's *Foreigners as Rulers* studies not only the
case of Alexis, but also those of Alexander the Great, Stilicho, Theodoric,
Mazarin, Napoleon, and the Greek and English royal families.

Chapter XIV

1. The phrase, which is often attributed to Mao Tse-tung, really belongs
to Philocrates, from whom Mao Tse-tung probably borrowed it. See the
article, "Tung Fang Hung" [The East Is Red], *People's Daily* (Feb. 26,
1966), and the curious allusion to "Alexis the pioneer" in a pamphlet in
honor of Chairman Mao published in Tiranë in 1968.
2. See B. and B. Twin, *Doubles in History* (Amphitryon Press, 1966),
pp. 66–99.
3. See above, ch. V, p. 41.
4. See Renan's *Vie d'Alexis*, Calmann-Lévy, *Oeuvres Complètes*, vol. IV,
p. 356.
5. The iconography of Helen and Alexis is inexhaustible. The best lists are
in *The Painters of Alexis* (Skira, 1962) and *Corpus des Peintures his-
toriques* (C.N.R.S., 1957–1968).
6. The fresco is now in a very bad state of deterioration. It is to be hoped
that the plans for restoring it, announced at various times by UNESCO
and Italy's Soprintendenza alle Gallerie ed alle Opere d'Arte, may soon be
set in motion to avert what would be an irreparable loss to the history of
Western art and to history itself.
7. Baldassare Peruzzi built the Farnesina on the banks of the Tiber between
1508 and 1511, for the banker Agostino Chigi, "the Magnificent," who
ruled over trade with the East. It contains works by Raphael and his
pupils, and is now the seat of the Accademia dei Lincei in the Via della
Lungara.
8. *Remembrance of Things Past*, trans. C. K. Scott Moncrieff (Chatto and
Windus), vol. IX, *The Captive*, pt. I, pp. 249–250.
9. Justus Dion, *Chronicles*, XX, 76.
10. Victor Hugo, "Naissance de Gavroche," in *Choses vues*.
11. A. W. Grock and Max Van Emden, "Jester, Trickster, Hamster," *American Anthropologist*, vol. 58 (1956), p. 503.

12. See above, ch. XI, 114–115.
13. Émile Bréhier, *Mélanges d'histoire et de philosophie* (P.U.F., 1959), p. 87.

Chapter XV

1. See above, ch. VII, p. 69.
2. See René Grousset, *L'Empire des steppes*, and Marcel Brion, *La Vie des Huns*.
3. Quoted above, ch. XIV, p. 176.
4. Justus Dion, *Chronicles*, XXXI, 32.
5. See *Actes des Troisièmes Journées du College de philosophie, de sociologie et d'histoire*, "Puissance et charisme dans l'Empire d'Alexis."

Chapter XVI

1. The present town of Székesfehérvár, Hungary, probably owes its name to a distant memory of the gathering of the barbarians in Asia.
2. American and English scholars have found references to ships belonging to Bruince's father in various documents and in stone and clay inscriptions.
3. *The State and Revolution* [Gosudarstvo i revolyutsiya] (1917), p. 31.
4. *L'Art de la guerre par principes et par règles* (1748).
5. *Essai de tactique générale* (1779).
6. *Vom Kriege* (posthumous).
7. *Die Geschichte der Kriegskunst im Rahmen der politischen Geschichte* (1919–1925).
8. *The Mind of the Army* [Mozg armii] (1929).
9. *Thoughts on War* (1944); *Strategy* (1955).
10. The scene is the subject of a painting by Géricault in Aragon's novel *La Semaine Sainte*.
11. Both Diderot, in his *Lettre sur les aveugles*, and Voltaire, in the entry "Aveugle" in the *Dictionnaire philosophique*, question whether Isidore was really blind, suggesting he had recovered his sight but said nothing about it so as to be able to use it to good purpose when the opportunity arose.
12. Justus Dion, *Chronicles*, XLIII, 27.
13. See above, ch. VII, p. 70.

Chapter XVII

1. Private collection.
2. See Maurice Rheims, *La Vie étrange des objets*, for the history of Alexis's letter to Balamir. On its adventures in the seventeenth century, see Paul Morand's book on Fouquet and Marcel Pagnol's on the Iron Mask.
3. See above, ch. V, pp. 44–46.

4. Renan, *La Réforme intellectuelle et morale*, p. 139.
5. See above, ch. XII, pp. 138–139. See below for the end of the story.

Chapter XVIII

1. See above, ch. IV, pp. 37–38, and ch. VII, p. 66.
2. Traditions vary on this subject. Some include 6 and 13 as "perfect numbers."
3. The number of divisors has always been important in mathematical philosophy. Plato, in the *Laws* (737e–738b), fixes the ideal population of the city at the strange figure of 5,040 households, because 5,040 is divisible by all numbers from 1 to 10 and by 49 others.
4. Readers may pursue this question in the monumental *Mathématiques de l'Empire*, by Jean-Claude Abreu and Macedonio Fernandez. There are also some interesting passages on Alexis in Léon Brunschvicg's *Étapes de la philosophie mathématique*.
5. Some authors arrive at a total of 122 or 123, including Corsica and Palestine, which for fiscal and other reasons (see ch. XXI, p. 310) were subject to special arrangements.
6. There is a detailed reconstruction of one of these ships in the Maritime Museum at Greenwich.
7. See above, ch. XIV, pp. 162–163.
8. *Le Figaro* (July 11, 1970).
9. Chamfort, *Maximes et pensées*, no. 525 (Livre de poche), p. 149.
10. See the remarkable historical and archeological note by Prof. Robert Weill-Pichon in the *Blue Guide* on the Empire.
11. Henri Focillon, *L'Art de l'Empire*, p. 85.
12. But recently it was reported in the *Times Literary Supplement* and in *Le Monde* that colored frescoes had been discovered that were thought to date from the Empire. An international team is soon to report on its investigations.
13. Georg Christoph Lichtenberg (1742–1799), *Aphorisms*, 127.
14. Conference on "History and Truth," held by the International Institute of Philosophy, Heidelberg, 1959.
15. On the influence of the two philosophers up to Aquinas, Bacon, and Descartes, see Jean-François Revel's *Histoire de la philosophie occidentale*.
16. Trans. J. Heinz.
17. Justus Dion, *Chronicles*, XXXIV, 21.

Chapter XIX

1. Justus Dion, *Chronicles*, LXI, 56.
2. See above, ch. I, p. 5.
3. *Essais*, III, 13.
4. See above, ch. XV, p. 193.
5. See above, ch. XVIII, pp. 246–247.

6. See above, ch. VII, pp. 67–68.
7. "Vom Wesen des Grundes und vom Kaiser Alexis," *Zeitschrift für philosophische Forschung*, vol. XXXII (1953), p. 57.
8. Hegel, *Vorlesungen über die Philosophie der Weltgeschichte*, addendum to §451.

Chapter XX

1. See above, ch. XIX, p. 275.
2. The fashion in painting and the decorative arts for elephants bearing obelisks or towers dates from this time. It was revived in Renaissance Rome and the Baroque period.
3. *Zafir Nameh*, IV, 11–15.
4. *Histoire de la littérature de l'Empire* (N.R.F., 1945), pp. 78, 134, 249.
5. At the end of his life Thomas Mann said *Death in Venice* had been influenced by Alexis's feelings toward Pomposa.
6. President de Brosses: "With great difficulty I read something of Dante on Alexis and Hadrian. . . . I must admit Dante pleases me rarely and tires me often." Flaubert: "One dares not say how dreary one finds that interminable description of the meeting between the emperor and the patriarch. This is a work of its time and not of all the ages."
7. See above, ch. XVII, pp. 229–230.
8. Amédée Thierry suggests it was August 14.
9. The event provides the setting for Julien Gracq's novel, *Le Rivage des Syrtes*.
10. See below, ch. XXII, p. 319.
11. Some Chinese sources call Ho K'iu-ping "the flying general," apparently in an effort to appropriate some of the prestige that the description enjoyed through a large part of Asia.
12. See Ch'oe Ch'aewon and Yi Chungu, *Choson myong 'innok* [Biographies of Eminent Personages in the History of Korea], and Futo-no-Yasumaro, *Kojiki* [Book of Ancient Things]. For Japanese representations of the invasion attempt, see Shizuya Fujikake, "On the Scroll Painting of the Mongol Invasion," *Kokka* (1921), nos. 371–379.
13. Now Fethiya, in Lycia.
14. See C. W. Ceram, *Des dieux, des tombeaux, des savants*, especially pp. 149–157 and 176–192. This work, almost in the form of a novel, should be regarded with caution. It has many inaccuracies, and the author's fancy sometimes runs away with him.
15. The modern Elath, on the Gulf of Aqaba.
16. SS Colonel Otto Skorzeny began a joint German-Japanese search for Balamir's treasure, a project in which both Hitler and Martin Bormann took great interest. It was abandoned when Colonel Skorzeny and his parachutists were sent to Italy to try to set Mussolini free.
17. The title of *mikado*, which originally meant the royal palace, not the emperor himself, is much more recent.

18. The fresco in the Campo Santo in Pisa (perhaps by Francesco Traini, but the attribution is debated), which depicted Balamir's funeral, was the chief victim of the air raid on July 27, 1944. Only the *sinopia*, or sketch, discovered under the debris, remains to give some idea of the original huge composition.

Chapter XXI

1. Abul Ghazi Bahadur Khan, *Chronicle*. See also the *Voyages* of Jean du Plan Carpin.
2. See above, ch. XVIII, p. 242.
3. Ch. XVIII, pp. 250–252.
4. See René Le Senne for a detailed analysis of Alexis's character. It is probable that he was closer to cyclothymia, perhaps to schizothymia or schizophrenia, than to the paranoia usually met with among emperors and other leaders.
5. Justus Dion's references to Logophilus and his views on the Emperor are confirmed by a scandalous but amusing tale called *Nights of the Empire* or *The Banquet of Logophilus*, probably the work of an Alexandrian or Syrian priest, which has been called one of the first novels in the history of literature.
6. See *The Will to Power*.

Chapter XXII

1. Justus Dion, *Chronicles*, XXXVII, 22; LV, 4; LXXI, 13.
2. It has been said he was the agent of Alexis's enemies—the priests, the barbarians, or the Pomposan merchants.
3. See the famous sonnet by Philippe Berthelot.
4. Recent studies, founding their argument on the observations of Justus Dion and other chroniclers, have suggested she may have died of cancer.
5. Stendhal's *Promenades dans Rome* describes pictures and statues of young women suffering horrible tortures or with seven swords piercing their hearts.
6. The question of whether Napoleon really existed has been examined by Whately in *Historical Doubts on Napoleon Bonaparte*, mentioned by J. L. Borges. In France itself, Charles Philippon in about 1840 reduced Napoleon to a solar myth.
7. Scattered references to the archpatriarch, and different views about his teachings, can be found by the learned reader in Bossuet, Voltaire, Pascal, and Marx.
8. Voltaire, Alexis's Prayer in *Traité sur la Tolérance*.
9. On the various aspects of the Empire after Alexis, aside from general works by Arnold Toynbee, Ferdinand Lot, Henri Pirenne, and André Malraux, see the more specialized works of P. Faure, *Vie économique et sociale à la fin de l'Empire*, and H. Baer, *Histoire de la littérature de l'Em-*

pire après Alexis. The author of the present work proposes, in so far as time and strength allow, to devote the years from now until about 1986 or 1987 to bringing out a history of the Empire in twenty-seven volumes, to be published by the Presses Universitaires de France.

10. See above, ch. XIX, p. 268.
11. René Grousset, *L'Empire des steppes*, p. 366.
12. Marco Polo, in Grousset, *op. cit.*, pp. 379–380.
13. *Ibid.*
14. *Ibid.*
15. *Ibid.*
16. Justus Dion, *Chronicles*, LXXXII, 6.
17. See above, ch. XVIII, pp. 256–257.
18. *Altaic* refers to the origins both of the peoples of the Empire and of the barbarians. Balamir was descended from tribes of Mongol origin who had long lived as nomads east of the Altai, whence had also come, many centuries earlier, the ancestors of the Porphyries and the Venostae (see ch. I, p. 7).
19. This name, adopted later by Pirenne, Burckhardt, and Toynbee, was given currency by Ranke and Mommsen, who probably borrowed it from the Benedictines of Saint-Maur and the learned Bollandists.
20. Justus Dion, *Chronicles*, CXXII, 27. The same words are attributed to Alexis in Firdausi's *Shah Nameh* (Book of Kings) and Hamd Allah al Mustawfi's *Zafir Nameh.*

Chapter XXIII

1. Justus Dion's actual expression is "from the golden age after the oak born of the eagle." See ch. I, p. 6.
2. Justus Dion, *Chronicles*, *CXXXIII*, 4; *Zafir Nameh*, III, 106.
3. "The Case of Alexis," Seminar on Diachrony, p. 1239.
4. See Dr. Annette Chardon-Cohen, *La Signification sexuelle d'un épisode historique: Alexis et la coïtus interruptus.* See also "névrose d'abandon" and "complexe d'Alexis" in *Vocabulaire de la psychanalyse*, by J. Laplanche and J.-B. Lefèvre-Pontalis (P.U.F.).
5. See Isaac Laquedem, *Alexis and the Legend of the Wandering Jew.*
6. This strange epilogue to the ceremony on the Capitol has been doubted by some, but there is much evidence to show that it actually happened. It is commemorated in countless works of art.
7. Three or four private collections have busts of Alexis that are of doubtful authenticity—e.g., the Hôtel Lambert on the Île Saint-Louis in Paris, and the Château de Ferrières, not far from the capital.
8. See above, ch. XXII, p. 332.
9. *Divina Commedia, Inferno*, Canto XXX, 64.
10. *Divina Commedia, Paradiso*, Canto II, 106.
11. Justus Dion, *Chronicles* (end), CXLIV, 12.
12. Dated April 27, 1869.

13. *Alexis* seems often to have been taken for a diminutive of *Alexander*, hence the suffix *djik*. The *al* in both names was taken by Arabs and Turks as a definite article; *-exander* became by distortion *Iskander*.
14. A somewhat vague figure in the Bayeux Tapestry is now thought to be a timid representation of Alexis.
15. Benvenuto Cellini, *Memoirs*, I, CXVIII, 22.
16. Letters from the Empress Alexandra Feodorovna to Grigori Efimovich Rasputin, March 22, 1905.
17. The Romanian fascist Iron Guard adapted this formula to perpetuate the memory of their leader, Corneliu Zelea Codreanu, after he was executed.
18. Lampidus, *The Story of Alexis*, trans. G. Lewes, 1847.
19. *Alexis the Great* was performed in Paris in 1966, with Laurence Olivier as the Emperor.
20. See above, ch. XII, p. 139, and ch. XIV, p. 175. One should also mention Cecil B. De Mille's "spectacle" *The King of Kings*.
21. See above, ch. XII, pp. 138–139.

Chapter XXIV

1. *The Glory of the Empire*, ch. XXIV, pp. 354–355.
2. In real life (see ch. XIX, p. 272) Helen never met Theodora.

BIBLIOGRAPHY

Out of the vast literature devoted to the Empire, we can only present here a very selective choice of essential works. The reader wishing to delve more deeply should refer to:

Évariste Martin-Clampier: *Bibliographie générale de l'Empire* (1966).

A. GENERAL WORKS

Sir Allan Carter-Bennett: *General History of the Empire* (7 volumes).
Robert Weill-Pichon: *Histoire de l'Empire*.
Bjöersen Bjöersenson: *Economic and Social Foundations of the Empire, From Basil the Great to Alexis*.
Helmuth Ritter: *Geschichte des Kaisertums*.
A 27-volume *History of the Empire* by the author of the present work is in preparation.

B. SOURCES

On the origins of the Empire:

The Empire of the Eagle and of the Tiger (selection of epic narratives).
Valerius: *The Onessiad, The Creation of the World, The Birth of the Empire, Loves*.
Archimandrites: *Fragments*.
Hermenides: *Works*.
Paraclitus: *Works*.

On Arsaphes:

Polyphilus: *Arsaphes and Heloise*.

On the reign of Basil:

The Master of Avignon (Mercutio da Verona): *Sonnets and Songs*.
The Chronicler of Famagusta: *Rélation de la vie, actions et déportements des princes en la rencontre de l'isle de Chypre déclarant tous les moyens tenus en icelle* (translated by Jacques Amyot).
Thaumas: *Works*.

Helen and Thaumas: *Correspondence.*
Philocrates and Isidore: *Correspondence.*

On the barbarians:

Monghol-un ni'utcha tobtchi'an ("Secret History of the Mongols").

On Alexis:

1. ALEXANDRIAN PERIOD:
   Helen and Philocrates: *Correspondence.*
   Lampidus: *Le Dict d'Alexis* (translated by E. Taillefert and J. Chenu).
   Turolde: *Alexis and Vanessa.*
2. CROSSING THE DESSERT:
   Manuscrits de Petra, Manuel des Enterrés, Connaissance d'Alexis (trans-
   lated by Paul Claudel), *Exile* or *Poem of Persia.*
3. APOGEE OF THE EMPIRE:
   Alexis: *The Banquet of the Soul.*
   Logophilus: *Plan for a Universal Calendar, Treatise on Versification,
   Treasury of the Language of the Empire.*
   Anonymous: *Nights of the Empire, or The Sigh of Logophilus.*
   Valerius: *Op. cit.*
   Philontes: *Works.*
   Aristo: *Works.*
   Isidore: *The Pleasures of Living.*
   Martian: *Summa, Contemplations.*
   Azkiri: *Book of Wisdom and Folly.*
   The Polititian: *Treatise on the Government of the Mind.*
   Polyphilus: *Tragedies.*
   Menalchas: *Tragedies.*
   Procopius of Caesarea: *History of the Wars of the Emperor Alexis.*
   Nicéphore Blemnydes: *Chronographie de l'Empire.*
   Georges Pachymère: *Annales de l'Empire.*
   Firdausi: *Shâh Nâmeh.*
   Hamd-Allah-al-Mustawfi: *Zafir Nâmeh.*
   Anonymous: *Iskanderdjik Nâmeh.*
   Nizami: *Sharaf Nâmeh.*
   Finally, the most basic source for Alexis's reign, and in fact the whole
   history of the Empire, is naturally:
   Justus Dion: *History* and *Chronicles.*

C. STUDIES

On the art:

Fulgence Tapir: *Annales universelles de la peinture, de la sculpture et de
l'architecture de l'Empire* (1908).

On the languages:

Noam Chomsky: *Syntactic Structures of the Languages of the Empire.*

On the origins:

Edmund Gibbon: *The Rise of the Empire.*
C. W. Ceram: *Gods, Graves and Scholars.*

On Kanabel:

Max and Moritz Struwwelpeter: "Der Erste Prinz von Onessa," *Zeitschrift für Geschichtwissenschaft und historische Forschung*, vol. XXII, pp. 722–791.

On the history of ideas:

Histoire de la Philosophie of l'Encyclopédie de la Pléiade (under the direction of Raymond Queneau), vol. I, pp. 117–118 and 123–126.
Bertrand Russell: *Hermenides* and *Paraclitus.*
Jean-Claude Abreu and Macedonio Fernandez: *Les Mathématiques de l'Empire.*
Léon Brunschvicg: *Les Étapes de la philosophie mathématique*, pp. 39–51.

On Arsaphes:

Oskar Adler: *Glück und Ende des Feldherren Arsaphos.*
Otto Rank: *Des Mythus des Todes des Helden.*
Special number of *Ucheniye zapiski Leningradskogo gosudarstvennogo ordena Lenina Universiteta* (ser. istor. nauk), CXI.

On the economic situation under Arsaphes and Basil:

Special number of *Diogène*, no. 208, summer 1963: *Routes, paysages, économie.*
Otto-Julius Brunnen and Herbert von Kaiserswasser: *L'Irrigation dans l'Empire.*

On Basil and Thaumas:

Algernon Queen: *The Sexual Background of a Historic Friendship.*

On Mercutio da Verona:

Gustave Lanson and Louis Petit de Julleville: *L'Œuvre méconnue du Maître d'Avignon.*

On Siméon:

Jean Laplanche: *Siméon, ou la question du fils.*

On Alexandria:

Pierre Celeyron: *Histoire générale des fêtes*, vol. I, pp. 97–151.

On Balamir and Khubilai:

René Grousset: *L'Empire des steppes, Les Barbares.*
Marcel Brion: *La Vie des Huns.*

On the conquests:

J. R. R. Tolkien: *The Wars of the Empire.*

On the role of priests and religion:

Marquis de Ségur: *Alexis et les prêtres.*

On Alexis's letter to Balamir:

Paul Morand: *Fouquet, ou le soleil offusqué.*
Marcel Pagnol: *Le Masque de fer.*
Maurice Rheims: *La Vie étrange des objets.*

On Hadrian:

Marguerite Yourcenar: *Memoirs of Hadrian.*

Studies devoted, throughout the centuries, to Bruince and especially to Alexis are too numerous for even an elementary choice to be made. We can only direct the reader back to the Notes, where several references are indicated, notably for chs. 14, 22, and 23.

To this let us only add—in particular on the government of the Empire:

Dietrich von Rieffenstahl: *Vorlesungen über den Ursprung des Staates des Kaisers Alexis.*

Hajime Kemamoto: *The Social and Economic Background of Alexis' Empire*, in *Sekai bunka-shi taikei* (Comprehensive Historical Studies of the Civilizations of the World).

Kasimierz Kostrowitzky: *La Genèse de l'Empire et ses bases économiques et sociales.*

Finally, the essential task remains of pointing out the innumerable references to the Empire or to Alexis in the classics of different literatures, from *Arsaphe et Héloïse* by Pierre Corneille to Turgenev and to Alexandre Dumas, from Madame de Sévigné and Saint-Simon to Lord Byron and to Villiers de L'Isle-Adam, from Voltaire to Karl Marx and Freud, from Amyot and Henri Estienne, Rabelais and Montaigne to Hugo and to Aragon, from Petrarch and Lope de Vega to Heinrich Heine and to Jorge Luis Borges. Naturally, it would be impossible to get an accurate impression of the role and place of Alexis without rereading Cervantes, Shakespeare, Goethe, Chateaubriand, and especially Dante.

The maps and illustrations are taken from:

Bertrand du Breuil: *Atlas historique de l'Empire.*
Henri Dorini: *Les Merveilles de l'Empire.*
Christian Latrille: *Médailles et monnaies de l'Empire.*

We express our grateful appreciation to the authors.

INDEX OF PRINCIPAL

HISTORICAL THEMES

Abdication, renunciation, 73, 194, 224–5, 312–13, 330–3, 335, 340–1, 349, 352–3

Administration, *see* Civil servants

Agriculture, 37–8, 174

Ambassadors, 4, 8, 39, 87, 178, 198, 199–200, 202, 233, 258, 267, 287, 296, 313, 316

Ambition, 45–6, 57, 79–80, 114–15, 116, 190, 194, 204–5, 274–5, 314, 316, 317, 320, 333

Anarchy, 12, 17, 43–4, 152–6

Anguish, 48, 97, 121, 124, 296, 300, 323

Apparitions, 165–6, 343–4, 347–8

Art, 12, 60–1, 167–70, 172, 226–7, 250–1, 265, 286–8, 309, 319–20, 323, 338, 341–3, 355–6, 364, 367

Artisans, 9–10, 36–7, 43, 66, 265, 339; *see also* Technology

Asceticism, 134–6, 138–43, 319–20, 322, 324; *see also* Moon, cult of the; Mysticism; Religion; Sun, cult of the

Assemblies, 53–4, 58, 199–200, 334–6

Astonishment, 209, 212, 335

Banquets, 50, 61, 80, 117–19, 121–2

Barbarians, *passim*

Bastardy, 90, 94, 96, 97, 99–100, 121, 139, 162, 167, 190

Battles, *see* Drawn battles; Naval battles

Beauty, 23, 47, 76, 111, 117, 123, 146–7, 252, 272, 290–1, 334, 345

Brigands, 44, 67, 107, 154, 317; *see also* Pirates

Brothers, rivalry of two, 11–12, 14–15, 19, 40, 190

Buddhism, 145, 147, 310, 329, 363

Calendar, 240–2, 264, 305

Caravans, 69, 155, 261–2, 307

Castles, 61–2

Censorship, 263–4

Ceremonies, 22–3, 53–4, 105, 109, 184, 196, 198–9, 234–5, 247, 269, 270–2, 287, 305–6, 316, 320–2, 327–8, 338–41; *see also* Festivals, holidays

Chance, 12, 64, 125, 354

Childhood, 76–81, 92–100, 102–8, 158, 159, 169–70, 190, 209, 317–18

Cities, *see* Alexandria (Egypt); Pomposa; Rome; City, the, *in the Index of Names and Places*

Civilization, culture, 9, 12, 16, 35–6, 123, 155–6, 254–6, 265, 281–2, 308–9, 316, 329–30, 349–52

Civil servants, 8, 38–9, 192, 244–6, 254, 308–9, 310, 311, 320

Climate, 3–4, 12, 51, 159–60, 187, 338, 344–5, 364

Coinage, 23, 240, 242, 310; *see also* Money

Commerce, 9–10, 12, 15, 34, 37–8, 116–17, 246, 307; *see also* Merchant princes; Merchants; Merchant warriors

Confidences, 23–4, 78

Conquests, 186, 188–9, 200, 232, 235, 288–9, 315
Conspiracies, 40–1, 161, 162–3, 173, 181, 214, 273–4
Contradiction, paradox, 16, 18–19, 164, 217, 231, 267–8, 280–1, 293–4, 314–15
Conversion, 145, 326–8, 350–1
Courage, 19, 33–4, 82, 277–8
Couriers, 308–9, 311
Courtesans, *see* Prostitutes, prostitution
Crimes, 3, 41, 43–4, 54–5, 62, 74, 78–9, 130–2, 172
Cults, *see* Moon, cult of the; Priests; Religion; Sun, cult of the

Dancing, 4, 49, 54, 253, 334
Death, 4, 10, 41, 74, 78, 82–3, 84, 86, 119, 130–2, 133, 139, 140, 151, 172, 180–1, 182, 222–3, 232–3, 237–8, 254–5, 280–1, 291–2, 305, 306, 321–4, 335, 345
Decadence, 17, 36, 152–7, 331, 336–7
Defeat, 17, 35, 300, 325–6, 330–1
Deserts, 75, 133, 134, 135, 139, 184
Dialects, *see* Languages
Discipline, 188, 202, 204
Discoveries, 134–5, 137–8, 141, 142, 241
Disembarkation, 17, 23, 276
Disorder, *see* Anarchy
Divorce, 48, 60; *see also* Marriage
Drawn battles, 5, 70–4, 206–7, 285–7
Dreams, 85–6, 97, 102, 110–11, 175, 184–5, 292
Drunkenness, 118, 121, 124, 127–9, 297
Duels, 198–213 *passim*

Eclipse of heroes, *see* Heroes, eclipse of
Education, 8–9, 77, 103–4, 135, 200, 203–4, 318
Elephants, 285, 292, 339, 371
Epidemics, *see* Leprosy; Plagues
Eroticism, 84–5, 111, 142, 220–1
Exile, 14, 133–51, 158–9

Expectation, 16, 23, 52, 82–4, 99, 210–11, 334–5

Famines, 44, 52, 151, 154–5, 237
Fate, *see* Chance
Fatherhood, 77–8, 94–5, 317–19
Festivals, holidays, 4–5, 22–3, 49, 54, 61–2, 66, 71, 74, 117–19, 121–9, 198–9, 234–5, 268–9, 338–41; *see also* Ceremonies
Fires, 25, 76, 87–9, 279, 297–8
Forbidden love, 22–4, 47, 48–9, 82–4, 111, 122–32
Forests, 62, 75–87, 91, 92, 97, 122, 167, 175, 184, 233
Forgetfulness, *see* Memory
Forgiveness, 57–8, 63, 286–7, 306, 320
Funerals, 4, 68, 301–5

Games, sports, 4–5, 16, 156, 268–71, 305–6; *see also* Festivals, holidays
Glory, 26–7, 85, 266, 274–5, 316, 337, 352–3, 355
God, gods, 9, 101, 106–7, 109, 113–14, 115, 156, 161, 166, 176–7, 188, 209, 244, 248–9, 266, 272, 300, 313–14, 316, 326–7, 335, 336
Golden age, 12, 17, 18–19, 30–1, 44, 103, 153, 246, 248, 266, 269, 307, 308; *see also* Myth
Grief, sorrow, 10, 62–3, 180, 300–1, 323–4, 330, 345–6, 391
Guile, 15, 19, 23–4, 34–5, 46, 51, 54–5, 62–4, 66, 71–3, 77–81, 152–3, 162, 166, 177, 178, 209–12, 220, 266

Happiness, 9, 12, 30, 48–9, 84, 98–9, 102, 105, 125, 135, 265–6, 314–15, 324, 337
Hatred, 14–15, 206, 208, 324, 335
Heirs, 29–30, 41–2, 64, 162, 184–5, 205, 218–19, 248–9, 268, 317–23, 335–6
Heresies, 9, 16, 103, 142

Heroes, eclipse of, 133–51, 158–60, 288, 363

High Council, 22, 24–5, 27, 30, 32–3, 39, 46, 287, 288–92, 307

History, 5–6, 14, 19, 56, 91, 265, 302, 331–3, 345, 354–6, 359

Homosexuality, 51, 86, 119, 147, 181–2, 325

Honesty, fairness, 68, 168, 178–9, 215–16, 281–2

Honor, 28–9, 59, 60, 179–80, 266

Hostages, 83, 94, 163, 178, 298–9

Humility, *see* Pride

Hunting, 76, 92, 95–6, 98–9, 119–20

Industry, *see* Technology

Injustice, *see* Justice

Intrigues, *see* Guile

Irrigation, *see* Water

Islam, 134–6, 336

Jealousy, 24, 190

Jews, 135, 137, 148, 341, 347, 349

Justice, 67, 76, 136, 157, 176–7, 179, 181, 220, 245–6, 263–4, 308, 309, 318, 330, 336, 346–7

Knowledge, learning, 8, 9, 57, 60, 97, 134, 137–8, 204, 236, 241–4, 361

Landscape, 11, 75, 92, 202–3, 254–5, 340, 344

Language, 7–8, 21, 49, 72, 73, 75, 155–6, 200, 226, 229, 309, 349–50, 362

Legend, 6–7, 11–12, 14–15, 41, 73–4, 83–4, 85, 94–5, 123–4, 131–2, 165, 171–2, 187, 279–80, 326, 350–1

Leprosy (particularly Leper prince), 322–4

Letters, 63, 106, 113–14, 176–7, 189–90, 225–9, 234, 346, 365

Literature, 14, 16, 22, 60–1, 84–5, 117, 123–4, 168–9, 171–2, 255–6, 261, 265

Lotteries, 119, 129–30, 321, 362

Love, 23–5, 47–8, 84–90, 122–32, 135, 149–50, 272, 359–60; *see also* Forbidden love

Madness, *passim*

Magi, *see* Priests

Marriage, 4, 29–30, 48–9, 64, 272; *see also* Divorce

Marxism, 5, 6, 106–7, 248, 314, 354, 364

Massacres, 15, 56–7, 90, 163, 187, 279, 293, 297–8

Master and disciple, 79–80, 103–5, 113–14, 116–17, 176–7, 179, 318

Mathematics, 15–16, 241–4, 366

Measures, *see* Weights and measures

Medicine, 62–4, 78, 241, 258

Meetings, 23, 48–51, 92, 106, 151, 167–70, 179, 188, 295–6

Melancholy, 306, 312–13, 316–17, 330–1

Memory, forgetfulness, 44, 91, 319–20, 355

Mercenaries, 18, 20–1, 23–4, 30, 32, 35, 38, 46–7, 50, 73–4, 159, 167, 171, 175, 198, 284, 285, 288

Merchant princes, 19, 23, 30, 32–3, 35, 39, 46, 50–1, 218–19, 233–4, 267, 276, 278–9, 283–4, 288–9, 308

Merchants, 15, 18, 25, 30, 33, 36, 39

Merchant warriors, 17, 21, 23, 25, 26, 50, 279–80

Messengers, 62–3, 80–2, 86, 89, 105, 223–4, 238–9, 322–3

Misery, poverty, 43, 44, 101–2, 154–5, 175–6, 336–7, 341

Money, 116–17, 240, 242, 329–30

Moon, cult of the, 142–4, 240–1, 319

Mother and son, 76–9, 83, 92, 94, 101–2, 162, 167–70, 194, 233, 319, 323

Murders, *see* Crimes

Music, *see* Singing; Dancing

Mysteries, secrets, 105, 106, 123, 125, 149, 163, 242–3, 295–6

Mystics, mysticism, 5, 108–9, 134–5, 138, 145–6, 190, 242, 294, 318, 324–5; *see also* Asceticism;

Moon, cult of the; Priests; Religion; Sun, cult of the
Myths, 6–7, 12, 14, 28–9, 41, 43, 91–2, 108–9, 133–4, 144, 166, 201, 346–7

Naval battles, 4, 16–17, 34–5, 246, 283–4
Nightmares, *see* Dreams

Omens, 53–4, 119, 156, 162, 316
Orgies, 115–18, 128–9, 270–1

Paradoxes, *see* Contradiction, paradox
Peace, *see* War
Peasants, 51–2, 57, 175–6, 315; *see also* Famines; Misery
Philosophy, 16, 103, 241, 242, 255, 257–60
Pilgrims, *see* Travelers
Pirates, 3, 66, 67–9, 79, 155, 275–7, 308; *see also* Brigands
Plagues, 4, 34, 74, 237–9, 263, 343
Pleasure, 4, 21, 69, 113–21 *passim*, 198; *see also* Banquets; Festivals, holidays; Orgies
Plots, *see* Conspiracies
Poetry, 8–9, 11–12, 14, 47, 148–51, 158–9, 254, 255–6, 261–3, 290–1
Poverty, *see* Misery
Pride and humility, 8, 288, 322, 324–5, 327, 337, 341, 352–3
Priestesses, *see* Priests
Priests, 5, 8–9, 32–3, 39, 41, 43, 46, 52, 53–4, 56–60, 67, 71, 76, 77, 79, 103–6, 108, 127–32, 136–7, 139–40, 153, 156–7, 161, 199, 205, 210, 219–22, 234–5, 244, 245, 247–8, 270, 293–6, 307, 310, 316, 320–1, 326, 328
Prisoners, 79, 85–6, 178–9, 222–4, 279–80, 286
Promise, 10, 17–18, 162, 178–83, 335
Prostitutes, prostitution, 32, 53, 95, 119, 120–2, 127, 268, 269, 270–1, 287, 290, 319, 324, 332, 360

Proverbs, *see* Sayings
Psychoanalysis, 6, 83–4, 92, 94, 233, 340–1, 368
Punishment, *see* Crimes; Torture; Massacres

Reconciliation, 162–3, 214–15, 244–5, 248
Religion, 5–6, 32–3, 71, 105, 106–7, 115, 188, 219–22, 247–9, 310–11, 325–8
Renunciation, *see* Abdication, renunciation
Revolt, 21, 24, 50, 152, 156–7, 161, 163–4, 171, 173, 175–6, 183, 273–4, 316–17
Riot, *see* Revolt
Rivalry, 50, 67–74, 154, 177–8, 247–8, 310
Roads, 37, 38, 66, 69, 239, 308

Sacrifice, 105, 108, 111–12, 127, 178–9, 209, 224–5, 324, 339
Sayings, proverbs, 72–4, 110, 124, 232, 245, 348
Schisms, *see* Heresies
Science, *see* Knowledge, learning
Sea, ships, shipping, 9, 15, 17, 34, 35, 50, 67–8, 116–17, 155–6, 246–7, 276–7, 278, 283–4, 300, 308
Sedition, *see* Revolt
Shamans, *see* Priests
Sieges, 81–90, 277–9, 283–4
Singing, 8, 54–5, 60, 253, 322, 334, 339
Slavery, 18–19, 36
Speeches, 48–9, 59, 178–9, 201, 228–9, 334–6
Steppes, 107, 186–7, 195–6, 208, 229, 277, 303, 308, 318, 328–9
Storms, 3, 102, 237–8, 278, 297–8, 300
Strategy, 34–5, 46, 163, 170–1, 201–2, 283–4, 285–7
Structuralism, 6, 248, 256–7
Suicide, 139, 163, 182, 260–1
Sun, cult of the, 6, 108–12, 113–14, 115, 123, 133, 139–42, 188, 220, 248, 271, 362

Symbols, 9, 142–3, 248–9, 319, 325, 348

Taoism, 145, 146, 257, 363
Taxation, 21, 39, 274, 309–11
Technology, 9–10, 12, 36–7, 244
Tempests, *see* Storms
Terror, 18, 20–1, 56–7, 157, 189, 201, 203, 206, 208, 335
Time, *passim*
Tolerance, 255–6, 310–11, 327, 330
Torture, 15, 22, 56–7, 131, 141, 157, 178–9, 181, 187, 222, 223–4, 288, 298
Tradition, 14, 46, 94, 108–9, 165, 187, 190, 219–20, 234–5, 316, 346
Travelers, 6, 61, 71, 74, 75, 97, 107–8, 143–4, 151, 157, 159–60, 165–6, 254, 271, 278, 296, 298, 344
Treason, 24, 41, 54–5, 83, 95, 190, 194, 197, 220–1, 339–40
Treasure, 265, 275, 277, 302–3

Triumph, 54–5, 184–5, 319, 338, 340, 343–4, 355–6
Truth, 104, 105, 106, 132, 176, 264, 354–5
Twins, 156, 158, 168

Unity, universality, 106–7, 231, 311, 312, 314, 326–7, 330, 333, 346–8

Vengeance, 15, 16, 24, 61, 67, 222, 288, 290–1, 300
Violence, 3, 178, 280–1, 305–6, 324, 330
Virginity, sacred, 109, 111–12, 122–3, 325–6
Visions, *see* Dreams

War, peace, *passim*
Water, 37–8, 66, 156, 239, 244
Weights and measures, 239–40, 242, 310

INDEX OF NAMES
AND PLACES

Abati, Bocca degli, 139
Abed, 134–5, 137
Abelard, 26, 117
Abraham, 174, 248, 326, 350
Abreu, Jean-Claude, 366
Achilles, 148, 363
Adelaide, Empress of Sicily, 47, 49, 50, 60, 153
Adeodatus, 117
Adler, Oskar, 360
Admetus, 363
Adrianople, 107, 285, 331, 355
Aegean Sea, 278, 284
Afghanistan, 134, 143, 268
Africa, 7, 16, 120, 198, 204, 215, 299, 304, 333
Agades, 356
Agrigentum, 47
Ahasuerus, 26, 341, 347
Ahmed, see Badalwi, Ahmed
Ahriman, 143
Ainus, 69, 186, 317
Ala-chan, 348
Alans, 80, 317, 319
Alaric (king of the Visigoths), 297
Alassio, 348
Al Azhar University, 135
Albania, 334
Alcibiades, 118, 225
Alès, 348
Aletsch glacier, 348
Alexain, 348
Alexander (father of Fabrician), 79
Alexander of Macedonia (Alexander the Great), 117, 148, 174, 225, 315, 364
Alexander VI (Borgia), Pope, 124, 348

Alexandria (Egypt), 105, 108, 109, 113–32, 139, 141, 147, 177, 184, 190, 192, 193, 198, 202, 268, 299, 305, 321, 322, 333, 340, 355, 362
Alexandria (Piedmont), 348
Alexeev, Admiral Yevgeni Ivano-vitch, 347
Alexis, 7, 18, 26, 31, 34, 41, 57, 64, 68, 90, 159–60, 173–4, 239, 241, 244, 284, 285, 364
 the bastard, see Bastardy in the Index of Principal Historical Themes
 childhood, 92, 94–100, 119
 youth, 115, 116–21
 maturity, 148–9
 old age, 267
 chronology, 133–4
 physical appearance, 92–3, 117, 146–8, 267
 an epileptic?, 148
 the healer, 148
 personality, 92–3, 108–9, 146–7, 159, 180, 183, 191–3, 205, 233, 312, 313–15, 321–2, 326, 340–1, 368
 double life, 148, 151
 the good, 280, 286, 341
 the beloved, 193
 the debauchee, see Banquets; Festivals, holidays; Orgies, in the Thematic Index. See also Alexandria
 and Vanessa, 112, 122–32, 160, 213, 232, 255, 288
 and the Yemenite, 149–50, 268
 and Theodora, 272–5, 277

the father, 317–22

the cruel, 279–80

commander in chief, 164–7, 201–3, 286–7

the politician, 176–8, 196–7, 212–13, 214, 230–3, 303–4

heir of the Porphyries, Venostae, Basil, Arsaphes, 31, 41, 45, 64, 68, 95, 159, 161–2, 165–6, 175, 184, 218, 230–1, 244

the judge, 224–5

the censor, 263–4

reorganizer of the Empire, 230–1, 236, 246–65 *passim*

defender of the arts and literature (the Age of Alexis), 8–9, 255–6, 290–1

the poet, 148–51, 158–9, 255–7, 282

and the gods, 108–12, 115, 248–9, 326–7, 335

Fool of God, mystic, saint, 139–47, 205, 232–3, 242, 345

unifier of the Empire, 281–2, 312; *see also* Father of the Peoples

Father of the Peoples, 213, 244, 337, 348

pseudo-Alexis, 164, 168

names by which he was known:
  Alachian, 140, 144
  Alechia, 140, 142, 144, 145
  Alaouis, 140, 142, 145
  Ha Li-Chien, 143–4
  Ha Lee-Chiang, 143–4, 145, 148

his legend, 346–8

cities and localities named after him:
  Alexain, Alixan, Alès, 348
  Alexkovo, Aletsch, Ala-chan, 348
  Alassio, 348

in art and literature, 167–70, 184, 206–7, 226–7, 287–8, 290–1, 295, 338, 342–3, 349–52, 369

our contemporary, 173–4, 175, 336–7

Alexkovo, 348

Alfarubeira, Don Pedro of, 284

Alfrania (mother of Philocrates), 101–2

Alixan, 348

Alpha (star), 348

Alph River, 155

Alps, 61, 198, 292, 308, 344

Altai Mountains, 7, 189, 196, 201, 216, 303, 328, 364, 369

Amaterasu (goddess), 300

America, 336

Ampère, J.-J., 84

Amphibolus, 5, 36, 37, 38, 41, 44–5, 51, 67, 70–4, 153, 154, 155, 173, 178, 179, 180, 182, 183, 186, 191, 194, 196, 201, 202, 213, 221, 223, 225, 281, 335

Amphyses River, 3, 15, 17, 36, 37, 41, 43, 51, 75, 154, 156, 171, 178, 184, 196, 252, 262, 299

Amu-Darya River, 196

Amyot, Jacques, 28, 118

Anagni, 298

Ancre, maréchal d', *see* Concini, Concino

Andersen, Hans Christian, 171

Angkor, 323

Anouilh, Jean, 24, 27

Antioch, 108, 119, 120, 137, 299, 305, 332, 333

Apollinaire, Guillaume, 84–5

Apollo, 363

Aqaba, Gulf of, 367

Aquileus, 6, 17, 36–7, 38, 39, 40, 41, 46, 50–5 *passim*, 57–9, 66, 68, 69, 71, 73, 75, 76, 79, 85, 95, 97, 106, 107, 109, 153, 155, 156, 161, 164, 166, 170, 177, 178, 180, 183, 184, 191, 194, 195, 205, 216, 217, 220–2, 234–5, 247, 248, 262, 293, 305, 306, 307, 309–10, 312, 317, 320–1, 328, 333, 335

Aquileus on the Adriatic, 287, 305

Aquitaine, 299

Arabia, 134, 135, 293, 312, 324, 325, 330, 333

Arachosia, 155, 303

Aragon, Louis, 361, 365

Aral Sea, 196, 303

Aranjuez, 299

Archimandrites, 15, 307

Argentina, 269

Arginous Islands, 17, 308

Ariosto, Ludovico, 351

Arismapians, 285, 286
Aristo, 241, 257–8, 295, 333, 356
Aristobulus, 349
Aristotle, 117, 225
Armenia, 310
Arno River, 344
Arrhideus, 155, 170–1, 178, 183, 187, 191, 201, 202
Arsaphes, 3, 9, 17, 21–2, 23, 25, 26–31, 32, 33, 34–5, 37–40 *passim*, 41, 43, 45, 47, 51, 52, 53, 56, 57, 69, 70, 73, 76, 94, 124, 138, 153, 162, 173, 175, 176, 184, 191, 201, 213, 217, 218, 221, 231, 234, 236, 239, 244, 247, 249, 265, 307, 308, 356
Artagnan, Charles de Batz or de Montesquiou, Comte d', 227
Arthur, King, 351
Ascoli Piceno, 167, 169
Ashurbanipal, 232, 315
Asia, 69, 71, 134, 144–7, 149, 158, 164, 177, 187–9, 196, 200–1, 203, 215–16, 231, 242, 246, 267–8, 276, 280, 299–304, 307, 328–9, 339, 341; *see also* Central Asia
Asoka, 174, 315
Aspasia, 21, 22, 23, 24, 29
Assisi, 344
Astakia, 155, 156, 170, 172, 173, 182, 183, 191, 202
Athens, 115, 198, 284, 307
Atlantis, 7
Atlas Mountains, 310, 317; Anti-Atlas, 317
Attavanti, Attavante degli, 338
Attila, 225
Auch, 227
Augustine, Saint, 117, 248, 263
Augustus, Emperor, 281
Auric, Georges, 124
Austerlitz, battle of, 207
Autun, 107
Avenches, 107
Avignon, 60
Aziri, 258, 259–60, 295, 324, 334

Babaji, *see* Sarabhavanamuktenand-āmanayagam, Swami Sri
Babiloth, 350

Babylon, 105, 142, 145, 302, 307, 350, 356
Bacon, Francis, 258, 366
Bactria, 7, 31, 35, 196, 285, 303, 305
Badalwi, Ahmed, 137, 142, 144
Baer, Hubert, 360, 369
Baghdad, 307, 351
Baikal, Lake, 196, 303
Baikonur, 200
Bajazet, 214
Balamir (Kha-Khan of the Oïghurs), 188–91, 194–5, 199–213, 214–17, 219–23, 225, 228–31, 234–5, 246, 268, 274–7, 279–82, 285–8, 291, 293, 296–306, 307, 312, 313, 320–3, 329, 333, 335, 340, 351, 356, 365, 367, 368, 369
Balearic slingers, 102, 202, 206, 285, 303, 320
Balkans, 245
Balkh, 75–90, 91, 107, 108, 157, 168, 174, 190, 195, 197, 202, 206, 288, 335, 355, 361
Balkhash, Lake, 196, 303
Balthazar (King, Magus), 288
Balzac, Honoré de, 271, 360
Bamian, 142, 143, 145, 148, 149
Barante, Prosper de, 84
Barbey d'Aurevilly, 118, 362
Barka, 299
Barrès, Maurice, 37, 85, 134, 157, 362
Barthélemy, Abbé, 172
Basilicata, the, 298
Basil the Great, Emperor, 3–4, 7, 8, 18, 34, 37, 38, 44–54, 56–64, 65–8, 70, 72–4, 75, 76, 79, 91, 94, 103, 114, 124, 152–3, 156, 162, 165, 173, 177, 184, 186, 196, 201, 203, 213, 217–21, 230, 231, 236, 239, 244, 246, 247, 249, 255, 269, 276, 277, 307–9, 312, 333, 356, 361, 362
Basques, 7, 269
Báthory, Stephen, 284
Bayan, 188
Bayet, Albert, 5
Befana, 347
Bengal, 320
Benghazi, 299
Benedict, Saint, 352

Beneventum Prince of, *see* Talley-rand-Périgord
Beneventum, 298
Benoist-Méchin, Jacques, 362
Berenson, Bernard, 226
Bergotte (character in Proust), 168–9
Bernay, Alexandre de, 350
Berthelot, Philippe, 368
Besançon, 257
Bibiena, 344
Bingham, Hiram, 12, 138, 359
Björsenson, Björsen, 5, 270
Black Forest, 346
Black Sea, 134, 284
Bleda, 188
Bloch, Marc, 6, 363
Blum, Léon, 177
Boccaccio, 271
Boccherini, Luigi, 352
Bodrum, 346
Bogomil, 35–6, 37, 38
Boileau, Nicolas, 264
Bologna, 63
Bolsena, Lake, 294–6
Bordighera, 348
Borges, Jorge Luis, 256, 362, 368
Borgia (Pope Alexander VI), *see* Alexander VI
Borgia, Cesare, 124
Borgia, Lucrezia, 124, 348
Borgo Pace, 294
Bormann, Martin, 367
Bossuet, 6, 139, 314, 368
Boucicault, Marshal, 284, 285
Bourbon, constable de, 297, 347
Bourdaille, Armand, 134–8, 139, 140–2, 143, 144, 148, 149
Bourget, Paul, 117
Bragmardo, General Hernani, 284–5
Bramante (Donato d'Angelo Lazzori), 250
Branciforte, Captain Jules, 284
Brantôme, Seigneur de (Pierre de Bourdelle), 271
Brasillach, Robert, 14, 28
Brazil, 7
Bréhier, Émile, 177, 365
Bréton, André, 291
Brittany, 7, 312, 330, 351
Brosses, President Charles de, 295, 367

Bruince, 5, 185, 201, 203–7, 214, 215, 218, 219, 224, 225, 235, 237, 239, 241, 247, 248, 250, 265, 268, 274, 276, 277, 287–8, 290, 295, 308, 310–13, 317, 319, 320–1, 327–8, 330, 333–4, 336–7, 341–3, 350, 355, 365
Brummell, George, 118
Brunschvicq, Léon, 366
Büchner, Georg, 328
Bucovina, 347
Buddha, 145, 146, 147, 363
Buffon, George Louis Leclerc, Comte de, 261
Bukhara, 77, 107, 148, 151, 192, 193, 328, 364
Buñuel, Luis, 139
Burgundians, 284–6
Burkhardt, Jacob, 369
Burnouf, Jean-Louis, 14, 134
Byblos, 275
Byron, George Gordon, Lord, 37, 85, 119, 174, 317
Byzantium, 216, 273, 307, 349

Cadore, 344
Caesar, Julius, 214, 225, 257, 350, 356
Caesarea, 79, 105
Caillois, Roger, 256, 363
Cairo, 135
California, University of, 140, 142
Callicles, 204
Callisthenes, 349
Camaldoli, 344
Cambaluc, *see* Peking
Camus, Albert, 260, 291
Canary Islands, 204
Cannae, battle of, 207
Canossa, 348
Cape Verde Islands, 204
Cappadocia, 346
Capua, 298
Caribbean Sea, 67
Carinthia, 283
Carnarvon, Lord, 302
Carpathians, 347
Carradine, Captain then Admiral, 277, 279, 287, 303, 333, 334, 350, 355

Carroll, Lewis, *see* Dodgson, Charles
Carter, Howard, 302
Carter-Bennett, Sir Allan, 40, 43, 45, 65–6, 114–15, 138, 139, 140–1, 144, 145, 153, 156, 159, 162, 213, 216, 219, 231, 241, 244, 245, 246, 249, 256, 267, 274, 280, 317, 319, 341, 362, 363
Carthage, 63, 67, 102, 107, 215, 305
Caspian Sea, 189
Catherine II (Empress of Russia), 273
Cato, 225
Caucasus Mountains, 187, 188, 189, 308
Cellini, Benvenuto, 347, 370
Central Asia, 75, 196, 200, 303, 328–9, 364
Ceram, C. W., 359, 367
Cerbical Islands, 246, 284, 308
Cervantes, Miguel de, 347, 351
Cesarion, 225
Ceylon, 329
Chalcis, 120
Chamfort (Nicolas Sébastien Roch), 249
Chantilly, chateau of, 338
Chaposhnikov, Marshal Boris Mikhailovitch, 206
Chardin, Jean, 25, 143
Chardon-Cohen, Dr. Annette, 369
Charlemagne, Emperor, 174, 326, 351
Charles V, Emperor, 214, 225, 297
Charles XII (King of Sweden), 174
Chasles, Michel, 225
Chateaubriand, François-René, Vicomte de, 37, 85, 174, 254
Châtillon, Gauthier de, 351
Cherubini, Luigi, 351
Chevreuse, Marie de Rohan-Montbazon, Duchesse de Luynes, then of, 227
Chicago, 228
Chigi, Agostino, 364
China, 7, 69, 143–5, 147, 186, 187, 188, 196, 200, 204, 215, 222, 226, 252, 258, 277, 288, 299–304, 312, 322, 325, 329
Ch'oe Ch'aewon, 367
Christ, *see* Jesus Christ
Cimarosa, Domenico, 351

Circassians, 285
Circe, 350
City, the, *passim* and particularly:
  founding, prosperity, golden age, 15, 16, 17–19, 31, 34, 103, 246
  as center for overland trade, 34, 35–6, 38–9
  harbor, 17, 21–2, 34, 39, 249–50
  capture of, 25–6, 31
  decadence, misery, 21, 31, 32, 34, 43, 153, 162
  renaissance and apogee, 246–7, 249, 307–8, 311
  as capital, administrative center, 247, 311–12
Ciudad Real, 299
Claudel, Paul, 134, 143, 291
Clausewitz, Karl von, 206
Clavijo, Ruy González de, 351
Cleopatra, 225, 273
Clitarchus, 349
Cnidus peninsula, 346
Cocteau, Jean, 305
Codreanu, Corneliu Zelea, 370
Coleridge, Samuel Taylor, 329
Cologne, 107
Comans, 187, 285
Comazon, 279
Comnena, Anna, 349
Como, 107, 199, 345
Concini, Concino (maréchal d'Ancre), 226–7
Confucius, 145, 148, 257
Constantine II, Emperor, 342, 362
Constantine (Porphyrogenete), 336–7
Constantinople, 336, 347
Coomaraswamy, A., 363
Cooper, James Fenimore, 171
Córdoba, 299
Corelli, Arcangelo, 352
Corinth, 284
Corneille, Pierre, 24, 28, 29, 30, 31
Coromandel Coast, 67
Corot, Camille, 344
Corsica, 303, 310, 366
Corvin, Mathias, 338
Cossacks, 285
Couchoud, 326
Crete, 102, 186, 199, 284, 303
Crussol d'Uzès family, 227
Ctesiphon, 79, 105, 303, 305, 320, 333, 335

Cuchulain monastery, 280
Cumaea, 199
Custine, Marquis de, 359
Cyclades Islands, 278
Cyprus, 7, 49, 102, 202, 203, 215,
    217, 219, 222, 229, 233–4, 267,
    268, 275–80, 283, 284
Cyrene, 299

Dalmatia, 283, 284, 286, 299
Damascus, 63, 134, 307, 351
Dante Alighieri, 85, 138–9, 294, 295,
    344, 352–3, 356, 367
Danube River, 61, 189, 284, 304,
    305, 310
Daudet, Alphonse, 226
Daudet, Léon, 281
David-Neel, Alexandra, 363
Debussy, Claude, 352
Defoe, Daniel, 171
Delaroche, Paul, 22
Delbos, Victor, 362
Delbrück, Hans, 206
della Robbia, Luca, 172
Delille, Abbé Jacques, 14
Delos, 302
Delphi, 102
Demetrios de Jamblée, 123
Demiéville, Paul, 363
Descartes, René, 117, 258, 366
Dickens, Charles, 171
Diderot, Denis, 365
Dingizik, 208–12, 218
Dion, see Justus Dion
Dionysus, 363
Djagatai, 285
Dnieper River, 317
Dodgson, Charles (Lewis Carroll),
    171
Dolomites, 344, 355
Domecq, Bustos, 362
Donatello (Donato di Betto Bardi),
    342
Don Juan, 119
Don River, 187, 317, 320
Dresden, 117, 252, 342
Drôme River, 348
Dryden, John, 359–60
Du Camp, Maxine, 143
Ducasse, Isidore, see Lautréamont

Du Guesclin, see Guesclin, Bertrand
    du
Dumas, Alexandre, 22, 92, 148
Dupont, Pierre, 6
Dura-Europos, 107, 142, 303
Dürer, Albrecht, 305
Duyvendak, J. J. L., 363
Dyushambe, 359
Dzungaria, 268

Edessa, 108, 141, 303, 333
Edith the swan-necked (mistress of
    Harold, King of England),
    347
Egypt, 7, 37, 204, 249, 302, 311
Eisenstein, Sergei, 175
Einstein, Albert, 174
Elam, 356
Eliot, T. S., 14
Elizabeth I (Queen of England),
    273
Elizabeth of Bohemia, Princess, 117
Ellis, Havelock, 362
Emden, Max Van, 364
Emesa, 108, 141
Émile (character in Rousseau), 204
Emmerich, Emma Katharina, 346
Ems, Rudolf von, 350
Engels, Friedrich, 106
England, 17, 63, 271
Enjolras (character in Hugo), 172
Entommeures, Prince of the, 285
Ephesus, 101, 335, 346
Epirus, 245
Eritrea, 199
Ertogrul, 188
Erythrean Sea, 318
Eschenbach, Ulrich von, 350
Este, Isabelle d', 273
Esther, 26
Estienne, Henri, 271
Estienne, Robert, 28
Esenin, Sergei Alexandrovich, 14
Étiemble, 363
Etruscans, 7
Euphrates River, 142, 273, 275, 276,
    284, 303, 311
Evcharisto, 38, 153, 156, 183, 333
Ezion-geber, 302

Fabrician, 79–84, 87–90, 95, 106, 109, 114, 124, 145, 148, 157, 162, 190, 197, 203, 219, 317
Famagusta, 49, 51, 65, 66, 188, 202, 219, 277, 321, 333
Faure, P., 360, 368–9
Federovsky, Igor, 361
Fénelon, François de Salignac de la Mothe-, 172
Feodorovna, Alexandra (Empress of Russia), 370
Fergama, 285
Fernandez, Macedonio, 362, 366
Ferrière, Alexandre de la, 135
Fethiya, *see* Telmessos
Feuerbach, Ludwig, 248
Fichte, Johann Gottlieb, 259
Ficino, Marsilio, 124
Fiesole, 226
Finale Ligure, 348
Firdussi, 349–50
Flaubert, Gustave, 295, 367
Fleuriot, Zénaïde, 172
Florence, 115, 123–4, 287–8, 305
Focillon, Henri, 252, 361
Ford, Henry, 174
Foscari, Francesco, 226
Foucauld, Charles de, 148
Foucault, Michel, 248
Fouquet, Marie-Madeleine, 227
Fouquet, Jean, 338
Fouquet, Nicolas, 227–8
France, 171, 172
France, Anatole, 225–6, 263
Francesca, Piero della, *see* Piero della Francesca
Francis of Assisi, Saint, 261
Francis I (King of France), 214
Frederick II of Hohenstaufen, Emperor, 96, 334
Freud, Sigmund, 94, 354, 362
Fujikake, Shizuya, 367
Füseli, 305
Futo-no-Yasumaro, 367

Gadaric, 187
Galigaï, Leonora, 226
Gance, Abel, 175
Gandolphus, 47, 50, 51, 58, 60, 64, 65–74, 79, 80–90, 92, 94, 107, 114, 152, 153, 165, 177, 190, 191, 197, 201, 202, 203, 310, 355, 356, 362
Ganelon, 351
Ganges River, 143, 303, 304
Garcia, Pauline Viardot-, 92
Gard River, 348
Garnier, Robert, 24
Garrett, Robert, 363
Gattamelata (Erasmo di Narni), 342
Gaulle, Gen. Charles de, 363
Gauls, 225, 297
Gautier, Théophile, 37, 157
Gavroche (character in Hugo), 172
Gazul, Clara, 334
Gedrosia, 155, 303
Geiseric (King of the Vandals), 297
Genghis Khan, 174, 232
Genlis, Stéphanie Félicité du Crest de Saint Aubin, Comtesse de, 172
Genoa, 120
George, Saint, 350
Géricault, Théodore, 365
Germany, 37, 63, 171, 231
Ghéon, Henri, 349
Gibbon, Edward, 359
Gibraltar, 299
Gide, André, 261, 263
Gildore, Cape, 34, 35, 37, 156, 173, 178, 184, 202, 208, 239, 276, 335
Giraudoux, Jean, 291
Glaucon, 204
Glendalough monastery, 280
Gobineau, Joseph Arthur, Comte de, 314
Goethe, Johann Wolfgang von, 203, 234, 252, 295, 351–2
Gozzoli, Benozzo, 287–8
Gracq, Julien, 367
Grado, 287
Granada, 299, 335
Greece, 7, 57, 97, 155–6, 242, 249, 251, 258, 284
Greenland, 67
Gregory VII, Saint, Pope, 328, 341, 343–4, 348
Grenier, Jean, 363
Grimm, Jacob and Wilhelm, 12, 95, 171
Grock, A. W., 172, 364

Grotius (Hugo de Groot), 258
Grousset, René, 359, 361, 369
Grüneveld, Professor von, 140
Guadalajara, 299, 304
Gubbio, 294, 344
Guesclin, Bertrand du, 225
Guignebert, Charles, 5
Guiscard, Robert, 297
Gurdjieff, 296

Hadrian VII (Archpatriarch),
    292–6, 298, 303, 310, 311,
    320–1, 323–8, 330, 334–6, 367
Hadrian, Emperor, 225, 340
Hahn, Reynaldo, 352
Halicarnassus, 302, 346
Hammurabi, 174
Handel, George Frederick, 352
Hannibal, 315
Harar, 134
Hardy, Alexandre, 351
Harold (King of England), 347
Hart, Liddell, 206
Hartlieb, Johannes, 350
Hastings, 347
Hegel, Friedrich, 259, 282, 335
Hegesippus, Prince, 285
Heidegger, Martin, 257, 280
Heine, Heinrich, 352
Helen, 76–90, 91–2, 94–7, 99, 100,
    107, 113, 114, 116, 124–25,
    145, 148, 162, 167–70, 171,
    173, 183, 184, 190, 194, 201–3,
    205, 212, 220, 233, 235, 268,
    272, 288, 295, 306, 319, 329,
    335, 340, 350, 355, 370
Heloise (wife of Abelard), 26, 117
Heloise (daughter of Nephaot, wife
    of Arsaphes), 22–3, 24, 25–31,
    39, 42, 94, 124
Herbolzheim, Berthold von, 350
Hermenides, 16, 35, 103, 109, 148,
    257–8, 295, 307
Hero, 26
Herod Antipas (Tetrarch of Gali-
    lee), 225
Heruli, 297
Himalaya Mountains, 144
Hindu Kush Mountains, 364
Hinstin, M., 117
Hitler, Adolf, 214, 232, 367

Hiung-Nus, 187, 189
Hobbits, 38
Hohenschwangau, castle of, 346
Holbein, Hans, 305
Ho K'iu-ping, 299, 367
Hondo, 300
Horeb, 324
Hubert-Michel, Michel, 361
Hugo, Victor, 85, 166, 172, 350,
    364
Huns, 187
Hunyadi, Jean, 284
Hu-Wuans, 187, 189
Hvar, island of, 346
Hvotan, 12
Hwang Ho River, 299, 348
Hyphasis, 303
Hyrcania, 155

ibn-Batuta, 134, 330
ibn-Khaldun, 134
Ibos, 317
Ikhnaton, 248, 294
Illyria, 362
Illysos River, 202
Imperia (courtesan), 120–1
Impruneta, 294
India, 7, 69, 122, 134, 144, 147, 186,
    200, 204, 229, 237, 252, 257,
    276, 325, 351
Indonesia, 334
Indus River, 142, 143, 145, 303, 304,
    324
Ingeburgh, Empress, 4, 47–9, 61–4,
    65–6, 68, 74, 124, 152, 153
Ireland, 67
Irene, Empress, 4, 54, 64, 153, 184
Isfahan, 142, 143, 144, 145, 149,
    318, 351
Isidore, 5, 106, 109, 133, 151, 157–8,
    161, 162, 166, 167, 177, 180,
    184, 185, 194, 201, 203, 205,
    209–12, 214, 218, 219, 235,
    248, 261–3, 265, 288, 295, 334,
    335, 339, 355, 363, 365
Italy, 171, 231
Ivoi, Paul d', 148
Izanagi (god), 300

Jammes, Francis, 261
Japan and the Japanese, 123, 131,
    268, 300–1, 304, 306, 333, 334

Jaxartes River, 196
Jayavarman VII, 323
Jerusalem, 284, 302, 307
Jester I, 158, 159, 161, 168–72, 174, 176, 180, 183, 184, 191, 235, 275, 288, 306
Jester II–VII, 171–2, 192–4, 197, 203, 205, 207, 209–12, 214, 218–19, 224–5, 228–35, 247, 272, 274, 275, 297, 306, 321
Jester VIII–IX, 306, 355
Jesus Christ, 134, 135, 225, 326, 363
Jimmu Tenno (Emperor of Japan), 300
Joan, Pope, 326
Joan of Arc, Saint, 225, 326, 363
John, Prester, 326
John, Saint (apostle), 136
Jones, E. T., 94
Jornandez, 210
Judas Iscariot, 225, 351
Julian the Apostate, Emperor, 174, 363
Julius II, della Rovere, Pope, 124, 174, 348
Jung, Carl Gustav, 370
Justinian, Emperor, 26, 174, 352
Justus Dion, 4, 8, 11, 23, 24, 25, 27, 28, 29, 31, 32, 56, 67, 69, 70, 73–4, 79, 83, 88, 94, 96, 97, 111, 133, 168, 170, 180, 182, 194, 209, 210, 216, 224, 241, 245, 248, 251, 256–7, 260–1, 263–6, 314, 317, 320, 330–2, 337, 338, 342–3, 345–6, 354, 356, 361, 364, 365, 366, 368, 369
Juvenal, Bishop, 346

Kabulistan, 285
Kadesh, 356
Kaisari, 12
Kaluga, 348
Kanabel, 12
Kandahar, 285
Kanishka, 155, 156, 161, 164, 170, 178–80, 182, 183, 191, 201, 202
Kant, Emmanuel, 259
Kaptchaks, 38, 187, 189
Karagoz (Turkish folklore character), 334

Karakoram, 328, 364
Karkemish, 356
Kereke Mountains, 196
Kerulen, 285
Kha-Khan of the Oïghurs, *see* Balamir
Khan, Abul Ghazi Bahadur, 368
Khan of the Oïghurs, 7, 46, 49, 155, 187–9, 191, 277
Khantaïskoia, Lake, 196
Khazars, 38, 187, 189
Khmers, 69, 186, 317, 323
Khorasan, 285
Khubilai, Emperor, 268, 329–31, 333, 334, 335–6, 337
Khwarizm, 285
Khyber Pass, 276, 303
Ki Lien-chan, *see* Székesfehérvár
Ki Liu-chan, 299
Kinsey, Alfred, 362
Kipling, Rudyard, 171
Kirghiz, 75, 156
Kleist, Heinrich von, 14
Königsee, 346
Kora-Kora, Mount, 3, 52, 156, 172
Korcula, island of, 346
Korea, 300–1, 304, 312, 330, 333
Kosovo, battle of, 347
Krafft-Ebing, Richard von, 362
Krk, island of, 346
Kuchan, 7
Kuchan, Prince, 303
Kuropatkin, Generalissimo Aleksei Nikolaevich, 347
Kyushu, 300

Labianus, 35–6, 38
Lacordaire, Henri, 139
Ladislas, King, 284
La Fontaine, Jean de, 261
Lagash, 356
Lägerlof, Selma, 171
Lahore, 303, 318
Lambrecht the priest, 349
Lampidus, 349, 362, 370
Lancelot of the Lake, 351
Languedoc, 299
Lao-tzu, 145
Laplanche, J., 369
Laquedem, Isaac, 369

Larsa, 356
Las Casas, Emmanuel, Comte de, 72
Las Navas de Tolosa, 299
Las Vegas, 228
Laurens, Jean-Paul, 22
Lautréamont, Isidore Ducasse, Comte de, 85, 117
Lauzun, Antonin Nompar de Caumont, Duc de, 227
Laval, 348
Lawrence, T. E., 148, 174
Lazarus, 225
Leal, Valdés, 305
Leander, 26
Le Corbusier (Edouard Jeanneret-Gris), 250
Ledoux, Claude Nicolas, 250
Lefèvre-Pontalis, J.-B., 369
Lefranc, Abel, 256
Leibnitz, Gottfried Wilhelm, 243
Lena River, 196, 201, 216
Lenin, Vladimir I., 174, 177, 206, 249, 268, 314
Leo I, Pope, 328
Leo X, Pope, 328, 338
León, 299
Le Senne, René, 368
Le Tors, Lambert, 350
Levaillant, Maurice, 85
Lévi-Strauss, Claude, 248
Libya, 21, 31, 333
Lichtenberg, Georg Christoph, 257, 366
Lindos, citadel of, 283, 331
Liszt, Franz, 92
Liu Kia-hway, 363
Liutpold (father of Empress Ingeburgh), 61-2, 63
Logophilus, 8, 239, 241, 264-5, 274, 277, 287, 290, 295, 303, 308-15, 317, 320-5, 327, 328, 331-4, 337, 340-3, 351, 355, 368
Loire River, 287, 310
Lombardy, 62
Lope de Vega Carpio, Felix, 85
Lot, Ferdinand, 368
Louis I of Wittenbach, 346
Louis II of Wittenbach, 346
Louis XI (King of France), 46, 338
Louis XIV, 227, 265
Lübeck, 351

Lusitanians, 284, 333
Luynes, Charles d'Albert, Duc de, 227
Lycia, 367
Lyly, John, 351

Maastricht, 227
Macedonia, 245, 284, 286
Machiavelli, Niccolo, 314
Maddalena Point, 17
Madeira, 204
Mademoiselle, the Grand, see Montpensier, Duchesse de
Madrid, 172
Maghreb, 134
Magnentius, Emperor, 362
Maguelonne, 155
Mala, Philippe de, 120
Malabar Coast, 67
Málaga, 299
Malaparte (Kurt Suckert, called "Curzio"), 174
Malea, Cape, 264, 284
Malherbe, François de, 118, 264
Malibran, Maria de la Felicidad Garcia-, 92
Malik, al-, see Saladin
Malot, Hector, 172
Malraux, André, 175, 368
Malta, 102
Manchuria, 347
Manfred (son of Alexis), 317-23, 324, 329, 333, 341
Mann, Thomas, 367
Mao Tse-tung, 299, 364
Mirandola, see Mirandolphus
Mirandole, see Pico de la Mirandola
Mirandolphus, 62-4
Marcian, 295, 324, 333
Marcus Aurelius, 342
Mardoch, 155, 156, 161, 170, 173, 178, 182, 183-4, 191, 202
Maria Theresa (Empress of Austria), 273
Marignano, battle of, 347
Marne, battle of the, 207
Marseilles, 199, 298
Martian, 258, 259-60, 356
Mary Magdalen, 225-6
Marx, Karl, 354, 368
Massagetans, 285

Mathiez, Albert, 235
Maulnier, Thierry, 28
Mauretania, 302, 320
Maurois, André, 85, 119
Maurya, King, 303
Mayakovsky, Vladimir, 14
Mayenne, 348
Mazarin, Jules Cardinal, 46, 364
Mazar-i-Sharif, 359
Medici, Jean de, *see* Leo X, Pope
Medici, Lorenzo de' (the Magnificent), 123–4, 174
Medici Dynasty, 115, 174, 226
Medina-Sidonia, 299
Mediterranean Sea, 144, 277, 283, 299, 303, 333
Memphis, 307, 356
Menalchas, 16, 255, 271, 282, 295, 321, 333–4, 342, 355
Menes, 174
Mentor, 117
Mercutio of Verona (Tybalt, Master of Avignon), 47, 48, 61
Mérida, 299
Mesa (Balamir's sister, Bruince's wife), 268
Mesopotamia, 319
Messina, 303
Messina, Antonello da, 226
Metagenes (architect), 249
Metastasio, Pietro, 351
Mexico, 7, 175
Mezzopotamo, 71, 153, 155, 164, 178, 183, 184, 195, 335
Michelangelo (Michelangelo Buonarroti), 342
Mies Van der Rohe, Ludwig, 250
Mieszko, King, 285
Milan, 272, 345
Mille, Cecil B. de, 370
Milton, John, 344
Mircea (voivode), 285, 286
Mithras, 294
Mljet, island of, 346
Moldovalacks, 285
Mohammed II, 174
Mommsen, Theodor, 369
Mongolia, Mongols, 21, 31, 268, 317
Monsalès, Marquis de, *see* Fouquet, Marie-Madeleine
Montaigne, Michel Eyquem de, 85, 203, 263, 271

Montalembert, Charles Forbes, Comte de, 139
Monte Carlo, 337
Montenegro, Gervasio, 362
Monte Oliveto Maggiore, 294
Montepulciano, 294, 304
Monteriggioni, 294
Montesquieu, Charles de Secondat, Baron de La Brède et de, 143, 360
Montesquiou-Fezensac, Robert, Comte de, 227
Montesquiou-Fezensac family, 227
Montpensier, Anne Marie Louise D'Orleans, the Grand Mademoiselle, Duchesse de, 228
Monsu Desiderio (painter), 250
Montez, Lola, 346
Morand, Paul, 365
Moscow, 348
Mugodjar-Aktiubinsk, *see* Székesfehérvár
Mukden, 347
Mun, Albert, Comte de, 135
Mundzuk, 187
Munich, 252, 342
Murillo, Bartolomé Esteban, 172
Mursa (Asia Minor), 79, 101–2, 103, 107, 109, 178, 362
Mursa on the Drava, 361
Musset, Alfred de, 64
Mussolini, Benito, 174, 367
Mustawfi, Hamd Allah al-, 369

Naiku, 300
Naktonggang River, 301, 303, 320, 327
Nandor, 77–9
Naples, 228, 250
Napoleon I, 38, 72, 174, 268, 326, 364, 368
Napoleon III, 214
Narni, Erasmo di, *see* Gattamelata
Nelson, Horatio (Duke of Bronte), Viscount, 246
Nepal, 134, 143
Nephaot (father of Heloise), 22, 23–4, 26, 29
Nephta River, 36, 37, 51, 68, 75, 154, 157, 162, 173, 196, 299, 363
Nera River, 344

Neuilly, 227
Neuschwanstein, castle of, 346
Neuville, Alphonse de, 22
Nevers, Count, 284
New York, 252, 272, 342
Nietzsche, Friedrich, 314
Nile River, 215
Nîmes, 305
Nineveh, 142, 307, 356
Niš, 284
Nizami, 350
Noailles, Natalie de, 254
Normans, 297
Norway, 351
Novokarkaralinsk, 361
Numidians, 35, 321
Nysa, 363

Odier, 35, 38
Odoacer (King of the Heruli), 297
Odoric Pordenone, 308
Oedipus, 363
Oïghurs, 38, 41, 49–50, 79, 187, 188,
    308, 334, 336
Oktar, 187
Olivier, Laurence, Lord, 370
Oman, Gulf of, 67
Onessa, 11, 14–19, 30, 31, 39, 40, 43,
    46, 47, 49–54, 57, 59, 61, 67,
    68, 74, 75, 76, 79, 85, 92, 106,
    138, 153–6, 162, 164, 183, 202,
    208, 218, 220, 238–9, 244, 247,
    254, 262, 293, 305, 306, 309,
    312, 335
Ophir, 302
Ormazd, 143
Orcagna, Andrea, 305
Orkhon River, 196, 285
Ormesson, Olivier Le Fèvre d', 227
Orontes River, 155
Ortega y Gasset, José, 370
Ossetes, 80
Ostrogoths, 297
Ottokar, King, 350
Oxford, 257
Oxus River, 196, 216

Padua, 63
Pagnol, Marcel, 365
Paisaye, 228

Paisiello, Giovanni, 351
Palermo, 47, 60, 199, 202, 228, 303,
    305
Palestine, 184, 310, 366
Palladio (Andrea di Pietro), 250,
    334
Palmyra, 305
Pamir, 7, 303, 364
Pannonia, 47, 362
Pantagruel, 204
Pantama, Cape, 4, 64, 68, 79, 308
Paraclitus, 16, 35, 103, 109, 148,
    257–8, 295, 307
Parapoli, 38, 71, 153, 155, 156, 164,
    183, 195, 333, 335
Paraponisus, 196, 303
Paris, 115
Parodi, Don Isidro, 362
Parthians, 35, 317
Pascal, Blaise, 106, 335, 368
Patmos, 246, 284, 308, 346
Patom Mountains, 196
Pauvert, J.-J., 361
Péguy, Charles, 259
Peking, 299–300, 307
Pelusium, 120
Penelope (nickname of Empress
    Ingeburgh in the sonnets of
    Mercutio of Verona), 47, 61
Pergamum, 101
Pericles, 225, 265
Persepolis, 307
Persia, 7, 21, 31, 57, 63, 142–3, 147,
    186, 187, 188, 200, 229, 237,
    251, 257, 258, 276, 277, 302,
    309, 310, 319, 333, 348, 359
Persian Gulf, 134, 310
Peruzzi, Baldassare, 364
Peshawar, 276, 303
Pétain, Marshal Philippe, 214, 369
Petchenegues, 187, 285
Peter, Saint, 328
Peter the Great, 174, 248–9
Peter the Hermit, 334
Petra, 137–8, 139–43, 363
Petrarch, 250
Phélippeaux, Antoine de, 370
Philippon, Charles, 368
Philocrates, 101–9, 112, 113–14, 130,
    131, 132, 133, 138, 139, 145,
    146, 151, 157–8, 161, 162, 163,
    166, 167, 174–83, 184, 185, 189–

90, 191, 193, 194, 205, 218, 219, 232, 234, 235, 264, 269, 281, 288, 290, 306, 313, 315, 317, 319, 326, 335, 350, 355, 362, 364
Philomena, 204
Philontes, 241, 257–8, 295, 321, 334, 356
Phoenicia, 8, 17, 57, 102, 246
Picasso, Pablo, 305
Pico della Mirandola, 179
Piedmont, 348
Pienza, 294
Piero della Francesca, 167, 168–70
Pinerolo, 227
Pirenne, Henri, 368, 369
Pirochole, 299
Pisa, 305, 368
Pistoia, 172
Plan Carpin, Jean du, 368
Plato, 248, 366
Pola, 287
Poland, 63, 198
Poldevians, 285
Politian, 124
Polititian, the, 258, 295, 308, 320, 333, 355–6
Polo, Marco, 226, 329, 330, 369
Polyphilius, 16, 24, 27, 255, 282, 295, 334, 342, 356
Pompeii, 298
Pomposa, 15, 16, 17–18, 19, 20–3, 26, 30, 31, 33, 34, 39, 40, 44, 46–7, 48–51, 50, 65–8, 117, 119, 155, 161, 186, 198–9, 202, 215, 217, 218, 229, 233, 234, 246, 265, 268, 275–80, 283–92, 296–7, 305, 306, 307, 339, 344, 345, 367
Poppi, 344
Pordenone, Odoric, *see* Odoric Pordenone
Pordoï, Passo del, 344
Po River, 287, 344
Porphyries, Dynasty of the, 11, 15, 17, 21, 26, 30, 31, 32, 35, 37, 40, 76, 95, 114, 148, 153, 154, 161–2, 165, 166, 175, 218, 221, 230, 244–5, 288, 335, 369
Princeton University, 94
Protus, 12
Proust, Marcel, 168–9, 227, 364

Provence, 225, 298, 310, 320
Provence, constable of, 284, 285, 286
Pufendorf, 258
Pulcheria, Empress, 346
Puvis de Chavannes, Pierre, 184
Puységur, Jacques François de Chastenet, Marquis de, 206
Pylos, 203
Pyrenees, 299

Queen, Algernon, 361
Queneau, Raymond, 359
Quilico de Spoleto, 350

Rab, island of, 346
Rabelais, François, 203, 225, 285, 299, 351
Racine, Jean, 351
Ramses II, 174, 315
Rank, Otto, 360
Ranke, Leopold von, 369
Raphael, 295, 296, 338, 364
Rasputin, Grigori Efimovich, 370
Réage, Pauline, 256
Red Sea, 135, 141
Regis II (King of Sicily), 7, 47–8, 49, 50, 60, 186, 333
Regium, 303
Renan, Ernest, 5, 106, 114, 115–16, 120, 134, 231, 261, 364, 366
Revel, Jean-François, 366
Rheims, Maurice, 365
Rhine River, 303, 304, 333
Rhodes, 102, 186, 203, 250, 283, 284, 346
Rhone River, 198, 292, 295, 310
Ricimer (King of the Suevians), 297
Rilke, Rainer Maria, 14
Rimbaud, Arthur, 134
Ritter, Helmuth, 28, 46, 93, 94, 95, 99, 138
Robbia, Luca della, *see* Della Robbia, Luca
Roderick, 76–90, 91–2, 94–6, 107, 114, 190, 212, 213, 268, 329
Rodzhestvensky, Admiral, 347
Rohan-Montbazon, *see* Chevreuse, Marie de Rohan-Montbazon

Rohe, Mies Van der, *see* Mies Van der Rohe, Ludwig
Roïlas, 187
Roland, 351
Romans-sur-Isère, 348
Rome, 115, 122, 167, 199, 229, 252, 265, 268, 307, 310, 317, 318, 320, 323–8, 332–3, 336, 338–44, 367
Rostopchin, Count Fyodor, 6
Rousseau, Jean-Jacques, 172, 203, 261
Rovere (Pope Julius II), *see* Julius II della Rovere
Roxana, 350
Rubempré, Lucien de (character in Balzac), 117
Rugghieri, Archbishop, 138–9
Russell, Bertrand, 257, 359
Russia, 351
Russo-Japanese War, 347

Sachs, Hans, 351
Sahara Desert, 304
Saint-Amarante, Comte de, 361
Saint Catherine, monastery of, 135
Saint-Fargeau, chateau of, 228
Saint-Gaudens, 134
Saint-Léger Léger, 364
Saint-Louis, Île, 370
Saint-Simon, Louis de Rouvroy, Duc de, 27, 227
Saïs, 125
Saitaphemes, 226
Saladin, 174, 334
Salamanca, 299
Samarkand, 107, 143, 144, 148, 149, 151, 180, 192, 193, 249, 262, 276, 293, 305, 313, 320, 321, 328, 332, 335, 339, 364
Samosata, 303
Samoyeds, 285, 317
Sand, George (Aurore Dupin, Baronne Dudevant), 92
Sangallo, 250
Sangimignano, 294
Sarabhavanamuktenandāmanayagam, Swami Sri (Babaji), 296
Saratov, 348
Sardinia, 102, 303
Sardou, Victorien, 22, 273

Sargon, 174
Sarmatia, 155
Sarmizegetusa, 51, 61, 62–3
Satie, Erik, 124
Saxony, 198, 330
Scala, Cangrande, Bartolomeo, Alboino, and Cansignorio della, 287
Scarlatti, Domenico, 352
Schelling, Friedrich Wilhelm Joseph von, 259
Schliemann, Heinrich, 12, 138, 359
Schnabel, J., 171
Schumann, Robert, 317–18
Scythia, 16, 31, 38, 87, 90, 155, 156, 188, 202, 320, 333
Seckendorff, Karl Sigmund von, 363
Segalen, Victor, 134
Segestam, 303
Ségur, Pierre, Marquis de, 247
Ségur, Sophie Rostopchina, Marquise de, 172
Seine River, 287
Selenga River, 196
Seleucia, 142
Selinus, 303
Sella, Passo di, 344
Sévigné, Marie de Rabutin-Chantal, Marquise de, 27–8
Seville, 305
Sforza, Catherine, 273
Shakespeare, 85, 164, 225, 352
Shaw, Bernard, 370
Sheba, Queen of, 273, 350
Shensi, 299
Siberia, Siberians, 134, 189, 285
Siddhartha Gautama, *see* Buddha
Sidon, 275
Sidonius Apollinaris, 225
Sicily, 16, 46–7, 50, 60, 67, 117, 155, 161, 186, 198–9, 202, 215, 217, 226, 234, 268, 277, 283–4, 287, 292–3, 300–1, 311, 333
Siemréap, 323
Siena, 294, 304
Sigismund, King, 284
Simeon, 77–86, 94–100, 107, 114, 133, 138, 162, 168, 189–91, 194–5, 197, 201–3, 207–13, 217, 218, 220, 232, 235, 268, 306, 313, 329, 340
Simon, Prince, 285

Simon the Angel, *see* Polititian, the
Simon the Clerk, 350
Sinai, 135, 137
Sipahis, 285
Sirmium, 287
Sixtus V, Pope, 328
Skorzeny, Colonel Otto, 367
Smith, Commodore Sidney, 370
Sodoma, Il (Giovanni Antonia
    Bazzi), 167, 169–70
Sogdiana, 155, 285, 311, 320
Solomon, King, 302, 326
Sommerfelt, Alf, 6
Sorel, Georges, 177
Sostratus (architect), 249
Soszla-Sczimonovski, Regnar, 364
Spain, 37, 271, 287, 299, 302, 304,
    309, 311, 351
Spalato, 287
Sphinx, 363
Spiesz, Johann, 352
Spinoza, Baruch de, 362
Spoleta, 294, 344
Sporades Islands, 278, 346
Stalin, Josef, 174, 232
Stalinabad, *see* Dyushambe
Stalingrad, 207, 348
Starnberger See, 346
Stendhal (Henri Beyle), 85, 298,
    360, 368
Stephen, King, 284, 286
Stevenson, Robert Louis, 171
Stilicho, 364
Struwwelpeter, Max and Moritz, 359
Suarès, André, 85
Sudan, 134
Suevians, 297
Sumer, 356, 359
Susa, 307
Susanoo (god), 300
Switzerland, 85
Syme, Sir Ronald, 37
Symē, island of, 346
Syracuse, 47, 155, 199, 202, 303, 306
Syr-Darya River, 196
Syria, Syrians, 7, 16, 31, 34, 35, 67,
    102, 134, 156, 202, 204, 249,
    258, 275, 285, 309, 310, 320,
    348
Syrte River, 299
Székesfehérvár (Asia), 200, 333
Székesfehérvár (Hungary), 200, 365

Taille, Jacques de la, 351
Taine, Hippolyte, 362
Talleyrand-Périgord, Charles Mau-
    rice de, Prince of Beneventum,
    72
Tamar, 363
Tamerlane, 174, 214, 232, 248, 315
Tancred (King of Sicily), 60
Tannenberg, battle of, 347
Taoism, 145, 146, 363
Tapir, Fulgence, 256
Tarkinos, 12
Tarsus, 108, 120
Tartars, 38, 75
Tavernier, Jean-Baptiste, 24, 143
Tcherkesses, 285
Tchitchi, 187
Tegernsee, 346
Teilhard de Chardin, Pierre, 248–9
Telemachus, 117
Telmessos, 301, 367
Thaumas, 5, 57–60, 64, 65–74, 77,
    79, 80, 86, 92, 105–6, 114, 116,
    152, 153, 154, 162, 165, 173,
    193, 196, 203, 205, 213, 218,
    219, 235, 246, 247, 265, 276,
    310, 317, 319, 355, 356, 361
Thebes, 307
Theodolinda (character in Alfred de
    Musset), *see* Ingeburgh
Theodomir, 188
Theodora, 26, 272–5, 277, 287, 309,
    312–13, 317, 319, 321, 323,
    327, 333, 341, 355, 370
Theodora (Empress of Byzantium),
    26
Theodora (Empress), 26, 272–5,
    277, 287, 309, 312, 313, 317,
    319, 321, 323, 327, 333, 341,
    355, 370
Theodoric, 174, 364
Theresa, Saint, 225
Thierry, Amédée, 297, 367
Thierry, Augustin, 64, 200
Thiers, Adolfe, 206
Thomas Aquinas, Saint, 248, 259,
    314, 335, 366
Thorvaldsen, Bertel, 252
Thrace, 286
Thule, 304
Tiberias, Lake, 135
Tiber River, 293, 327, 364

Tibet, 134, 143, 145, 329
Tigris River, 141, 142, 143, 273, 303
Timgad, 305
Tiranë, 364
Todi, 294
Togo, Admiral Heihachiro, 347
Tokhars, 285
Toledo, 299, 304, 332, 339
Totila (King of the Ostrogoths), 297
Toynbee, Arnold, 230, 368, 369
Traini, Francesco, 368
Trajan, Emperor, 352
Transoxiana, 285
Transylvania, 284, 347
Triboulet (character in Hugo), 172
Trier, 107, 305
Tristan, 351
Troy, 350
Tsarkozy-Wilozlaw, 92
Tsushima Island, 347
Tula, 348
Turgenev, Ivan, 92
Turkey, 348
Turolde, 123
Tutankhamen, King, 320
Twin, B. and B., 364
Tybalt, *see* Mercutio of Verona
Tyre, 17, 120, 137, 203, 275, 299, 305, 332, 335

Uccello (Paolo di Dono), 286
Ugek, 187
Ugolino (della Gherardesca), 139
Ur, 356
Ural Mountains, 216, 303
Urban II, Pope, 334
Urbino, 294
Uruk, 356

Valais, 348
Valerius, 8, 11, 14, 44, 123, 248, 255, 256, 264, 282, 321, 333, 337, 341, 342, 355, 361
Valéry, Paul, 253–5
Vallombrosa, 294, 344
Vandals, 297
Vanessa, 112, 122–32, 141, 145, 149, 150, 160, 164, 184, 213, 220, 232, 235, 255, 268, 271, 288, 299, 306, 319, 322
Vanini, Vanina ("La Pasticcierina"), 226
Varangians, 134, 237, 239
Varus, Count, 284
Vasari, Giorgio, 250
Vaugelas, Claude Favre, Baron de Pérouges, Seigneur de, 118
Vautrin, Abbá Carlos Herrera, 117
Vaux-le-Vicomte, chateau of, 227
Venosta Dynasty, 11, 15, 19, 21, 30, 40, 45, 46, 119, 153, 154, 162, 184, 218, 230, 244–5, 369
Venice, 17, 115, 342
Vercingetorix, 214, 225
Verdi, Giuseppe, 172
Verna, 344
Verona, 60, 287, 305, 331, 344, 345
Verrocchio (Andrea di Cione), 342
Viardot-Garcia, Pauline, *see* Garcia, Pauline Viardot-
Vicenza, 334, 344
Victoria, Queen, 273
Vienna, 107, 305, 320
Vienne, 305
Villiers de l'Isle-Adam, Auguste, Comte de, 361
Virgil (Publius Virgilius Maro), 352, 356
Visigoths, 297
Viterbo, 294
Vitry, Nicolas, marquis then duc de (Captain of the King's guards, then Marshal of France), 227
Vivaldi, Antonio, 352
Voltaire (François Marie Arouet), 6, 95, 143, 249, 327, 360, 365, 368
Voronezh, 348
Vrain-Lucas (Vrin Lucas), Denis, 225–6

Wagner, Richard, 346
Weil, Simone, 317
Weill-Pichon, Robert, 6, 17, 26, 65, 114, 138, 159, 164, 172, 213, 217, 218, 219, 256, 268, 317, 330, 362, 366
Wenceslaus II of Bohemia, King, 350
Whitman, Walt, 254

Wilde, Oscar, 370
Wilhelm I, Emperor, 214
William the Conqueror, 347
Winckelmann, Johann Joachim, 252
Wright, Frank Lloyd, 250
Wyss, Johann Rudolf, 171

Xanadu (Khubilai's capital), 155,
    329
Xanthus, 301
Xenophon, 349

Yalu River, 317
Yangtze River, 329
Yemen, 134, 141

Yenisei River, 196
Yeni-tcheris, 285, 286
Yen-ngang, 299
Yi Chungu, 367
Yong-lo (Emperor of China), 226
Yonne, 228
Yturri, Gabriel, 227

Zapata, Emiliano, 175
Zenobia (Alexis's sister, Balamir's
    wife), 268, 329
Zenobia (Queen of Palmyra), 273
Zévaco, Michel, 148
Zingara, 142
Zoroaster, 143, 310, 321

Jean d'Ormesson—youngest member of the Académie française; Chairman of the Board of the great newspaper *Figaro;* Deputy Secretary General of the International Council on Philosophy for UNESCO's Humanities Division; director of the philosophical-historical journal *Diogenes*—is the author of two nonfiction books and four novels. *The Glory of the Empire* won the Grand Prize for fiction from the Académie française.

A NOTE ON THE TYPE

This book was set in Monticello, a Linotype revival of the original Roman No. 1 cut by Archibald Binny and cast in 1796 by the Philadelphia type foundry Binny & Ronaldson. The face was named Monticello in honor of its use in the monumental fifty-volume *Papers of Thomas Jefferson*, published by Princeton University Press. Monticello is a transitional type design, embodying certain features of Bulmer and Baskerville, but it is a distinguished face in its own right.

This book was composed, printed and bound
by American Book–Stratford Press, Inc., New York, N.Y.

Typography and binding design by Camilla Filancia